PENGUIN CLASSICS

SELECTED WRITINGS

WILLIAM HAZLITT was born in 1778 at Maidstone. His parents were revolutionaries and intellectual deists familiar with the works of Priestley, Price and Godwin. In 1783 the family emigrated to America, but they found life there disappointing and returned to England in 1788, settling at Wem in Shropshire. Hazlitt rejected his father's wish that he should become a Unitarian Minister, but in 1798 he heard Coleridge's last sermon, which proved a turning-point in his career. Coleridge encouraged him to pursue his interest in philosophy and Hazlitt later wrote several such works, including *An Essay on the Principles of Human Action* (1805), *An Abridgement of 'The Light of Nature pursued by Abraham Tucker'* (1807) and his great attack on Malthus, *A Reply to the Essay on Population* (1807). Art was one of his greatest passions and his training in Paris left its mark on his writing. Unlike his literary contemporaries, such as Wordsworth and Coleridge, Hazlitt remained a radical all his life, and this commitment made him many enemies. Much of his writing is ephemeral, but there is a body of literary and social criticism which holds an important place in English literature. A great essayist, he handled a wide range of styles, from the abstract and formal ideas in 'On Reason and Imagination' to the colloquialism of 'The Fight'. In 1812 he became Parliamentary Reporter for the *Morning Chronicle* and was soon filling its columns with essays on diverse subjects and brilliant accounts of the London stage. His collected essays from the *Examiner*, published under the title of *The Round Table*, are a notable contribution to the literature of radical protest. In 1820 he began submitting essays to the *London Magazine*, which were to become the first volume of *Table Talk* (2 vols., 1821–2). In the same year he fell in love with a young girl, and this disastrous period in his life is recounted in *Liber Amoris*. Hazlitt recovered and began writing again, and in 1825 *The Spirit of the Age* was published. His last great task was *The Life of Napoleon Buonaparte* (4 vols., 1828–30). William Hazlitt died in 1830.

RONALD BLYTHE, critic and writer, is the author of *The Age of Illusion*, a social history of England between the wars, *Akenfield: Portrait of an*

English Village, The View in Winter, From the Headlands, Divine Landscapes and, most recently, *Word from Wormingford*. He is editor of *Writing in a War*, originally published as *Components of the Scene*), *The Penguin Book of Diaries* and *Private Words: Letters and Diaries from the Second World War*. Many of these are published by Penguin. He has edited Jane Austen's *Emma*, Thomas Hardy's *Far From the Madding Crowd*, Henry James's *The Awkward Age*, and William Hazlitt's *Selected Writings* for the Penguin Classics.

CONTENTS

*Titles in italic are those supplied by the Editor

ACKNOWLEDGEMENTS

I am much indebted to the great edition of Hazlitt's Works which P. P. Howe published in 1930–34, and which is itself based on the edition produced by A. R. Waller and A. Glover. I would also like to acknowledge the usefulness of P. P. Howe's excellent *Life of William Hazlitt* (Hamish Hamilton, 1947) and of Catherine Macdonald Maclean's biography, *Born Under Saturn* (Collins, 1943). My thanks are due too to the City Librarian of Nottingham.

INTRODUCTION

A CONSPIRACY of caution has grown up around William Hazlitt. Unquestionably a 'great author' in the system which measures writers for posterity, he has to be admitted, yet grudgingly, warningly. An impression persists of a man at odds with all and everything, someone to whom his friends had to offer an almost saintly response if they were not to get their heads bitten off. He was a bitter creature, a malcontent. Equally persistent is the hint of scandal: a rumour about making a fool of himself over young girls which, in the case of Herrick, say, carries with it amusement and forgiveness, but which in connexion with Hazlitt is loaded with Sunday newspaper innuendo. He was an irritant and a grit in the eye of his contemporaries. But he wrote as marvellously as any essayist who was not Montaigne could, so his work has always received high praise. Yet, in spite of this, most of the assessments of Hazlitt have a certain maggoty quality and are eaten through with reservation.

In the many editions of his work there are numerous attempts to present him in the best light. Because there was in his fretful nature a sublime streak of joy and serenity which allowed him to write perfectly about human happiness, the essays in which he does so have been singled out for constant reprinting, with the result that the average Hazlitt-taster has not met the real flavour of this extraordinary man. His great hedge of thorny comment, which runs parallel with the retreat-from-revolution politics of the early nineteenth century, has too often been chopped away in order to show a calm view of a journalist-philosopher hanging 'Great Thoughts' on the type-line and meditating on such absolutes as fame, time, death, nature, etc. Yet the very essence of Hazlitt is his dangerousness, and not only with respect to the reactionary climate of his own day but when and wherever freedom and truth are compromised by those actions which are summed up as the 'art of the possible'. These were what he called 'the lie' and it was his refusal to either take or give 'the lie' which turned him into the uncomfortable creature he was. This, the very kernel of his character, has been seen as a kind of aberrant grumpiness, a tiresome failing in an otherwise excellent prose stylist. So his work has been tilted until it squares up to what is expected of an inexhaustible aphorist and again it is wholesome Hazlitt, rather than whole Hazlitt, which is presented.

What was it, both in his own day and after, which makes him one of literature's separated brethren, which sees to it that he is critically acclaimed but which leaves him outside the full warm fellowship of what were once called trusted writers? 'I want to know why everybody has such a dislike of me?' he asked Leigh Hunt. Edmund Gosse, giving the general nineteenth-century answer, put it all down to cussedness: 'Eccentricity, violence and a disregard of the conventions were at no time unsympathetic to Hazlitt.' Except for his telling inclusion of that key-word 'violence', the rest of Gosse's statement takes up the central position and is a nervous cheer for a writer who made the Olympian winning-post, though handicapped. 'In his own time and way he was a transmitter of the sacred fire.' Like so many critics before and since, Gosse tries to stay neutral. But Hazlitt leaves no one neutral. Disturbed himself by every ecstatic, political and tragic aspect of the human condition, he could never believe that there were those who managed to get through life without feeling and knowing these things in all their intensity. He could not understand the rules of selection which made some of the subjects on which he wrote praiseworthy and socially acceptable – art, Shakespeare (although once his analysis of Desdemona brought shouts of 'obscenity!'), the countryside – and others – class, war, money, slavery, sex – taboo. His England had been at war with France for twenty years and had, like the rest of Europe, been fed on cruelties. His London was famous for its prostitutes. The great mass of his fellow men were near starvation. Yet he was to be polite in print and draw the line. It was impossible.

'Hazlitt was not one of those non-committal writers who shuffle off in a mist and die of their own insignificance,' wrote Virginia Woolf.

His essays are emphatically himself. He has no reticence and he has no shame. He tells us exactly what he thinks, and he tells us – the confidence is less seductive – what he feels. As of all men he had the most intense consciousness of his own existence, since never a day passed without inflicting on him a pang of hate or of jealousy, some thrill of anger or pleasure, we cannot read him for long without coming in contact with a very singular character – ill-conditioned yet high-minded; mean yet noble; intensely egotistical yet inspired by the most genuine passion for the rights and liberties of mankind. . . . So thin is the veil of the essay as Hazlitt wore it, his very look comes before us. ... No man could read him and maintain a simple and uncompounded idea of him.

There is a noticeable broadening of judgement here but it is still 'less seductive' to know what Hazlitt feels than what he thinks. He is all right until he allows his private life to run so unchecked onto the page. But of course it is when Hazlitt is most privately concerned that he touches on those public affairs which involve political, sensual, happiness-seeking, disappointment-finding mankind. The reader, encountering this form of literary nakedness, must either acknowledge its reality or join the prissy mob which defines what is permissible. But whatever his reaction to that 'brow-hanging, shoe-contemplative, *strange*' creature of Cole-ridge's jittery description, ordinary conforming, tax-paying, shibboleth-swallowing man must inevitably encounter guilt, cowardice and regret when he encounters William Hazlitt. The oil which runs the smooth society was not for him. Nor did he ever pretend otherwise.

I am not in the ordinary acceptance of the term, *a good-natured man*, that is, many things annoy me besides what interferes with my own ease and interest. I hate a lie; a piece of injustice wounds me to the quick, though nothing but the report of it reaches me. Therefore I have made many enemies and few friends; for the public know nothing of well-wishers and keep a wary eye on those that would reform them.

William Hazlitt was born in Maidstone on 10 April 1778, the fourth child of an Irish Unitarian minister. The Reverend William Hazlitt and Grace his wife were revolu-tionaries and intellectual deists, thoroughly familiar with the teachings of Franklin, Priestley, Price and Godwin. Having such direct access to this radical spring was to create in their son what he described as 'that unfortunate attachment to a set of abstract phrases, such as liberty, truth, justice, human-ity, honour. . . .' Weaned on absolutes, quite unable to judge anything without the use of both head and heart, Hazlitt inherited a code which lacked all social flexibility. What was not truth was a lie. And what made the world swing, far more terribly than merrily when the movement was honestly examined, was, for him, chiefly a set of myths. What was not liberty was slavery. Where and what was compromise? It was a word on which he stumbled, never seeing it, never able to convince himself of its uses. 'If we only think justly,' the good simple father told the son, 'we shall easily foil all the advocates of tyranny.' Hazlitt believed this and con-tinued to believe it to the end of his life; and long after the great dream of replacing kingdoms (government by superstition) with republics (government by reason) was being repudiated as a kind of youthful excess by his friends. For them it was just a phase and to remind them of it became a breach of good manners. Students and young writers said wild things. The sign for them to accept the world as it was came when Napoleon crowned himself in Notre Dame. Their loyalties, they then knew, were elsewhere.

Hazlitt, dedicated to the revolution, became a lone voice speaking against the full blast of windy rhetoric needed to prosecute a national war. Allied to his revolutionary politics there were notions of personal freedom which not only disturbed and shocked, but which could endanger the kind of blanket patriotism required during a national emergency. He insisted that to deny discussion of any aspect of the human condition was cant. His contemporaries disagreed. What they could not bear in the public sense they called 'sedition' and what they shrank from in the personal sense they termed 'filth'. Hazlitt met invective with invective. His abuse was an art in itself. It coruscated with brilliant side issues. This was the Hazlitt who believed 'in the theoretical benevolence, and practical malignity of man', and who was able to turn every dirty thrust with such skill and panache that reading his rage and abuse at this length of time is as exhilarating as watching an immense gale from a safe room. Both enemy and friend hoped that these periodic great uproars, with their close engagement with life as it was, would somehow loosen Hazlitt from his untenable ideals and bring him into the ordinary arena of debate. Somewhere where his white face and black looks did not spoil the comfort of the day. But he could not be drawn into any cosy circle. He remained on the edge to remind friends who had done a deal with the establishment of the time when they would have refused to settle for little improvements on earth and pious hopes of heaven. Humanity might have had its heart's desire, as the young Wordsworth had plainly stated,

> Not in Utopia ...
> But in the very world, which is the world
> Of all of us – the place where in the end
> We find our happiness, or not at all !

The chance to 'find happiness in the world of all of us' had occurred in a rare and wonderful way during Hazlitt's lifetime. Then had come this blank refusal on the part of the very heralds of change. How could they have gone back on all the bright promises? He was unable either to understand or to forgive.

I have never given the lie to my own soul. If I have felt any impression once, I feel it more strongly a second time; and I have no wish to revile or discard my best thoughts. There is at least a thorough *keeping* in what I write – not a line that betrays a principle or disguises a feeling.

Hazlitt's youth had spanned an incredibly ecstatic moment in human history. Shackling traditions were being over-hauled; the status quo questioned. The American colonies had freed themselves with surprising ease from Britain and the French people had rejected the hereditary principle in government. He was still a boy when Captain Tournay had ridden against the very symbol of the old power, the Bastille, and it had fallen. Hope reached out far beyond Paris at this event and involved change-makers everywhere in the actual possibility of creating a society which up until this moment had seemed to belong to the geography of romance, or the hereafter. It was the first of Hazlitt's personality-shaking, soul-forming experiences. Others were to come and each would exalt and afflict him for the rest of his days. His anger was only equalled by his astonishment when, later on, others were to describe similar experiences and the com-monsense way they had grown out of them. Enthusiasm –

a word then used to sum up a well-meaning but weak-headed eagerness – should not be applied to the new and the non-traditional. Yet some had never presented enthusiasm more magnificently:

> For mighty were the auxiliars which then stood
> Upon our side, we who were strong in love!
> Bliss was it in that dawn to be alive
> But to be young was very heaven!

This was the clear trumpet-note which Hazlitt heard in his head and felt in his heart until he died. He had stayed, the rest had retreated. (He had actually advanced, that was his trouble. Although so exactly late-Georgian Man, there was that in his nature which anticipated radical concepts and behaviour which are only now being accepted as possible alternatives to the existing structure.) He was often so far ahead that he was fighting evils which his contemporaries simply could not see. He called their conduct cant – a favourite epithet – but it was true that they often did not know what he was so angry about. When his strictures became too much, too outside anything they could comprehend, it became charitable to call him mad.

But for him there were worse things than being called mad. Nicknames. 'A nickname is the hardest stone that the devil can throw at a man. It will knock down any man's resolution. It will stagger his reason. It will tame his pride. ... The unfavourable opinion of others gives you a bad opinion of yourself.' As so often happens, the least apt, the most moronically inspired nickname cut deepest. In March 1818 he was described as 'Pimpled Hazlitt' in *Blackwood's Magazine*. The fact of his notoriously sharp, set face with its pale clear skin became irrelevant. He believed that his entire image in the eyes of the world had become pustulate and obscene because of this false description. It heralded the grand attack on him and he met it with the most dazzling set pieces of invective which, with the exception of Swift's, can be found in the language. But the damage was done all the same and, as he confessed to Bryan Procter ('Barry Cornwall'), 'it nearly put me underground'. Procter tragically summed it up when he said that Hazlitt 'was crowned by defamation'. There was another young friend who had reason to take sides with the figure in the pillory. Why should not Hazlitt speak out on anything and everything? What was the fear – it could be nothing less – which made the *Quarterly*, for instance, attempt to reduce his influence by declaring that his essays were dished up in 'broken English' and left behind them a trail of 'slime and filth'? Since when was the world unable to endure the truth? 'Hazlitt,' cried John Keats '... is your only good damner, and if ever I am damn'd – damn me if I shouldn't like him to damn me.'

But however deep the wounding, Hazlitt was never changed by it. Society was never to teach him a lesson. Sweet reason and threats alike could not sway his commitment, whether to an individual or a cause. 'These bargains are for life,' he said of his decisions, once made. Had not his father been equally uncompromising? Old Mr Hazlitt's outspokenness had forced him out of his comfortable living at Maidstone, and his protests about the barbarous treatment given by the English garrison to American prisoners of war in Ireland had made it necessary for him to leave that country. Greatly daring, he had in 1783 emigrated to the new and hopeful republic of the United States of America, only to find as much bigotry in Boston as in Kent or County Cork. William, aged eight, thought so little of his new land that, writing to his father, he said, 'that it would have been a great deal better if the white people had not found it out'. His only memory of America, from which he returned a year later, was the taste of barberries. In 1788 the family settled in Wem, Shropshire. Mr Hazlitt's gradual withdrawal from 'the world of all of us' to a dreamier habitation is described by William with absolute tenderness, and without accusation. A note of wistfulness too intrudes. Hazlitt, though never an agnostic, has parted from the comfort of his father's God. There will be no such retreat for him when the world becomes unendurable.

> After being tossed about from congregation to congregation ... he had been relegated to an obscure village, where he was to spend the last thirty years of his life, far from the only converse that he loved, the talk about disputed texts of Scripture, and the cause of civil and religious liberty. Here he passed his days, repining but resigned, in the study of the Bible, and the perusal of the Commentators – huge folios, not easily got through, one of which would outlast a winter! ... Here were 'no figures nor no fantasies' – neither poetry nor philosophy – nothing to dazzle, nothing to excite modern curiosity; but to his lack-lustre eyes there appeared ... the sacred name JEHOVAH in capitals: pressed down by the weight of style, worn to the last fading thinness of the understanding, there were glimpses, glimmering notions of the patriarchal wanderings, with palm-trees hovering in the horizon, and processions of camels at the distance of three thousand years ... questions as to the date of the creation, predictions of the end of all things; the great lapses of time, the strange mutations of the globe were unfolded with the voluminous leaf, as it turned over; and though the soul might slumber with an hieroglyphic veil of inscrutable mysteries drawn over it, yet it was in a slumber ill-exchanged for all the sharpened realities of sense, wit, fancy or reason. My father's life was comparatively a dream; but it was a dream of infinity and eternity, of death, the resurrection, and a judgment to come!

Although Hazlitt had, at fifteen, rejected his father's wish that he should become a Unitarian minister, his awakening to faith had about it much of the detail of the classic Christian conversion, word, angel and all. The latter had luminous eyes, a mighty brow and large, soft childish lips only partly concealing bad teeth. At twenty-six, Samuel Taylor

Coleridge had not had the same difficulties as Hazlitt in combining religion with intellectual freedom, and in 1797 was considering the offer of a Unitarian living in Shrewsbury. In January 1798 Hazlitt, who was now nineteen and had done little since leaving college four years before except to hide away in his room or in a field and read *Tom Jones* (another bargain for life), Rousseau and Burke, having read Coleridge's *Ode on the Departing Year*, and having heard that he was a revolutionary, walked the ten miles from Wem to Shrewsbury to hear him preach. Neither he nor the world as yet knew that this magical young man had completed *The Ancient Mariner* or that he had begun the regular use of drugs. The sermon was spectacular. Coleridge's text was 'And he went up into the mountain to pray, HIM-SELF, ALONE.' It was about the real Christ-path, about pacifism (Britain was expecting to be invaded by Napoleon), poetry and isolation. Hazlitt listened and was both crushed and elated by the personal implications the sermon had for him. The following Tuesday Coleridge came to Wem for a dinner of Welsh mutton and boiled turnips, and stayed the night. Hazlitt walked with the poet as far as the sixth milestone when he returned to Shrewsbury in the morning. Hazlitt's walk was straight and Coleridge's meandering and constantly crossing the younger man's path. Hazlitt saw that they did not collide and listened to the quite unimaginable flood of talk. All was changed, all was new. His confusion and dullness had gone. His joy in Coleridge was almost like that of a lover at times, making him sick and exhilarated by turn. When, on parting, the poet invited him to visit him in Somerset, where he and Wordsworth were collaborating on a book of poems (*Lyrical Ballads*), Hazlitt's happiness was overwhelming.

Years later, in one of the most wonderful descriptions of a turning-point in life – 'My First Acquaintance With Poets' – Hazlitt recalled the moment exactly.

On my way back, I had a sound in my ears, it was the voice of Fancy: I had a light before me, it was the face of Poetry. . . . I had an uneasy, pleasurable sensation all the time, till I was to visit him. During these months the chill breath of winter gave me a welcoming; the vernal air was balm and inspiration to me. The golden sunsets, the silver star of evening, lighten me on my way to new hopes and prospects. *I was to visit Coleridge in the spring*. This circumstance was never absent from my thoughts, and mingled with all my feelings. I wrote to him at the time proposed, and received an answer postponing my intended visit for a week or two, but very cordially urging me to complete my promise then. This delay did not damp, but rather increased my ardour. In the meantime I went to Llangollen Vale, by way of initiating myself in the mysteries of natural scenery; and I must say I was enchanted with it. . . . That valley was to me (in a manner) the cradle of a new existence . . . !

Thus the first meeting with Coleridge and Wordsworth possessed all the dramatic power of a curtain rising on a tragedy whose first scene is the deceptive and lulling idyll. Yet, in spite of what was to follow, when Wordsworth, sunk deep in reaction and apprehensive of what the world would think of his youthful friendship with a man who was now a notorious radical, was not above spreading gossip about Hazlitt's sex life in an effort to discredit him, and Coleridge, as marvellous during this period as his own drinker of the milk of Paradise, had sunk into a comfort-seeking hulk, the essayist allowed nothing to dim or qualify the glory of his twentieth year. 'What I have once set my hand to, I take the consequences of ...' We see Coleridge at this moment as one who commits others to great doctrines which he is unable to follow himself, and we see Hazlitt's frightening vulnerability for the first time. 'My First Acquaintance With Poets' reveals, as well as happiness, that ultimate defencelessness which marks all his writing.

It was art, however, and not literature which received its

fillip from this meeting, although in Hazlitt's mind at this time the two activities had begun their inseparable fascination for him – 'Till I began to paint, or till I became acquainted with the author of *The Ancient Mariner*, I could neither write nor speak.' But painting for Hazlitt was to be neither a career nor mere interest. Mania might best describe it. It is doubtful if any words – his beloved Shakespeare's excepted – were ever to involve him heart and soul as did Rembrandt, Titian and Raphael. Throughout his life he thrust these masters forward like a salvation-bringing icon, insisting, 'Believe! believe!' It was not enough that he should become rapturous in picture galleries, he had to bring others to this state, for he knew nothing to equal it. A few weeks after meeting the poets he left home to become an art student in London. His hero now – for Hazlitt was a man who insisted on heroes – was James Northcote.

Hazlitt's conception of painting was strictly retrospective. The nearer it turned back to its sublime source – Titian, Rembrandt, Raphael – the greater it became. Northcote's special attraction was that he had known Sir Joshua Reynolds and his circle, and, as one who had had direct contact with an artist who had reaffirmed the inviolable laws of art, he possessed a special mystique for Hazlitt. Eventually he Boswellized the gossipy old man in *Conversations with Northcote*, a book which contains many amusing anecdotes including one about Romney and a painter friend first seeing the Sistine Chapel, and the friend gasping, 'Egad, George, we're bit!' Hazlitt, the entirely open and inquiring, the radical and the sceptic in most matters connected with human activity, became fiercely orthodox and academic the moment he entered a gallery. Nor could he ever see a picture without needing to place a written description beside it. He quite baffled old Northcote – 'Very odd – very odd! I can make nothing of him. He is the strangest being I ever met with.' But when, in 1821, he published his essay *On the*

Pleasure of Painting, the need for such an enthusiasm is explained. Reading it in the light of his multiple tragedy, his inability to relate to everything from the accepted pattern of politics to the average notions of love, we see his faith in painting as a great stabilizing factor in his sad, triumphant life. Old Mr Hazlitt, after half a lifetime's engagement with callousness, had sought Jehovah's arm. His son, fighting the same evils but never to know a moment's rest, found in landscapes and portraits harmonious statements from which he could draw strength. Art was for Hazlitt a mixture of religion and medicine, and he envied those engaged in it.

No one thinks of disturbing a landscape painter at his task: he seems a kind of magician, the privileged genius of the place. Whenever a Claude, a Wilson, has introduced his own portrait in the foreground of a picture, we look at it with interest (however ill it may be done) feeling that it is the portrait of one who was quite happy at the time, and how glad we should be to change places with him.

Where his own painting was concerned, Hazlitt was a fundamentalist, restating the dictums of the old masters as faithfully as he could. He painted his father in the manner of Rembrandt and Charles Lamb in the style of Titian. On two occasions, in 1802 and 1824, he visited the Louvre. No one in search of Europe's great pictures need have gone further, for Napoleon had looted the Continental galleries and palaces of their treasures and had heaped them up in Paris. There had never been so great a concentration of the major European schools before and certainly not one so easily available to the ordinary people. Hazlitt, a shabby student of twenty-four when he first sat copying one of his beloved Titians in rooms so recently closed to all but the privileged few, felt that he was present at some kind of break-through in the frustrating rules governing humanity. 'You have enriched the museum of Paris with 300 masterpieces ... which

it required thirty centuries to produce,' Napoleon had told
his troops. For Hazlitt, this was not the customary spoils of
war but a taking of art out of the exclusive hereditary sector
and making it available to all. In France, he heard tales of
the Emperor's taste, charm, courage and general superiority
at every hand, and there began that process – and one involving the hero of all heroes – by which he could accept
Napoleon as the enemy of absolutism and all the stale systems devolving from it.

Wordsworth, who was also in France in 1802 – the Peace
of Amiens had brought the British across the Channel in
their thousands, all eager to see this sensationally transformed nation – watched Napoleon's imperialism and lost
all belief in revolution. He wrote sneeringly of the eagerness
of the recent destroyers of the Bourbons to

> bend the knee
> In France, before the new-born Majesty!

For Hazlitt, Napoleon remained the hope of the world and
when, at Waterloo, the final crushing came, his despair was
terrifying. 'It is not to be believed how the destruction of
Napoleon affected him,' wrote Benjamin Robert Haydon.
'He seemed prostrated in mind and body, he walked about
unwashed, unshaved, hardly sober by day and always in-
toxicated by night, literally, without exaggeration, for
weeks; until at length, wakening as it were from a stupor,
he at once left off all stimulating liquors, and never touched
them after.' (This latter teetotalism was not the good thing
it might appear, for Hazlitt took to drinking green tea of
such strength and in such quantities that it probably contributed to the stomach cancer which was to kill him.) Another witness of Hazlitt at this time was Thomas Talfourd,
the first biographer of Lamb. 'When I first met Hazlitt in
the year 1815,' he wrote, 'he was staggering under the blow
of Waterloo. The reappearance of his imperial idol on the

coast of France, and his triumphant march to Paris, like a fairy vision, had excited his admiration and sympathy to the utmost pitch; and though in many respects sturdily English in feeling, he could scarcely forgive the valour of the conquerors ...' He added, 'On this subject only was he "eaten up with passion", on all others, he was the fairest, the most candid of reasoners.'

Hazlitt's last great task was a monumental *Life of the Emperor*. It was mostly written in Paris and he intended it as both a vindication of Bonaparte and the pinnacle of his own career. He also relied on it to bring him some real money and to put a stop, at least for some time, to the hand-to-mouth existence of essay-writing. But whereas these had seemed to simply fly into print with no difficulty beyond that created by Rightist claques, the great *Life of Napoleon* seemed hardly able to totter from the press. Nor was this all. Like some hideously uncalled-for blow from a person for whose sake one has endured much, the publishers went bankrupt, involving Hazlitt in a loss of £200 when, with his last illness approaching, he was in desperate need of money. The Emperor who had alighted like the bird of promise had turned into an albatross. Hazlitt could have found reasons for getting Napoleon off his neck. It would have made life easier. It would certainly have widened his influence as a radical journalist, for there were those who saw his defence of Napoleon as something which at the best was irrational and at the worst, mad. But as he wrote to William Gifford:

The reason why I have not changed my principle with some of the persons alluded to [Wordsworth, Coleridge and Southey] is, that I had a natural inveteracy of understanding which did not bend to fortune or circumstances. I was not a poet, but a metaphysician; and I suppose that the conviction of an abstract principle is alone a match for the prejudices of absolute power. The love of truth is the best foundation for the love of liberty. In this sense, I might have repeated –

> 'Love is not love that alteration finds:
> O, no! it is an ever-fixed mark
> That looks on tempests and is never shaken.'

Besides, I had another reason. I owed something to truth, for she had done something for me. Early in life I had made (what I thought) a metaphysical discovery; and after that it was too late to think of retracting. My pride forbad it: my understanding revolted at it. I could not do better than go on as I had begun. I too, worshipped at no unhallowed shrine, and served in no mean presence. I had laid my hand on the ark, and could not turn back!

To trace the second disastrous strand in Hazlitt's life, we have to return to his second meeting with the poets. This occurred in the summer of 1803. They were kind and welcoming but they were *different*. They sat to the almost penniless artist for their portraits, but when they introduced him to their benefactor, Sir George Beaumont, a famous patron, he disgraced them by airing his radical views and contradicting Coleridge, Sir George's latest protégée, in his – Sir George's – actual presence. Other complications followed. Hazlitt drifted along with the poets, now including Southey, all that autumn, becoming more and more bewildered by the great change which had come over his friends, and feeling upset. On 14 December 1803 he left. Southey, writing at the time, makes it sound a perfectly ordinary departure and even goes so far as to describe Hazlitt as a painter 'of real genius'. Wordsworth, writing twelve years later, had a very different tale to tell. Hazlitt, the moralist on all things, had when staying with the poets in the Lake District attempted to violate a village girl against her will and it was only through the generosity of his friends that he had escaped from the indignant country youths, and possibly from transportation! Charles Lamb, who received this news from Wordsworth in December 1814, laughingly reduced it to a pastoral frolic but Henry

Crabb Robinson, who actually heard the details from Wordsworth's own lips, was so fascinated by them that, in the selfish manner of educated prudes, he resorted to Latin when setting them down in his diary. An obscene gossip proliferated at once from this story and from now until the close of his life Hazlitt's name carried with it the overtones of depravity.

Wordsworth's motive for making the serious charge stemmed from his volte-face politics of 1802–3. Both he and Coleridge had sided with France during the first half of the Napoleonic war because they regarded their own country's action as a war against the birth of democracy. But they were able to change sides when the second war was decided upon because they saw that Napoleon was no more democratic than the Bourbons and was in fact planning a great imperial military adventure. Eagerness to begin this second war, which had actually been declared by the time Hazlitt reached Keswick, was rowdily apparent and he saw, to his disgust, that Coleridge of all people was in the van of 'the war-whoop', as he called it. Coleridge had, in fact, invented Napoleon's most damaging nickname – 'the Corsican'. Such fervent patriotism was reassuring to Coleridge's new patron, the High Tory Sir George Beaumont, and came as a natural relief to Wordsworth in his new mood of Olympian withdrawal to the Cumberland mountains. Hazlitt's disgust at their revised positions when he arrived in 1803 was one thing, but his morbid pursuit of them in print as turncoats – something they could not have imagined the confused young artist would ever be able to do – was another. Hazlitt, fighting his own private war for liberty, was a menace. The note of accusation never ceased. The accuser needed to be accused – but of what?

Because his enemies so often reached through his private life in order to discredit his politics and, in Wordsworth's case, even his literary opinions – for one reason why the

Lakes escapade was made public in 1814 was fear of what Hazlitt might write about *The Excursion*, which was published that year – it is necessary to take a brief look at Hazlitt and women. They were very important to him but his neglect of 'manner' in his approach to them and what seemed like a tacit assumption on his part that they would reciprocate his feelings without going through the usual charade of high-flown talk and artificial gestures, got him nowhere. His lack of success, and subsequent fear and hostility towards 'young ladies', was well-known among his friends, who found it very amusing. Crabb Robinson had seen his nervous confusion and shock when, still a boy, some well-bred girls had teased him during a holiday at Bury St Edmunds. It enabled the diarist to state, when the outcry against him as an immoralist was at its height, that 'Like other gross sensualists, he had a horror of the society of ladies, especially of smart and handsome and modest young women.'

Hazlitt was married twice, each time to a 'lady'. But an early Rousseau-like idealization of simple, unsophisticated girls, a conception of companionship which at first had for him a dreamy innocence, grew naturally into a sexual desire for such women. Although they let him down every bit as much as the ladies, his forgiveness of their inability to accept him as a lover showed that in these encounters he was not self-blind. P. P. Howe, his best biographer, sees the Keswick incident as the sketch, as it were, of the marvellous and remorselessly worked-out *Liber amoris* story in which both the bathos and the splendour of obsessional sexual love have been set down on the page in their entirety. It is the type of love which those who have not experienced it call infatuation because to them it is undignified and pathetic. Hazlitt in love was, to his friends, a comic sight, to his enemies, a disgusting one. Hazlitt did not pretend to find love, as he recognized it, in either of his wives. The first union, to

Sarah Stoddart, was almost as much an arranged marriage (by Charles and Mary Lamb) as if the bride and groom had been Chinese. Lamb, for whom Hazlitt's sex life was the only thing about his friend he could never take seriously, laughed so much during the wedding that he was nearly turned out of church. Sarah was to bring Hazlitt little happiness in herself but she gave him a son, whom he both mothered and fathered, his wife being cold in such matters and, anyway, frequently away from home on great walking tours. Neither lover nor home-maker, she was yet what he vaguely wanted a woman to be – a free agent, an untrammelled soul. Sarah Hazlitt was, in fact, a New Woman born a century before her time. How she would have enjoyed 'rational' clothes for all that hiking! By the time of their – inevitable – divorce, in Edinburgh, her craving for the open road forced her to walk nearly 150 miles through the Scottish countryside during the proceedings. As well as his adored son, she gave her husband one other thing that pleased him, a small cottage in Winterslow, Wiltshire.

It was from this address, immediately after his marriage in 1808, that he began to bombard the London editors with outlines for literary projects, and that he wrote his *Life of Holcroft*. The choice of subject was interesting. Thomas Holcroft, who had died the year before, had been a friend of Tom Paine and a believer in Godwin's revolutionary ideas. He had also been a stable-boy who had become a successful novelist and playwright.

But neither painting, his wife's fortune of £80 a year, nor the solid books he was managing to turn out, met the expenses of married life, and in the autumn of 1812 Hazlitt, with Lamb's help, became Parliamentary reporter for the *Morning Chronicle*, a Whig newspaper edited by James Perry, whose snobbery and scant scholarship did not prevent him from becoming one of the most progressive figures in nineteenth-century journalism. Within a year of accepting

this job, Hazlitt was filling the columns of the *Morning
Chronicle* with far more exciting things than could be heard
in the House of Commons, essays such as *On the Love of
Life* and brilliant accounts of what was taking place on the
London stage. Both these discursive essays, in which profound and extraordinary matters were dealt with wittily
and with a personal conviction which made an immediate
contact with the reader, and the dramatic criticism, were
of a kind previously unknown to journalism. The excellence
and unusualness of his work provided Hazlitt, now in his
early thirties, with the influence which he could never
have hoped to have derived from any other literary activity.
Whatever the world thought of his politics, both his style
and the strangely intimate tone of his arguments were things
which no one cared to miss. 'Once he had started,' says
P. P. Howe, 'we find his dramatic criticisms, art criticisms,
political letters and leading articles, "Common-places", and
contributions from "An English Metaphysician", all going
up together in Mr Perry's columns.'

As this hardly-to-be-expected burst of literary power and
excellence coincided with such national self-examinings as
the meaning of patriotism, inquests on the value of the
French Revolution and what to do with Napoleon, a reactionary Britain – including the Lake District – saw with
horror that a Daniel had come to judgement. Worse, Hazlitt's very catholicity, his perverse refusal – or inability – to
specialize in a subject, as other men did, made him hard to
handle. A piece that, when produced by the eighteenth-
century essayists and their followers, would have contained
a few ounces of elegantly wrapped morality, often contained
an ethical explosion when it left Hazlitt's hand. He lacked
all restraint. Anything which threatened the total liberty of
the individual, the little deceits by which society managed to
get by, the areas of human behaviour which it was 'civilized'
to ignore, speciousness of all kinds and *cant* – his four-letter

word for describing the talk which covered the naked truth – these were his natural targets. He attacked them with a mixture of gaiety and rage. Those who had reason to fear waited nervously for his blow. His concept of truth as a once-revealed thing to which a man remained loyal no matter what happened later on placed everybody in the somewhat religious position of either the 'faithful' or the 'apostates'. Southey, who at nineteen had written a revolutionary play called *Wat Tyler*, was aghast to find something he hoped the world had forgotten being reissued by a pirate-publisher at the very moment he had accepted the Laureateship. Hazlitt gave no quarter in this affair, and others with radical pasts which, up to now, they thought well-buried, shivered. He was no believer in the woolliness which society permitted to shelter public and private lives, but however much people might deplore his stark honesty, they could not forbear to look.

Yet he was never simply out for a scoop, and journalism in the ordinary sense of news-plus-comment meant little to him. A magnificent writer who would have preferred to work quietly on metaphysical treatises in the tradition of Locke and Hobbes, he was driven to the newspapers and the magazines by the need to make money. He wrote spasmodically and with a certain resentment. He was daydreaming and indolent. His real pleasure never stemmed from work but from drifting, idling, unplanned days made up of lying on the chalky turf of the Wiltshire downs, playing racquets on the St Martin's Street court and chatting to strangers or chance acquaintances. Like so many artists, he was never reconciled to one or other of the country-versus-the-town choice. His compassion for the village people of England during their extreme misery of the 1820s also showed indications of his personal fear of them. As a village-intellectual, on and off for the best part of his life, he could not forget the countryman's narrowness and meanness of spirit, and as a townsman he could never be sufficiently man of the world to exist without shock amidst scenes of accepted greed, indifference and hypocrisy. In both village and town he recovered his shaken belief in life by reading the poets and by looking at pictures.

Yet, although shy of contact with the masses and often scathing about them, he saw them as few people did at the time – as the real England, crushed by the land evictions, reduced and starved by the famine caused by the war, and tragically inarticulate. His emergence as a trenchant and controversial writer, in 1807, came with *A Reply to the Essay on Population*, when his attack on Malthus revealed his brilliant radical pen. The Reverend T. R. Malthus was exactly what the establishment needed after the drums of revolution had petered out, a clergyman-prophet able to supply fact and figure for the inevitability of inequality in human society. For the ruling class Malthus had provided a mandate for going on as before. To back his theory he had put forward a plan for dealing with 'the poor', that inconvenient nine-tenths of the nation. This included, among many other things, notions for restraining fatherhood among the rural males and the blue-print for the extensions of the Poor Law which was to harass countless simple families right up to the First World War. Hazlitt's attack on Malthus was violent and emotional but it displayed his freedom, and less apprehensive friends than Wordsworth and Coleridge came forward to acknowledge him. Among these was Charles Lamb, Hazlitt's senior by only three and a half years, but in whose (much tried) relationship there was a stable, protective element suggesting a much older man. The great difference, in fact, between Lamb and Hazlitt was that the former seemed to have received the gift of perpetual early middle-age and the latter, with his moodiness, his iconoclasm, his physical energy, his hero-worship, his passionate love and his general recklessness, appeared to have been cursed with everlasting youth. To outgrow innocence – i.e., one's initial reflexes to important matters – was for Hazlitt a sin. James Knowles, one of his disciple-like young friends, said, 'There was ore in him, and rich, but his maturer friends were blind to it. I saw it. He was a man to whom I would have submitted my life.'

From 1816 onwards Hazlitt's work has to be seen against the churning unrest which provoked the government to suspend Habeas Corpus in 1817 and which was violently epitomized in the massacre at Peterloo on 16 August 1819. His collected essays from the *Examiner* were published under the title of *The Round Table*, and dedicated to Lamb. The essays so excelled the usual literature of radical protest that one critic described it as being 'like a whale's back in a sea of prose'. We have a number of glimpses of him at this period, including the one Haydon painted in his enormous *Entry into Jerusalem*, where Hazlitt is shown 'looking at Christ as an investigator'. The same year as this portrait appeared, Wordsworth was writing to the artist, 'The miscreant Hazlitt continues, I have heard, to abuse Southey, Coleridge and myself in the *Examiner*. I hope you do not associate with the Fellow, he is not a proper person to be admitted into respectable society ...' A less hostile witness gives this vivid description.

His face was indeed indifferent, and his movements shy and awkward; but there was something in his earnest irritable face, his restless eyes, his black hair, combed backwards and curling (not too resolutely) about a well-shaped head, that was very striking. ... At home, his style of dress (or undress) was perhaps slovenly, because there was no one to please; but he always presented a very clean and neat appearance when he went abroad. His mode of walking was loose, weak and unsteady; although his arms displayed strength, which he used to put forth when he played at raquets with Martin Burney and others. ... His violence (if violence he had), was of very rare occurrence. He was extremely patient. ... Had he been as temperate in his political views as in his cups, he would have escaped the slander that pursued him through life.

Temperance, however, was not something which Hazlitt understood. 'When I see a spirit of intolerance I see a great Devil,' he said.

This, then, was how he looked at the moment when he was at the height of his power as a writer. The man who in life so disliked being touched and human contact generally, and accepted friendship on chilling terms – and then complained of lack of warmth : 'I want to know why everybody has such a dislike of me' – was, on the page, to generate a glow which admitted the reader at once to his intimate presence.

In 1820 Hazlitt and Lamb were contributing to the *London Magazine* the wonderful essays which were to become, respectively, the first volume of *Table Talk* and the *Essays of Elia*. It was also the year of disaster. Hazlitt lost all hope – 'I believe in the theoretical benevolence and practical malignity of man' – and eventually almost lost his reason. Why? Because at forty-three he had fallen in love at first sight with the nineteen-year-old girl who waited on him in the two back rooms of a lodging-house in Southampton Buildings. 'Love at first sight is only realising an imagination that has always haunted us ... our dream is out at last ...' At twenty-six, the Lakes girl had led him on, laughing, and (according to Wordsworth) he had struck her. Now he was middle-aged, Sarah Walker was to do the same, with 'mock embraces' and lips 'as common as the stairs'. Yet sometimes she smiled, and in analysing the effect this had on him, he had immortalized her. His refusal not to treat the situation rationally – with a straightforward sexuality – bewildered Sarah and puzzled his friends, to whom he was compelled to pour out his troubles. Strangers, too, had to listen to every

humiliating detail of the affair, for he was an obsessed creature – 'the fool of love'. It was the kind of behaviour which
appeared to justify De Quincey's later verdict that Hazlitt
'wilfully placed himself in collision with all the interests
that were in the sunshine of this world ...' The love affair,
grotesquely compounded with divorce proceedings concerning the other Sarah, and followed by a nervous breakdown
during which he considered suicide, produced the extraordinary *Liber amoris*. Once he had been merely bitter
when a simple girl let him down – 'Choose a mistress from
among your equals. ... Those in an inferior station to yourself will doubt your good intentions. ... They will be ignorant of the meaning of half you say, and laugh at the rest'
– now he gave himself up to a total declaration of the nature
of the only sexual love he understood. The *Liber amoris*
endorsed posterity's claim to distrust him long after his politics had ceased to offend. Robert Louis Stevenson thought
of writing Hazlitt's biography, then discovered this book
and withdrew in horror. Augustus Birrell was simply
astonished that a grown man could let himself in for anything so idiotic – 'The loves of the middle-aged are never
agreeable subject matter ... a fool at forty is a fool indeed ...' He added, '*Liber amoris* now sinks below the
stage, and joins the realm of things unspeakable ...' Charles
Morgan, in an excellent introduction to the book (1948),
reminds us that Hazlitt's unguarded account of love and
sexual madness was published at the same time as Stendhal's
De l'amour, and he says that 'the whole story of the *Liber
amoris* is a flawless example of Stendahl's theory of crys-
talization'. To write it, Hazlitt had to abandon the only
thing which could have made it even remotely socially
acceptable – dignity. It was not 'manly' declared *Blackwood's*. This it all too shatteringly was. Love is frequently a
pitiable state.

Recovered from the débâcle, he settled down to his familiar

unsettled life, working when he must but now with a greater sense of his own coherence. In 1825 came *The Spirit of the Age* and a year abroad with his second wife, the all but unknown Isabella Bridgwater. Also a meeting with Stendhal – 'my friend Mr Beyle'. He returned looking ill. His writing grew in its intensity, breaking in on the privacy of those who read it with irresistible and sometimes unbearable news. There was no escape from his meaning; the language which conveyed it shone with precision – 'I hate to see a load of bandboxes go along the street, and I hate to see a parcel of big words without anything in them.' The exposition of an idea would start out on the page in light, happy phrases which threatened no man's complacency, and then the skilful strengthening would begin, and intellectual involvement would bind the reader. Each essay shows the build-up of numerous small climaxes, such as are sometimes employed in the novel. Excitement and expectation mount. Hazlitt is the word-juggler who never misses; his almost casual use of ornament, epigram and fancy is hypnotic. Some, like De Quincey, resented that they should be morally got at by this 'abrupt, insulated, capricious ... and non-sequacious style'. Hazlitt's method of writing essays had something in common with his action on the St Martin's Street fives-court. He would begin by pleasantly spinning his subject around, work along various entertaining possibilities until he found a possible break-through, then score for all he was worth. He never regarded journalism as an inferior literary activity. His only regret was the voracious way it had of swallowing up work, and thus the time he would have preferred to spend in a kind of unambitious reverie. 'All that is worth remembering of life is the poetry of it.' Yet it was, as Virginia Woolf saw, the chafing and goading of many of life's unpoetic asides which kept Hazlitt on the stretch. One of his most amazing accomplishments is his abolition of the time barrier, not for himself – he is primarily the spokesman for the inarticulate, the exploited, the self-deceived and the less brave inhabitants of George IV's England; the conscience of an era – but for future readers. He has an uncanny ability to involve us across the generations in his hopes, hates, enthusiasms, fury and sensuality. It is also possible to see in him the warring extremes of the Puritan nature. He is a writer who must always remain more than 'works' and it is both thrilling and sobering when one investigates the latter to find so much flesh and blood, so much anger and so very much love. His was a uniquely unsublimated life. For him, writing never took the place of living.

He died of cancer on 18 September 1830 in a poor little room at 6 Frith Street, Soho. Bryan Procter heard him speaking his last words in a voice 'resembling the faint scream I have heard from birds'. He was fifty-two.

R. B.

THE BIBLIOGRAPHY OF
WILLIAM HAZLITT

1805 An Essay on the Principles of Human Action

1806 Free Thoughts on Public Affairs

1807 Abridgement of Tucker's 'The Light of Nature Pursued'

1807 The Eloquence of the British Senate

1807 A Reply to the Essay on Population by the Rev. T. R. Malthus

1810 A New and Improved Grammar of the English Tongue

1816 Memoirs of Thomas Holcroft

1817 The Round Table, 2 Volumes (from the *Examiner*)

1817 Characters of Shakespeare's Plays

1818 A View of the English Stage

1818 Lectures on the English Poets

1819 A Letter to William Gifford, Esq.

1819 Lectures on the English Comic Writers

1819–22 Political Essays, with sketches of Public Characters

1820 Lectures on the Age of Elizabeth

1821–2 Table-Talk

1823 Liber amoris

1823 Characteristics in the Manner of Rochefoucauld's Maxims

1824 Sketches of the Principle Picture Galleries in England

1825 The Spirit of the Age, or Contemporary Portraits

1825 Select Poets of Great Britain, with Critical Notices

1826 The Plain Speaker

1826 Notes on a Journey Through France and Italy

1826–7 Boswell Redivivus

1828–30 The Life of Napoleon Buonaparte (4 volumes)

1830 Conversations with James Northcote

1836 Literary Remains

1839 Sketches and Essays (now first collected, and republished as *Men and Manners* in 1852)

1843–4 Criticisms on Art, etc.

1850 Winterslow. Essays and Characters written there

1930–34 Complete Works, edited by P. P. Howe

BIOGRAPHY

Contemporaries: Henry Crabb Robinson, *Diary*
John Keats, *Letters*
William Wordsworth, *Letters*
Leigh Hunt, *Autobiography*
B. R. Haydon, *Autobiography*
Miss Mitford, *Life and Letters*
W. C. Hazlitt (Son), *Memoirs of William Hazlitt*
P. G. Patmore, *My Friends and Acquaintances*
Thomas De Quincey, *Collected Works*
Mrs (Sarah) Hazlitt's *Diary*

The definitive Life is that by P. P. Howe, first published in 1922. *Born Under Saturn* by Catherine Macdonald Maclean (Collins, 1943) contains a full social and political description of the background to Hazlitt's life, and *The Fool of Love* by Hesketh Pearson (Hamish Hamilton, 1934) is mainly a study of Hazlitt in the context of the *Liber amoris* story.

NOTE ON THE TEXT

This selection is based on the most authoritative text we have of Hazlitt's work, that followed in the 1930–34 edition by P. P. Howe. In making the selection I have not attempted a strict chronological order but have placed certain essays so that they form the main outline of Hazlitt's life. Examples of his literary and dramatic criticism, those brilliant carefree writings such as *The Fight* and *The Indian Jugglers* which were often composed when he was most wretched, his talent for invective and his opinions on politics, religion, class, fashion, hate, love, are arranged within this outline. At the centre of the book is his astonishing account of the sexual crisis which, in his own words, 'nearly finished me'. This selection also contains a fresh supplement of Hazlitt's epigrams and aphorisms.

SELECTED WRITINGS

MY FIRST ACQUAINTANCE
WITH POETS

M y father was a Dissenting Minister at W—m[1] in Shropshire; and in the year 1798 (the figures that compose that
date are to me like the 'dreaded name of Demogorgon')
Mr Coleridge came to Shrewsbury, to succeed Mr Rowe in
the spiritual charge of a Unitarian Congregation there. He
did not come till late on the Saturday afternoon before he
was to preach; and Mr Rowe, who himself went down to
the coach in a state of anxiety and expectation, to look for
the arrival of his successor, could find no one at all answering the description but a round-faced man in a short black
coat (like a shooting jacket) which hardly seemed to have
been made for him, but who seemed to be talking at a great
rate to his fellow-passengers. Mr Rowe had scarce returned
to give an account of his disappointment, when the round-
faced man in black entered, and dissipated all doubts on the
subject, by beginning to talk. He did not cease while he
staid; nor has he since, that I know of. He held the good
town of Shrewsbury in delightful suspense for three weeks
that he remained there, 'fluttering the *proud Salopians* like
an eagle in a dove-cote;' and the Welch mountains that skirt
the horizon with their tempestuous confusion, agree to have
heard no such mystic sounds since the days of

'High-born Hoel's harp or soft Llewellyn's lay!'

As we passed along between W—m and Shrewsbury, and I
eyed their blue tops seen through the wintry branches, or the
red rustling leaves of the sturdy oak-trees by the road-side, a
sound was in my ears as of a Siren's song; I was stunned,
startled with it, as from deep sleep; but I had no notion then
that I should ever be able to express my admiration to others

in motley imagery or quaint allusion, till the light of his genius shone into my soul, like the sun's rays glittering in the puddles of the road. I was at that time dumb, inarticulate, helpless, like a worm by the way-side, crushed, bleeding, lifeless; but now, bursting from the deadly bands that 'bound them,

'With Styx nine times round them,'

my ideas float on winged words, and as they expand their plumes, catch the golden light of other years. My soul has indeed remained in its original bondage, dark, obscure, with longings infinite and unsatisfied; my heart, shut up in the prison-house of this rude clay, has never found, nor will it ever find, a heart to speak to; but that my understanding also did not remain dumb and brutish, or at length found a language to express itself, I owe to Coleridge. But this is not to my purpose.

My father lived ten miles from Shrewsbury, and was in the habit of exchanging visits with Mr Rowe, and with Mr Jenkins of Whitchurch (nine miles farther on) according to the custom of Dissenting Ministers in each other's neighbourhood. A line of communication is thus established, by which the flame of civil and religious liberty is kept alive, and nourishes its smouldering fire unquenchable, like the fires in the Agamemnon of Æschylus, placed at different stations, that waited for ten long years to announce with their blazing pyramids the destruction of Troy. Coleridge had agreed to come over to see my father, according to the courtesy of the country, as Mr Rowe's probable successor; but in the meantime I had gone to hear him preach the Sunday after his arrival. A poet and a philosopher getting up into a Unitarian pulpit to preach the Gospel, was a romance in these degenerate days, a sort of revival of the primitive spirit of Christianity, which was not to be resisted.

It was in January, 1798, that I rose one morning before

daylight, to walk ten miles in the mud, and went to hear this celebrated person preach. Never, the longest day I have to live, shall I have such another walk as this cold, raw, comfortless one, in the winter of the year 1798. *Il y a des impressions que ni le tems ni les circonstances peuvent effacer. Dusse-je vivre des siècles entiers, le doux tems de ma jeunesse ne peut renaître pour moi, ni s'effacer jamais dans ma mémoire.* When I got there, the organ was playing the 100th psalm, and, when it was done, Mr Coleridge rose and gave out his text, 'And he went up into the mountain to pray, HIMSELF, ALONE.' As he gave out his text, his voice 'rose like a steam of rich distilled perfumes,' and when he came to the two last words, which he pronounced loud, deep, and distinct, it seemed to me, who was then young, as if the sounds had echoed from the bottom of the human heart, and as if that prayer might have floated in solemn silence through the universe. The idea of St John came into mind, 'of one crying in the wilderness, who had his loins girt about, and whose food was locusts and wild honey.' The preacher then launched into his subject, like an eagle dallying with the wind. The sermon was upon peace and war; upon church and state – not their alliance, but their separation – on the spirit of the world and the spirit of Christianity, not as the same, but as opposed to one another. He talked of those who had 'inscribed the cross of Christ on banners dripping with human gore.' He made a poetical and pastoral excursion, – and to shew the fatal effects of war, drew a striking contrast between the simple shepherd boy, driving his team afield, or sitting under the hawthorn, piping to his flock, 'as though he should never be old,' and the same poor country-lad, crimped, kidnapped, brought into town, made drunk at an alehouse, turned into a wretched drummer-boy, with his hair sticking on end with powder and pomatum, a long cue at his back, and tricked out in the loathsome finery of the profession of blood.

'Such were the notes our once-lov'd poet sung.'

And for myself, I could not have been more delighted if I had heard the music of the spheres. Poetry and Philosophy had met together. Truth and Genius had embraced, under the eye and with the sanction of Religion. This was even beyond my hopes. I returned home well satisfied. The sun that was still labouring pale and wan through the sky, obscured by thick mists, seemed an emblem of the *good cause*; and the cold dank drops of dew that hung half melted on the beard of the thistle, had something genial and refreshing in them; for there was a spirit of hope and youth in all nature, that turned every thing into good. The face of nature had not then the brand of JUS DIVINUM on it:

'Like to that sanguine flower inscrib'd with woe.'

On the Tuesday following, the half-inspired speaker came. I was called down into the room where he was, and went half-hoping, half-afraid. He received me very graciously, and I listened for a long time without uttering a word. I did not suffer in his opinion by my silence. 'For those two hours,' he afterwards was pleased to say, 'he was conversing with W. H.'s forehead!' His appearance was different from what I had anticipated from seeing him before. At a distance, and in the dim light of the chapel, there was to me a strange wildness in his aspect, a dusky obscurity, and I thought him pitted with the small-pox. His complexion was at that time clear, and even bright —

'As are the children of yon azure sheen.'

His forehead was broad and high, light as if built of ivory, with large projecting eyebrows, and his eyes rolling beneath them like a sea with darkened lustre. 'A certain tender bloom his face o'erspread,' a purple tinge as we see it in the pale thoughtful complexions of the Spanish portrait-painters, Murillo and Velasquez. His mouth was gross, voluptuous, open, eloquent; his chin good-humoured and round; but his nose, the rudder of the face, the index of the will, was small, feeble, nothing – like what he has done. It might seem that the genius of his face as from a height surveyed and projected him (with sufficient capacity and huge aspiration) into the world unknown of thought and imagination, with nothing to support or guide his veering purpose, as if Columbus had launched his adventurous course for the New World in a scallop, without oars or compass. So at least I comment on it after the event. Coleridge in his person was rather above the common size, inclining to the corpulent, or like Lord Hamlet, 'somewhat fat and pursy.' His hair (now, alas! grey) was then black and glossy as the raven's, and fell in smooth masses over his forehead. This long pendulous hair is peculiar to enthusiasts, to those whose minds tend heavenward; and is traditionally inseparable (though of a different colour) from the pictures of Christ. It ought to belong, as a character, to all who preach *Christ crucified*, and Coleridge was at that time one of those!

It was curious to observe the contrast between him and my father, who was a veteran in the cause, and then declining into the vale of years. He had been a poor Irish lad, carefully brought up by his parents, and sent to the University of Glasgow (where he studied under Adam Smith) to prepare him for his future destination. It was his mother's proudest wish to see her son a Dissenting Minister. So if we look back to past generations (as far as eye can reach) we see the same hopes, fears, wishes, followed by the same disappointments, throbbing in the human heart; and so we may see them (if we look forward) rising up for ever, and disappearing, like vapourish bubbles, in the human breast! After being tossed about from congregation to congregation in the heats of the Unitarian controversy, and squabbles about the American war, he had been relegated to an obscure village, where he was to spend the last thirty years of

his life, far from the only converse that he loved, the talk
about disputed texts of Scripture and the cause of civil and
religious liberty. Here he passed his days, repining but resigned, in the study of the Bible, and the perusal of the
Commentators, – huge folios, not easily got through, one
of which would outlast a winter! Why did he pore on these
from morn to night (with the exception of a walk in the
fields or a turn in the garden to gather broccoli-plants or
kidney-beans of his own rearing, with no small degree of
pride and pleasure)? – Here were 'no figures nor no fantasies,' – neither poetry nor philosophy – nothing to dazzle,
nothing to excite modern curiosity; but to his lack-lustre
eyes there appeared, within the pages of the ponderous, un-
wieldly, neglected tomes, the sacred name of JEHOVAH in
Hebrew capitals: pressed down by the weight of the style,
worn to the last fading thinness of the understanding, there
were glimpses, glimmering notions of the patriarchal wanderings, with palm-trees hovering in the horizon, and pro-
cessions of camels at the distance of three thousand years;
there was Moses with the Burning Bush, the number of the
Twelve Tribes, types, shadows, glosses on the law and the
prophets; there were discussions (dull enough) on the age of
Methuselah, a mighty speculation! there were outlines, rude
guesses at the shape of Noah's Ark and of the riches of
Solomon's Temple; questions as to the date of the creation,
predictions of the end of all things; the great lapses of time,
the strange mutations of the globe were unfolded with the
voluminous leaf, as it turned over; and though the soul
might slumber with an hieroglyphic veil of inscrutable mysteries drawn over it, yet it was in a slumber ill-exchanged
for all the sharpened realities of sense, wit, fancy, or reason.
My father's life was comparatively a dream; but it was a
dream of infinity and eternity, of death, the resurrection,
and a judgment to come!

No two individuals were ever more unlike than were the

host and his guest. A poet was to my father a sort of non-descript: yet whatever added grace to the Unitarian cause was to him welcome. He could hardly have been more surprised or pleased, if our visitor had worn wings. Indeed, his thoughts had wings; and as the silken sounds rustled round our little wainscoted parlour, my father threw back his spectacles over his forehead, his white hairs mixing with its sanguine hue; and a smile of delight beamed across his rugged cordial face, to think that Truth had found a new ally in Fancy!* Besides, Coleridge seemed to take considerable notice of me, and that of itself was enough. He talked very familiarly, but agreeably, and glanced over a variety of subjects. At dinner-time he grew more animated, and dilated in a very edifying manner on Mary Wolstonecraft and Mackintosh. The last, he said, he considered (on my father's speaking of his *Vindiciæ Gallicæ* as a capital performance) as a clever scholastic man – a master of the topics, – or as the ready warehouseman of letters, who knew exactly where to lay his hand on what he wanted, though the goods were not his own. He thought him no match for Burke, either in style or matter. Burke was a metaphysician, Mackintosh a mere logician. Burke was an orator (almost a poet) who reasoned in figures, because he had an eye for nature: Mackintosh, on the other hand, was a rhetorician, who had only an eye to common-places. On this I ventured to say that I had always entertained a great opinion of Burke, and that (as far as I could find) the speaking of him with contempt might be made the test of a vulgar democratical mind. This was the first observation I ever made to Coleridge, and he said it was a very just and striking one. I remember the leg of Welsh

---

*My father was one of those who mistook his talent after all. He used to be very much dissatisfied that I preferred his Letters to his Sermons. The last were forced and dry; the first came naturally from him. For ease, half-plays on words, and a supine, monkish, indolent pleasantry, I have never seen them equalled.

mutton and the turnips on the table that day had the finest flavour imaginable. Coleridge added that Mackintosh and Tom Wedgwood [2] (of whom, however, he spoke highly) had expressed a very indifferent opinion of his friend Mr Wordsworth, on which he remarked to them – 'He strides on so far before you, that he dwindles in the distance!' God- win had once boasted to him of having carried on an argu- ment with Mackintosh for three hours with dubious suc- cess; Coleridge told him – 'If there had been a man of genius in the room, he would have settled the question in five minutes.' He asked me if I had ever seen Mary Wolstone- craft, and I said, I had once for a few moments, and that she seemed to me to turn off Godwin's objections to something she advanced with quite a playful, easy air. He replied, that 'this was only one instance of the ascendancy which people of imagination exercised over those of mere intellect.' He did not rate Godwin very high * (this was caprice or preju- dice, real or affected) but he had a great idea of Mrs Wol- stonecraft's powers of conversation, none at all of her talent for book-making. We talked a little about Holcroft. He had been asked if he was not much struck *with* him, and he said, he thought himself in more danger of being struck *by* him. I complained that he would not let me get on at all, for he required a definition of even the commonest word, ex- claiming, 'What do you mean by a *sensation*, Sir? What do you mean by an *idea*?' This, Coleridge said, was barrica- doing the road to truth: – it was setting up a turnpike-gate at every step we took. I forget a great number of things, many more than I remember; but the day passed off pleas- antly, and the next morning Mr Coleridge was to return to

* He complained in particular of the presumption of attempting to establish the future immortality of man 'without' (as he said) 'know- ing what Death was or what Life was' – and the tone in which he pronounced these two words seemed to convey a complete image of both.

Shrewsbury. When I came down to breakfast, I found that he had just received a letter from his friend T. Wedgwood, making him an offer of 150 *l.* a-year if he chose to wave his present pursuit, and devote himself entirely to the study of poetry and philosophy. Coleridge seemed to make up his mind to close with this proposal in the act of tying on one of his shoes. It threw an additional damp on his departure. It took the wayward enthusiast quite from us to cast him into Deva's winding vales, or by the shores of old romance. Instead of living at ten miles distance, of being the pastor of a Dissenting congregation at Shrewsbury, he was henceforth to inhabit the Hill of Parnassus, to be a shepherd on the Delectable Mountains. Alas! I knew not the way thither, and felt very little gratitude for Mr Wedgwood's bounty. I was presently relieved from this dilemma; for Mr Coleridge, asking for a pen and ink, and going to a table to write something on a bit of card, advanced towards me with undulating step, and giving me the precious document, said that that was his address, *Mr Coleridge, Nether-Stowey, Somersetshire*; and that he should be glad to see me there in a few weeks' time, and, if I chose, would come half-way to meet me. I was not less surprised than the shepherd-boy (this simile is to be found in Cassandra) when he sees a thunder-bolt fall close at his feet. I stammered out my acknowledgements and acceptance of this offer (I thought Mr Wedgwood's annuity a trifle to it) as well as I could; and this mighty business being settled, the poet-preacher took leave, and I accompanied him six miles on the road. It was a fine morning in the middle of winter, and he talked the whole way. The scholar in Chaucer is described as going

– 'Sounding on his way.'

So Coleridge went on his. In digressing, in dilating, in passing from subject to subject, he appeared to me to float in air, to slide on ice. He told me in confidence (going along)

that he should have preached two sermons before he accepted the situation at Shrewsbury, one on Infant Baptism, the other on the Lord's Supper, shewing that he could not administer either, which would have effectually disqualified him for the object in view. I observed that he continually crossed me on the way by shifting from one side of the footpath to the other. This struck me as an odd movement; but I did not at that time connect it with any instability of purpose or involuntary change of principle, as I have done since. He seemed unable to keep on in a strait line. He spoke slightingly of Hume (whose Essay on Miracles he said was stolen from an objection started in one of South's sermons — *Credat Judæus Apella!*) I was not very much pleased at this account of Hume, for I had just been reading, with infinite relish, that completest of all metaphysical *choke-pears*, his *Treatise on Human Nature*, to which the *Essays*, in point of scholastic subtlety and close reasoning, are mere elegant trifling, light summer-reading. Coleridge even denied the excellence of Hume's general style, which I think betrayed a want of taste or candour. He however made me amends by the manner in which he spoke of Berkeley. He dwelt particularly on his *Essay on Vision* as a masterpiece of analytical reasoning. So it undoubtedly is. He was exceedingly angry with Dr Johnson for striking the stone with his foot, in allusion to this author's Theory of Matter and Spirit, and saying, 'Thus I confute him, Sir.' Coleridge drew a parallel (I don't know how he brought about the connection) between Bishop Berkeley and Tom Paine. He said the one was an instance of a subtle, the other of an acute mind, than which no two things could be more distinct. The one was a shop-boy's quality, the other the characteristic of a philosopher. He considered Bishop Butler as a true philosopher, a profound and conscientious thinker, a genuine reader of nature and of his own mind. He did not speak of his *Analogy* but of his *Sermons at the Rolls' Chapel*, of which I had never heard. Coleridge somehow always contrived to prefer the *unknown* to the *known*. In this instance he was right. The *Analogy* is a tissue of sophistry, of wiredrawn, theological special-pleading; the *Sermons* (with the Preface to them) are in a fine vein of deep, matured reflection, a candid appeal to our observation of human nature, without pedantry and without bias. I told Coleridge I had written a few remarks, and was sometimes foolish enough to believe that I had made a discovery on the same subject (the *Natural Disinterestedness of the Human Mind*) – and I tried to explain my view of it to Coleridge, who listened with great willingness, but I did not succeed in making myself understood. I sat down to the task shortly afterwards for the twentieth time, got new pens and paper, determined to make clear work of it, wrote a few meagre sentences in the skeleton-style of a mathematical demonstration, stopped half-way down the second page; and, after trying in vain to pump up any words, images, notions, apprehensions, facts, or observations, from that gulph of abstraction in which I had plunged myself for four or five years preceding, gave up the attempt as labour in vain, and shed tears of helpless despondency on the blank unfinished paper. I can write fast enough now. Am I better than I was then? Oh no! One truth discovered, one pang of regret at not being able to express it, is better than all the fluency and flippancy in the world. Would that I could go back to what I then was! Why can we not revive past times as we can revisit old places? If I had the quaint Muse of Sir Philip Sidney to assist me, I would write a *Sonnet to the Road between W—m and Shrewsbury*, and immortalise every step of it by some fond enigmatical conceit. I would swear that the very milestones had ears, and that Harmer-hill stooped with all its pines, to listen to a poet, as he passed! I remember but one other topic of discourse in this walk. He mentioned Paley, praised the naturalness and clearness of his style, but condemned his sentiments, thought him a mere time-serving casuist, and said that 'the fact of his work on Moral and Political Philosophy being made a text-book in our Universities was a disgrace to the national character.' We parted at the six-mile stone; and I returned homeward pensive but much pleased. I had met with unexpected notice from a person, whom I believed to have been prejudiced against me. 'Kind and affable to me had been his condescension, and should be honoured ever with suitable regard.' He was the first poet I had known, and he certainly answered to that inspired name. I had heard a great deal of his powers of conversation, and was not disappointed. In fact, I never met with any thing at all like them, either before or since. I could easily credit the accounts which were circulated of his holding forth to a large party of ladies and gentlemen, an evening or two before, on the Berkeleian Theory, when he made the whole material universe look like a transparency of fine words; and another story (which I believe he has somewhere told himself) of his being asked to a party at Birmingham, of his smoking tobacco and going to sleep after dinner on a sofa, where the company found him to their no small surprise, which was increased to wonder when he started up of a sudden, and rubbing his eyes, looked about him, and launched into a three-hours' description of the third heaven, of which he had had a dream, very different from Mr Southey's Vision of Judgment, and also from that other Vision of Judgment,[3] which Mr Murray, the Secretary of the Bridge-street Junto, has taken into his especial keeping!

On my way back, I had a sound in my ears, it was the voice of Fancy: I had a light before me, it was the face of Poetry. The one still lingers there, the other has not quitted my side! Coleridge in truth met me half-way on the ground of philosophy, or I should not have been won over to his imaginative creed. I had an uneasy, pleasurable sensation all the time, till I was to visit him. During those months the chill breath of winter gave me a welcoming; the vernal air was balm and inspiration to me. The golden sunsets, the silver star of evening, lighted me on my way to new hopes and prospects. *I was to visit Coleridge in the spring*. This circumstance was never absent from my thoughts, and mingled with all my feelings. I wrote to him at the time proposed, and received an answer postponing my intended visit for a week or two, but very cordially urging me to complete my promise then. This delay did not damp, but rather increased my ardour. In the meantime, I went to Llangollen Vale,⁴ by way of initiating myself in the mysteries of natural scenery; and I must say I was enchanted with it. I had been reading Coleridge's description of England in his fine *Ode on the Departing Year*, and I applied it, *con amore*, to the objects before me. That valley was to me (in a manner) the cradle of a new existence: in the river that winds through it, my spirit was baptised in the waters of Helicon!

I returned home, and soon after set out on my journey with unworn heart and untried feet. My way lay through Worcester and Gloucester, and by Upton, where I thought of Tom Jones and the adventure of the muff.⁵ I remember getting completely wet through one day, and stopping at an inn (I think it was at Tewkesbury) where I sat up all night to read Paul and Virginia. Sweet were the showers in early youth that drenched my body, and sweet the drops of pity that fell upon the books I read! I recollect a remark of Coleridge's upon this very book, that nothing could shew the gross indelicacy of French manners and the entire corruption of their imagination more strongly than the behaviour of the heroine in the last fatal scene, who turns away from a person on board the sinking vessel, that offers to save her life, because he has thrown off his clothes to assist him in swimming. Was this a time to think of such a circumstance?

I once hinted to Wordsworth, as we were sailing in his boat on Grasmere lake, that I thought he had borrowed the idea of his *Poems on the Naming of Places* from the local inscriptions of the same kind in Paul and Virginia. He did not own the obligation, and stated some distinction without a difference, in defence of his claim to originality. Any the slightest variation would be sufficient for this purpose in his mind; for whatever *he* added or omitted would inevitably be worth all that any one else had done, and contain the marrow of the sentiment. I was still two days before the time fixed for my arrival, for I had taken care to set out early enough. I stopped these two days at Bridgewater, and when I was tired of sauntering on the banks of its muddy river, returned to the inn, and read Camilla. So have I loitered my life away, reading books, looking at pictures, going to plays, hearing, thinking, writing on what pleased me best. I have wanted only one thing to make me happy; but wanting that, have wanted everything!

I arrived, and was well received. The country about Nether Stowey is beautiful, green and hilly, and near the sea-shore. I saw it but the other day, after an interval of twenty years, from a hill near Taunton. How was the map of my life spread out before me, as the map of the country lay at my feet! In the afternoon, Coleridge took me over to All-Foxden, a romantic old family-mansion of the St Aubins, where Wordsworth lived. It was then in the possession of a friend of the poet's who gave him the free use of it. [6] Somehow that period (the time just after the French Revolution) was not a time when *nothing was given for nothing*. The mind opened, and a softness might be perceived coming over the heart of individuals, beneath 'the scales that fence' our self-interest. Wordsworth himself was from home, but his sister kept house, and set before us a frugal repast; and we had free access to her brother's poems, the *Lyrical Ballads*, which were still in manuscript, or in the form of *Sybilline Leaves*. I dipped into a few of these with great satisfaction, and with the faith of a novice. I slept that night in an old room with blue hangings, and covered with the round-faced family-portraits of the age of George 1. and 11., and from the wooded declivity of the adjoining park that overlooked my window, at the dawn of day, could

'– hear the loud stag speak.'

In the outset of life (and particularly at this time I felt it so) our imagination has a body to it. We are in a state between sleeping and waking, and have indistinct but glorious glimpses of strange shapes, and there is always something to come better than what we see. As in our dreams the fulness of the blood gives warmth and reality to the coinage of the brain, so in youth our ideas are clothed, and fed, and pampered with our good spirits; we breathe thick with thoughtless happiness, the weight of future years presses on the strong pulses of the heart, and we repose with undisturbed faith in truth and good. As we advance, we exhaust our fund of enjoyment and of hope. We are no longer wrapped in *lamb's-wool*, lulled in Elysium. As we taste the pleasures of life, their spirit evaporates, the sense palls; and nothing is left but the phantoms, the lifeless shadows of what *has been*!

That morning, as soon as breakfast was over, we strolled out into the park, and seating ourselves on the trunk of an old ash-tree that stretched along the ground, Coleridge read aloud with a sonorous and musical voice, the ballad of *Betty Foy*.[7] I was not critically or sceptically inclined. I saw touches of truth and nature, and took the rest for granted. But in the *Thorn*, the *Mad Mother*, and the *Complaint of a Poor Indian Woman*, I felt that deeper power and pathos which have been since acknowledged,

'In spite of pride, in erring reason's spite,'

as the characteristics of this author; and the sense of a new style and a new spirit in poetry came over me. It had to me something of the effect that arises from the turning up of the fresh soil, or of the first welcome breath of Spring,

> 'While yet the trembling year is unconfirmed.'

Coleridge and myself walked back to Stowey that evening, and his voice sounded high

> 'Of Providence, foreknowledge, will, and fate,
> Fix'd fate, free-will, foreknowledge absolute,'

as we passed through echoing grove, by fairy stream or waterfall, gleaming in the summer moonlight! He lamented that Wordsworth was not prone enough to believe in the traditional superstitions of the place, and that there was a something corporeal, a *matter-of-fact-ness*, a clinging to the palpable, or often to the petty, in his poetry, in consequence. His genius was not a spirit that descended to him through the air; it sprung out of the ground like a flower, or unfolded itself from a green spray, on which the gold-finch sang. He said, however (if I remember right), that this objection must be confined to his descriptive pieces, that his philosophic poetry had a grand and comprehensive spirit in it, so that his soul seemed to inhabit the universe like a palace, and to discover truth by intuition, rather than by deduction. The next day Wordsworth arrived from Bristol at Coleridge's cottage. I think I see him now. He answered in some degree to his friend's description of him, but was more gaunt and Don Quixote-like. He was quaintly dressed (according to the *costume* of that unconstrained period) in a brown fustian jacket and striped pantaloons. There was something of a roll, a lounge in his gait, not unlike his own Peter Bell. There was a severe, worn pressure of thought about his temples, a fire in his eye (as if he saw something in objects more than the outward appearance), an intense high narrow forehead, a Roman nose, cheeks furrowed by strong purpose and feeling, and a convulsive inclination to laughter about the mouth, a good deal at variance with the solemn, stately expression of the rest of his face. Chantry's bust wants the marking traits; but he was teazed into making it regular and heavy: Haydon's head of him,[8] introduced into the *Entrance of Christ into Jerusalem*, is the most like his drooping weight of thought and expression. He sat down and talked very naturally and freely, with a mixture of clear gushing accents in his voice, a deep guttural intonation, and a strong tincture of the northern *burr*, like the crust on wine. He instantly began to make havoc of the half of a Cheshire cheese on the table, and said triumphantly that 'his marriage with experience had not been so unproductive as Mr Southey's in teaching him a knowledge of the good things of this life.' He had been to see the *Castle Spectre* by Monk Lewis, while at Bristol, and described it very well. He said 'it fitted the taste of the audience like a glove.' This *ad captandum* merit was however by no means a recommendation of it, according to the severe principles of the new school, which reject rather than court popular effect. Wordsworth, looking out of the low, latticed window, said, 'How beautifully the sun sets on that yellow bank!' I thought within myself, 'With what eyes these poets see nature!' and ever after, when I saw the sun-set stream upon the objects facing it, conceived I had made a discovery, or thanked Mr Wordsworth for having made one for me! We went over to All-Foxden again the day following, and Wordsworth read us the story of Peter Bell in the open air; and the comment made upon it by his face and voice was very different from that of some later critics! Whatever might be thought of the poem, 'his face was as a book where men might read strange matters,' and he announced the fate of his hero in prophetic tones. There is a *chaunt* in the recitation both of Coleridge and Wordsworth, which acts as a spèll upon the hearer, and disarms the judgment. Perhaps they have deceived themselves by making habitual use of this ambiguous accompaniment. Coleridge's manner is more full, animated, and varied; Wordsworth's more equable, sustained, and internal. The one might be termed more *dramatic*, the other more *lyrical*. Coleridge has told me that he himself liked to compose in walking over uneven ground, or breaking through the straggling branches of a copse-wood; whereas Wordsworth always wrote (if he could) walking up and down a straight gravel-walk, or in some spot where the continuity of his verse met with no collateral interruption. Returning that same evening, I got into a metaphysical argument with Wordsworth, while Coleridge was explaining the different notes of the nightingale to his sister, in which we neither of us succeeded in making ourselves perfectly clear and intelligible. Thus I passed three weeks at Nether Stowey and in the neighbourhood, generally devoting the afternoons to a delightful chat in an arbour made of bark by the poet's friend Tom Poole, sitting under two fine elm-trees, and listening to the bees humming round us, while we quaffed our *flip*. It was agreed, among other things, that we should make a jaunt down the Bristol-Channel, as far as Linton. We set off together on foot, Coleridge, John Chester, and I. This Chester was a native of Nether Stowey, one of those who were attracted to Coleridge's discourse as flies are to honey, or bees in swarming-time to the sound of a brass pan. He 'followed in the chase, like a dog who hunts, not like one that made up the cry.' He had on a brown cloth coat, boots, and corduroy breeches, was low in stature, bow-legged, had a drag in his walk like a drover, which he assisted by a hazel switch, and kept on a sort of trot by the side of Coleridge, like a running footman by a state coach, that he might not lose a syllable or sound that fell from Coleridge's lips. He told me his private opinion, that Coleridge was a wonderful

man. He scarcely opened his lips, much less offered an
opinion the whole way: yet of the three, had I to chuse during that journey, I would be John Chester. He afterwards
followed Coleridge into Germany, where the Kantean philosophers were puzzled how to bring him under any of their
categories. When he sat down at table with his idol, John's
felicity was complete; Sir Walter Scott's, or Mr Blackwood's, when they sat down at the same table with the King,
was not more so. We passed Dunster on our right, a small
town between the brow of a hill and the sea. I remember
eyeing it wistfully as it lay below us: contrasted with the
woody scene around, it looked as clear, as pure, as *em-
browned* and ideal as any landscape I have seen since, of
Gaspar Poussin's or Domenichino's. We had a long day's
march — (our feet kept time to the echoes of Coleridge's
tongue) — through Minehead and by the Blue Anchor, and
on to Linton, which we did not reach till near midnight, and
where we had some difficulty in making a lodgment. We
however knocked the people of the house up at last, and we
were repaid for our apprehensions and fatigue by some excellent rashers of fried bacon and eggs. The view in coming
along had been splendid. We walked for miles and miles on
dark brown heaths overlooking the Channel, with the
Welsh hills beyond and at times descended into little sheltered valleys close by the seaside, with a smuggler's face
scowling by us, and then had to ascend conical hills with a
path winding up through a coppice to a barren top, like a
monk's shaven crown, from one of which I pointed out to
Coleridge's notice the bare masts of a vessel on the very edge
of the horizon and within the red-orbed disk of the setting
sun, like his own spectre-ship, in the *Ancient Mariner*. At
Linton the character of the sea-coast becomes more marked
and rugged. There is a place called the *Valley of Rocks* (I
suspect this was only the poetical name for it) bedded among
precipices overhanging the sea, with rocky caverns beneath,

into which the waves dash, and where the sea-gull for ever wheels its screaming flight. On the tops of these are huge stones thrown transverse, as if an earthquake had tossed them there, and behind these is a fretwork of perpendicular rocks, something like the *Giant's Causeway*. A thunder-storm came on while we were at the inn, and Coleridge was running out bare-headed to enjoy the commotion of the elements in the *Valley of Rocks*, but as if in spite, the clouds only muttered a few angry sounds, and let fall a few refreshing drops. Coleridge told me that he and Wordsworth were to have made this place the scene of a prose-tale, which was to have been in the manner of, but far superior to, the *Death of Abel*, but they had relinquished the design. In the morning of the second day, we breakfasted luxuriously in an old-fashioned parlour, on tea, toast, eggs, and honey, in the very sight of the bee-hives from which it had been taken, and a garden full of thyme and wild flowers that had produced it. On this occasion Coleridge spoke of Virgil's Georgics, but not well. I do not think he had much feeling for the classical or elegant. It was in this room that we found a little worn-out copy of the *Seasons*, lying in a window-seat, on which Coleridge exclaimed, '*That* is true fame!' He said Thomson was a great poet, rather than a good one; his style was as meretricious as his thoughts were natural. He spoke of Cowper as the best modern poet. He said the *Lyrical Ballads* were an experiment about to be tried by him and Wordsworth, to see how far the public taste would endure poetry written in a more natural and simple style than had hitherto been attempted; totally discarding the artifices of poetical diction, and making use only of such words as had probably been common in the most ordinary language since the days of Henry II. Some comparison was introduced between Shakespear and Milton. He said 'he hardly knew which to prefer. Shakespear appeared to him a mere stripling in the art; he was as tall and as strong, with infinitely more activity than Milton, but he never appeared to have come to man's estate; or if he had, he would not have been a man, but a monster.' He spoke with contempt of Gray, and with intolerance of Pope. He did not like the versification of the latter. He observed that 'the ears of these couplet-writers might be charged with having short memories, that could not retain the harmony of whole passages.' He thought little of Junius as a writer; he had a dislike of Dr Johnson, and a much higher opinion of Burke as an orator and politician, than of Fox or Pitt. He however thought him very inferior in richness of style and imagery to some of our elder prose-writers, particularly Jeremy Taylor. He liked Richardson, but not Fielding; nor could I get him to enter into the merits of *Caleb Williams.*[9] In short, he was profound and discriminating with respect to those authors whom he liked, and where he gave his judgment fair play; capricious, perverse, and prejudiced in his antipathies and distastes. We loitered on the 'ribbed sea-sands,' in such talk as this, a whole morning, and I recollect met with a curious sea-weed, of which John Chester told us the country name! A fisherman gave Coleridge an account of a boy that had been drowned the day before, and that they had tried to save him at the risk of their own lives. He said 'he did not know how it was that they ventured, but, Sir, we have a *nature* towards one another.' This expression, Coleridge remarked to me, was a fine illustration of that theory of disinterestedness which I (in common with Butler) had adopted. I broached to him an argument of mine to prove that *likeness* was not mere association of ideas. I said that the mark in the sand put one in mind of a man's foot, not because it was part of a former impression of a man's foot (for it was quite new) but because it was like the shape of a man's foot. He assented to the justness of this distinction (which I have explained at length elsewhere, for the benefit of the curious) and John Chester listened; not from any interest in the subject, but because he was astonished that I should be able to suggest any thing to Coleridge that he did not already know. We returned on the third morning, and Coleridge remarked the silent cottage-smoke curling up the valleys where, a few evenings before, we had seen the lights gleaming through the dark.

In a day or two after we arrived at Stowey, we set out, I on my return home, and he for Germany. It was a Sunday morning, and he was to preach that day for Dr Toulmin of Taunton. I asked him if he had prepared any thing for the occasion? He said he had not even thought of the text, but should as soon as we parted. I did not go near him, – this was a fault – but we met in the evening at Bridgewater. The next day we had a long day's walk to Bristol, and sat down, I recollect, by a well-side on the road, to cool ourselves and satisfy our thirst, when Coleridge repeated to me some descriptive lines from his tragedy of Remorse; which I must say became his mouth and that occasion better than they, some years after, did Mr Elliston's and the Drury-lane boards, –

> 'Oh memory! shield me from the world's poor strife,
> And give those scenes thine everlasting life.'

I saw no more of him for a year or two, during which period he had been wandering in the Hartz Forest in Germany; and his return was cometary, meteorous, unlike his setting out. It was not till some time after that I knew his friends Lamb and Southey. The last always appears to me (as I first saw him) with a common-place book under his arm, and the first with a *bon-mot* in his mouth. It was at Godwin's that I met him with Holcroft and Coleridge, where they were disputing fiercely which was the best – *Man as he was, or man as he is to be.* 'Give me,' says Lamb, 'man as he is *not* to be.' This saying was the beginning of a

friendship between us, which I believe still continues. –
Enough of this for the present.

> 'But there is matter for another rhyme,
> And I to this may add a second tale.'

From *The Liberal* (1823), reprinted by Hazlitt's
son in *Literary Remains* (1836).

ON THE PLEASURE OF PAINTING

'THERE is a pleasure in painting which none but painters know.' In writing, you have to contend with the world; in painting, you have only to carry on a friendly strife with Nature. You sit down to your task, and are happy. From the moment that you take up the pencil, and look Nature in the face, you are at peace with your own heart. No angry passions rise to disturb the silent progress of the work, to shake the hand, or dim the brow: no irritable humours are set afloat: you have no absurd opinions to combat, no point to strain, no adversary to crush, no fool to annoy – you are actuated by fear or favour to no man. There is 'no juggling here,' no sophistry, no intrigue, no tampering with the evidence, no attempt to make black white, or white black: but you resign yourself into the hands of a greater power, that of Nature, with the simplicity of a child, and the devotion of an enthusiast – 'study with joy her manner, and with rapture taste her style.' The mind is calm, and full at the same time. The hand and eye are equally employed. In tracing the commonest object, a plant or the stump of a tree, you learn something every moment. You perceive unexpected differences, and discover likenesses where you looked for no such thing. You try to set down what you see – find out your error, and correct it. You need not play tricks, or purposely mistake: with all your pains, you are still far short of the mark. Patience grows out of the endless pursuit, and turns it into a luxury. A streak in a flower, a wrinkle in a leaf, a tinge in a cloud, a stain in an old wall or ruin grey, are seized with avidity as the *spolia optima* of this sort of mental warfare, and furnish out labour for another half day. The hours pass away untold, without chagrin, and without weariness; nor would you ever wish to pass them otherwise. Innocence is joined with industry, pleasure with business; and the mind is satisfied, though it is not engaged in thinking or in doing harm.*

I have not much pleasure in writing these Essays, or in reading them afterwards; though I own I now and then meet with a phrase that I like, or a thought that strikes me as a true one. But after I begin them, I am only anxious to get to the end of them, which I am not sure I shall do, for I seldom see my way a page or even a sentence beforehand; and when I have as by a miracle escaped, I trouble myself little more about them. I sometimes have to write them

---

*There is a passage in Werter which contains a very pleasing illustration of this doctrine, and is as follows

'About a league from the town is a place called Walheim. It is very agreeably situated on the side of a hill: from one of the paths which leads out of the village, you have a view of the whole country; and there is a good old woman who sells wine, coffee, and tea there: but better than all this are two lime-trees before the church, which spread their branches over a little green, surrounded by barns and cottages. I have seen few places more retired and peaceful. I send for a chair and table from the old woman's, and there I drink my coffee and read Homer. It was by accident that I discovered this place one fine afternoon: all was perfect stillness; every body was in the fields, except a little boy about four years old, who was sitting on the ground, and holding between his knees a child of about six months; he pressed it to his bosom with his little arms, which made a sort of great chair for it, and notwithstanding the vivacity which sparkled in his eyes, he sat perfectly still. Quite delighted with the scene, I sat down on a plough opposite, and had great pleasure in drawing this little picture of brotherly tenderness. I added a bit of the hedge, the barn-door, and some broken cart-wheels, without any order, just as they happened to lie; and in about an hour I found I had made a drawing of great expression and very correct design, without having put in any thing of my own. This confirmed me in the resolution I had made before, only to copy nature for the future. Nature is inexhaustible, and alone forms the greatest masters. Say what you will of rules, they alter the true features, and the natural expression.'

twice over: then it is necessary to read the *proof*, to prevent mistakes by the printer; so that by the time they appear in a tangible shape, and one can con them over with a conscious, sidelong glance to the public approbation, they have lost their gloss and relish, and become 'more tedious than a twice-told tale.' For a person to read his own works over with any great delight, he ought first to forget that he ever wrote them. Familiarity naturally breeds contempt. It is, in fact, like poring fondly over a piece of blank paper: from repetition, the words convey no distinct meaning to the mind, are mere idle sounds, except that our vanity claims an interest and property in them. I have more satisfaction in my own thoughts than in dictating them to others: words are necessary to explain the impression of certain things upon me to the reader, but they rather weaken and draw a veil over than strengthen it to myself. However I might say with the poet, 'My mind to me a kingdom is,' yet I have little ambition 'to set a throne or chair of state in the understandings of other men.' The ideas we cherish most, exist best in a kind of shadowy abstraction,

'Pure in the last recesses of the mind;'

and derive neither force nor interest from being exposed to public view. They are old established acquaintance, and any change in them, arising from the adventitious ornaments of style or dress, is hardly to their advantage. After I have once written on a subject, it goes out of my mind: my feelings about it have been melted down into words, and *them* I forget. I have, as it were, discharged my memory of its old habitual reckoning, and rubbed out the score of real sentiment. In future, it exists only for the sake of others. – But I cannot say, from my own experience, that the same process takes place in transferring our ideas to canvas; they gain more than they lose in the mechanical transformation. One is never tired of painting, because you have to set down not what you knew already, but what you have just discovered. In the former case, you translate feelings into words; in the latter, names into things. There is a continual creation out of nothing going on. With every stroke of the brush, a new field of inquiry is laid open; new difficulties arise, and new triumphs are prepared over them. By comparing the imitation with the original, you see what you have done, and how much you have still to do. The test of the senses is severer than that of fancy, and an over-match even for the delusions of our self-love. One part of a picture shames another, and you determine to paint up to yourself, if you cannot come up to nature. Every object becomes lustrous from the light thrown back upon it by the mirror of art: and by the aid of the pencil we may be said to touch and handle the objects of sight. The air-wove visions that hover on the verge of existence have a bodily presence given them on the canvas: the form of beauty is changed into a substance: the dream and the glory of the universe is made 'palpable to feeling as to sight.' – And see! a rainbow starts from the canvas, with all its humid train of glory, as if it were drawn from its cloudy arch in heaven. The spangled landscape glitters with drops of dew after the shower. The 'fleecy fools' show their coats in the gleams of the setting sun. The shepherds pipe their farewell notes in the fresh evening air. And is this bright vision made from a dead dull blank, like a bubble reflecting the mighty fabric of the universe? Who would think this miracle of Rubens' pencil possible to be performed? Who, having seen it, would not spend his life to do the like? See how the rich fallows, the bare stubble-field, the scanty harvest-home, drag in Rembrandt's landscapes! How often have I looked at them and nature, and tried to do the same, till the very 'light thickened,' and there was an earthiness in the feeling of the air! There is no end of the refinements of art and nature in this respect. One may look at the misty glimmering horizon till the eye dazzles and the imagination is lost, in hopes to transfer the whole interminable expanse at one blow upon the canvas. Wilson said,[1] he endeavoured to paint the effect of the motes dancing in the setting sun. At another time, a friend coming into his painting-room, when he was sitting on the ground in a melancholy posture, observed that his picture looked like a landscape after a shower: he started up with the greatest delight, and said, 'That is the effect I intended to represent, but thought I had failed.' Wilson was neglected; and, by degrees, neglected his art to apply himself to brandy. His hand became unsteady, so that it was only by repeated attempts that he could reach the place, or produce the effect he aimed at; and when he had done a little to a picture, he would say to any acquaintance who chanced to drop in, 'I have painted enough for one day: come, let us go somewhere.' It was not so Claude left his pictures, or his studies on the banks of the Tiber, to go in search of other enjoyments, or ceased to gaze upon the glittering sunny vales and distant hills; and while his eye drank in the clear sparkling hues and lovely forms of nature, his hand stamped them on the lucid canvas to remain there for ever! — One of the most delightful parts of my life[2] was one fine summer, when I used to walk out of an evening to catch the last light of the sun, gemming the green slopes or russet lawns, and gilding tower or tree, while the blue sky gradually turning to purple and gold, or skirted with dusky grey, hung its broad marble pavement over all, as we see it in the great master of Italian landscape. But to come to a more particular explanation of the subject.

The first head I ever tried to paint[3] was an old woman with the upper part of the face shaded by her bonnet, and I certainly laboured it with great perseverance. It took me numberless sittings to do it. I have it by me still, and sometimes look at it with surprise, to think how much pains were thrown away to little purpose, — yet not altogether in vain, if it taught me to see good in every thing, and to know that there is nothing vulgar in nature seen with the eye of science or of true art. Refinement creates beauty everywhere: it is the grossness of the spectator that discovers nothing but grossness in the object. Be this as it may, I spared no pains to do my best. If art was long, I thought that life was so too at that moment. I got in the general effect the first day; and pleased and surprised enough I was at my success. The rest was a work of time – of weeks and months (if need were) of patient toil and careful finishing. I had seen an old head by Rembrandt at Burleigh-House, and if I could produce a head at all like Rembrandt in a year, in my life-time, it would be glory and felicity and wealth and fame enough for me! The head I had seen at Burleigh was an exact and wonderful fac-simile of nature, and I resolved to make mine (as nearly as I could) an exact fac-simile of nature. I did not then, nor do I now believe with Sir Joshua, that the perfection of art consists in giving general appearances without individual details, but in giving general appearances with individual details. Otherwise, I had done my work the first day. But I saw something more in nature than general effect, and I thought it worth my while to give it in the picture. There was a gorgeous effect of light and shade: but there was a delicacy as well as depth in the *chiaro-scuro*, which I was bound to follow into all its dim and scarce perceptible variety of tone and shadow. Then I had to make the transition from a strong light to as dark a shade, preserving the masses, but gradually softening off the intermediate parts. It was so in nature: the difficulty was to make it so in the copy. I tried, and failed again and again; I strove harder, and succeeded, as I thought. The wrinkles in Rembrandt were not hard lines; but broken and irregular. I saw the same appearance in nature, and strained every nerve to give it. If I could hit off this crumbling appearance, and insert the reflected light in the furrows of old age in half a morning, I did not think I had lost a day. Beneath the shrivelled yellow parchment look of the skin, there was here and there a streak of blood-colour tinging the face; this I made a point of conveying, and did not cease to compare what I saw with what I did (with jealous, lynx-eyed watchfulness) till I succeeded to the best of my ability and judgment. How many revisions were there! How many attempts to catch an expression which I had seen the day before! How often did we strive to get the old position, and wait for the return of the same light! There was a puckering up of the lips, a cautious introversion of the eye under the shadow of the bonnet, indicative of the feebleness and suspicion of old age, which at last we managed, after many trials and some quarrels, to a tolerable nicety. The picture was never finished, and I might have gone on with it to the present hour.* I used to set it on the ground when my day's work was done, and saw revealed to me with swimming eyes the birth of new hopes, and of a new world of objects. – The painter thus learns to look at nature with different eyes. He before saw her 'as in a glass darkly, but now face to face.' He understands the texture and meaning of the visible universe, and 'sees into the life of things,' not by the help of mechanical instruments, but of the improved exercise of his faculties, and an intimate sympathy with nature. The meanest thing is not lost upon him, for he looks at it with an eye to itself, not merely to his own vanity or interest, or the opinion of the world. Even where there is neither beauty nor use – if that ever were – still there is truth, and a sufficient source of gratification in the indulgence of curiosity and activity of mind. The humblest painter is a true scholar; and the best of scholars – the scholar of nature. For myself, and for the real comfort and satisfaction

* It is at present covered with a thick slough of oil and varnish (the perishable vehicle of the English school) like an envelope of goldbeaters' skin, so as to be hardly visible.

of the thing, I had rather have been Jan Steen, or Gerard Dow, than the greatest casuist or philologer that ever lived. The painter does not view things in clouds or 'mist, the common gloss of theologians,' but applies the same standard of truth and disinterested spirit of inquiry, that influence his daily practice, to other subjects. He perceives form; he distinguishes character. He reads men and books with an intuitive glance. He is a critic as well as a connoisseur. The conclusions he draws are clear and convincing, because they are taken from actual experience. He is not a fanatic, a dupe, or a slave: for the habit of seeing for himself also disposes him to judge for himself. The most sensible men I know (taken as a class) are painters; that is, they are the most lively observers of what passes in the world about them, and the closest observers of what passes in their own minds. From their profession they in general mix more with the world than authors; and if they have not the same fund of acquired knowledge, are obliged to rely more on individual sagacity. I might mention the names of Opie, Fuseli, Northcote, as persons distinguished for striking description and acquaintance with the subtle traits of character.* Painters in ordinary society, or in obscure situations where their value is not known, and they are treated with neglect and indifference, have sometimes a forward self-sufficiency of manner: but this is not so much their fault as that of others. Perhaps their want of regular education may also be in fault in such cases. Richardson,[4] who is very tenacious of the respect in which the profession ought to be held, tells a story of Michael Angelo, that after a quarrel between him and Pope

---

*Men in business, who are answerable with their fortunes for the consequences of their opinions, and are therefore accustomed to ascertain pretty accurately the grounds on which they act, before they commit themselves on the event, are often men of remarkably quick and sound judgments. Artists in like manner must know tolerably well what they are about, before they can bring the result of their observations to the test of ocular demonstration.

Julius II. 'upon account of a slight the artist conceived the pontiff had put upon him, Michael Angelo was introduced by a bishop, who, thinking to serve the artist by it, made it an argument that the Pope should be reconciled to him, because men of his profession were commonly ignorant, and of no consequence otherwise: his holiness, enraged at the bishop, struck him with his staff, and told him, it was he that was the blockhead, and affronted the man himself would not offend; the prelate was driven out of the chamber, and Michael Angelo had the Pope's benediction accompanied with presents. This bishop had fallen into the vulgar error, and was rebuked accordingly.'

Besides the employment of the mind, painting exercises the body. It is a mechanical as well as a liberal art. To do any thing, to dig a hole in the ground, to plant a cabbage, to hit a mark, to move a shuttle, to work a pattern, – in a word, to attempt to produce any effect, and to *succeed*, has something in it that gratifies the love of power, and carries off the restless activity of the mind of man. Indolence is a delightful but distressing state: we must be doing something to be happy. Action is no less necessary than thought to the instinctive tendencies of the human frame; and painting combines them both incessantly.* The hand furnishes a practical test of the correctness of the eye; and the eye, thus admonished, imposes fresh tasks of skill and industry upon the hand. Every stroke tells, as the verifying of a new truth; and every new observation, the instant it is made, passes into an act and emanation of the will. Every step is nearer what we wish, and yet there is always more to do. In spite of the facility, the fluttering grace, the evanescent hues, that play round the pencil of Rubens and Vandyke, however I may admire, I do not envy them this power so much as I do

---

*The famous Schiller used to say, that he found the great happiness of life, after all, to consist in the discharge of some mechanical duty.

the slow, patient, laborious execution of Correggio, Leonardo da Vinci, and Andrea del Sarto, where every touch appears conscious of its charge, emulous of truth, and where the painful artist has so distinctly wrought.

'That you might also say his picture thought!'

In the one case, the colours seem breathed on the canvas as by magic, the work and the wonder of a moment: in the other, they seem inlaid in the body of the work, and as if it took the artist years of unremitting labour, and of delightful never-ending progress to perfection.* Who would wish ever to come to the close of such works, – not to dwell on them, to return to them, to be wedded to them to the last? Rubens, with his florid, rapid style, complained that when he had just learned his art, he should be forced to die. Leonardo, in the slow advances of his, had lived long enough!

Painting is not, like writing, what is properly understood by a sedentary employment. It requires not indeed a strong, but a continued and steady exertion of muscular power. The precision and delicacy of the manual operation makes up for the want of vehemence, – as to balance himself for any time in the same position the rope-dancer must strain every nerve. Painting for a whole morning gives one as excellent an appetite for one's dinner, as old Abraham Tucker acquired for his by riding over Banstead Downs. It is related of Sir Joshua Reynolds, that 'he took no other exercise than what he used in his painting-room,' – the writer means, in walking backwards and forwards to look at his picture; but the act of painting itself, of laying on the colours in the proper place and proper quantity, was a much harder exercise than this alternate receding from and returning to the picture. The last would be rather a relaxation and relief than an

* The rich *impasting* of Titian and Giorgione combines something of the advantages of both these styles, the felicity of the one with the carefulness of the other, and is perhaps to be preferred to either.

effort. It is not to be wondered at, that an artist like Sir Joshua, who delighted so much in the sensual and practical part of his art, should have found himself at a considerable loss when the decay of his sight precluded him, for the last year or two of his life, from the following up of his profession, – 'the source,' according to his own remark, 'of thirty years uninterrupted enjoyment and prosperity to him.' It is only those who never think at all, or else who have accustomed themselves to brood invariably on abstract ideas, that never feel *ennui*.

To give one instance more, and then I will have done with this rambling discourse. One of my first attempts was a picture of my father, who was then in a green old age, with strong-marked features, and scarred with the small-pox. I drew it with a broad light crossing the face, looking down, with spectacles on, reading. The book was Shaftesbury's Characteristics, in a fine old binding, with Gribelin's etchings. My father would as lieve it had been any other book; but for him to read was to be content, was 'riches fineless.' The sketch promised well; and I set to work to finish it, determined to spare no time nor pains. My father was willing to sit as long as I pleased; for there is a natural desire in the mind of man to sit for one's picture, to be the object of continued attention, to have one's likeness multiplied; and besides his satisfaction in the picture, he had some pride in the artist, though he would rather I should have written a sermon than painted like Rembrandt or like Raphael! Those winter days, with the gleams of sunshine coming through the chapel-windows, and cheered by the notes of the robin-redbreast in our garden (that 'ever in the haunch of winter sings') – as my afternoon's work drew to a close, – were among the happiest of my life. When I gave the effect I intended to any part of the picture for which I had prepared my colours, when I imitated the roughness of the skin by a lucky stroke of the pencil, when I hit the clear pearly tone of a vein, when I gave the ruddy complexion of health, the blood circulating under the broad shadows of one side of the face, I thought my fortune made; or rather it was already more than made, in my fancying that I might one day be able to say with Correggio, '*I also am a painter!*' It was an idle thought, a boy's conceit; but it did not make me less happy at the time. I used regularly to set my work in the chair to look at it through the long evenings; and many a time did I return to take leave of it, before I could go to bed at night. I remember sending it with a throbbing heart to the Exhibition, and seeing it hung up there by the side of one of the Honourable Mr Skeffington[5] (now Sir George). There was nothing in common between them, but that they were the portraits of two very good-natured men. I think, but am not sure, that I finished this portrait (or another afterwards) on the same day that the news of the battle of Austerlitz came; I walked out in the afternoon, and, as I returned, saw the evening star set over a poor man's cottage with other thoughts and feelings than I shall ever have again. Oh for the revolution of the great Platonic year, that those times might come over again! I could sleep out the three hundred and sixty-five thousand intervening years very contentedly! – The picture is left: the table, the chair, the window where I learned to construe Livy, the chapel where my father preached,[6] remain where they were; but he himself is gone to rest,[7] full of years, of faith, of hope, and charity!

From *The London Magazine* (December 1820), reprinted in *Table-Talk* (1821).

THE FIGHT

'– The *fight*, the *fight's* the thing,
Wherein I'll catch the conscience of the king.'

Where there's a will, there's a way – I said to myself, as I
walked down Chancery-lane, about half-past six o'clock on
Monday the 10th of December, to inquire at Jack Randall's
where the fight the next day was to be; and I found 'the
proverb' nothing 'musty' in the present instance. I was determined to see this fight, come what would, and see it I did,
in great style. It was my *first fight*, yet it more than
answered my expectations. Ladies – it is to you I dedicate
this description; nor let it seem out of character for the fair
to notice the exploits of the brave. Courage and modesty are
the old English virtues; and may they never look cold and
askance on one another! Think, ye fairest of the fair, loveliest of the lovely kind, ye practisers of soft enchantment,
how many more ye kill with poisoned baits than ever fell in
the ring; and listen with subdued air and without shuddering, to a tale tragic only in appearance, and sacred to the
FANCY!

I was going down Chancery-lane, thinking to ask at Jack
Randall's where the fight was to be, when looking through
the glass-door of the *Hole in the Wall*, I heard a gentleman
asking the same question *at* Mrs Randall, as the author of
Waverley would express it. Now Mrs Randall stood answering the gentleman's question, with the authenticity of the
lady of the Champion of the Light Weights. Thinks I, I'll
wait till this person comes out, and learn from him how it
is. For to say a truth, I was not fond of going into this

house of call for heroes and philosophers, ever since the owner of it (for Jack is no gentleman) threatened once upon a time to kick me out of doors for wanting a mutton-chop at his hospitable board, when the conqueror in thirteen battles was more full of *blue ruin* than of good manners. I was the more mortified at this repulse, inasmuch as I had heard Mr James Simpkins, hosier in the Strand, one day when the character of the *Hole in the Wall* was brought in question, observe – 'The house is a very good house, and the company quite genteel: I have been there myself!' Remembering this unkind treatment of mine host, to which mine hostess was also a party, and not wishing to put her in unquiet thoughts at a time jubilant like the present, I waited at the door, when, who should issue forth but my friend Joe Toms, and turning suddenly up Chancery-lane with that quick jerk and impatient stride which distinguishes a lover of the FANCY, I said, 'I'll be hanged if that fellow is not going to the fight, and is on his way to get me to go with him.' So it proved in effect, and we agreed to adjourn to my lodgings to discuss measures with that cordiality which makes old friends like new, and new friends like old, on great occasions. We are cold to others only when we are dull in ourselves, and have neither thoughts nor feelings to impart to them. Give a man a topic in his head, a throb of pleasure in his heart, and he will be glad to share it with the first person he meets. Toms and I, though we seldom meet, were an *alter idem* on this memorable occasion, and had not an idea that we did not candidly impart; and 'so carelessly did we fleet the time,' that I wish no better, when there is another fight, than to have him for a companion on my journey down, and to return with my friend Jack Pigott talking of what was to happen or of what did happen, with a noble subject always at hand, and liberty to digress to others whenever they offered. Indeed, on my repeating the lines from Spenser in an involuntary fit of enthusiasm,

'What more felicity can fall to creature,
      Than to enjoy delight with liberty?'

my last-named ingenious friend stopped me by saying that
this, translated into the vulgate, meant '*Going to see a fight.*'

Joe Toms and I could not settle about the method of going
down. He said there was a caravan, he understood, to start
from Tom Belcher's at two, which would go there *right out*
and back again the next day. Now I never travel all night,
and said I should get a cast to Newbury by one of the mails.
Joe swore the thing was impossible, and I could only answer
that I had made up my mind to it. In short, he seemed to me
to waver, said he only came to see if I was going, had letters
to write, a cause coming on the day after, and faintly said at
parting (for I was bent on setting out that moment) – 'Well,
we meet at Philippi!' I made the best of my way to Piccadilly. The mail coach stand was bare. 'They are all gone,'
said I – 'this is always the way with me – in the instant I
lose the future – if I had not stayed to pour out that last cup
of tea, I should have been just in time' – and cursing my
folly and ill-luck together, without inquiring at the coach-
office whether the mails were gone or not, I walked on in
despite, and to punish my own dilatoriness and want of determination. At any rate, I would not turn back : I might
get to Hounslow, or perhaps farther, to be on my road the
next morning. I passed Hyde Park Corner (my Rubicon),
and trusted to fortune. Suddenly I heard the clattering of a
Brentford stage, and the fight rushed full upon my fancy. I
argued (not unwisely) that even a Brentford coachman was
better company than my own thoughts (such as they were
just then), and at his invitation mounted the box with
him. I immediately stated my case to him – namely, my
quarrel with myself for missing the Bath or Bristol mail, and
my determination to get on in consequence as well as I
could, without any disparagement or insulting comparison
between longer or shorter stages. It is a maxim with

me that stage-coaches, and consequently stage-coachmen, are respectable in proportion to the distance they have to travel: so I said nothing on that subject to my Brentford friend. Any incipient tendency to an abstract proposition, or (as he might have construed it) to a personal reflection of this kind, was however nipped in the bud; for I had no sooner declared indignantly that I had missed the mails, than he flatly denied that they were gone along, and lo! at the instant three of them drove by in rapid, provoking, orderly succession, as if they would devour the ground before them. Here again I seemed in the contradictory situation of the man in Dryden who exclaims,

'I follow Fate, which does too hard pursue!'

If I had stopped to inquire at the White Horse Cellar, which would not have taken me a minute, I should now have been driving down the road in all the dignified unconcern and *ideal* perfection of mechanical conveyance. The Bath mail I had set my mind upon, and I had missed it, as I missed every thing else, by my own absurdity, in putting the will for the deed, and aiming at ends without employing means. 'Sir,' said he of the Brentford, 'the Bath mail will be up presently, my brother-in-law drives it, and I will engage to stop him if there is a place empty.' I almost doubted my good genius; but, sure enough, up it drove like lightning, and stopped directly at the call of the Brentford Jehu. I would not have believed this possible, but the brother-in-law of a mail-coach driver is himself no mean man. I was transferred without loss of time from the top of one coach to that of the other, desired the guard to pay my fare to the Brentford coachman for me as I had no change, was accommodated with a great coat, put up my umbrella to keep off a drizzling mist, and we began to cut through the air like an arrow. The mile-stones disappeared one after another, the rain kept off; Tom Turtle, the trainer, sat before me on the coach-box, with whom I exchanged civilities as a gentleman going to the fight; the passion that had transported me an hour before was subdued to pensive regret and conjectural musing on the next day's battle; I was promised a place inside at Reading, and upon the whole, I thought myself a lucky fellow. Such is the force of imagination! On the outside of any other coach on the 10th of December, with a Scotch mist drizzling through the cloudy moonlight air, I should have been cold, comfortless, impatient, and, no doubt, wet through; but seated on the Royal mail, I felt warm and comfortable, the air did me good, the ride did me good, I was pleased with the progress we had made, and confident that all would go well through the journey. When I got inside at Reading, I found Turtle and a stout valetudinarian, whose costume bespoke him one of the FANCY, and who had risen from a three months' sick bed to get into the mail to see the fight. They were intimate, and we fell into a lively discourse. My friend the trainer was confined in his topics to fighting dogs and men, to bears and badgers; beyond this he was 'quite chap-fallen,' had not a word to throw at a dog, or indeed very wisely fell asleep, when any other game was started. The whole art of training (I, however, learnt from him) consists in two things, exercise and abstinence, abstinence and exercise, repeated alternately and without end. A yolk of an egg with a spoonful of rum in it is the first thing in a morning, and then a walk of six miles till breakfast. This meal consists of a plentiful supply of tea and toast and beef-steaks. Then another six or seven miles till dinner-time, and another supply of solid beef or mutton with a pint of porter, and perhaps, at the utmost, a couple of glasses of sherry. Martin trains on water, but this increases his infirmity on another very dangerous side. The Gas-man takes now and then a chirping glass (under the rose) to console him, during a six weeks' probation, for the absence of Mrs Hickman – an agreeable woman, with (I understand) a pretty fortune of two hundred pounds. How matter presses on me! What stubborn things are facts! How inexhaustible is nature and art! 'It is well,' as I once heard Mr Richmond[1] observe, 'to see a variety.' He was speaking of cock-fighting as an edifying spectacle. I cannot deny but that one learns more of what *is* (I do not say of what *ought to be*) in this desultory mode of practical study, than from reading the same book twice over, even though it should be a moral treatise. Where was I? I was sitting at dinner with the candidate for the honours of the ring, 'where good digestion waits on appetite, and health on both.' Then follows an hour of social chat and native glee; and afterwards, to another breathing over healthy hill or dale. Back to supper, and then to bed, and up by six again – Our hero

> 'Follows so the ever-running sun
> With profitable *ardour*' –

to the day that brings him victory or defeat in the green fairy circle. Is not this life more sweet than mine? I was going to say; but I will not libel any life by comparing it to mine, which is (at the date of these presents) bitter as coloquintida and the dregs of aconitum!

The invalid in the Bath mail soared a pitch above the trainer, and did not sleep so sound, because he had 'more figures and more fantasies.' We talked the hours away merrily. He had faith in surgery, for he had had three ribs set right, that had been broken in a *turn-up* at Belcher's, but thought physicians old women, for they had no antidote in their catalogue for brandy. An indigestion is an excellent common-place for two people that never met before. By way of ingratiating myself, I told him the story of my doctor, who, on my earnestly representing to him that I thought his regimen had done me harm, assured me that the whole pharmacopeia contained nothing comparable to the prescription he had given me; and, as a proof of its undoubted efficacy,

said that, 'he had had one gentleman with my complaint under his hands for the last fifteen years.' This anecdote
made my companion shake the rough sides of his three
great coats with boisterous laughter; and Turtle, starting
out of his sleep, swore he knew how the fight would go, for
he had had a dream about it. Sure enough the rascal told us
how the three first rounds went off, but 'his dream,' like
others, 'denoted a foregone conclusion.' He knew his men.
The moon now rose in silver state, and I ventured, with
some hesitation, to point out this object of placid beauty,
with the blue serene beyond, to the man of science, to which
his ear he 'seriously inclined,' the more as it gave promise
d'un beau jour for the morrow, and showed the ring un-
drenched by envious showers, arrayed in sunny smiles. Just
then, all going on well, I thought on my friend Toms,
whom I had left behind, and said innocently, 'There was a
blockhead of a fellow I left in town, who said there was no
possibility of getting down by the mail, and talked of going
by a caravan from Belcher's at two in the morning, after he
had written some letters.' 'Why,' said he of the lapells, 'I
should not wonder if that was the very person we saw running about like mad from one coach-door to another, and
asking if any one had seen a friend of his, a gentleman going
to the fight, whom he had missed stupidly enough by staying to write a note.' 'Pray, Sir,' said my fellow-traveller,
'had he a plaid-cloak on?' – 'Why, no,' said I, 'not at the
time I left him, but he very well might afterwards, for he
offered to lend me one.' The plaid-cloak and the letter decided the thing. Joe, sure enough, was in the Bristol mail,
which preceded us by about fifty yards. This was droll
enough. We had now but a few miles to our place of destination, and the first thing I did on alighting at Newbury,
both coaches stopping at the same time, was to call out,
'Pray, is there a gentleman in that mail of the name of
Toms?' 'No,' said Joe, borrowing something of the vein of

Gilpin, 'for I have just got out.' 'Well!' says he, 'this is lucky; but you don't know how vexed I was to miss you; for,' added he, lowering his voice, 'do you know when I left you I went to Belcher's to ask about the caravan, and Mrs Belcher said very obligingly she couldn't tell about that, but there were two gentlemen who had taken places by the mail and were gone on in a landau, and she could frank us. It's a pity I didn't meet with you; we could then have got down for nothing. But *mum's the word*.' It's the devil for any one to tell me a secret, for it's sure to come out in print. I do not care so much to gratify a friend, but the public ear is too great a temptation to me.

Our present business was to get beds and a supper at an inn; but this was no easy task. The public-houses were full, and where you saw a light at a private house, and people poking their heads out of the casement to see what was going on, they instantly put them in and shut the window, the moment you seemed advancing with a suspicious overture for accommodation. Our guard and coachman thundered away at the outer gate of the Crown for some time without effect – such was the greater noise within; – and when the doors were unbarred, and we got admittance, we found a party assembled in the kitchen round a good hospitable fire, some sleeping, others drinking, others talking on politics and on the fight. A tall English yeoman (something like Matthews in the face, and quite as great a wag) –

'A lusty man to ben an abbot able,' –

was making such a prodigious noise about rent and taxes, and the price of corn now and formerly, that he had prevented us from being heard at the gate. The first thing I heard him say was to a shuffling fellow who wanted to be off a bet for a shilling glass of brandy and water – 'Confound it, man, don't be *insipid*!' Thinks I, that is a good phrase. It was a good omen. He kept it up so all night, nor flinched with the approach of morning. He was a fine fellow, with sense, wit, and spirit, a hearty body and a joyous mind, free-spoken, frank, convivial – one of that true English breed that went with Harry the Fifth to the siege of Harfleur – 'standing like greyhounds in the slips,' &c. We ordered tea and eggs (beds were soon found to be out of the question) and this fellow's conversation was *sauce piquante*. It did one's heart good to see him brandish his oaken towel and to hear him talk. He made mince-meat of a drunken, stupid, red-faced, quarrelsome, *frowsy* farmer, whose nose 'he moralised into a thousand similes,' making it out a fire-brand like Bardolph's. 'I'll tell you what, my friend,' says he, 'the landlady has only to keep you here to save fire and candle. If one was to touch your nose, it would go off like a piece of charcoal.' At this the other only grinned like an idiot, the sole variety in his purple face being his little peering eyes and yellow teeth; called for another glass, swore he would not stand it; and after many attempts to provoke his humorous antagonist to single combat, which the other turned off (after working him up to a ludicrous pitch of choler) with great adroitness, he fell quietly asleep with a glass of liquor in his hand, which he could not lift to his head. His laughing persecutor made a speech over him, and turning to the opposite side of the room, where they were all sleeping in the midst of this 'loud and furious fun,' said, 'There's a scene, by G—d, for Hogarth to paint. I think he and Shakespear were our two best men at copying life.' This confirmed me in my good opinion of him. Hogarth, Shakespear, and Nature, were just enough for him (indeed for any man) to know. I said, 'You read Cobbett, don't you? At least,' says I, 'you talk just as well as he writes.' He seemed to doubt this. But I said, 'We have an hour to spare: if you'll get pen, ink, and paper, and keep on talking, I'll write down what you say; and if it doesn't make a capital Political Register, I'll forfeit my head. You have kept me alive to-night, however. I don't know what I should have done without you.' He did not dislike this view of the thing, nor my asking if he was not about the size of Jem Belcher; and told me soon afterwards, in the confidence of friendship, that 'the circumstance which had given him nearly the greatest concern in his life, was Cribb's beating Jem after he had lost his eye by racket-playing.' – The morning dawns; that dim but yet clear light appears, which weighs like solid bars of metal on the sleepless eyelids; the guests drop down from their chambers one by one – but it was too late to think of going to bed now (the clock was on the stroke of seven), we had nothing for it but to find a barber's (the pole that glittered in the morning sun lighted us to his shop), and then a nine miles' march to Hungerford. The day was fine, the sky was blue, the mists were retiring from the marshy ground, the path was tolerably dry, the sitting-up all night had not done us much harm – at least the cause was good; we talked of this and that with amicable difference, roving and sipping of many subjects, but still invariably we returned to the fight. At length, a mile to the left of Hungerford, on a gentle eminence, we saw the ring surrounded by covered carts, gigs, and carriages, of which hundreds had passed us on the road; Toms gave a youthful shout, and we hastened down a narrow lane to the scene of action.

Reader, have you ever seen a fight? If not, you have a pleasure to come, at least if it is a fight like that between the Gas-man and Bill Neate. The crowd was very great when we arrived on the spot; open carriages were coming up, with streamers flying and music playing, and the country-people were pouring in over hedge and ditch in all directions, to see their hero beat or be beaten. The odds were still on Gas, but only about five to four. Gully had been down to try Neate, and had backed him considerably, which was a damper to the sanguine confidence of the adverse party. About two hundred thousand pounds were pending. The

Gas says, he has lost 3000*l*. which were promised him by different gentlemen if he had won. He had presumed too much on himself, which had made others presume on him. This spirited and formidable young fellow seems to have taken for his motto the old maxim, that 'there are three things necessary to success in life – *Impudence! Impudence! Impudence!*' It is so in matters of opinion, but not in the FANCY, which is the most practical of all things, though even here confidence is half the battle, but only half. Our friend had vapoured and swaggered too much, as if he wanted to grin and bully his adversary out of the fight. 'Alas! the Bristol man was not so tamed!' – 'This is *the grave-digger*' (would Tom Hickman exclaim in the moments of intoxication from gin and success, shewing his tremendous right hand), 'this will send many of them to their long homes; I haven't done with them yet!' Why should he – though he had licked four of the best men within the hour, yet why should he threaten to inflict dishonourable chastisement on my old master Richmond, a veteran going off the stage, and who has borne his sable honours meekly? Magnanimity, my dear Tom, and bravery, should be inseparable. Or why should he go up to his antagonist, the first time he ever saw him at the Fives Court, and measuring him from head to foot with a glance of contempt, as Achilles surveyed Hector, say to him, 'What, are you Bill Neate? I'll knock more blood out of that great carcase of thine, this day fortnight, than you ever knock'd out of a bullock's!' It was not manly, 'twas not fighter-like. If he was sure of the victory (as he was not), the less said about it the better. Modesty should accompany the FANCY as its shadow. The best men were always the best behaved. Jem Belcher, the Game Chicken (before whom the Gas-man could not have lived) were civil, silent men. So is Cribb, so is Tom Belcher, the most elegant of sparrers, and not a man for every one to take by the nose. I enlarged on this topic in the mail (while Turtle was asleep), and said very wisely (as I thought) that impertinence was a part of no profession. A boxer was bound to beat his man, but not to thrust his fist, either actually or by implication, in every one's face. Even a highwayman, in the way of trade, may blow out your brains, but if he uses foul language at the same time, I should say he was no gentleman. A boxer, I would infer, need not be a blackguard or a coxcomb, more than another. Perhaps I press this point too much on a fallen man – Mr Thomas Hickman has by this time learnt that first of all lessons. 'That man was made to mourn.' He has lost nothing by the late fight but his presumption; and that every man may do as well without! By an over-display of this quality, however, the public had been prejudiced against him, and the *knowing-ones* were taken in. Few but those who had bet on him wished Gas to win. With my own prepossessions on the subject, the result of the 11th of December appeared to me as fine a piece of poetical justice as I had ever witnessed. The difference of weight between the two combatants (14 stone to 12) was nothing to the sporting men. Great, heavy, clumsy, long-armed Bill Neate kicked the beam in the scale of the Gas-man's vanity. The amateurs were frightened at his big words, and thought that they would make up for the difference of six feet and five feet nine. Truly, the F A N C Y are not men of imagination. They judge of what has been, and cannot conceive of any thing that is to be. The Gas-man had won hitherto, therefore he must beat a man half as big again as himself – and that to a certainty. Besides, there are as many feuds, factions, prejudices, pedantic notions in the F A N C Y as in the state or in the schools. Mr Gully is almost the only cool, sensible man among them, who exercises an unbiassed discretion, and is not a slave to his passions in these matters. But enough of reflections, and to our tale. The day, as I have said, was fine for a December morning. The grass was wet, and the ground miry, and ploughed up with multitudinous feet, except that, within the ring itself, there was a spot of virgin-green closed in and unprofaned by vulgar tread, that shone with dazzling brightness in the mid-day sun. For it was now noon, and we had an hour to wait. This is the trying time. It is then the heart sickens, as you think what the two champions are about, and how short a time will determine their fate. After the first blow is struck, there is no opportunity for nervous apprehensions; you are swallowed up in the immediate interest of the scene – but

> 'Between the acting of a dreadful thing
> And the first motion, all the interim is
> Like a phantasma, or a hideous dream.'

I found it so as I felt the sun's rays clinging to my back, and saw the white wintry clouds sink below the verge of the horizon. 'So,' I thought, 'my fairest hopes have faded from my sight! – so will the Gas-man's glory, or that of his adversary, vanish in an hour.' The *swells* were parading in their white box-coats, the outer ring was cleared with some bruises on the heads and shins of the rustic assembly (for the *cockneys* had been distanced by the sixty-six miles); the time drew near, I had got a good stand; a bustle, a buzz, ran through the crowd, and from the opposite side entered Neate, between his second and bottle-holder. He rolled along, swathed in his loose great coat, his knock-knees bending under his huge bulk; and, with a modest cheerful air, threw his hat into the ring. He then just looked round, and began quietly to undress; when from the other side there was a similar rush and an opening made, and the Gas-man came forward with a conscious air of anticipated triumph, too much like the cock-of-the-walk. He strutted about more than became a hero, sucked oranges with a supercilious air, and threw away the skin with a toss of his head, and went up and looked at Neate, which was an act of supererogation. The only sensible thing he did was, as he strode away from the modern Ajax, to fling out his arms, as if he wanted to try whether they would do their work that day. By this time they had stripped, and presented a strong contrast in appearance. If Neate was like Ajax, 'with Atlantean shoulders, fit to bear' the pugilistic reputation of all Bristol, Hickman might be compared to Diomed, light, vigorous, elastic, and his back glistened in the sun, as he moved about, like a panther's hide. There was now a dead pause – attention was awe-struck. Who at that moment, big with a great event, did not draw his breath short – did not feel his heart throb? All was ready. They tossed up for the sun, and the Gas-man won. They were led up to the *scratch* – shook hands, and went at it.

In the first round every one thought it was all over. After making play a short time, the Gas-man flew at his adversary like a tiger, struck five blows in as many seconds, three first, and then following him as he staggered back, two more, right and left, and down he fell, a mighty ruin. There was a shout, and I said, 'There is no standing this.' Neate seemed like a lifeless lump of flesh and bone, round which the Gas-man's blows played with the rapidity of electricity or lightning, and you imagined he would only be lifted up to be knocked down again. It was as if Hickman held a sword or a fire in that right hand of his, and directed it against an unarmed body. They met again, and Neate seemed, not cowed, but particularly cautious. I saw his teeth clenched together and his brows knit close against the sun. He held out both his arms at full length straight before him, like two sledge-hammers, and raised his left an inch or two higher. The Gas-man could not get over this guard – they struck mutually and fell, but without advantage on either side. It was the same in the next round; but the balance of power was thus restored – the fate of the battle was suspended. No one could tell how it would end. This was the only moment in which opinion was divided; for, in the next, the Gas-man aiming a mortal blow at his adversary's neck, with his right hand, and failing from the length he had to reach, the other returned it with his left at full swing, planted a tremendous blow on his cheek-bone and eyebrow, and made a red ruin of that side of his face. The Gas-man went down, and there was another shout – a roar of triumph as the waves of fortune rolled tumultuously from side to side. This was a settler. Hickman got up, and 'grinned horrible a ghastly smile,' yet he was evidently dashed in his opinion of himself; it was the first time he had ever been so punished; all one side of his face was perfect scarlet, and his right eye was closed in dingy blackness, as he advanced to the fight, less confident, but still determined. After one or two rounds, not receiving another such remembrancer, he rallied and went at it with his former impetuosity. But in vain. His strength had been weakened, – his blows could not tell at such a distance, – he was obliged to fling himself at his adversary, and could not strike from his feet; and almost as regularly as he flew at him with his right hand, Neate warded the blow, or drew back out of its reach, and felled him with the return of his left. There was little cautious sparring – no half-hits – no tapping and trifling, none of the *petit-maîtreship* of the art – they were almost all knock-down blows: – the fight was a good stand up fight. The wonder was the half-minute time. If there had been a minute or more allowed between each round, it would have been intelligible how they should by degrees recover strength and resolution; but to see two men smashed to the ground, smeared with gore, stunned, senseless, the breath beaten out of their bodies; and then, before you recover from the shock, to see them rise up with new strength and courage, stand steady to inflict or receive mortal offence, and rush upon each other 'like two clouds over the Caspian' – this is the most astonishing thing of all: – this is the high and heroic state of man! From this time forward the event became more certain every round; and about the twelfth it seemed as ·if it must have been over. Hickman generally stood with his back to me; but in the scuffle, he had changed positions, and Neate just then made a tremendous lunge at him, and hit him full in the face. It was doubtful whether he would fall backwards or forwards; he hung suspended for a second or two, and then fell back, throwing his hands in the air, and with his face lifted up to the sky. I never saw any thing more terrific than his aspect just before he fell. All traces of life, of natural expression, were gone from him. His face was like a human skull, a death's head, spouting blood. The eyes were filled with blood, the nose streamed with blood, the mouth gaped blood. He was not like an actual man, but like a preternatural, spectral appearance, or like one of the figures in Dante's *Inferno*. Yet he fought on after this for several rounds, still striking the first desperate blow, and Neate standing on the defensive, and using the same cautious guard to the last, as if he had still all his work to do; and it was not till the Gas-man was so stunned in the seventeenth or eighteenth round, that his senses forsook him, and he could not come to time, that the battle was declared over.* Ye who despise the FANCY, do something to shew as much *pluck*, or as much self-possession as this, before you assume a superiority which you have never given a single proof of by any one action in the whole course of your lives! – When the Gas-man came to himself, the first words he uttered were, 'Where am I? What is the matter?' 'Nothing is the matter, Tom – you have lost the

---

* Scroggins said of the Gas-man, that he thought he was a man of that courage, that if his hands were cut off, he would still fight on with the stumps – like that of Widrington, –

> – 'In doleful dumps,
> Who, when his legs were smitten off
> Still fought upon his stumps.'

battle, but you are the bravest man alive.' And Jackson whispered to him, 'I am collecting a purse for you, Tom.' – Vain sounds, and unheard at that moment! Neate instantly went up and shook him cordially by the hand, and seeing some old acquaintance, began to flourish with his fists, calling out, 'Ah, you always said I couldn't fight – What do you think now?' But all in good-humour, and without any appearance of arrogance; only it was evident Bill Neate was pleased that he had won the fight. When it was over, I asked Cribb if he did not think it was a good one? He said, '*Pretty well!*' The carrier-pigeons now mounted into the air, and one of them flew with the news of her husband's victory to the bosom of Mrs Neate. Alas, for Mrs Hickman!

Mais au revoir, as Sir Fopling Flutter says. I went down with Toms; I returned with Jack Pigott, whom I met on the ground. Toms is a rattle-brain; Pigott is a sentimentalist. Now, under favour, I am a sentimentalist too – therefore I say nothing, but that the interest of the excursion did not flag as I came back. Pigott and I marched along the causeway leading from Hungerford to Newbury, now observing the effect of a brilliant sun on the tawny meads or moss-coloured cottages, now exulting in the fight, now digressing to some topic of general and elegant literature. My friend was dressed in character for the occasion, or like one of the FANCY; that is, with a double portion of great coats, clogs, and overhauls: and just as we had agreed with a couple of country-lads to carry his superfluous wearing-apparel to the next town, we were overtaken by a return post-chaise, into which I got, Pigott preferring a seat on the bar. There were two strangers already in the chaise, and on their observing they supposed I had been to the fight, I said I had, and concluded they had done the same. They appeared, however, a little shy and sore on the subject; and it was not till after several hints dropped, and questions put, that it turned out that they had missed it. One of these friends had undertaken to drive the other there in his gig: they had set out, to make sure work, the day before at three in the afternoon. The owner of the one-horse vehicle scorned to ask his way, and drove right on to Bagshot, instead of turning off at Hounslow: there they stopped all night, and set off the next day across the country to Reading, from whence they took coach, and got down within a mile or two of Hungerford, just half an hour after the fight was over. This might be safely set down as one of the miseries of human life. We parted with these two gentlemen who had been to see the fight, but had returned as they went, at Wolhampton, where we were promised beds (an irresistible temptation, for Pigott had passed the preceding night at Hungerford as we had done at Newbury), and we turned into an old bow-windowed parlour with a carpet and a snug fire; and after devouring a quantity of tea, toast, and eggs, sat down to consider, during an hour of philosophic leisure, what we should have for supper. In the midst of an Epicurean deliberation between a roasted fowl and mutton chops with mashed potatoes, we were interrupted by an inroad of Goths and Vandals – *O procul este profani* – not real flash-men, but interlopers, noisy pretenders, butchers from Tothill-fields, brokers from Whitechapel, who called immediately for pipes and tobacco, hoping it would not be disagreeable to the gentlemen, and began to insist that it was *a cross*. Pigott withdrew from the smoke and noise into another room, and left me to dispute the point with them for a couple of hours *sans intermission* by the dial. The next morning we rose refreshed; and on observing that Jack had a pocket volume in his hand, in which he read in the intervals of our discourse, I inquired what it was, and learned to my particular satisfaction that it was a volume of the New Eloise. Ladies, after this, will you contend that a love for the FANCY is incompatible with the cultivation of sentiment? – We jogged on as before, my friend setting me up in a genteel drab great coat and green silk handkerchief (which I must say became me exceedingly), and after stretching our legs for a few miles, and seeing Jack Randall, Ned Turner, and Scroggins, pass on the top of one of the Bath coaches, we engaged with the driver of the second to take us to London for the usual fee. I got inside, and found three other passengers. One of them was an old gentleman with an aquiline nose, powdered hair, and a pigtail, and who looked as if he had played many a rubber at the Bath rooms. I said to myself, he is very like Mr Windham; I wish he would enter into conversation, that I might hear what fine observations would come from those finely-turned features. However, nothing passed, till, stopping to dine at Reading, some inquiry was made by the company about the fight, and I gave (as the reader may believe) an eloquent and animated description of it. When we got into the coach again, the old gentleman, after a graceful exordium, said, he had, when a boy, been to a fight between the famous Broughton and George Stevenson, who was called the *Fighting Coachman*, in the year 1770, with the late Mr Windham. This beginning flattered the spirit of prophecy within me and rivetted my attention. He went on – 'George Stevenson was coachman to a friend of my father's. He was an old man when I saw him some years afterwards. He took hold of his own arm and said, "there was muscle here once, but now it is no more than this young gentleman's." He added, "Well, no matter; I have been here long, I am willing to go hence, and I hope I have done no more harm than another man." Once,' said my unknown companion, 'I asked him if he had ever beat Broughton? He said Yes; that he had fought with him three times, and the last time he fairly beat him, though the world did not allow it. "I'll tell you how it was, master. When the seconds lifted us up in the last round, we were so exhausted that neither of us could stand, and we fell upon one another, and as Master Broughton fell uppermost, the mob gave it in his favour, and he was said to have won the battle. But," says he, "the fact was, that as his second (John Cuthbert) lifted him up, he said to him, 'I'll fight no more, I've had enough;' which," says Stevenson, "you know gave me the victory. And to prove to you that this was the case, when John Cuthbert was on his death-bed, and they asked him if there was any thing on his mind which he wished to confess, he answered, 'Yes, that there was one thing he wished to set right, for that certainly Master Stevenson won that last fight with Master Broughton; for he whispered him as he lifted him up in the last round of all, that he had had enough.'"' 'This,' said the Bath gentleman, 'was a bit of human nature;' and I have written this account of the fight on purpose that it might not be lost to the world. He also stated as a proof of the candour of mind in this class of men, that Stevenson acknowledged that Broughton could have beat him in his best day; but that he (Broughton) was getting old in their last rencounter. When we stopped in Piccadilly, I wanted to ask the gentleman some questions about the late Mr Windham, but had not courage. I got out, resigned my coat and green silk handkerchief to Pigott (loth to part with these ornaments of life), and walked home in high spirits.

P.S. Toms called upon me the next day, to ask me if I did not think the fight was a complete thing? I said I thought it was. I hope he will relish my account of it.

From *The New Monthly Magazine* (February 1822), reprinted by Hazlitt's son in *Literary Remains* (1836).

ON THE KNOWLEDGE OF CHARACTER

It is astonishing, with all our opportunities and practice, how little we know of this subject. For myself, I feel that the more I learn, the less I understand it.

I remember, several years ago, a conversation in the *Diligence* coming from Paris, in which, on its being mentioned that a man had married his wife after thirteen years' courtship, a fellow-countryman of mine observed, that 'then, at least, he would be acquainted with her character;' when a Monsieur P—, inventor and proprietor of the *Invisible Girl*, made answer, 'No, not at all; for that the very next day she might turn out the very reverse of the character that she had appeared in during all the preceding time.' * I could not help admiring the superior sagacity of the French juggler, and it struck me then that we could never be sure when we had got at the bottom of this riddle.

There are various ways of getting at a knowledge of character – by looks, words, actions. The first of these, which seems the most superficial, is perhaps the safest, and least liable to deceive: nay, it is that which mankind, in spite of their pretending to the contrary, are generally governed by. Professions pass for nothing, and actions may be counterfeited: but a man cannot help his looks. 'Speech,' said a celebrated wit, 'was given to man to conceal his thoughts.' Yet I do not know that the greatest hypocrites are the least silent. The mouth of Cromwell is pursed up in the portraits of him, as if he was afraid to trust himself with words. Lord Chesterfield advises us, if we wish to know the real sentiments of the person we are conversing with, to look

* 'It is not a year or two shows us a man.'—ÆMILIA, in OTHELLO.

in his face, for he can more easily command his words than his features. A man's whole life may be a lie to himself and others: and yet a picture painted of him by a great artist would probably stamp his true character on the canvas, and betray the secret to posterity. Men's opinions were divided, in their life-times, about such prominent personages as Charles v. and Ignatius Loyola, partly, no doubt, from passion and interest, but partly from contradictory evidence in their ostensible conduct: the spectator, who has ever seen their pictures by Titian, judges of them at once, and truly. I had rather leave a good portrait of myself behind me than have a fine epitaph. The face, for the most part, tells what we have thought and felt – the rest is nothing. I have a higher idea of Donne from a rude, half-effaced outline [1] of him prefixed to his poems than from any thing he ever wrote. Cæsar's Commentaries would not have redeemed him in my opinion, if the bust of him had resembled the Duke of W—. [2] My old friend, Fawcett, used to say, that if Sir Isaac Newton himself had lisped, he could not have thought any thing of him. So I cannot persuade myself that any one is a great man, who looks like a blockhead. In this I may be wrong.

First impressions are often the truest, as we find (not unfrequently) to our cost, when we have been wheedled out of them by plausible professions or studied actions. A man's look is the work of years, it is stamped on his countenance by the events of his whole life, nay, more, by the hand of nature, and it is not to be got rid of easily. There is, as it has been remarked repeatedly, something in a person's appearance at first sight which we do not like, and that gives us an odd twinge, but which is overlooked in a multiplicity of other circumstances, till the mask is taken off, and we see this lurking character verified in the plainest manner in the sequel. We are struck at first, and by chance, with what is peculiar and characteristic; also with permanent *traits* and general effect; these afterwards go off in a set of unmeaning, common-place details. This sort of *prima facie* evidence, then, shows what a man is, better than what he says or does; for it shows us the habit of his mind, which is the same under all circumstances and disguises. You will say, on the other hand, that there is no judging by appearances, as a general rule. No one, for instance, would take such a person for a very clever man, without knowing who he was. Then, ten to one, he is not; he may have got the reputation, but it is a mistake. You say, there is Mr —, undoubtedly a person of great genius: yet, except when excited by something extraordinary, he seems half dead. He has wit at will, yet wants life and spirit. He is capable of the most generous acts, yet meanness seems to cling to every motion. He looks like a poor creature – and in truth he is one! The first impression he gives you of him answers nearly to the feeling he has of his personal identity; and this image of himself, rising from his thoughts, and shrouding his faculties, is that which sits with him in the house, walks out with him into the street, and haunts his bed-side. The best part of his existence is dull, cloudy, leaden: the flashes of light that proceed from it, or streak it here and there, may dazzle others, but do not deceive himself. Modesty is the lowest of the virtues, and is a real confession of the deficiency it indicates. He who undervalues himself is justly undervalued by others. Whatever good properties he may possess are, in fact, neutralised by a 'cold rheum' running through his veins, and taking away the zest of his pretensions, the pith and marrow of his performances. What is it to me that I can write these TABLE-TALKS? It is true I can, by a reluctant effort, rake up a parcel of half-forgotten observations, but they do not float on the surface of my mind, nor stir it with any sense of pleasure, nor even of pride. Others have more property in them than I have: *they* may reap the benefit, *I* have only had the pain. Otherwise, they are to me as if they had never existed: nor should I know that I had ever thought at all, but that I am reminded of it by the strangeness of my appearance, and my unfitness for every thing else. Look in C—'s [3] face while he is talking. His words are such as might 'create a soul under the ribs of death.' His face is a blank. Which are we to consider as the true index of his mind? Pain, languor, shadowy remembrances are the uneasy inmates there: his lips move mechanically!

There are people whom we do not like, though we may have known them long, and have no fault to find with them, except that 'their appearance is so much against them.' That is not all, if we could find it out. There is generally, a reason for this prejudice; for nature is true to itself. They may be very good sort of people, too, in their way, but still something is the matter. There is a coldness, a selfishness, a levity, an insincerity, which we cannot fix upon any particular phrase or action, but we see it in their whole persons and deportment. One reason that we do not see it in any other way may be, that they are all the time trying to conceal this defect by every means in their power. There is, luckily, a sort of *second sight* in morals: we discern the lurking indications of temper and habit a long while before their palpable effects appear. I once used to meet with a person at an ordinary, a very civil, good-looking man in other respects, but with an odd look about his eyes, which I could not explain, as if he saw you under their fringed lids, and you could not see him again: this man was a common sharper. The greatest hypocrite I ever knew [4] was a little, demure, pretty, modest-looking girl, with eyes timidly cast upon the ground, and an air soft as enchantment; the only circumstance that could lead to a suspicion of her true character was a cold, sullen, watery, glazed look about the eyes, which she bent on vacancy, as if determined to avoid all explanation with yours. I might have spied in their glittering, motionless surface, the rocks and quicksands that awaited me below! We do not feel quite at ease in the company or friendship of those who have any natural obliquity or imperfection of person. The reason is, they are not on the best terms with themselves, and are sometimes apt to play off on others the tricks that nature has played them. This, however, is a remark that, perhaps, ought not to have been made. I know a person to whom it has been objected as a disqualification for friendship, that he never shakes you cordially by the hand. I own this is a damper to sanguine and florid temperaments, who abound in these practical demonstrations and 'compliments extern.' The same person, who testifies the least pleasure at meeting you, is the last to quit his seat in your company, grapples with a subject in conversation right earnestly, and is, I take it, backward to give up a cause or a friend. Cold and distant in appearance, he piques himself on being the king of *good haters*, and a no less zealous partisan. The most phlegmatic constitutions often contain the most inflammable spirits – as fire is struck from the hardest flints.

And this is another reason that makes it difficult to judge of character. Extremes meet; and qualities display themselves by the most contradictory appearances. Any inclination, in consequence of being generally suppressed, vents itself the more violently when an opportunity presents itself: the greatest grossness sometimes accompanies the greatest refinement, as a natural relief, one to the other; and we find the most reserved and indifferent tempers at the beginning of an entertainment, or an acquaintance, turn out the most communicative and cordial at the end of it. Some spirits exhaust themselves at first: others gain strength by progression. Some minds have a greater facility of throwing off impressions, and are, as it were, more transparent or porous than others. Thus the French present a marked contrast to the English in this respect. A Frenchman addresses you at once with a sort of lively indifference; an English-

man is more on his guard, feels his way, and is either exceedingly silent, or lets you into his whole confidence,
which he cannot so well impart to an entire stranger. Again,
a Frenchman is naturally humane: an Englishman is, I
should say, only friendly by habit. His virtues and his vices
cost him more than they do his more gay and volatile neighbours. An Englishman is said to speak his mind more
plainly than others: — yes, if it will give you pain to hear it.
He does not care whom he offends by his discourse: a
foreigner generally strives to oblige in what he says. The
French are accused of promising more than they perform.
That may be, and yet they may perform as many good-
natured acts as the English, if the latter are as averse to perform as they are to promise. Even the professions of the
English may be sincere at the time, or arise out of the impulse of the moment; though their desire to serve you may
be neither very violent nor very lasting. I cannot think, notwithstanding, that the French are not a serious people; nay,
that they are not a more reflecting people than the common
run of the English. Let those who think them merely light
and mercurial, explain that enigma, their everlasting prosing tragedy. The English are considered as comparatively a
slow, plodding people. If the French are quicker, they are
also more plodding. See, for example, how highly finished
and elaborate their works of art are! How systematic and
correct they aim at being in all their productions of a graver
cast! 'If the French have a fault,' as Yorick said, 'it is that
they are too grave.' With wit, sense, cheerfulness, patience,
good-nature and refinement of manners, all they want is
imagination and sturdiness of moral principle! Such are
some of the contradictions in the character of the two
nations, and so little does the character of either appear to
have been understood! Nothing can be more ridiculous indeed than the way in which we exaggerate each other's vices
and extenuate our own. The whole is an affair of prejudice

on one side of the question, and of partiality on the other. Travellers who set out to carry back a true report of the case appear to lose not only the use of their understandings, but of their senses, the instant they set foot in a foreign land. The commonest facts and appearances are distorted, and discoloured. They go abroad with certain preconceived notions on the subject, and they make every thing answer, in reason's spite, to their favourite theory. In addition to the difficulty of explaining customs and manners foreign to our own, there are all the obstacles of wilful prepossession thrown in the way. It is not, therefore, much to be wondered at that nations have arrived at so little knowledge of one another's characters; and that, where the object has been to widen the breach between them, any slight differences that occur are easily blown into a blaze of fury by repeated misrepresentations, and all the exaggerations that malice or folly can invent!

This ignorance of character is not confined to foreign nations: we are ignorant of that of our own countrymen in a class a little below or above ourselves. We can hardly pretend to pronounce magisterially on the good or bad qualities of strangers; and, at the same time, we are ignorant of those of our friends, of our kindred, and of our own. We are in all these cases either too near or too far off the object to judge of it properly.

Persons, for instance, in a higher or middle rank of life know little or nothing of the characters of those below them, as servants, country people, &c. I would lay it down in the first place as a general rule on this subject, that all uneducated people are hypocrites. Their sole business is to deceive. They conceive themselves in a state of hostility with others, and stratagems are fair in war. The inmates of the kitchen and the parlour are always (as far as respects their feeling and intentions towards each other) in Hobbes's 'state of nature.' Servants and others in that line of life have nothing to exercise their spare talents for invention upon but those about them. Their superfluous electrical particles of wit and fancy are not carried off by those established and fashionable conductors, novels and romances. Their faculties are not buried in books, but all alive and stirring, erect and bristling like a cat's back. Their coarse conversation sparkles with 'wild wit, invention ever new.' Their betters try all they can to set themselves up above them, and they try all they can to pull them down to their own level. They do this by getting up a little comic interlude, a daily, domestic, homely drama out of the odds and ends of the family failings, of which there is in general a pretty plentiful supply, or make up the deficiency of materials out of their own heads. They turn the qualities of their masters and mistresses inside out, and any real kindness or condescension only sets them the more against you. They are not to be taken in in that way – they will not be baulked in the spite they have to you. They only set to work with redoubled alacrity, to lessen the favour or to blacken your character. They feel themselves like a degraded *caste*, and cannot understand how the obligations can be all on one side, and the advantages all on the other. You cannot come to equal terms with them – they reject all such overtures as insidious and hollow – nor can you ever calculate upon their gratitude or good-will, any more than if they were so many strolling Gipsies or wild Indians. They have no fellow-feeling, they keep no faith with the more privileged classes. They are in your power, and they endeavour to be even with you by trick and cunning, by lying and chicanery. In this they have nothing to restrain them. Their whole life is a succession of shifts, excuses, and expedients. The love of truth is a principle with those only who have made it their study, who have applied themselves to the pursuit of some art or science, where the intellect is severely tasked, and learns by habit to take a pride in, and to set a just value on, the correctness of its conclusions. To have a disinterested regard for truth, the mind must have contemplated it in abstract and remote questions; whereas the ignorant and vulgar are only conversant with those things in which their own interest is concerned. All their notions are local, personal, and consequently gross and selfish. They say whatever comes uppermost – turn whatever happens to their own account – and invent any story, or give any answer that suits their purposes. Instead of being bigoted to general principles, they trump up any lie for the occasion, and the more of a *thumper* it is, the better they like it; the more unlooked-for it is, why, so much the more of a *God-send!* They have no conscience about the matter; and if you find them out in any of their manoeuvres, are not ashamed of themselves, but angry with you. If you remonstrate with them, they laugh in your face. The only hold you have of them is their interest – you can but dismiss them from your employment; and *service is no inheritance*. If they affect any thing like decent remorse, and hope you will pass it over, all the while they are probably trying to recover the wind of you. Persons of liberal knowledge or sentiments have no kind of chance in this sort of mixed intercourse with these barbarians in civilised life. You cannot tell, by any signs or principles, what is passing in their minds. There is no common point of view between you. You have not the same topics to refer to, the same language to express yourself. Your interests, your feelings are quite distinct. You take certain things for granted as rules of action : they take nothing for granted but their own ends, pick up all their knowledge out of their own occasions, are on the watch only for what they can catch – are

> 'Subtle as the fox for prey :
> Like warlike as the wolf, for what they eat.'

They have indeed a regard to their character, as this last may affect their livelihood or advancement, none as it is connected with a sense of propriety; and this sets their motherwit and native talents at work upon a double file of expedients, to bilk their consciences, and salve their reputation. In short, you never know where to have them, any more than if they were of a different species of animals; and in trusting to them, you are sure to be betrayed and over-reached. You have other things to mind, they are thinking only of you, and how to turn you to advantage. Give and take is maxim here. You can build nothing on your own moderation or on their false delicacy. After a familiar conversation with a waiter at a tavern, you over-hear him calling you by some provoking nickname. If you make a present to the daughter of the house where you lodge, the mother is sure to recollect some addition to her bill. It is a running fight. In fact, there is a principle in human nature not willingly to endure the idea of a superior, a sour jacobinical disposition to wipe out the score of obligation, or efface the tinsel of external advantages – and where others have the opportunity of coming in contact with us, they generally find the means to establish a sufficiently marked degree of degrading equality. No man is a hero to his valet-de-chambre, is an old maxim. A new illustration of this principle occurred the other day. While Mrs Siddons was giving her readings of Shakespear to a brilliant and admiring drawing-room, one of the servants in the hall below was saying, 'What, I find the old lady is making as much noise as ever!' So little is there in common between the different classes of society, and so impossible is it ever to unite the diversities of custom and knowledge which separate them.

Women, according to Mrs Peachum, are 'bitter bad judges' of the characters of men; and men are not much better of theirs, if we can form any guess from their choice in marriage. Love is proverbially blind. The whole is an affair of whim and fancy. Certain it is, that the greatest favourites

with the other sex are not those who are most liked or respected among their own. I never knew but one clever man
who was what is called a *lady's man*; and he (unfortunately
for the argument) happened to be a considerable coxcomb.
It was by this irresistible quality, and not by the force of his
genius, that he vanquished. Women seem to doubt their
own judgments in love, and to take the opinion which a
man entertains of his own prowess and accomplishments
for granted. The wives of poets are (for the most part) mere
pieces of furniture in the room. If you speak to them of their
husbands' talents or reputation in the world, it is as if you
made mention of some office that they held. It can hardly be
otherwise, when the instant any subject is started or conversation arises, in which men are interested, or try one
another's strength, the women leave the room, or attend to
something else. The qualities then in which men are ambitious to excel, and which ensure the applause of the world,
eloquence, genius, learning, integrity, are not those which
gain the favour of the fair. I must not deny, however, that
wit and courage have this effect. Neither is youth or beauty
the sole passport to their affections.

> 'The way of woman's will is hard to find,
> 　Harder to hit.'

Yet there is some clue to this mystery, some determining
cause; for we find that the same men are universal favourites
with women, as others are uniformly disliked by them. Is
not the load-stone that attracts so powerfully, and in all circumstances, a strong and undisguised bias towards them, a
marked attention, a conscious preference of them to every
other passing object or topic? I am not sure, but I incline to
think so. The successful lover is the *cavalier servente* of all
nations. The man of gallantry behaves as if he had made an
assignation with every woman he addresses. An argument
immediately draws off the scholar's attention from the pret-

tiest woman in the room. He accordingly succeeds better in argument – than in love! – I do not think that what is called *Love at first sight* is so great an absurdity as it is sometimes imagined to be. We generally make up our minds beforehand to the sort of person we should like, grave or gay, black, brown, or fair; with golden tresses or with raven locks; – and when we meet with a complete example of the qualities we admire, the bargain is soon struck. We have never seen any thing to come up to our newly discovered goddess before, but she is what we have been all our lives looking for. The idol we fall down and worship is an image familiar to our minds. It has been present to our waking thoughts, it has haunted us in our dreams, like some fairy vision. Oh! thou, who, the first time I ever beheld thee, didst draw my soul into the circle of thy heavenly looks,[5] and wave enchantment round me, do not think thy conquest less complete because it was instantaneous; for in that gentle form (as if another Imogen had entered) I saw all that I had ever loved of female grace, modesty, and sweetness!

I cannot say much of friendship as giving an insight into character, because it is often founded on mutual infirmities and prejudices. Friendships are frequently taken up on some sudden sympathy, and we see only as much as we please of one another's characters afterwards. Intimate friends are not fair witnesses to character, any more than professed enemies. They cool, indeed, in time – part, and retain only a rankling grudge at past errors and oversights. Their testimony in the latter case is not quite free from suspicion.

One would think that near relations, who live constantly together, and always have done so, must be pretty well acquainted with one another's character. They are nearly in the dark about it. Familiarity confounds all traits of distinction: interest and prejudice take away the power of judging. We have no opinion on the subject, any more than of one another's faces. The Penates, the household-gods, are veiled. We do not see the features of those we love, nor do we clearly distinguish their virtues or their vices. We take them as they are found in the lump: – by weight, and not by measure. We know all about the individuals, their senti- ments, history, manners, words, actions, every thing: but we know all these too much as facts, as inveterate, habitual impressions, as clothed with too many associations, as sancti- fied with too many affections, as woven too much into the web of our hearts, to be able to pick out the different threads, to cast up the items of the debtor and creditor account, or to refer them to any general standard of right and wrong. Our impressions with respect to them are too strong, too real, too much *sui generis*, to be capable of a comparison with any thing but themselves. We hardly inquire whether those for whom we are thus interested, and to whom we are thus knit, are *better* or *worse* than others – the question is a kind of profanation – all we know is, they are *more* to us than any one else can be. Our sentiments of this kind are rooted and grow in us, and we cannot eradicate them by volun- tary means. Besides, our judgments are bespoke, our in- terests take part with our blood. If any doubt arises, if the veil of our implicit confidence is drawn aside by any acci- dent for a moment, the shock is too great, like that of a dis- located limb, and we recoil on our habitual impressions again. Let not that veil ever be rent entirely asunder, so that those images may be left bare of reverential awe, and lose their religion: for nothing can ever support the desolation of the heart afterwards!

The greatest misfortune that can happen among relations is a different way of bringing up, so as to set one another's opinions and characters in an entirely new point of view. This often lets in an unwelcome day-light on the subject, and breeds schisms, coldness, and incurable heart-burnings in families. I have sometimes thought whether the progress of society and march of knowledge does not do more harm in this respect, by loosening the ties of domestic attachment, and preventing those who are most interested in, and anxious to think well of one another, from feeling a cordial sympathy and approbation of each other's sentiments, manners, views, &c. than it does good by any real advantage to the community at large. The son, for instance, is brought up to the church, and nothing can exceed the pride and pleasure the father takes in him, while all goes on well in his favourite direction. His notions change, and he imbibes a taste for the Fine Arts. From this moment there is an end of any thing like the same unreserved communication between them. The young man may talk with enthusiasm of his 'Rembrandts, Correggios, and stuff:' it is all *Hebrew* to the elder; and whatever satisfaction he may feel in hearing of his son's progress, or good wishes for his success, he is never reconciled to the new pursuit, he still hankers after the first object that he had set his mind upon. Again, the grandfather is a Calvinist, who never gets the better of his disappointment at his son's going over to the Unitarian side of the question. The matter rests here, till the grand-son, some years after, in the fashion of the day and 'infinite agitation of men's wit,' comes to doubt certain points in the creed in which he has been brought up, and the affair is all abroad again. Here are three generations made uncomfortable and in a manner set at variance, by a veering point of theology, and the officious meddling biblical critics! Nothing, on the other hand, can be more wretched or common than that upstart pride and insolent good fortune which is ashamed of its origin; nor are there many things more awkward than the situation of rich and poor relations. Happy, much happier, are those tribes and people who are confined to the same *caste* and way of life from sire to son, where prejudices are transmitted like instincts, and where the same unvarying standard of opinion and refinement blends countless generations in its improgressive, everlasting mould!

Not only is there a wilful and habitual blindness in near kindred to each other's defects, but an incapacity to judge from the quantity of materials, from the contradictoriness of the evidence. The chain of particulars is too long and massy for us to lift it or put it into the most approved ethical scales. The concrete result does not answer to any abstract theory, to any logical definition. There is black, and white, and grey, square and round – there are too many anomalies, too many redeeming points in poor human nature, such as it actually is, for us to arrive at a smart, summary decision on it. We know too much to come to any hasty or partial conclusion. We do not pronounce upon the present act, because a hundred others rise up to contradict it. We suspend our judgments altogether, because in effect one thing unconsciously balances another; and perhaps this obstinate, pertinacious indecision would be the truest philosophy in other cases, where we dispose of the question of character easily, because we have only the smallest part of the evidence to decide upon. Real character is not one thing, but a thousand things; actual qualities do not conform to any factitious standard in the mind, but rest upon their own truth and nature. The dull stupor under which we labour in respect of those whom we have the greatest opportunities of inspecting nearly, we should do well to imitate, before we give extreme and uncharitable verdicts against those whom we only see in passing, or at a distance. If we knew them better, we should be disposed to say less about them.

In the truth of things, there are none utterly worthless, none without some drawback on their pretensions, or some alloy of imperfection. It has been observed that a familiarity with the worst characters lessens our abhorrence of them; and a wonder is often expressed that the greatest criminals look like men. The reason is that *they are like other men in many respects*. If a particular individual was merely the wretch we read of, or conceive in the abstract, that is, if he was the mere personified idea of the criminal brought to the bar, he would not disappoint the spectator, but would look like what he would be – a monster! But he has other qualities, ideas, feelings, nay, probably virtues, mixed up with the most profligate habits or desperate acts. This need not lessen our abhorrence of the crime, though it does of the criminal; for it has the latter effect only by showing him to us in different points of view, in which he appears a common mortal, and not the caricature of vice we took him for, nor spotted all over with infamy. I do not at the same time think this a lax or dangerous, though it is a charitable view of the subject. In my opinion, no man ever answered in his own mind (except in the agonies of conscience or of repentance, in which latter case he throws the imputation from himself in another way) to the abstract idea of a *murderer*. He may have killed a man in self-defence, or 'in the trade of war,' or to save himself from starving, or in revenge for an injury, but always 'so as with a difference,' or from mixed and questionable motives. The individual, in reckoning with himself, always takes into the account the considerations of time, place, and circumstance, and never makes out a case of unmitigated, unprovoked villany, of 'pure defecated evil' against himself. There are degrees in real crimes: we reason and moralise only by names and in classes. I should be loth, indeed, to say, that 'whatever is, is right;' but almost every actual choice inclines to it, with some sort of imperfect, unconscious bias. This is the reason, besides the ends of secresy, of the invention of *slang* terms for different acts of profligacy committed by thieves, pickpockets, &c. The common names suggest associations of disgust in the minds of others, which those who live by them do not willingly recognise, and which they wish to sink in a technical phraseology. So there is a story of a fellow who, as he was writing down his confession of a murder, stopped to ask how the word *murder* was spelt; this, if true, was partly because his imagination was staggered by the recollection of the thing, and partly because he shrunk from the verbal admission of it. '*Amen* stuck in his throat!' The defence made by Eugene Aram of himself against a charge of murder, some years before, shows that he in imagination completely flung from himself the *nominal* crime imputed to him : he might, indeed, have staggered an old man with a blow, and buried his body in a cave, and lived ever since upon the money he found upon him, but there was 'no malice in the case, none at all,' as Peachum says. The very coolness, subtlety, and circumspection of his defence (as masterly a legal document as there is upon record) prove that he was guilty of the act, as much as they prove that he was unconscious of the *crime*.* In the same spirit, and I conceive with great metaphysical truth, Mr Coleridge, in his tragedy of *Remorse*, makes Ordonio (his chief character) waive the acknowledgment of his meditated guilt to his own mind, by putting into his mouth that striking soliloquy :

> Say, I had lay'd a body in the sun !
> Well ! in a month there swarm forth from the corse
> A thousand, nay, ten thousand sentient beings
> In place of that one man. Say I had *kill'd* him !
> Yet who shall tell me, that each one and all
> Of these ten thousand lives is not as happy
> As that one life, which being push'd aside,
> Made room for these unnumber'd. – Act ii. sc. ii.

I am not sure, indeed, that I have not got this whole train of speculation from him; but I should not think the worse of it on that account. That gentleman, I recollect, once asked

---

*The bones of the murdered man were dug up in an old hermitage. On this, as one instance of the acuteness which he displayed all through the occasion, Aram remarks 'Where would you expect to find the bones of a man sooner than in a hermit's cell, except you were to look for them in a cemetery?' See Newgate Calendar for the year 1758 or 9.

me whether I thought that the different members of a family really liked one another so well, or had so much attachment as was generally supposed: and I said that I conceived the regard they had towards each other was expressed by the word interest, rather than by any other; which he said was the true answer. I do not know that I could mend it now. Natural affection is not pleasure in one another's company, nor admiration of one another's qualities; but it is an intimate and deep knowledge of the things that affect those, to whom we are bound by the nearest ties, with pleasure or pain; it is an anxious, uneasy, fellow-feeling with them, a jealous watchfulness over their good name, a tender and unconquerable yearning for their good. The love, in short, we bear them, is the nearest to that we bear ourselves. *Home*, according to the old saying, *is home, be it never so homely*. We love ourselves, not according to our deserts, but our cravings after good: so we love our immediate relations in the next degree (if not even sometimes in a higher one) because we know best what they have suffered and what sits nearest to their hearts. We are implicated, in fact, in their welfare, by habit and sympathy, as we are in our own.

If our devotion to our own interests is much the same as to theirs, we are ignorant of our own characters for the same reason. We are parties too much concerned to return a fair verdict, and are too much in the secret of our own motives or situation not to be able to give a favourable turn to our actions. We exercise a liberal criticism upon ourselves, and put off the final decision to a late day. The field is large and open. Hamlet exclaims, with a noble magnanimity, 'I count myself indifferent honest, and yet I could accuse me of such things!' If you could prove to a man that he is a knave, it would not make much difference in his opinion; his self-love is stronger than his love of virtue. Hypocrisy is generally used as a mask to deceive the world, not to impose on ourselves: for once detect the delinquent in his knavery, and he laughs in your face or glories in his iniquity. This at least happens except where there is a contradiction in the character, and our vices are involuntary, and at variance with our convictions. One great difficulty is to distinguish ostensible motives, or such as we acknowledge to ourselves, from tacit or secret springs of action. A man changes his opinion readily, he thinks it candour: it is levity of mind. For the most part, we are stunned and stupid in judging of ourselves. We are callous by custom to our defects or excellencies, unless where vanity steps in to exaggerate or extenuate them. I cannot conceive how it is that people are in love with their own persons, or astonished at their own performances, which are but a nine days' wonder to every one else. In general it may be laid down that we are liable to this twofold mistake in judging of our own talents: we, in the first place, nurse the rickety bantling, we think much of that which has cost us much pains and labour and which goes against the grain; and we also set little store by what we do with most ease to ourselves, and therefore best. The works of the greatest genius are produced almost unconsciously, with an ignorance on the part of the persons themselves that they have done any thing extraordinary. Nature has done it for them. How little Shakespear seems to have thought of himself or of his fame! Yet, if 'to know another well, were to know one's self,' he must have been acquainted with his own pretensions and character, 'who knew all qualities with a learned spirit.' His eye seems never to have been bent upon himself, but outwards upon nature. A man, who thinks highly of himself, may almost set it down that it is without reason. Milton, notwithstanding, appears to have had a high opinion of himself, and to have made it good. He was conscious of his powers, and great by design. Perhaps his tenaciousness, on the score of his own merit, might arise from an early habit of polemical writing, in which his pretensions were continually called to the bar of prejudice and party-spirit, and he had to plead not guilty to the indictment. Some men have died unconscious of immortality, as others have almost exhausted the sense of it in their life-times. Correggio might be mentioned as an instance of the one, Voltaire of the other.

There is nothing that helps a man in his conduct through life more than a knowledge of his own characteristic weaknesses (which, guarded against, become his strength), as there is nothing that tends more to the success of a man's talents than his knowing the limits of his faculties, which are thus concentrated on some practicable object. One man can do but one thing. Universal pretensions end in nothing. Or, as Butler has it, too much wit requires

'As much again to govern it.'

There are those who have gone, for want of this self-knowledge, strangely out of their way, and others who have never found it. We find many who succeed in certain departments, and are yet melancholy and dissatisfied, because they failed in the one to which they first devoted themselves, like discarded lovers who pine after their scornful mistress. I will conclude with observing, that authors in general overrate the extent and value of posthumous fame: for what (as it has been asked) is the amount even of Shakespear's fame? That in that very country which boasts his genius and his birth, perhaps scarce one person in ten has ever heard of his name, or read a syllable of his writings!

From *Table-Talk* (1821).

THE INDIAN JUGGLERS

COMING forward and seating himself on the ground in his white dress and tightened turban, the chief of the Indian Jugglers begins with tossing up two brass balls, which is what any of us could do, and concludes with keeping up four at the same time, which is what none of us could do to save our lives, nor if we were to take our whole lives to do it in. Is it then a trifling power we see at work, or is it not something next to miraculous? It is the utmost stretch of human ingenuity, which nothing but the bending the faculties of body and mind to it from the tenderest infancy with incessant, ever-anxious application up to manhood, can accomplish or make even a slight approach to. Man, thou art a wonderful animal, and thy ways past finding out! Thou canst do strange things, but thou turnest them to little account! – To conceive of this effort of extraordinary dexterity distracts the imagination and makes admiration breathless. Yet it costs nothing to the performer, any more than if it were a mere mechanical deception with which he had nothing to do but to watch and laugh at the astonishment of the spectators. A single error of a hair's-breadth, of the smallest conceivable portion of time, would be fatal: the precision of the movements must be like a mathematical truth, their rapidity is like lightning. To catch four balls in succession in less than a second of time, and deliver them back so as to return with seeming consciousness to the hand again, to make them revolve round him at certain intervals, like the planets in their spheres, to make them chase one another like sparkles of fire, or shoot up like flowers or meteors, to throw them behind his back and twine them round his neck like ribbons or like serpents, to do what appears an impossibility, and to do it with all the ease, the grace, the carelessness imaginable, to laugh at, to play with the glittering mockeries, to follow them with his eye as if he could fascinate them with its lambent fire, or as if he had only to see that they kept time with the music on the stage – there is something in all this which he who does not admire may be quite sure he never really admired any thing in the whole course of his life. It is skill surmounting difficulty, and beauty triumphing over skill. It seems as if the difficulty once mastered naturally resolved itself into ease and grace, and as if to be overcome at all, it must be overcome without an effort. The smallest awkwardness or want of pliancy or self-possession would stop the whole process. It is the work of witchcraft, and yet sport for children. Some of the other feats are quite as curious and wonderful, such as the balancing the artificial tree and shooting a bird from each branch through a quill; though none of them have the elegance or facility of the keeping up of the brass balls. You are in pain for the result, and glad when the experiment is over; they are not accompanied with the same unmixed, unchecked delight as the former; and I would not give much to be merely astonished without being pleased at the same time. As to the swallowing of the sword, the police ought to interfere to prevent it. When I saw the Indian Juggler do the same things before, his feet were bare, and he had large rings on the toes, which keep turning round all the time of the performance, as if they moved of themselves. – The hearing a speech in Parliament, drawled or stammered out by the Honourable Member or the Noble Lord, the ringing the changes on their common-places, which any one could repeat after them as well as they, stirs me not a jot, shakes not my good opinion of myself: but the seeing the Indian Juggler does. It makes me ashamed of myself. I ask what there is that I can do as well as this? Nothing. What have I been doing all my life? Have I been idle, or have I nothing to shew for all my labour and pains? Or have I passed my time in pouring words like water into empty sieves, rolling a stone up a hill and then down again, trying to prove an argument in the teeth of facts, and looking for causes in the dark, and not finding them? Is there no one thing in which I can challenge competition, that I can bring as an instance of exact perfection, in which others cannot find a flaw? The utmost I can pretend to is to write a description of what this fellow can do. I can write a book: so can many others who have not even learned to spell. What abortions are these Essays! What errors, what ill-pieced transitions, what crooked reasons, what lame conclusions! How little is made out, and that little how ill! Yet they are the best I can do. I endeavour to recollect all I have ever observed or thought upon a subject, and to express it as nearly as I can. Instead of writing on four subjects at a time, it is as much as I can manage to keep the thread of one discourse clear and unentangled. I have also time on my hands to correct my opinions, and polish my periods: but the one I cannot, and the other I will not do. I am fond of arguing: yet with a good deal of pains and practice it is often as much as I can do to beat my man; though he may be a very indifferent hand. A common fencer would disarm his adversary in the twinkling of an eye, unless he were a professor like himself. A stroke of wit will sometimes produce this effect, but there is no such power or superiority in sense or reasoning. There is no complete mastery of execution to be shewn there: and you hardly know the professor from the impudent pretender or the mere clown.*

---

* The celebrated Peter Pindar (Dr Wolcot) first discovered and brought out the talents of the late Mr Opie, the painter. He was a poor Cornish boy, and was out at work in the fields, when the poet went in search of him. 'Well, my lad, can you go and bring me your

I have always had this feeling of the inefficacy and slow progress of intellectual compared to mechanical excellence, and it has always made me somewhat dissatisfied. It is a great many years since I saw Richer, the famous rope-dancer, perform at Sadler's Wells. He was matchless in his art, and added to his extraordinary skill exquisite ease, and unaffected natural grace. I was at that time employed in copying a half-length picture of Sir Joshua Reynolds's; and it put me out of conceit with it. How ill this part was made out in the drawing! How heavy, how slovenly this other was painted! I could not help saying to myself, 'If the rope-dancer had performed his task in this manner, leaving so many gaps and botches in his work, he would have broke his neck long ago; I should never have seen that vigorous elasticity of nerve and precision of movement!' – Is it then so easy an undertaking (comparatively) to dance on a tight-rope? Let any one, who thinks so, get up and try. There is the thing. It is that which at first we cannot do at all, which in the end is done to such perfection. To account for this in some degree, I might observe that mechanical dexterity is confined to doing some one particular thing, which you can repeat as often as you please, in which you know whether you succeed or fail, and where the point of perfection consists in succeeding in a given undertaking. – In mechanical efforts, you improve by perpetual practice, and you do so infallibly, because the object to be attained is not a matter of taste or fancy or opinion, but of actual experiment, in which

---

very best picture?' The other flew like lightning, and soon came back with what he considered as his master-piece. The stranger looked at it, and the young artist, after waiting for some time without his giving any opinion, at length exclaimed eagerly, 'Well, what do you think of it?' – 'Think of it?' said Wolcot, 'why I think you ought to be ashamed of it – that you who might do so well, do no better!' The same answer would have applied to this artist's latest performances, that had been suggested by one of his earliest efforts.

you must either do the thing or not do it. If a man is put to aim at a mark with a bow and arrow, he must hit it or miss it, that's certain. He cannot deceive himself, and go on shooting wide or falling short, and still fancy that he is making progress. The distinction between right and wrong, between true and false, is here palpable; and he must either correct his aim or persevere in his error with his eyes open, for which there is neither excuse nor temptation. If a man is learning to dance on a rope, if he does not mind what he is about, he will break his neck. After that, it will be in vain for him to argue that he did not make a false step. His situation is not like that of Goldsmith's pedagogue. –

> 'In argument they own'd his wondrous skill,
> And e'en though vanquish'd, he could argue still.'

Danger is a good teacher, and makes apt scholars. So are disgrace, defeat, exposure to immediate scorn and laughter. There is no opportunity in such cases for self-delusion, no idling time away, no being off your guard (or you must take the consequences) – neither is there any room for humour or caprice or prejudice. If the Indian Juggler were to play tricks in throwing up the three case-knives, which keep their positions like the leaves of a crocus in the air, he would cut his fingers. I can make a very bad antithesis without cutting my fingers. The tact of style is more ambiguous than that of double-edged instruments. If the Juggler were told that by flinging himself under the wheels of the Jaggernaut, when the idol issues forth on a gaudy day, he would immediately be transported into Paradise, he might believe it, and nobody could disprove it. So the Brahmins may say what they please on that subject, may build up dogmas and mysteries without end, and not be detected: but their ingenious countryman cannot persuade the frequenters of the Olympic Theatre that he performs a number of astonishing feats without actually giving proofs of what he says. – There is then in this sort of manual dexterity, first a gradual aptitude acquired to a given exertion of muscular power, from constant repetition, and in the next place, an exact knowledge how much is still wanting and necessary to be supplied. The obvious test is to increase the effort or nicety of the operation, and still to find it come true. The muscles ply instinctively to the dictates of habit. Certain movements and impressions of the hand and eye, having been repeated together an infinite number of times, are unconsciously but unavoidably cemented into closer and closer union; the limbs require little more than to be put in motion for them to follow a regular track with ease and certainty; so that the mere intention of the will acts mathematically, like touching the spring of a machine, and you come with Locksley in Ivanhoe, in shooting at a mark, 'to allow for the wind.'

Farther, what is meant by perfection in mechanical exercises is the performing certain feats to a uniform nicety, that is, in fact, undertaking no more than you can perform. You task yourself, the limit you fix is optional, and no more than human industry and skill can attain to: but you have no abstract, independent standard of difficulty or excellence (other than the extent of your own powers). Thus he who can keep up four brass balls does this *to perfection*; but he cannot keep up five at the same instant, and would fail every time he attempted it. That is, the mechanical performer undertakes to emulate himself, not to equal another.* But the artist undertakes to imitate another, or to do what nature has done, and this it appears is more difficult, *viz.* to copy what she has set before us in the face of nature or 'human face divine,' entire and without a blemish, than to keep up four brass balls at the same instant; for the one is done by the power of human skill and industry, and the

* If two persons play against each other at any game, one of them necessarily fails.

other never was nor will be. Upon the whole, therefore, I have more respect for Reynolds, than I have for Richer: for, happen how it will, there have been more people in the world who could dance on a rope like the one than who could paint like Sir Joshua. The latter was but a bungler in his profession to the other, it is true; but then he had a harder task-master to obey, whose will was more wayward and obscure, and whose instructions it was more difficult to practise. You can put a child apprentice to a tumbler or rope-dancer with a comfortable prospect of success, if they are but sound of wind and limb: but you cannot do the same thing in painting. The odds are a million to one. You may make indeed as many H—s and H—s, [1] as you put into that sort of machine, but not one Reynolds amongst them all, with his grace, his grandeur, his blandness of *gusto*, 'in tones and gestures hit,' unless you could make the man over again. To snatch this grace beyond the reach of art is then the height of art – where fine art begins, and where mechanical skill ends. The soft suffusion of the soul, the speechless breathing eloquence, the looks 'commercing with the skies,' the ever-shifting forms of an eternal principle, that which is seen but for a moment, but dwells in the heart always, and is only seized as it passes by strong and secret sympathy, must be taught by nature and genius, not by rules or study. It is suggested by feeling, not by laborious microscopic inspection: in seeking for it without, we lose the harmonious clue to it within: and in aiming to grasp the substance, we let the very spirit of art evaporate. In a word, the objects of fine art are not the objects of sight but as these last are the objects of taste and imagination, that is, as they appeal to the sense of beauty, of pleasure, and of power in the human breast, and are explained by that finer sense, and revealed in their inner structure to the eye in return. Nature is also a language. Objects, like words, have a meaning; and the true artist is the interpreter of this language, which he can only do by knowing its application to a thousand other objects in a thousand other situations. Thus the eye is too blind a guide of itself to distinguish between the warm or cold tone of a deep blue sky, but another sense acts as a monitor to it, and does not err. The colour of the leaves in autumn would be nothing without the feeling that accompanies it; but it is that feeling that stamps them on the canvas, faded, seared, blighted, shrinking from the winter's flaw, and makes the sight as true as touch –

> 'And visions, as poetic eyes avow,
> Cling to each leaf and hang on every bough.'

The more ethereal, evanescent, more refined and sublime part of art is the seeing nature through the medium of sentiment and passion, as each object is a symbol of the affections and a link in the chain of our endless being. But the unravelling this mysterious web of thought and feeling is alone in the Muse's gift, namely, in the power of that trembling sensibility which is awake to every change and every modification of its ever-varying impressions, that,

> 'Thrills in each nerve, and lives along the line.'

This power is indifferently called genius, imagination, feeling, taste; but the manner in which it acts upon the mind can neither be defined by abstract rules, as is the case in science, nor verified by continual unvarying experiments, as is the case in mechanical performances. The mechanical excellence of the Dutch painters in colouring and handling is that which comes the nearest in fine art to the perfection of certain manual exhibitions of skill. The truth of the effect and the facility with which it is produced are equally admirable. Up to a certain point, every thing is faultless. The hand and eye have done their part. There is only a want of taste and genius. It is after we enter upon that enchanted ground that the human mind begins to droop and flag as in a strange road, or in a thick mist, benighted and making little way with many attempts and many failures, and that the best of us only escape with half a triumph. The undefined and the imaginary are the regions that we must pass like Satan, difficult and doubtful, 'half flying, half on foot.' The object in sense is a positive thing, and execution comes with practice.

Cleverness is a certain *knack* or aptitude at doing certain things, which depend more on a particular adroitness and off-hand readiness than on force or perseverance, such as making puns, making epigrams, making extempore verses, mimicking the company, mimicking a style, &c. Cleverness is either liveliness and smartness, or something answering to *sleight of hand*, like letting a glass fall sideways off a table, or else a trick, like knowing the secret spring of a watch. Accomplishments are certain external graces, which are to be learnt from others, and which are easily displayed to the admiration of the beholder, *viz.* dancing, riding, fencing, music, and so on. These ornamental acquirements are only proper to those who are at ease in mind and fortune. I know an individual who if he had been born to an estate of five thousand a year, would have been the most accomplished gentleman of the age. He would have been the delight and envy of the circle in which he moved – would have graced by his manners the liberality flowing from the openness of his heart, would have laughed with the women, have argued with the men, have said good things and written agreeable ones, have taken a hand at piquet or the lead at the harpsichord, and have set and sung his own verses – *nugae canorae* – with tenderness and spirit; a Rochester without the vice, a modern Surrey! As it is, all these capabilities of excellence stand in his way. He is too versatile for a professional man, not dull enough for a political drudge, too gay to be happy, too thoughtless to be rich. He wants the enthusiasm of the poet, the severity of the prose-writer, and the application of the man of business. – Talent is the capacity of doing any thing that depends on application and industry, such as writing a criticism, making a speech, studying the law. Talent differs from genius, as voluntary differs from involuntary power. Ingenuity is genius in trifles, greatness is genius in undertakings of much pith and moment. A clever or ingenious man is one who can do any thing well, whether it is worth doing or not: a great man is one who can do that which when done is of the highest importance. Themistocles said he could not play on the flute, but that he could make of a small city a great one. This gives one a pretty good idea of the distinction in question.

Greatness is great power, producing great effects. It is not enough that a man has great power in himself, he must shew it to all the world in a way that cannot be hid or gainsaid. He must fill up a certain idea in the public mind. I have no other notion of greatness than this two-fold definition, great results springing from great inherent energy. The great in visible objects has relation to that which extends over space: the great in mental ones has to do with space and time. No man is truly great, who is great only in his life-time. The test of greatness is the page of history. Nothing can be said to be great that has a distinct limit, or that borders on something evidently greater than itself. Besides, what is short-lived and pampered into mere notoriety, is of a gross and vulgar quality in itself. A Lord Mayor is hardly a great man. A city orator or patriot of the day only shew, by reaching the height of their wishes, the distance they are at from any true ambition. Popularity is neither fame nor greatness. A king (as such) is not a great man. He has great power, but it is not his own. He merely wields the lever of the state, which a child, an idiot, or a madman can do. It is the office, not the man we gaze at. Any one else in the same situation would be just as much an object of abject curiosity. We laugh at the country girl who having seen a king expressed her disappointment by saying, 'Why, he is only a man!' Yet, knowing this, we run to see a king as if he was something more than a man. – To display the greatest powers, unless they are applied to great purposes, makes nothing for the character of greatness. To throw a barley-corn through the eye of a needle, to multiply nine figures by nine in the memory, argues infinite dexterity of body and capacity of mind, but nothing comes of either. There is a surprising power at work, but the effects are not proportionate, or such as take hold of the imagination. To impress the idea of power on others, they must be made in some way to feel it. It must be communicated to their understandings in the shape of an increase of knowledge, or it must subdue and overawe them by subjecting their wills. Admiration, to be solid and lasting, must be founded on proofs from which we have no means of escaping; it is neither a slight nor a voluntary gift. A mathematician who solves a profound prob-lem, a poet who creates an image of beauty in the mind that was not there before, imparts knowledge and power to others, in which his greatness and his fame consists, and on which it reposes. Jedediah Buxton will be forgotten; but Napier's bones will live.[2] Lawgivers, philosophers, founders of religion, conquerors and heroes, inventors and great geniuses in arts and sciences, are great men; for they are great public benefactors, or formidable scourges to man-kind. Among ourselves, Shakespear, Newton, Bacon, Mil-ton, Cromwell, were great men; for they shewed great power by acts and thoughts, which have not yet been con-signed to oblivion. They must needs be men of lofty stature, whose shadows lengthen out to remote posterity. A great farce-writer may be a great man; for Moliere was but a great farce-writer. In my mind, the author of Don Quixote was a great man. So have there been many others. A great chess-player it not a great man, for he leaves the world as he found it. No act terminating in itself constitutes greatness.

This will apply to all displays of power or trials of skill, which are confined to the momentary, individual effort, and construct no permanent image or trophy of themselves without them. Is not an actor then a great man, because 'he dies and leaves the world no copy?' I must make an exception for Mrs Siddons, or else give up my definition of greatness for her sake. A man at the top of his profession is not therefore a great man. He is great in his way, but that is all, unless he shews the marks of a great moving intellect, so that we trace the master-mind, and can sympathise with the springs that urge him on. The rest is but a craft or *mystery*. John Hunter[3] was a great man – *that* any one might see without the smallest skill in surgery. His style and manner shewed the man. He would set about cutting up the carcase of a whale with the same greatness of *gusto* that Michael Angelo would have hewn a block of marble. Lord Nelson was a great naval commander; but for myself, I have not much opinion of a sea-faring life. Sir Humphry Davy is a a great chemist, but I am not sure that he is a great man. I am not a bit the wiser for any of his discoveries, nor I never met with any one that was. But it is in the nature of greatness to propagate an idea of itself, as wave impels wave, circle without circle. It is a contradiction in terms for a coxcomb to be a great man. A really great man has always an idea of something greater than himself. I have observed that certain sectaries and polemical writers have no higher compliment to pay their most shining lights than to say that 'Such a one was a considerable man in his day.' Some new elucidation of a text sets aside the authority of the old interpretation, and a 'great scholar's memory outlives him half a century,' at the utmost. A rich man is not a great man, except to his dependants and his steward. A lord is a great man in the idea we have of his ancestry, and probably of himself, if we know nothing of him but his title. I have heard a story of two bishops, one of whom said (speaking of St

Peter's at Rome) that when he first entered it, he was rather awe-struck, but that as he walked up it, his mind seemed to swell and dilate with it, and at last to fill the whole building – the other said that as he saw more of it, he appeared to himself to grow less and less every step he took, and in the end to dwindle into nothing. This was in some respects a striking picture of a great and little mind – for greatness sympathises with greatness, and littleness shrinks into itself. The one might have become a Wolsey; the other was only fit to become a Mendicant Friar – or there might have been court-reasons for making him a bishop. The French have to me a character of littleness in all about them; but they have produced three great men that belong to every country, Moliere, Rabelais, and Montaigne.

To return from this digression, and conclude the Essay. A singular instance of manual dexterity was shewn in the person of the late John Cavanagh, whom I have several times seen. His death was celebrated at the time in an article in the Examiner newspaper (Feb. 7, 1819), written apparently between jest and earnest: but as it is *pat* to our purpose, and falls in with my own way of considering such subjects, I shall here take leave to quote it.

'Died at his house in Burbage-street, St Giles's, John Cavanagh, the famous hand fives-player. When a person dies, who does any one thing better than any one else in the world, which so many others are trying to do well, it leaves a gap in society. It is not likely that any one will now see the game of fives played in its perfection for many years to come – for Cavanagh is dead, and has not left his peer behind him. It may be said that there are things of more importance than striking a ball against a wall – there are things indeed which make more noise and do as little good, such as making war and peace, making speeches and answering them, making verses and blotting them; making money and throwing it away. But the game of fives is what no one despises who has ever played at it. It is the finest exercise for the body, and the best relaxation for the mind. The Roman poet said that "Care mounted behind the horse-man and stuck to his skirts." But this remark would not have applied to the fives-player. He who takes to playing at fives is twice young. He feels neither the past nor future "in the instant." Debts, taxes, "domestic reason, foreign levy, nothing can touch him further." He has no other wish, no other thought, from the moment the game begins, but that of striking the ball, of placing it, of *making* it! This Cava-nagh was sure to do. Whenever he touched the ball, there was an end of the chase. His eye was certain, his hand fatal, his presence of mind complete. He could do what he pleased, and he always knew exactly what to do. He saw the whole game, and played it; took instant advantage of his adversary's weakness, and recovered balls, as if by a miracle and from sudden thought, that every one gave for lost. He had equal power and skill, quickness, and judgment. He could either out-wit his antagonist by finesse, or beat him by main strength. Sometimes, when he seemed preparing to send the ball with the full swing of his arm, he would by a slight turn of his wrist drop it within an inch of the line. In general, the ball came from his hand, as if from a racket, in a straight horizontal line; so that it was in vain to attempt to overtake or stop it. As it was said of a great orator that he never was at a loss for a word, and for the properest word, so Cavanagh always could tell the degree of force necessary to be given to a ball, and the precise direction in which it should be sent. He did his work with the greatest ease; never took more pains than was necessary; and while others were fagging themselves to death, was as cool and collected as if he had just entered the court. His style of play was as remarkable as his power of execution. He had no affectation, no trifling. He did not throw away the game to show off an attitude, or try an experiment. He was a fine, sensible, manly player, who did what he could, but that was more than any one else could even affect to do. His blows were not undecided and ineffectual – lumbering like Mr Wordsworth's epic poetry, nor wavering like Mr Coleridge's lyric prose, nor short of the mark like Mr Brougham's speeches, nor wide of it like Mr Canning's wit, nor foul like the *Quarterly*, not *let* balls like the *Edinburgh Review*. Cobbett and Junius together would have made a Cavanagh. He was the best *up-hill* player in the world; even when his adversary was fourteen, he would play on the same or better, and as he never flung away the game through carelessness and conceit, he never gave it up through laziness or want of heart. The only peculiarity of his play was that he never *volleyed*, but let the balls hop; but if they rose an inch from the ground, he never missed having them. There was not only nobody equal, but nobody second to him. It is supposed that he could give any other player half the game, or beat him with his left hand. His service was tremendous. He once played Woodward and Meredith together (two of the best players in England) in the Fives-court, St Martin's-street, and made seven and twenty aces following by services alone – a thing unheard of. He another time played Peru, who was considered a first-rate fives-player, a match of the best out of five games, and in the first three games, which of course decided the match, Peru got only one ace. Cavanagh was an Irishman by birth, and a house-painter by profession. He had once laid aside his working-dress, and walked up, in his smartest clothes, to the Rosemary Branch[4] to have an afternoon's pleasure. A person accosted him, and asked him if he would have a game. So they agreed to play for half-a-crown a game, and a bottle of cider. The first game began – it was seven, eight, ten, thirteen, fourteen, all. Cavanagh won it. The next was the same. They played on, and each game was hardly contested. "There," said the unconscious fives-player, "there was a stroke that Cavanagh could not take: I never played better in my life, and yet I can't win a game. I don't know how it is." However, they played on, Cavanagh winning every game, and the by-standers drinking the cider, and laughing all the time. In the twelfth game, when Cavanagh was only four, and the stranger thirteen, a person came in, and said, "What! are you here, Cavanagh?" The words were no sooner pronounced than the astonished player let the ball drop from his hand, and saying, "What! have I been breaking my heart all this time to beat Cavanagh?" refused to make another effort. "And yet, I give you my word," said Cavanagh, telling the story with some triumph, "I played all the while with my clenched fist." – He used frequently to play matches at Copenhagen-house[4] for wagers and dinners. The wall against which they play is the same that supports the kit-chen-chimney, and when the wall resounded louder than usual, the cooks exclaimed, "Those are the Irishman's balls," and the joints trembled on the spit! – Goldsmith consoled himself that there were places where he too was admired: and Cavanagh was the admiration of all the fives-courts, where he ever played. Mr Powell,[5] when he played matches in the Court in St Martin's-street, used to fill his gallery at half a crown a head, with amateurs and admirers of talent in whatever department it is shown. He could not have shown himself in any ground in England, but he would have been immediately surrounded with inquisitive gazers, trying to find out in what part of his frame his un-rivalled skill lay, as politicians wonder to see the balance of Europe suspended in Lord Castlereagh's face, and admire the trophies of the British Navy lurking under Mr Croker's hanging brow. Now Cavanagh was as good-looking a man as the Noble Lord, and much better looking than the Right Hon. Secretary. He had a clear, open countenance, and did not look sideways or down, like Mr Murray the bookseller. He was a young fellow of sense, humour, and courage.

He once had a quarrel with a waterman at Hungerford-stairs, and, they say, served him out in great style. In a word, there are hundreds at this day, who cannot mention his name without admiration, as the best fives-player that perhaps ever lived (the greatest excellence of which they have any notion) – and the noisy shout of the ring happily stood him in stead of the unheard voice of posterity! – The only person who seems to have excelled as much in another way as Cavanagh did in his, was the late John Davies,[6] the racket-player. It was remarked of him that he did not seem to follow the ball, but the ball seemed to follow him. Give him a foot of wall, and he was sure to make the ball. The four best racket-players of that day were Jack Spines, Jem Harding, Armitage, and Church. Davies could give any one of these two hands a time, that is, half the game, and each of these, at their best, could give the best player now in London the same odds. Such are the gradations in all exertions of human skill and art. He once played four capital players together, and beat them. He was also a first-rate tennis-player, and excellent fives-player. In the Fleet or King's Bench, he would have stood against Powell, who was reckoned the best open-ground player of his time. This last-mentioned player is at present the keeper of the Fives-court, and we might recommend to him for a motto over his door – "Who enters here, forgets himself, his country, and his friends." And the best of it is, that by the calculation of the odds, none of the three are worth remembering! – Cavanagh died from the bursting of a blood-vessel, which prevented him from playing for the last two or three years. This, he was often heard to say, he thought hard upon him. He was fast recovering, however, when he was suddenly carried off, to the regret of all who knew him. As Mr Peel made it a qualification of the present Speaker, Mr Manners Sutton, that he was an excellent moral character, so Jack Cavanagh was a zealous Catholic, and could not be persuaded to eat meat on a Friday, the day on which he died. We have paid this willing tribute to his memory.

"Let no rude hand deface it,
And his forlorn '*Hic Jacet*' " '

From *Table-Talk* (1821).

ON GOING A JOURNEY

ONE of the pleasantest things in the world is going a journey; but I like to go by myself. I can enjoy society in a room; but out of doors, nature is company enough for me. I am then never less alone than when alone.

> 'The fields his study, nature was his book.'

I cannot see the wit of walking and talking at the same time. When I am in the country, I wish to vegetate like the country. I am not for criticising hedge-rows and black cattle. I go out of town in order to forget the town and all that is in it. There are those who for this purpose go to watering-places, and carry the metropolis with them. I like more elbow-room, and fewer incumbrances. I like solitude, when I give myself up to it, for the sake of solitude; nor do I ask for

> – 'a friend in my retreat,
> Whom I may whisper solitude is sweet.'

The soul of a journey is liberty, perfect liberty, to think, feel, do just as one pleases. We go a journey chiefly to be free of all impediments and of all inconveniences; to leave ourselves behind, much more to get rid of others. It is because I want a little breathing-space to muse on indifferent matters, where Contemplation

> 'May plume her feathers and let grow her wings,
> That in the various bustle of resort
> Were all too ruffled, and sometimes impair'd,'

that I absent myself from the town for awhile, without feeling at a loss the moment I am left by myself. Instead of a friend in a postchaise or in a tilbury, to exchange good things with, and vary the same stale topics over again, for once let me have a truce with impertinence. Give me the clear blue sky over my head, and the green turf beneath my feet, a winding road before me, and a three hours' march to dinner – and then to thinking! It is hard if I cannot start some game on these lone heaths. I laugh, I run, I leap, I sing for joy. From the point of yonder rolling cloud, I plunge into my past being, and revel there, as the sun-burnt Indian plunges headlong into the wave that wafts him to his native shore. Then long-forgotten things, like 'sunken wrack and sumless treasuries,' burst upon my eager sight, and I begin to feel, think, and be myself again. Instead of an awkward silence, broken by attempts at wit or dull com-mon-places, mine is that undisturbed silence of the heart which alone is perfect eloquence. No one likes puns, alli-terations, antitheses, argument, and analysis better than I do; but I sometimes had rather be without them. 'Leave, oh, leave me to my repose!' I have just now other business in hand, which would seem idle to you, but is with me 'the very stuff of the conscience.' Is not this wild rose sweet with-out a comment? Does not this daisy leap to my heart, set in its coat of emerald? Yet if I were to explain to you the cir-cumstance that has so endeared it to me, you would only smile: Had I not better then keep it to myself, and let it serve me to brood over, from here to yonder craggy point, and from thence onward to the far-distant horizon? I should be but bad company all that way, and therefore prefer being alone. I have heard it said that you may, when the moody fit comes on, walk or ride on by yourself, and indulge your reveries. But this looks like a breach of manners, a neglect of others, and you are thinking all the time that you ought to rejoin your party. 'Out upon such half-faced fellowship,' say I. I like to be either entirely to myself, or entirely at the disposal of others; to talk or be silent, to walk or sit still, to be sociable or solitary. I was pleased with an observation of Mr Cobbett's, that 'he thought it a bad French custom to drink our wine with our meals, and that an Englishman ought to do only one thing at a time.' So I cannot talk and think, or indulge in melancholy musing and lively conversation by fits and starts. 'Let me have a companion of my way,' says Sterne, 'were it but to remark how the shadows lengthen as the sun goes down.' It is beautifully said: but in my opinion, this continual comparing of notes interferes with the involuntary impression of things upon the mind, and hurts the sentiment. If you only hint what you feel in a kind of dumb show, it is insipid: if you have to explain it, it is making a toil of a pleasure. You cannot read the book of nature, without being perpetually put to the trouble of translating it for the benefit of others. I am for the synthetical method on a journey, in preference to the analytical. I am content to lay in a stock of ideas then, and to examine and anatomise them afterwards. I want to see my vague notions float like the down of the thistle before the breeze, and not to have them entangled in the briars and thorns of controversy. For once, I like to have it all my own way; and this is impossible unless you are alone, or in such company as I do not covet. I have no objection to argue a point with any one for twenty miles of measured road, but not for pleasure. If you remark the scent of a beanfield crossing the road, perhaps your fellow-traveller has no smell. If you point to a distant object, perhaps he is short-sighted, and has to take out his glass to look at it. There is a feeling in the air, a tone in the colour of a cloud which hits your fancy, but the effect of which you are unprepared to account for. There is then no sympathy, but an uneasy craving after it, and a dissatisfaction which pursues you on the way, and in the end probably produces ill humour. Now I never quarrel with myself, and take all my own conclusions for granted till I find it necessary to defend them against objections. It is not merely that you may not be of accord on the objects and circumstances that present themselves before you – they may recal a number of ideas, and lead to associations too delicate and refined to be possibly communicated to others. Yet these I love to cherish, and sometimes still fondly clutch them, when I can escape from the throng to do so. To give way to our feelings before company, seems extravagance or affectation; on the other hand, to have to unravel this mystery of our being at every turn, and to make others take an equal interest in it (otherwise the end is not answered) is a task to which few are competent. We must 'give it an understanding, but no tongue.' My old friend C—,[1] however, could do both. He could go on in the most delightful explanatory way over hill and dale, a summer's day, and convert a landscape into a didactic poem or a Pindaric ode. 'He talked far above singing.' If I could so clothe my ideas in sounding and flowing words, I might perhaps wish to have some one with me to admire the swelling theme; or I could be more content, were it possible for me still to hear his echoing voice in the woods of All-Foxden. They had 'that fine madness in them which our first poets had;' and if they could have been caught by some rare instrument, would have breathed such strains as the following.

> – 'Here be woods as green
> As any, air likewise as fresh and sweet
> As when smooth Zephyrus plays on the fleet
> Face of the curled stream, with flow'rs as many
> As the young spring gives, and as choice as any;
> Here be all new delights, cool streams and wells,
> Arbours o'ergrown with woodbine, caves and dells:
> Choose where thou wilt, while I sit by and sing,
> Or gather rushes to make many a ring
> For thy long fingers; tell thee tales of love,
> How the pale Phœbe, hunting in a grove,

First saw the boy Endymion, from whose eyes
She took eternal fire that never dies;
How she convey'd him softly in a sleep,
His temples bound with poppy, to the steep
Head of old Latmos, where she stoops each night,
Gilding the mountain with her brother's light,
To kiss her sweetest' —

FAITHFUL SHEPHERDESS.

Had I words and images at command like these, I would
attempt to wake the thoughts that lie slumbering on golden
ridges in the evening clouds: but at the sight of nature my
fancy, poor as it is, droops and closes up its leaves, like
flowers at sunset. I can make nothing out on the spot: — I
must have time to collect myself.

In general, a good thing spoils out-of-door prospects: it
should be reserved for Table-talk. L—[2] is for this reason, I
take it, the worst company in the world out of doors; because he is the best within. I grant, there is one subject on
which it is pleasant to talk on a journey; and that is, what
one shall have for supper when we get to our inn at night.
The open air improves this sort of conversation or friendly
altercation, by setting a keener edge on appetite. Every mile
of the road heightens the flavour of the viands we expect
at the end of it. How fine it is to enter some old town,
walled and turreted, just at the approach of night-fall, or
to come to some straggling village, with the lights streaming
through the surrounding gloom; and then after inquiring
for the best entertainment that the place affords, to 'take
one's ease at one's inn!' These eventful moments in our
lives are in fact too precious, too full of solid, heart-felt
happiness to be frittered and dribbled away in imperfect
sympathy. I would have them all to myself, and drain them
to the last drop: they will do to talk of or to write about
afterwards. What a delicate speculation it is, after drinking
whole goblets of tea,

'The cups that cheer, but not inebriate,'

and letting the fumes ascend into the brain, to sit considering what we shall have for supper – eggs and a rasher, a rab-
bit smothered in onions, or an excellent veal-cutlet! Sancho
in such a situation once fixed upon cow-heel; and his choice,
though he could not help it, is not to be disparaged. Then
in the intervals of pictured scenery and Shandean contemplation, to catch the preparation and the stir in the kitchen –
Procul, O procul este profani! These hours are sacred to
silence and to musing, to be treasured up in the memory,
and to feed the source of smiling thoughts hereafter. I would
not waste them in idle talk; or if I must have the integrity
of fancy broken in upon, I would rather it were by a stranger
than a friend. A stranger takes his hue and character from
the time and place; he is a part of the furniture and costume
of an inn. If he is a Quaker, or from the West Riding of
Yorkshire, so much the better. I do not even try to sympathise with him, and *he breaks no squares*. I associate nothing with my travelling companion but present objects and
passing events. In his ignorance of me and my affairs, I in a
manner forget myself. But a friend reminds one of other
things, rips up old grievances, and destroys the abstraction
of the scene. He comes in ungraciously between us and our
imaginary character. Something is dropped in the course of
conversation that gives a hint of your profession and pursuits; or from having some one with you that knows the
less sublime portions of your history, it seems that other
people do. You are no longer a citizen of the world: but
your 'unhoused free condition is put into circumscription
and confine.' The *incognito* of an inn is one of its striking
privileges – 'lord of one's-self, uncumber'd with a name.'
Oh! it is great to shake off the trammels of the world and
of public opinion – to lose our importunate, tormenting,
everlasting personal identity in the elements of nature, and

become the creature of the moment, clear of all ties – to hold
to the universe only by a dish of sweet-breads, and to owe
nothing but the score of the evening – and no longer seeking
for applause and meeting with contempt, to be known by no
other title than *the Gentleman in the parlour!* One may
take one's choice of all characters in this romantic state of
uncertainty as to one's real pretensions, and become inde-
finitely respectable and negatively right-worshipful. We
baffle prejudice and disappoint conjecture; and from being
so to others, begin to be objects of curiosity and wonder even
to ourselves. We are no more those hackneyed common-
places that we appear in the world: an inn restores us to the
level of nature, and quits scores with society! I have certainly spent some enviable hours at inns – sometimes when I
have been left entirely to myself, and have tried to solve
some metaphysical problem, as once at Witham-common,
where I found out the proof that likeness is not a case of the
association of ideas – at other times, when there have been
pictures in the room, as at St Neot's, (I think it was) where
I first met with Gribelin's engravings of the Cartoons,[3] into
which I entered at once; and at a little inn on the borders of
Wales, where there happened to be hanging some of
Westall's drawings, which I compared triumphantly (for a
theory that I had, not for the admired artist) with the figure
of a girl who had ferried me over the Severn, standing up in
the boat between me and the fading twilight – at other times
I might mention luxuriating in books, with a peculiar interest in this way, as I remember sitting up half the night to
read Paul and Virginia,[4] which I picked up at an inn at
Bridgewater, after being drenched in the rain all day; and
at the same place I got through two volumes of Madame
D'Arblay's Camilla.[5] It was on the tenth of April, 1798,
that I sat down to a volume of the New Eloise, at the inn at
Llangollen, over a bottle of sherry and a cold chicken. The
letter I chose was that in which St Preux describes his feel-

ings as he first caught a glimpse from the heights of the Jura of the Pays de Vaud, which I had brought with me as a *bonne bouche* to crown the evening with. It was my birthday, and I had for the first time come from a place in the neighbourhood to visit this delightful spot. The road to Llangollen turns off between Chirk and Wrexham; and on passing a certain point, you come all at once upon the valley, which opens like an amphitheatre, broad, barren hills rising in majestic state on either side, with 'green upland swells that echo to the bleat of flocks' below, and the river Dee babbling over its stony bed in the midst of them. The valley at this time 'glittered green with sunny showers,' and a budding ash-tree dipped its tender branches in the chiding stream. How proud, how glad I was to walk along the high road that commanded the delicious prospect, repeating the lines which I have just quoted from Mr Coleridge's poems! But besides the prospect which opened beneath my feet, another also opened to my inward sight, a heavenly vision, on which were written, in letters large as Hope could make them, these four words, LIBERTY, GENIUS, LOVE, VIRTUE; which have since faded into the light of common day, or mock my idle gaze.

'The beautiful is vanished, and returns not.'

Still I would return some time or other to this enchanted spot; but I would return to it alone. What other self could I find to share that influx of thoughts, of regret, and delight, the traces of which I could hardly conjure up to myself, so much have they been broken and defaced! I could stand on some tall rock, and overlook the precipice of years that separates me from what I then was. I was at that time going shortly to visit the poet whom I have above named. Where is he now? Not only I myself have changed; the world, which was then new to me, has become old and incorrigible. Yet will I turn to thee in thought, O sylvan Dee, as then thou wert, in joy, in youth and gladness; and thou shalt always be to me the river of Paradise, where I will drink of the waters of life freely!

There is hardly any thing that shows the short-sightedness or capriciousness of the imagination more than travelling does. With change of place we change our ideas; nay, our opinions and feelings. We can by an effort indeed transport ourselves to old and long-forgotten scenes, and then the picture of the mind revives again; but we forget those that we have just left. It seems that we can think but of one place at a time. The canvas of the fancy has only a certain extent, and if we paint one set of objects upon it, they immediately efface every other. We cannot enlarge our conceptions; we only shift our point of view. The landscape bares its bosom to the enraptured eye; we take our fill of it; and seem as if we could form no other image of beauty or grandeur. We pass on, and think no more of it: the horizon that shuts it from our sight also blots it from our memory like a dream. In travelling through a wild barren country, I can form no idea of a woody and cultivated one. It appears to me that all the world must be barren, like what I see of it. In the country we forget the town, and in town we despise the country. 'Beyond Hyde Park,' says Sir Fopling Flutter, 'all is a desert.' All that part of the map that we do not see before us is a blank. The world in our conceit of it is not much bigger than a nutshell. It is not one prospect expanded into another, county joined to county, kingdom to kingdom, lands to seas, making an image voluminous and vast; — the mind can form no larger idea of space than the eye can take in at a single glance. The rest is a name written on a map, a calculation of arithmetic. For instance, what is the true signification of that immense mass of territory and population, known by the name of China to us? An inch of paste-board on a wooden globe, of no more account than a China orange! Things near us are seen of the size of life: things at a distance are diminished to the size of the understanding. We measure the universe by ourselves, and even comprehend the texture of our own being only piece-meal. In this way, however, we remember an infinity of things and places. The mind is like a mechanical instrument that plays a great variety of tunes, but it must play them in succession. One idea recalls another, but it at the same time excludes all others. In trying to renew old recollections, we cannot as it were unfold the whole web of our existence; we must pick out the single threads. So in coming to a place where we have formerly lived and with which we have intimate associations, every one must have found that the feeling grows more vivid the nearer we approach the spot, from the mere anticipation of the actual impression: we remember circumstances, feelings, persons, faces, names, that we had not thought of for years; but for the time all the rest of the world is forgotten! – To return to the question I have quitted above.

I have no objection to go to see ruins, aqueducts, pictures, in company with a friend or a party, but rather the contrary, for the former reason reversed. They are intelligible matters, and will bear talking about. The sentiment here is not tacit, but communicable and overt. Salisbury Plain is barren of criticism, but Stonehenge will bear a discussion antiquarian, picturesque, and philosophical. In setting out on a party of pleasure, the first consideration always is where we shall go: in taking a solitary ramble, the question is what we shall meet with by the way. The mind then is 'its own place;' nor are we anxious to arrive at the end of our journey. I can myself do the honours indifferently well to works of art and curiosity. I once took a party to Oxford with no mean *éclat* – shewed them the seat of the Muses at a distance,

'With glistering spires and pinnacles adorn'd' –

descanted on the learned air that breathes from the grassy

quadrangles and stone walls of halls and colleges – was at home in the Bodleian; and at Blenheim quite superseded the powdered Cicerone that attended us, and that pointed in vain with his wand to common-place beauties in match-less pictures. – As another exception to the above reasoning, I should not feel confident in venturing on a journey in a foreign country without a companion. I should want at in-tervals to hear the sound of my own language. There is an involuntary antipathy in the mind of an Englishman to foreign manners and notions that requires the assistance of social sympathy to carry it off. As the distance from home in-creases, this relief, which was at first a luxury, becomes a passion and an appetite. A person would almost feel stifled to find himself in the deserts of Arabia without friends and countrymen: there must be allowed to be something in the view of Athens or old Rome that claims the utterance of speech; and I own that the Pyramids are too mighty for any single contemplation. In such situations, so opposite to all one's ordinary train of ideas, one seems a species by one's-self, a limb torn off from society, unless one can meet with instant fellowship and support. – Yet I did not feel this want or craving very pressing once, when I first set my foot on the laughing shores of France. Calais was peopled with novelty and delight. The confused, busy murmur of the place was like oil and wine poured into my ears; nor did the mariners' hymn, which was sung from the top of an old crazy vessel in the harbour, as the sun went down, send an alien sound into my soul. I breathed the air of general humanity. I walked over 'the vine-covered hills and gay regions of France,' erect and satisfied; for the image of man was not cast down and chained to the foot of arbitrary thrones. I was at no loss for language, for that of all the great schools of painting was open to me. The whole is vanished like a shade. Pictures, heroes, glory, freedom, all are fled: nothing remains but the Bourbons and the French people! – There is undoubtedly a sensation in travelling into foreign parts that is to be had nowhere else: but it is more pleasing at the time than lasting. It is too remote from our habitual associations to be a common topic of discourse or reference, and, like a dream or another state of existence, does not piece into our daily modes of life. It is an animated but a momentary hallucination. It demands an effort to exchange our actual for our ideal identity; and to feel the pulse of our old transports revive very keenly, we must 'jump' all our present comforts and connexions. Our romantic and itinerant character is not to be domesticated. Dr Johnson remarked how little foreign travel added to the facilities of conversation in those who had been abroad. In fact, the time we have spent there is both delightful and in one sense instructive; but it appears to be cut out of our substantial, downright existence, and never to join kindly on to it. We are not the same, but another, and perhaps more enviable individual, all the time we are out of our own country. We are lost to ourselves, as well as to our friends. So the poet somewhat quaintly sings,

> 'Out of my country and myself I go.'

Those who wish to forget painful thoughts, do well to absent themselves for a while from the ties and objects that recal them: but we can be said only to fulfil our destiny in the place that gave us birth. I should on this account like well enough to spend the whole of my life in travelling abroad, if I could any where borrow another life to spend afterwards at home!

From *Table-Talk* (1821).

WHY DISTANT OBJECTS PLEASE

DISTANT objects please, because, in the first place, they imply an idea of space and magnitude, and because, not being obtruded too close upon the eye, we clothe them with the indistinct and airy colours of fancy. In looking at the misty mountain-tops that bound the horison, the mind is as it were conscious of all the conceivable objects and interests that lie between; we imagine all sorts of adventures in the interim; strain our hopes and wishes to reach the air-drawn circle, or to 'descry new lands, rivers, and mountains,' stretching far beyond it: our feelings carried out of themselves lose their grossness and their husk, are rarefied, expanded, melt into softness and brighten into beauty, turning to 'ethereal mould, sky-tinctured.' We drink the air before us, and borrow a more refined existence from objects that hover on the brink of nothing. Where the landscape fades from the dull sight, we fill the thin, viewless space with shapes of unknown good, and tinge the hazy prospect with hopes and wishes and more charming fears.

> 'But thou, oh Hope, with eyes so fair,
> What was this delightful measure?
> Still it whisper'd promised pleasure,
> And bade the lovely scenes at distance hail!'

Whatever is placed beyond the reach of sense and knowledge, whatever is imperfectly discerned, the fancy pieces out at its leisure; and all but the present moment, but the present spot, passion claims for its own, and brooding over it with wings outspread, stamps it with an image of itself. Passion is lord of infinite space, and distant objects please because they border on its confines, and are moulded by its touch. When I was a boy, I lived within sight of a range of lofty hills, whose blue tops blending with the setting sun had often tempted my longing eyes and wandering feet. At last I put my project in execution, and on a nearer approach, instead of glimmering air woven into fantastic shapes, found them huge lumpish heaps of discoloured earth. I learnt from this (in part) to leave 'Yarrow unvisited,' and not idly to disturb a dream of good!

Distance of time has much the same effect as distance of place. It is not surprising that fancy colours the prospect of the future as it thinks good, when it even effaces the forms of memory. Time takes out the sting of pain; our sorrows after a certain period have been so often steeped in a medium of thought and passion, that they 'unmould their essence;' and all that remains of our original impressions is what we would wish them to have been. Not only the untried steep ascent before us, but the rude, unsightly masses of our past experience presently resume their power of deception over the eye: the golden cloud soon rests upon their heads, and the purple light of fancy clothes their barren sides! Thus we pass on, while both ends of our existence touch upon Heaven! – There is (so to speak) 'a mighty stream of tendency' to good in the human mind, upon which all objects float and are imperceptibly borne along: and though in the voyage of life we meet with strong rebuffs, with rocks and quicksands, yet there is 'a tide in the affairs of men,' a heaving and a restless aspiration of the soul, by means of which, 'with sails and tackle torn,' the wreck and scattered fragments of our entire being drift into the port and haven of our desires! In all that relates to the affections, we put the will for the deed: – the instant the pressure of unwelcome circumstances is removed, the mind recoils from their grasp, recovers its elasticity, and re-unites itself to that image of good, which is but a reflection and configuration of its own nature. Seen in the distance, in the long perspective of waning years, the meanest incidents, enlarged and enriched by countless recollections, become interesting; the most painful, broken and softened by time, soothe. How any object, that unexpectedly brings back to us old scenes and associations, startles the mind! What a yearning it creates within us; what a longing to leap the intermediate space! How fondly we cling to, and try to revive the impression of all that we then were!

'Such tricks hath strong Imagination!'

In truth, we impose upon ourselves, and know not what we wish. It is a cunning artifice, a quaint delusion, by which, in pretending to be what we were at a particular moment of time, we could fain be all that we have since been, and have our lives to come over again. It is not the little, glimmering, almost annihilated speck in the distance, that rivets our attention and 'hangs upon the beatings of our hearts:' it is the interval that separates us from it, and of which it is the trembling boundary, that excites all this coil and mighty pudder in the breast. Into that great gap in our being 'come thronging soft desires' and infinite regrets. It is the contrast, the change from what we then were, that arms the half-extinguished recollection with its giant-strength, and lifts the fabric of the affections from its shadowy base. In contemplating its utmost verge, we overlook the map of our existence, and re-tread, in apprehension, the journey of life. So it is that in early youth we strain our eager sight after the pursuits of manhood; and, as we are sliding off the stage, strive to gather up the toys and flowers that pleased our thoughtless childhood.

When I was quite a boy, my father used to take me to the Montpelier Tea-gardens at Walworth. Do I go there now? No; the place is deserted, and its borders and its beds o'erturned. Is there, then, nothing that can

'Bring back the hour
Of glory in the grass, of splendour in the flower?'

Oh! yes. I unlock the casket of memory, and draw back the warders of the brain; and there this scene of my faint wanderings still lives unfaded, or with fresher dyes. A new sense comes upon me, as in a dream; a richer perfume, brighter colours start out; my eyes dazzle; my heart heaves with its new load of bliss, and I am a child again. My sensations are all glossy, spruce, voluptuous, and fine: they wear a candied coat, and are in holiday trim. I see the beds of larkspur with purple eyes; tall holy-oaks, red and yellow; the broad sunflowers, caked in gold, with bees buzzing round them; wildernesses of pinks, and hot-glowing pionies; poppies run to seed; the sugared lily, and faint mignionette, all ranged in order, and as thick as they can grow; the box-tree borders; the gravel-walks, the painted alcove, the confectionary, the clotted cream: – I think I see them now with sparkling looks; or have they vanished while I have been writing this description of them? No matter; they will return again when I least think of them. All that I have observed since, of flowers and plants, and grass-plots, and of suburb delights, seems, to me, borrowed from 'that first garden of my innocence' – to be slips and scions stolen from that bed of memory. In this manner the darlings of our childhood burnish out in the eye of after-years, and derive their sweetest perfume from the first heartfelt sigh of pleasure breathed upon them,

– 'like the sweet south,
That breathes upon a bank of violets,
Stealing and giving odour!'

If I have pleasure in a flower-garden, I have in a kitchen-garden too, and for the same reason. If I see a row of cabbage-plants or of peas or beans coming up, I immediately think of those which I used so carefully to water of an evening at W—m, when my day's tasks were done, and of the pain with which I saw them droop and hang down their leaves in the morning's sun. Again, I never see a child's kite in the air, but it seems to pull at my heart. It is to me a 'thing of life.' I feel the twinge at my elbow, the flutter and palpitation, with which I used to let go the string of my own, as it rose in the air and towered among the clouds. My little cargo of hopes and fears ascended with it; and as it made a part of my own consciousness then, it does so still, and appears 'like some gay creature of the element,' my playmate when life was young, and twin-born with my earliest recollections. I could enlarge on this subject of childish amusements, but Mr Leigh Hunt has treated it so well,[1] in a paper in the *Indicator*, on the productions of the toy-shops of the metropolis, that if I were to insist more on it, I should only pass for an imitator of that ingenious and agreeable writer, and for an indifferent one into the bargain.

Sounds, smells, and sometimes tastes, are remembered longer than visible objects, and serve, perhaps, better for links in the chain of association. The reason seems to be this: they are in their nature intermittent, and comparatively rare; whereas objects of sight are always before us, and, by their continuous succession, drive one another out. The eye is always open; and between any given impression and its recurrence a second time, fifty thousand other impressions have, in all likelihood, been stamped upon the sense and on the brain. The other senses are not so active or vigilant. They are but seldom called into play. The ear, for example, is oftener courted by silence than noise; and the sounds that break that silence sink deeper and more durably into the mind. I have, for this reason, a more present and lively recollection of certain scents, tastes, and sounds than I have of mere visible images, because they are more original, and less worn by frequent repetition. Where there is nothing interposed between any two impressions, whatever the distance of time that parts them, they naturally seem to touch; and the renewed impression recalls the former one in full force, without distraction or competition. The taste of barberries, which have hung out in the snow² during the severity of a North American winter, I have in my mouth still, after an interval of thirty years; for I have met with no other taste, in all that time, at all like it. It remains by itself, almost like the impression of a sixth sense. But the colour is mixed up indiscriminately with the colours of many other berries, nor should I be able to distinguish it among them. The smell of a brick-kiln carries the evidence of its own identity with it: neither is it to me (from peculiar associations) unpleasant. The colour of brick-dust, on the contrary, is more common, and easily confounded with other colours. Raphael did not keep it quite distinct from his flesh-colour. I will not say that we have a more perfect recollection of the human voice than of that complex picture, the human face; but I think the sudden hearing of a well-known voice has something in it more affecting and striking than the sudden meeting with the face: perhaps, indeed, this may be because we have a more familiar remembrance of the one than the other, and the voice takes us more by surprise on that account. I am by no means certain (generally speaking) that we have the ideas of the other senses so accurate and well-made out as those of visible form: what I chiefly mean is, that the feelings belonging to the sensations of our other organs, when accidentally recalled, are kept more separate and pure. Musical sounds, probably, owe a good deal of their interest and romantic effect to the principle here spoken of. Were they constant, they would become indifferent, as we may find with respect to disagreeable noises, which we do not hear after a time. I know no situation more pitiable than that of a blind fiddler, who has but one sense left (if we except the sense of snuff-taking *) and who has that stunned or deafened by his own villainous noises. Shakespear says,

'How silver-sweet sound lovers' tongues by night!'

It has been suggested, in explanation of this passage, that it is because in the day-time lovers are occupied with one another's faces, but that at night they can only distinguish the sound of each other's voices. I know not how this may be: but I have, ere now, heard a voice break so upon the silence,

'To angels 'twas most like,'

and charm the moonlight air with its balmy essence, while the budding leaves trembled to its accents. Would I might have heard it once more whisper peace and hope (as erst when it was mingled with the breath of spring), and with its soft pulsations lift winged fancy to heaven! But it has ceased, or turned where I no more shall hear it! – Hence, also, we see what is the charm of the shepherd's pastoral reed; and why we hear him, as it were, piping to his flock, even in a picture. Our ears are fancy-stung! I remember once strolling along the margin of a stream, skirted with willows and plashy sedges, in one of those low sheltered valleys on Salisbury Plain, where the monks of former ages had planted chapels and built hermits' cells. There was a little parish-church near; but tall elms and quivering alders hid it from my sight, when, all of a sudden, I was startled by the sound of the full organ pealing on the ear, accompanied by rustic voices, and the willing quire of village-maids, and children. It rose, indeed, 'like an exhalation of rich distilled perfumes.' The dew from a thousand pastures was gathered in its softness; the silence of a thousand years spoke in it. It came upon the heart like the calm beauty of death: fancy caught the sound, and faith mounted on it to the skies. It

* See Wilkie's Blind Fiddler.[3]

filled the valley like a mist, and still poured out its endless chaunt, and still it swells upon the ear, and wraps me in a golden trance, drowning the noisy tumult of the world!

There is a curious and interesting discussion, on the comparative distinctness of our visual and other external impressions, in Mr Fearn's Essay on Consciousness, with which I shall try to descend from this rhapsody to the ground of common sense and plain reasoning again. After observing, a little before, that 'nothing is more untrue than that sensations of vision do necessarily leave more vivid and durable ideas than those of grosser senses,' he proceeds to give a number of illustrations in support of this position. 'Notwithstanding,' he says, 'the advantages here enumerated in favour of sight, I think there is no doubt that a man will come to forget acquaintance, and many other visible objects, noticed in mature age, before he will in the least forget tastes and smells, of only moderate interest, encountered either in his childhood, or at any time since.

'In the course of voyaging to various distant regions, it has several times happened that I have eaten once or twice of different things that never came in my way before nor since. Some of these have been pleasant, and some scarce better than insipid; but I have no reason to think I have forgot, or much altered the ideas left by those single impulses of taste; though here the memory of them certainly has not been preserved by repetition. It is clear I must have seen, as well as tasted those things; and I am decided that I remember the tastes with more precision than I do the visual sensations.

'I remember having once, and only once, eat Kangaroo in New Holland; and having once smelled a baker's shop, having a peculiar odour, in the city of Bassorah. Now both these gross ideas remain with me as vivid as any visual ideas of those places; and this could not be from repetition, but really from interest in the sensation.

'Twenty-eight years ago, in the island of Jamaica, I

partook (perhaps twice) of a certain fruit, of the taste of which I have now a very fresh idea; and I could add other instances of that period.

'I have had repeated proofs of having lost retention of visual objects, at various distances of time, though they had once been familiar. I have not, during thirty years, forgot the delicate, and in itself most trifling sensation, that the palm of my hand used to convey, when I was a boy, trying the different effects of what boys call *light* and *heavy* tops; but I cannot remember within several shades of the brown coat which I left off a week ago. If any man thinks he can do better, let him take an ideal survey of his wardrobe, and then actually refer to it for proof.

'After retention of such ideas, it certainly would be very difficult to persuade me that feeling, taste, and smell can scarce be said to leave ideas, unless indistinct and obscure ones . . .

'Shew a Londoner correct models of twenty London churches, and, at the same time, a model of each, which differs, in several considerable features, from the truth, and I venture to say he shall not tell you, in any instance, which is the correct one, except by mere chance.

'If he is an architect, he may be much more correct than any ordinary person : and this obviously is, because he has felt an interest in viewing these structures, which an ordinary person does not feel : and here interest is the sole reason of his remembering more correctly than his neighbour.

'I once heard a person quaintly ask another, How many trees there are in St Paul's churchyard? The question itself indicates that many cannot answer it; and this is found to be the case with those who have passed the church an hundred times : whilst the cause is, that every individual in the busy stream which glides past St Paul's is engrossed in various other interests.

'How often does it happen that we enter a well-known

apartment, or meet a well-known friend, and receive some vague idea of visible difference, but cannot possibly find out *what* it is; until at length we come to perceive (or perhaps must be told) that some ornament or furniture is removed, altered, or added in the apartment; or that our friend has cut his hair, taken a wig, or has made any of twenty considerable alterations in his appearance. At other times, we have no perception of alteration whatever, though the like has taken place.

'It is, however, certain, that sight, apposited with interest, can retain tolerably exact copies of sensations, especially if not too complex; such as of the human countenance and figure. Yet the voice will convince us, when the countenance will not; and he is reckoned an excellent painter, and no ordinary genius, who can make a tolerable likeness from memory. Nay, more, it is a conspicuous proof of the inaccuracy of visual ideas, that it is an effort of consummate art, attained by many years' practice, to take a strict likeness of the human countenance, even when the object is present; and among those cases, where the wilful cheat of flattery has been avoided, we still find in how very few instances the best painters produce a likeness up to the life, though practice and interest join in the attempt.

'I imagine an ordinary person would find it very difficult, supposing he had some knowledge of drawing, to afford, from memory, a tolerable sketch of such a familiar object as his curtain, his carpet, or his dressing-gown, if the pattern of either be at all various or irregular; yet he will instantly tell, with precision, either if his snuff or his wine has not the same character it had yesterday, though both these are compounds.

'Beyond all this I may observe, that a draper, who is in the daily habit of such comparisons, cannot carry in his mind the particular shade of a colour during a second of time; and has no certainty of tolerably matching two simple colours, except by placing the patterns in contact.' – *Essay on Consciousness*, p. 303.

I will conclude the subject of this Essay with observing, that a nearer and more familiar acquaintance with persons has a different and more favourable effect than that with places or things. The latter improve by being removed to a distance, for we have no interest in *backbiting* them: the former gain by being brought nearer and more home to us, and thus stripped of artful and ill-natured misrepresentations. Report or imagination very seldom raises any individual so high in our estimation as to disappoint us greatly when we are introduced to him: prejudice and malice constantly exaggerate defects beyond the reality. Ignorance alone makes monsters or bugbears: our actual acquaintances are all very common-place people. The thing is, that as a matter of hearsay or conjecture, we make abstractions of particular vices, and irritate ourselves against some particular quality or action of the person we dislike: – whereas, individuals are concrete existences, not arbitrary denominations or nicknames; and have innumerable other qualities, good, bad, and indifferent, besides the damning feature with which we fill up the portrait or caricature, in our previous fancies. We can scarcely hate any one that we know. An acute observer complained,[4] that if there was any one to whom he had a particular spite, and a wish to let him see it, the moment he came to sit down with him, his enmity was disarmed by some unforeseen circumstance. If it was a Quarterly Reviewer, he was in other respects like any other man. Suppose, again, your adversary turns out a very ugly man, or wants an eye, you are balked in that way: – he is not what you expected, the object of your abstract hatred and implacable disgust. He may be a very disagreeable person, but he is no longer the same. If you come into a room where a man is, you find, in general, that he has a nose upon his face. 'There's sympathy!' This alone is a diversion to your unqualified contempt. He is stupid, and says nothing, but he seems to have something in him when he laughs. You had conceived of him as a rank Whig or Tory – yet he talks upon other subjects. You knew that he was a virulent party-writer; but you find that the man himself is a tame sort of animal enough. He does not bite. That's something. In short, you can make nothing of it. Even opposite vices balance one another. A man may be pert in company, but he is also dull; so that you cannot, though you try, hate him cordially, merely for the wish to be offensive. He is a knave. Granted. You learn, on a nearer acquaintance, what you did not know before – that he is a fool as well; so you forgive him. On the other hand, he may be a profligate public character, and may make no secret of it; but he gives you a hearty shake by the hand, speaks kindly to servants, and supports an aged father and mother. Politics apart, he is a very honest fellow. You are told that a person [5] has carbuncles on his face; but you have ocular proofs that he is sallow, and pale as a ghost. This does not much mend the matter; but it blunts the edge of the ridicule, and turns your indignation against the inventor of the lie; but he is —, the editor of a Scotch magazine; so you are just where you were. I am not very fond of anonymous criticism; I want to know who the author can be: but the moment I learn this, I am satisfied. Even — would do well to come out of his disguise. It is the mask only that we dread and hate: the man may have something human about him! The notions, in short, which we entertain of people at a distance, or from partial representations, or from guess-work, are simple, uncompounded ideas, which answer to nothing in reality: those which we derive from experience are mixed modes, the only true, and, in general, the most favourable ones. Instead of naked deformity, or abstract perfection –

'Those faultless monsters which the world ne'er saw,' –

'the web of our lives is of a mingled yarn, good and ill together: our virtues would be proud, if our faults whipt them not; and our vices would despair, if they were not encouraged by our virtues.' This was truly and finely said long ago, by one who knew the strong and weak points of human nature: but it is what sects, and parties, and those philosophers whose pride and boast it is to classify by nicknames, have yet to learn the meaning of!

From *Table-Talk* (1821).

ON DIFFERENT SORTS OF FAME

THERE is a half serious, half ironical argument in Melmoth's *Fitz-Osborn's Letters*, to shew the futility of posthumous fame, which runs thus: 'The object of any one who is inspired with this passion is to be remembered by posterity with admiration and delight, as having been possessed of certain powers and excellences which distinguish him above his contemporaries. But posterity, it is said, can know nothing of the individual but from the memory of these qualities which he has left behind him. All that we know of Julius Cæsar, for instance, is that he was the person who performed certain actions, and wrote a book called his *Commentaries*. When, therefore, we extol Julius Cæsar for his actions or his writings, what do we say but that the person who performed certain things did perform them; that the author of such a work was the person who wrote it; or, in short, that Julius Cæsar was Julius Cæsar? Now this is a mere truism, and the desire to be the subject of such an identical proposition must, therefore, be an evident absurdity.' The sophism is a tolerably ingenious one, but it is a sophism, nevertheless. It would go equally to prove the nullity, not only of posthumous fame, but of living reputation; for the good or the bad opinion which my next-door neighbour may entertain of me is nothing more than his conviction that such and such a person having certain good or bad qualities is possessed of them; nor is the figure, which a Lord-Mayor elect, a prating demagogue, or popular preacher, makes in the eyes of the admiring multitude — *himself*, but an image of him reflected in the minds of others, in connection with certain feelings of respect and wonder. In fact, whether the admiration we seek is to last for a day or for eternity, whether we are to have it while living or after we are dead, whether it is to be expressed by our contemporaries or by future generations, the principle of it is the same – *sympathy with the feelings of others* – and the necessary tendency which the idea or consciousness of the approbation of others has to strengthen the suggestions of our self-love.* We are all inclined to think well of ourselves, of our sense and capacity in whatever we undertake; but from this very desire to think well of ourselves, we are (as *Mrs Peachum* says) '*bitter* bad judges' of own pretensions; and when our vanity flatters us most, we ought in general to suspect it most. We are, therefore, glad to get the good opinion of a friend, but that may be partial; the good word of a stranger is likely to be more sincere, but he may be a blockhead; the multitude will agree with us, if we agree with them; accident, the caprice of fashion, the prejudice of the moment, may give a fleeting reputation; our only certain appeal, therefore, is to posterity; the voice of fame is alone the voice of truth. In proportion, however, as this award is final and secure, it is remote and uncertain. Voltaire said to some one, who had addressed an Epistle to Posterity, 'I am afraid, my friend, this letter will never be delivered according to its direction.' It can exist only in imagination; and we can only presume upon our claim to it, as we prefer the hope of lasting fame to every thing else. The love of fame is almost another name for the love of excellence; or it is the ambition to attain the highest excellence, sanctioned by the highest authority, that of time. Vanity, and the love of fame, are quite distinct from each other; for the one is voracious of the most obvious and doubtful applause, whereas the other rejects or overlooks every kind of applause but that which is purified from every mixture of flattery, and identified with

*Burns, when about to sail for America after the first publication of his poems, consoled himself with 'the delicious thought of being regarded as a clever fellow, though on the other side of the Atlantic.'

truth and nature itself. There is, therefore, something disinterested in this passion, inasmuch as it is abstracted and ideal, and only appeals to opinion as a standard of truth; it is this which 'makes ambition virtue.' Milton had as fine an idea as any one of true fame; and Dr Johnson has very beautifully described his patient and confident anticipations of the success of his great poem in the account of *Paradise Lost*. He has, indeed, done the same thing himself in *Lycidas*:

> 'Fame is the spur that the clear spirit doth raise
> (That last infirmity of noble mind)
> To scorn delights, and live laborious days;
> But the fair Guerdon when we hope to find,
> And think to burst out into sudden blaze,
> Comes the blind Fury with th' abhorred shears,
> And slits the thin-spun life. But not the praise,
> Phœbus replied, and touch'd my trembling ears.'

None but those who have sterling pretensions can afford to refer them to time; as persons who live upon their means cannot well go into Chancery. No feeling can be more at variance with the true love of fame than that impatience which we have sometimes witnessed to 'pluck its fruits, unripe and crude,' before the time, to make a little echo of popularity mimic the voice of fame, and to convert a prize-medal or a newspaper-puff into a passport to immortality.

When we hear any one complaining that he has not the same fame as some poet or painter who lived two hundred years ago, he seems to us to complain that he has not been dead these two hundred years. When his fame has undergone the same ordeal, that is, has lasted as long, it will be as good, if he really deserves it. We think it equally absurd, when we sometimes find people objecting, that such an acquaintance of theirs, who has not an idea in his head, should be so much better off in the world than they are. But it is for this very reason; they have preferred the indulgence of their ideas to the pursuit of realities. It is but fair that he who has no ideas should have something in their stead. If he who has devoted his time to the study of beauty, to the pursuit of truth, whose object has been to govern opinion, to form the taste of others, to instruct or to amuse the public, succeeds in this respect, he has no more right to complain that he has not a title or a fortune, than he who has not purchased a ticket, that is, who has taken no means to the end, has a right to complain that he has not a prize in the lottery.

In proportion as men can command the immediate and vulgar applause of others, they become indifferent to that which is remote and difficult of attainment. We take pains only when we are compelled to do it. Little men are remarked to have courage; little women to have wit; and it is seldom that a man of genius is a coxcomb in his dress. Rich men are contented not to be thought wise; and the Great often think themselves well off, if they can escape being the jest of their acquaintance. Authors were actuated by the desire of the applause of posterity, only so long as they were debarred of that of their contemporaries, just as we see the map of the gold-mines of Peru hanging in the room of Hogarth's *Distressed Poet.* In the midst of the ignorance and prejudices with which they were surrounded, they had a sort of *forlorn hope* in the prospect of immortality. The spirit of universal criticism has superseded the anticipation of posthumous fame, and instead of waiting for the award of distant ages, the poet or prose-writer receives his final doom from the next number of the *Edinburgh* or *Quarterly Review.* According as the nearness of the applause increases, our impatience increases with it. A writer in a weekly journal engages with reluctance in a monthly publication: and again, a contributor to a daily paper sets about his task with greater spirit than either of them. It is like prompt payment. The effort and the applause go together. We, indeed, have known a man of genius and eloquence, to whom, from a habit of excessive talking, the certainty of seeing what he wrote in print the next day was too remote a stimulus for his imagination, and who constantly laid aside his pen in the middle of an article, if a friend dropped in, to finish the subject more effectually aloud, so that the approbation of his hearer, and the sound of his own voice might be co-instantaneous. Members of Parliament seldom turn authors, except to print their speeches when they have not been distinctly heard or understood; and great orators are generally very indifferent writers, from want of sufficient inducement to exert themselves, when the immediate effect on others is not perceived, and the irritation of applause or opposition ceases.

There have been in the last century two singular examples of literary reputation, the one of an author without a name, and the other of a name without an author. We mean the author of *Junius's Letters*,[1] and the translator of the mottos to the *Rambler*, whose name was Elphinstone. The *Rambler* was published in the year 1750, and the name of Elphinstone prefixed to each paper is familiar to every literary reader, since that time, though we know nothing more of him. We saw this gentleman, since the commencement of the present century, looking over a clipped hedge in the country, with a broad-flapped hat, a venerable countenance, and his dress cut out with the same formality as his evergreens. His name had not only survived half a century in conjunction with that of Johnson, but he had survived with it, enjoying all the dignity of a classical reputation, and the ease of a literary sinecure, on the strength of his mottos. The author of *Junius's Letters* is, on the contrary, as remarkable an instance of a writer who has arrived at all the public honours of literature, without being known by name to a single individual, and who may be said to have realised all the pleasure of posthumous fame, while living, without the smallest gratification of personal vanity. An anonymous

writer may feel an acute interest in what is said of his productions, and a secret satisfaction in their success, because it
is not the effect of personal considerations, as the overhearing
any one speak well of us is more agreeable than a direct
compliment. But this very satisfaction will tempt him to
communicate his secret. This temptation, however, does not
extend beyond the circle of his acquaintance. With respect
to the public, who know an author only by his writings, it is
of little consequence whether he has a real or a fictitious
name, or a signature, so that they have some clue by which
to associate the works with the author. In the case of *Junius*,
therefore, where other personal considerations of interest or
connections might immediately counteract and set aside this
temptation, the triumph over the mere vanity of authorship
might not have cost him so dear as we are at first inclined
to imagine. Suppose it to have been the old Marquis of —?
It is quite out of the question that he should keep his places
and not keep his secret. If ever the King should die, we
think it not impossible that the secret may out. Certainly the
accouchement of any princess in Europe would not excite an
equal interest. 'And you, then, Sir, are the author of
Junius!' What a recognition for the public and the author!
That between Yorick and the Frenchman was a trifle to it.

We have said that we think the desire to be known by
name as an author chiefly has a reference to those to whom
we are known personally, and is strongest with regard to
those who know most of our persons and least of our capacities. We wish to *subpœna* the public to our characters.
Those who, by great services or great meannesses, have attained titles, always take them from the place with which
they have the earliest associations, and thus strive to throw a
veil of importance over the insignificance of their original
pretensions, or the injustice of fortune. When Lord Nelson
was passing over the quay at Yarmouth, to take possession
of the ship to which he had been appointed, the people ex-

claimed, 'Why make that little fellow a captain?' He thought of this when he fought the battles of the Nile and Trafalgar. The same sense of personal insignificance which made him great in action made him a fool in love. If Bonaparte had been six inches higher, he never would have gone on that disastrous Russian expedition, nor 'with that addition' would he ever have been Emperor and King. For our own parts, one object which we have in writing these Essays, is to send them in a volume to a person who took some notice of us when children, and who augured, perhaps, better of us than we deserved. In fact, the opinion of those who know us most, who are a kind of second self in our recollections, is a sort of second conscience; and the approbation of one or two friends is all the immortality *we* pretend to.

From *The Round Table* (1817).

ON A SUN-DIAL

'To carve out dials quaintly, point by point.'
SHAKESPEAR.

Horas non numero nisi serenas – is the motto of a sun-dial near Venice. There is a softness and a harmony in the words and in the thought unparalleled. Of all conceits it is surely the most classical. 'I count only the hours that are serene.' What a bland and care-dispelling feeling! How the shadows seem to fade on the dial-plate as the sky lours, and time presents only a blank unless as its progress is marked by what is joyous, and all that is not happy sinks into oblivion! What a fine lesson is conveyed to the mind – to take no note of time but by its benefits to watch only for the smiles and neglect the frowns of fate, to compose our lives of bright and gentle moments, turning always to the sunny side of things, and letting the rest slip from our imaginations, unheeded or forgotten! How different from the common art of self-tormenting! For myself, as I rode along the Brenta, while the sun shone hot upon its sluggish, slimy waves, my sensations were far from comfortable; but the reading this inscription on the side of a glaring wall in an instant restored me to myself; and still, whenever I think of or repeat it, it has the power of wafting me into the region of pure and blissful abstraction. I cannot help fancying it to be a legend of Popish superstition. Some monk of the dark ages must have invented and bequeathed it to us, who, loitering in trim gardens and watching the silent march of time, as his fruits ripened in the sun or his flowers scented the balmy air, felt a mild languor pervade his senses, and having little to do or to care for determined (in imitation of his sun-dial) to efface that little from his thoughts or draw a veil over it, making of his life one long dream of quiet! *Horas non numero nisi serenas* – he might repeat, when the heavens were overcast and the gathering storm scattered the falling leaves, and turn to his books and wrap himself in his golden studies! Out of some such mood of mind, indolent, elegant, thoughtful, this exquisite device (speaking volumes) must have originated.

Of the several modes of counting time, that by the sun-dial is perhaps the most apposite and striking, if not the most convenient or comprehensive. It does not obtrude its observations, though it 'morals on the time,' and, by its stationary character, forms a contrast to the most fleeting of all essences. It stands *sub dio* – under the marble air, and there is some connexion between the image of infinity and eternity. I should also like to have a sunflower growing near it with bees fluttering round.* It should be of iron to denote duration, and have a dull-leaden look. I hate a sun-dial made of wood, which is rather calculated to show the variations of the seasons, than the progress of time, slow, silent, imperceptible, chequered with light and shade. If our hours were all serene, we might probably take almost as little note of them, as the dial does of those that are clouded. It is the shadow thrown across, that gives us warning of their flight. Otherwise, our impressions would take the same undistinguishable hue; we should scarce be conscious of our existence. Those who have had none of the cares of this life to harass and disturb them, have been obliged to have recourse to the hopes and fears of the next to enliven the prospect before them. Most of the methods for measuring the lapse of time have, I believe, been the contrivance of monks and religious recluses, who, finding time hang heavy on their

---

* Is this a verbal fallacy? Or in the close, retired, sheltered scene which I have imagined to myself, is not the sun-flower a natural accompaniment of the sun-dial?

hands, were at some pains to see how they got rid of it. The hour-glass is, I suspect, an older invention; and it is certainly the most defective of all. Its creeping sands are not indeed an unapt emblem of the minute, countless portions of our existence; and the manner in which they gradually slide through the hollow glass and diminish in number till not a single one is left, also illustrates the way in which our years slip from us by stealth: but as a mechanical invention, it is rather a hindrance than a help, for it requires to have the time, of which it pretends to count the precious moments, taken up in attention to itself, and in seeing that when one end of the glass is empty, we turn it round, in order that it may go on again, or else all our labour is lost, and we must wait for some other mode of ascertaining the time before we can recover our reckoning and proceed as before. The philosopher in his cell, the cottager at her spinning-wheel must, however, find an invaluable acquisition in this 'companion of the lonely hour,' as it has been called,* which not only serves to tell how the time goes, but to fill up its vacancies. What a treasure must not the little box seem to hold, as if it were a sacred deposit of the very grains and fleeting sands of life! What a business, in lieu of other more important avocations, to see it out to the last sand, and then to renew the process again on the instant, that there may not be the least flaw or error in the account! What a strong sense must be brought home to the mind of the value and irrecoverable nature of the time that is fled; what a thrilling, incessant consciousness of the slippery tenure by which we hold what remains of it! Our very existence must seem crumbling to atoms, and running down (without a miraculous reprieve) to the last fragment. 'Dust to dust and ashes to ashes' is a text that might be fairly in-

---

* 'Once more, companion of the lonely hour,
     I'll turn thee up again.'
          Bloomfield's Poems – The Widow to her Hour-glass.

scribed on an hour-glass: it is ordinarily associated with the scythe of Time and a Death's head, as a *Memento mori*; and has no doubt, furnished many a tacit hint to the apprehensive and visionary enthusiast in favour of a resurrection to another life!

The French give a different turn to things, less *sombre* and less edifying. A common and also a very pleasing ornament to a clock, in Paris, is a figure of Time seated in a boat which Cupid is rowing along, with the motto, *L'Amour fait passer le Tems* – which the wits again have travestied into *Le Tems fait passer L'Amour*. All this is ingenious and well; but it wants sentiment. I like a people who have something that they love and something that they hate, and with whom every thing is not alike a matter of indifference or *pour passer le tems*. The French attach no importance to any thing, except for the moment; they are only thinking how they shall get rid of one sensation for another; all their ideas are *in transitu*. Every thing is detached, nothing is accumulated. It would be a million years before a Frenchman would think of the *Horas non numero nisi serenas*. Its impassioned repose and *ideal* voluptuousness are as far from their breasts as the poetry of that line in Shakespear – 'How sweet the moonlight sleeps upon that bank!' They never arrive at the classical – or the romantic. They blow the bubbles of vanity, fashion, and pleasure; but they do not expand their perceptions into refinement, or strengthen them into solidity. Where there is nothing fine in the ground-work of the imagination, nothing fine in the superstructure can be produced. They are light, airy, fanciful (to give them their due) – but when they attempt to be serious (beyond mere good sense) they are either dull or extravagant. When the volatile salt has flown off, nothing but a *caput mortuum* remains. They have infinite crotchets and caprices with their clocks and watches, which seem made for any thing but to tell the hour – gold-repeaters, watches with metal covers, clocks with hands to count the seconds. There is no escaping from quackery and impertinence, even in our attempts to calculate the waste of time. The years gallop fast enough for me, without remarking every moment as it flies; and farther, I must say I dislike a watch (whether of French or English manufacture) that comes to me like a footpad with its face muffled, and does not present its clear, open aspect like a friend, and point with its finger to the time of day. All this opening and shutting of dull, heavy cases (under pretence that the glass-lid is liable to be broken, or lets in the dust or air and obstructs the movement of the watch) is not to husband time, but to give trouble. It is mere pomposity and self-importance, like consulting a mysterious oracle that one carries about with one in one's pocket, instead of asking a common question of an acquaintance or companion. There are two clocks which strike the hour in the room where I am. This I do not like. In the first place, I do not want to be reminded twice how the time goes (it is like the second tap of a saucy servant at your door when perhaps you have no wish to get up): in the next place, it is starting a difference of opinion on the subject, and I am averse to every appearance of wrangling and disputation. Time moves on the same, whatever disparity there may be in our mode of keeping count of it, like true fame in spite of the cavils and contradictions of the critics. I am no friend to repeating watches. The only pleasant association I have with them is the account given by Rousseau[1] of some French lady, who sat up reading the *New Heloise* when it first came out, and ordering her maid to sound the repeater, found it was too late to go to bed, and continued reading on till morning. Yet how different is the interest excited by this story from the account which Rousseau somewhere else gives of his sitting up with his father reading romances, when a boy, till they were startled by the swallows twittering in their nests at day-break, and the father cried out, half angry and ashamed – '*Allons, mon fils; je suis plus enfant que toi!*' In general, I have heard repeating watches sounded in stage-coaches at night, when some fellow-traveller suddenly awaking and wondering what was the hour, another has very deliberately taken out his watch, and pressing the spring, it has counted out the time; each petty stroke acting like a sharp puncture on the ear, and informing me of the dreary hours I had already passed, and of the more dreary ones I had to wait till morning.

The great advantage, it is true, which clocks have over watches and other dumb reckoners of time is, that for the most part they strike the hour – that they are as it were the mouth-pieces of time; that they not only point it to the eye, but impress it on the ear; that they 'lend' it both an understanding and a tongue.' Time thus speaks to us in an audible and warning voice. Objects of sight are easily distinguished by the sense, and suggest useful reflections to the mind; sounds, from their intermittent nature, and perhaps other causes, appeal more to the imagination, and strike upon the heart. But to do this, they must be unexpected and involuntary – there must be no trick in the case – they should not be squeezed out with a finger and a thumb; there should be nothing optional, personal in their occurrence; they should be like stern, inflexible monitors, that nothing can prevent from discharging their duty. Surely, if there is any thing with which we should not mix up our vanity and self-consequence, it is with Time, the most independent of all things. All the sublimity, all the superstition that hang upon this palpable mode of announcing its flight, are chiefly attached to this circumstance. Time would lose its abstracted character, if we kept it like a curiosity or in a jack-in-a-box: its prophetic warnings would have no effect, if it obviously spoke only at our prompting, like a paltry ventriloquism. The clock that tells the coming, dreaded hour – the castle bell, that 'with its brazen throat

and iron tongue, sounds one unto the drowsy ear of night' –
the curfew, 'swinging slow with sullen roar' o'er wizard
stream or fountain, are like a voice from other worlds, big
with unknown events. The last sound, which is still kept up
as an old custom in many parts of England, is a great favourite with me. I used to hear it when a boy. It tells a tale of
other times. The days that are past, the generations that are
gone, the tangled forest glades and hamlets brown of my
native country, the woodsman's art, the Norman warrior
armed for the battle or in his festive hall, the conqueror's
iron rule and peasant's lamp extinguished, all start up at
the clamorous peal, and fill my mind with fear and wonder.
I confess, nothing at present interests me but what has been
– the recollection of the impressions of my early life, or events
long past, of which only the dim traces remain in a smouldering ruin or half-obsolete custom. That *things should be
that are now no more*, creates in my mind the most un-
feigned astonishment. I cannot solve the mystery of the past,
nor exhaust my pleasure in it. The years, the generations to
come, are nothing to me. We care no more about the world
in the year 2300 than we do about one of the planets. Even
George IV. is better than the Earl of Windsor. We might as
well make a voyage to the moon as think of stealing a march
upon Time with impunity. *De non apparentibus et non
existentibus eadem est ratio.* Those who are to come after
us and push us from the stage seem like upstarts and pretenders, that may be said to exist *in vacuo*, we know not
upon what, except as they are blown up with vain and self
conceit by their patrons among the moderns. But the ancients are true and *bonâ-fide* people, to whom we are bound
by aggregate knowledge and filial ties, and in whom seen by
the mellow light of history we feel our own existence doubled
and our pride consoled, as we ruminate on the vestiges of
the past. The public in general, however, do not carry this
speculative indifference about the future to what is to hap-

pen to themselves, or to the part they are to act in the busy scene. For my own part, I do; and the only wish I can form, or that ever prompts the passing sigh, would be to live some of my years over again – they would be those in which I enjoyed and suffered most!

The ticking of a clock in the night has nothing very interesting nor very alarming in it, though superstition has magnified it into an omen. In a state of vigilance or debility, it preys upon the spirits like the persecution of a teazing pertinacious insect; and haunting the imagination after it has ceased in reality, is converted into the death-watch. Time is rendered vast by contemplating its minute portions thus repeatedly and painfully urged upon our attention, as the ocean in its immensity is composed of water-drops. A clock striking with a clear and silver sound is a great relief in such circumstances, breaks the spell, and resembles a sylph-like and friendly spirit in the room. Foreigners, with all their tricks and contrivances upon clocks and time-pieces, are strangers to the sound of village-bells, though perhaps a people that can dance may dispense with them. They impart a pensive wayward pleasure to the mind, and are a kind of chronology of happy events, often serious in the retrospect – births, marriages, and so forth. Coleridge calls them 'the poor man's only music.' A village spire in England peeping from its cluster of trees is always associated in imagination with this cheerful accompaniment, and may be expected to pour its joyous tidings on the gale. In Catholic countries, you are stunned with the everlasting tolling of bells to prayers or for the dead. In the Apennines, and other wild and mountainous districts of Italy, the little chapel-bell with its simple tinkling sound has a romantic and charming effect. The Monks in former times appear to have taken a pride in the construction of bells as well as churches; and some of those of the great cathedrals abroad (as at Cologne and Rouen) may be fairly said to be hoarse with counting the flight of ages. The chimes in Holland are a nuisance. They dance in the hours and the quarters. They leave no respite to the imagination. Before one set has done ringing in your ears, another begins. You do not know whether the hours move or stand still, go backwards or forwards, so fantastical and perplexing are their accompaniments. Time is a more staid personage, and not so full of gambols. It puts you in mind of a tune with variations, or of an embroidered dress. Surely, nothing is more simple than time. His march is straightforward; but we should have leisure allowed us to look back upon the distance we have come, and not be counting his steps every moment. Time in Holland is a foolish old fellow with all the antics of a youth, who 'goes to church in a coranto, and lights his pipe in a cinque-pace.' The chimes with us, on the contrary, as they come in every three or four hours, are like stages in the journey of the day. They give a fillip to the lazy, creeping hours, and relieve the lassitude of country-places. At noon, their desultory, trivial song is diffused through the hamlet with the odour of rashers of bacon; at the close of day they send the toil-worn sleepers to their beds. Their discontinuance would be a great loss to the thinking or unthinking public. Mr Wordsworth has painted their effect on the mind when he makes his friend Matthew, in a fit of inspired dotage,

> 'Sing those witty rhymes
> About the crazy old church-clock
> And the bewilder'd chimes.'

The tolling of the bell for deaths and executions is a fearful summons, though, as it announces, not the advance of time but the approach of fate, it happily makes no part of our subject. Otherwise, the 'sound of the bell' for Macheath's execution in the 'Beggar's Opera,' or for that of the Conspirators in 'Venice Preserved,' with the roll of the drum at a soldier's funeral, and a digression to that of my Uncle

Toby, as it is so finely described by Sterne, would furnish ample topics to descant upon. If I were a moralist, I might disapprove the ringing in the new and ringing out the old year.

'Why dance ye, mortals, o'er the grave of Time?'

St Paul's bell tolls only for the death of our English kings, or a distinguished personage or two, with long intervals between.*

Those who have no artificial means of ascertaining the progress of time, are in general the most acute in discerning its immediate signs, and are most retentive of individual dates. The mechanical aids to knowledge are not sharpeners of the wits. The understanding of a savage is a kind of natural almanac, and more true in its prognostication of the future. In his mind's eye he sees what has happened or what is likely to happen to him, 'as in a map the voyager his course.' Those who read the times and seasons in the aspect of the heavens and the configurations of the stars, who count by moons and know when the sun rises and sets, are by no means ignorant of their own affairs or of the common concatenation of events. People in such situations have not their faculties distracted by any multiplicity of inquiries beyond what befalls themselves, and the outward appearances that mark the change. There is, therefore, a simplicity and clearness in the knowledge they possess, which often puzzles the more learned. I am sometimes surprised at a shepherd-boy by the roadside, who sees nothing but the earth and sky, asking me the time of day – he ought to know so much better than any one how far the sun is above the horizon. I suppose he wants to ask a question of a passenger, or to see if he has a watch. Robinson Crusoe lost his reckoning in the

* Rousseau has admirably described the effect of bells on the imagination in a passage in the Confessions, beginning '*Les son des cloches m'a toujours singulièrement affecté,*' &c.

monotony of his life and that bewildering dream of solitude, and was fain to have recourse to the notches in a piece of wood. What a diary was his! And how time must have spread its circuit round him, vast and pathless as the ocean!

For myself, I have never had a watch nor any other mode of keeping time in my possession, nor ever wish to learn how times goes. It is a sign I have had little to do, few avocations, few engagements. When I am in a town, I can hear the clock; and when I am in the country, I can listen to the silence. What I like best is to lie whole mornings on a sunny bank on Salisbury Plain, without any object before me, neither knowing nor caring how time passes, and thus 'with light-winged toys of feathered Idleness' to melt down hours to moments. Perhaps some such thoughts as I have here set down float before me like motes before my half-shut eyes, or some vivid image of the past by forcible contrast rushes by me – 'Diana and her fawn, and all the glories of the antique world;' then I start away to prevent the iron from entering my soul, and let fall some tears into that stream of time which separates me farther and farther from all I once loved! At length I rouse myself from my reverie, and home to dinner, proud of killing time with thought, nay even without thinking. Somewhat of this idle humour I inherit from my father, though he had not the same freedom from *ennui*, for he was not a metaphysician; and there were stops and vacant intervals in his being which he did not know how to fill up. He used in these cases, and as an obvious resource, carefully to wind up his watch at night, and 'with lacklustre eye' more than once in the course of the day look to see what o'clock it was. Yet he had nothing else in his character in common with the elder Mr Shandy. Were I to attempt a sketch of him, for my own or the reader's satisfaction, it would be after the following manner: – but now I recollect, I have done something of the kind once before, and were I to resume the subject here, some bat or owl of a critic, with spectacled gravity, might swear I had stolen the whole of this Essay from myself – or (what is worse) from him! So I had better let it go as it is.

From *The New Monthly Magazine* (October 1827), reprinted in *Sketches and Essays* (1839).

ON GOOD-NATURE

LORD SHAFTESBURY somewhere remarks,[1] that a great many people pass for very good-natured persons, for no other reason than because they care about nobody but themselves; and, consequently, as nothing annoys them but what touches their own interest, they never irritate themselves unnecessarily about what does not concern them, and seem to be made of the very milk of human kindness.

Good-nature, or what is often considered as such, is the most selfish of all the virtues: it is nine times out of ten mere indolence of disposition. A good-natured man is, generally speaking, one who does not like to be put out of his way; and as long as he can help it, that is, till the provocation comes home to himself, he will not. He does not create fictitious uneasiness out of the distresses of others; he does not fret and fume, and make himself uncomfortable about things he cannot mend, and that no way concern him, even if he could: but then there is no one who is more apt to be disconcerted by what puts him to any personal inconvenience, however trifling; who is more tenacious of his selfish indulgences, however unreasonable; or who resents more violently any interruption of his ease and comforts, the very trouble he is put to in resenting it being felt as an aggravation of the injury. A person of this character feels no emotions of anger or detestation, if you tell him of the devastation of a province, or the massacre of the inhabitants of a town, or the enslaving of a people; but if his dinner is spoiled by a lump of soot falling down the chimney, he is thrown into the utmost confusion, and can hardly recover a decent command of his temper for the whole day. He thinks nothing can go amiss, so long as he is at his ease, though a pain in his little finger makes him so peevish and quarrelsome, that nobody can come near him. Knavery and injustice in the abstract are things that by no means ruffle his temper, or alter the serenity of his countenance, unless he is to be the sufferer by them; nor is he ever betrayed into a passion in answering a sophism, if he does not think it immediately directed against his own interest.

On the contrary, we sometimes meet with persons who regularly heat themselves in an argument, and get out of humour on every occasion, and make themselves obnoxious to a whole company about nothing. This is not because they are ill-tempered, but because they are in earnest. Goodnature is a hypocrite: it tries to pass off its love of its own ease and indifference to everything else for a particular softness and mildness of disposition. All people get in a passion, and lose their temper, if you offer to strike them, or cheat them of their money, that is, if you interfere with that which they are really interested in. Tread on the heel of one of these good-natured persons, who do not care if the whole world is in flames, and see how he will bear it. If the truth were known, the most disagreeable people are the most amiable. They are the only persons who feel an interest in what does not concern them. They have as much regard for others as they have for themselves. They have as many vexations and causes of complaint as there are in the world. They are general righters of wrongs, and redressers of grievances. They not only are annoyed by what they can help, by an act of inhumanity done in the next street, or in a neighbouring country by their own countrymen, they not only do not claim any share in the glory, and hate it the more, the more brilliant the success, – but a piece of injustice done three thousand years ago touches them to the quick. They have an unfortunate attachment to a set of abstract phrases, such as *liberty*, *truth*, *justice*, *humanity*, *honour*, which are continually abused by knaves, and misunderstood by fools, and they can hardly contain themselves for spleen. They have something to keep them in perpetual hot water. No sooner is one question set at rest than another rises up to perplex them. They wear themselves to the bone in the affairs of other people, to whom they can do no manner of service, to the neglect of their own business and pleasure. They tease themselves to death about the morality of the Turks, or the politics of the French. There are certain words that afflict their ears, and things that lacerate their souls, and remain a plague-spot there forever after. They have a fellow-feeling with all that has been done, said, or thought in the world. They have an interest in all science and in all art. They hate a lie as much as a wrong, for truth is the foundation of all justice. Truth is the first thing in their thoughts, then mankind, then their country, last themselves. They love excellence, and bow to fame, which is the shadow of it. Above all, they are anxious to see justice done to the dead, as the best encouragement to the living, and the lasting inheritance of future generations. They do not like to see a great principle undermined, or the fall of a great man. They would sooner forgive a blow in the face than a wanton attack on acknowledged reputation. The contempt in which the French hold Shakespeare is a serious evil to them; nor do they think the matter mended, when they hear an Englishman, who would be thought a profound one, say that Voltaire was a man without wit. They are vexed to see genius playing at Tom Fool, and honesty turned bawd. It gives them a cutting sensation² to see a number of things which, as they are unpleasant to see, we shall not here repeat. In short, they have a passion for truth; they feel the same attachment to the idea of what is right, that a knave does to his interest, or that a good-natured man does to his ease; and they have as many sources of uneasiness as there are actual or supposed deviations from this standard in the sum of things, or as there is a possibility of folly and mischief in the world.

Principle is a passion for truth; an incorrigible attachment to a general proposition. Good-nature is humanity that costs nothing. No good-natured man was ever a martyr to a cause, in religion or politics. He has no idea of striving against the stream. He may become a good courtier and a loyal subject; and it is hard if he does not, for he has nothing to do in that case but to consult his ease, interest, and outward appearances. The Vicar of Bray was a good-natured man. What a pity he was but a vicar! A good-natured man is utterly unfit for any situation or office in life that requires integrity, fortitude, or generosity, – any sacrifice, except of opinion, or any exertion, but to please. A good-natured man will debauch his friend's mistress, if he has an opportunity; and betray his friend, sooner than share disgrace or danger with him. He will not forego the smallest gratification to save the whole world. He makes his own convenience the standard of right and wrong. He avoids the feeling of pain in himself, and shuts his eyes to the sufferings of others. He will put a malefactor or an innocent person (no matter which) to the rack, and only laugh at the uncouthness of the gestures, or wonder that he is so unmannerly as to cry out. There is no villainy to which he will not lend a helping hand with great coolness and cordiality, for he sees only the pleasant and profitable side of things. He will assent to a falsehood with a leer of complacency, and applaud any atrocity that comes recommended in the garb of authority. He will betray his country to please a Minister, and sign the death-warrant of thousands of wretches, rather than forfeit the congenial smile, the well-known squeeze of the hand. The shrieks of death, the torture of mangled limbs, the last groans of despair, are things that shock his smooth humanity too much ever to make an impression on it: his good-nature sympathizes only with the smile, the bow, the gracious

salutation, the fawning answer: vice loses its sting, and
corruption its poison, in the oily gentleness of his disposition. He will not hear of any thing wrong in Church or
State. He will defend every abuse by which any thing is to
be got, every dirty job, every act of every Minister. In an
extreme case, a very good-natured man indeed may try to
hang twelve honester men than himself to rise at the Bar,
and forge the seal of the realm to continue his colleagues a
week longer in office. He is a slave to the will of others, a
coward to their prejudices, a tool of their vices. A good-
natured man is no more fit to be trusted in public affairs,
than a coward or a woman is to lead an army. Spleen is the
soul of patriotism and of public good. Lord Castlereagh is a
good-natured man, Lord Eldon is a good-natured man,
Charles Fox was a good-natured man. The last instance is
the most decisive. The definition of a true patriot is *a good
hater*.[3]

A king, who is a good-natured man, is in a fair way of
being a great tyrant. A king ought to feel concern for all to
whom his power extends; but a good-natured man cares
only about himself. If he has a good appetite, eats and sleeps
well, nothing in the universe besides can disturb him. The
destruction of the lives or liberties of his subjects will not
stop him in the least of his caprices, but will concoct well
with his bile, and 'good digestion wait on appetite, and
health on both.' He will send out his mandate to kill and
destroy with the same indifference or satisfaction that he performs any natural function of his body. The consequences
are placed beyond the reach of his imagination, or would
not affect him if they were not, for he is a fool, and good-
natured. A good-natured man hates more than any one else
whatever thwarts his will, or contradicts his prejudices; and
if he has the power to prevent it, depend upon it, he will use
it without remorse and without control.

There is a lower species of this character which is what is

usually understood by a *well-meaning man*. A well-meaning man is one who often does a great deal of mischief without any kind of malice. He means no one any harm, if it is not for his interest. He is not a knave, nor perfectly honest. He does not easily resign a good place. Mr Vansittart is a well-meaning man.[4]

The Irish are a good-natured people; they have many virtues, but their virtues are those of the heart, not of the head. In their passions and affections they are sincere, but they are hypocrites in understanding. If they once begin to calculate the consequences, self-interest prevails. An Irishman who trusts to his principles, and a Scotchman who yields to his impulses, are equally dangerous. The Irish have wit, genius, eloquence, imagination, affections: but they want coherence of understanding, and consequently have no standard of thought or action. Their strength of mind does not keep pace with the warmth of their feelings, or the quickness of their conceptions. Their animal spirits run away with them: their reason is a jade. There is something crude, indigested, rash, and discordant, in almost all that they do or say. They have no system, no abstract ideas. They are 'everything by starts, and nothing long.' They are a wild people. They hate whatever imposes a law on their understandings, or a yoke on their wills. To betray the principles they are most bound by their own professions and the expectations of others to maintain, is with them a reclamation of their original rights, and to fly in the face of their benefactors and friends, an assertion of their natural freedom of will. They want consistency and good faith. They unite fierceness with levity. In the midst of their headlong impulses, they have an undercurrent of selfishness and cunning, which in the end gets the better of them. Their feelings, when no longer excited by novelty or opposition, grow cold and stagnant. Their blood, if not heated by passion, turns to poison. They have a rancour in their hatred of any object they have abandoned, proportioned to the attachment they have professed to it. Their zeal, converted against itself, is furious. The late Mr Burke was an instance of an Irish patriot and philosopher. He abused metaphysics, because he could make nothing out of them, and turned his back upon liberty, when he found he could get nothing more by her. – See to the same purpose the winding up of the character of *Judy* in Miss Edgeworth's *Castle Rackrent*.

From the *Examiner* (9 June 1816) reprinted in *The Round Table* (1817).

ON THE DISADVANTAGES OF
INTELLECTUAL SUPERIORITY

THE chief disadvantages of knowing more and seeing farther than others, is not to be generally understood. A man is, in consequence of this, liable to start paradoxes, which immediately transport him beyond the reach of the common-place reader. A person speaking once in a slighting manner of a very original-minded man, received for answer – 'He strides on so far before you, that he dwindles in the distance!'

Petrarch complains, that 'Nature had made him different from other people' – *singular' d'altra genti.* The great happiness of life, is, to be neither better nor worse than the general run of those you meet with. If you are beneath them, you are trampled upon; if you are above them, you soon find a mortifying level in their indifference to what you particularly pique yourself upon. What is the use of being moral in a night-cellar, or wise in Bedlam? 'To be honest, as this world goes, is to be one man picked out of ten thousand.' So says Shakespear; and the commentators have not added that, under these circumstances, a man is more likely to become the butt of slander than the mark of admiration for being so. 'How now, thou particular fellow*?' is the common answer to all such out-of-the-way pretensions. By not doing as those at Rome do, we cut ourselves off from good-fellowship and society. We speak another language, have notions of our own, and are treated as of a different species. Nothing can be more awkward than to intrude with any such far-fetched ideas among the common herd, who will be sure to

* Jack Cade's salutation to one who tries to recommend himself by saying he can write and read. – See HENRY VI. Part Second.

– 'Stand all astonied, like a sort of steers,
'Mongst whom some beast of strange and foreign race
Unwares is chanced, far straying from his peers:
So will their ghastly gaze betray their hidden fears.'

Ignorance of another's meaning is a sufficient cause of
fear, and fear produces hatred: hence the suspicion and rancour entertained against all those who set up for greater
refinement and wisdom than their neighbours. It is in vain
to think of softening down this spirit of hostility by simplicity of manners, or by condescending to persons of low
estate. The more you condescend, the more they will presume upon it; they will fear you less, but hate you more;
and will be the more determined to take their revenge on
you for a superiority as to which they are entirely in the
dark, and of which you yourself seem to entertain considerable doubts. All the humility in the world will only pass for
weakness and folly. They have no notion of such a thing.
They always put their best foot forward; and argue that
you would do the same if you had any such wonderful
talents as people say. You had better, therefore, play off the
great man at once – hector, swagger, talk big, and ride the
high horse over them: you may by this means extort outward respect or common civility; but you will get nothing
(with low people) by forbearance and good-nature but open
insult or silent contempt. C—[1] always talks to people about
what they don't understand: I, for one, endeavour to talk
to them about what they do understand, and find I only get
the more ill-will by it. They conceive I do not think them
capable of any thing better; that I do not think it worth
while, as the vulgar saying is, to *throw a word to a dog.* I
once complained of this to C—, thinking it hard I should
be sent to Coventry for not making a prodigious display. He
said, 'As you assume a certain character, you ought to produce your credentials. It is a tax upon people's good nature
to admit superiority of any kind, even where there is the

most evident proof of it: but it is too hard a task for the imagination to admit it without any apparent ground at all.'

There is not a greater error than to suppose that you avoid the envy, malice, and uncharitableness, so common in the world, by going among people without pretensions. There are no people who have no pretensions; or the fewer their pretensions, the less they can afford to acknowledge yours without some sort of value received. The more information individuals possess, or the more they have refined upon any subject, the more readily can they conceive and admit the same kind of superiority to themselves that they feel over others. But from the low, dull, level sink of ignorance and vulgarity, no idea or love of excellence can arise. You think you are doing mighty well with them; that you are laying aside the buckram of pedantry and pretence, and getting the character of a plain, unassuming, good sort of fellow. It will not do. All the while that you are making these familiar advances, and wanting to be at your ease, they are trying to recover the wind of you. You may forget that you are an author, an artist, or what not – they do not forget that they are nothing, nor bate one jot of their desire to prove you in the same predicament. They take hold of some circumstance in your dress; your manner of entering a room is different from that of other people; you do not eat vegetables – that's odd; you have a particular phrase, which they repeat, and this becomes a sort of standing joke; you look grave, or ill; you talk, or are more silent than usual; you are in or out of pocket: all these petty, inconsiderable circumstances, in which you resemble, or are unlike other people, form so many counts in the indictment which is going on in their imaginations against you, and are so many contradictions in your character. In any one else they would pass unnoticed, but in a person of whom they had heard so much, they cannot make them out at all. Meanwhile, those things in which you may really excel, go for nothing, because they cannot judge of them. They speak highly of some book which you do not like, and therefore you make no answer. You recommend them to go and see some picture, in which they do not find much to admire. How are you to convince them that you are right? Can you make them perceive that the fault is in them, and not in the picture, unless you could give them your knowledge? They hardly distinguish the difference between a Correggio and a common daub. Does this bring you any nearer to an understanding? The more you know of the difference, the more deeply you feel it, or the more earnestly you wish to convey it, the farther do you find yourself removed to an immeasurable distance from the possibility of making them enter into views and feelings of which they have not even the first rudiments. You cannot make them see with your eyes, and they must judge for themselves.

Intellectual is not like bodily strength. You have no hold of the understanding of others but by their sympathy. Your knowing, in fact, so much more about a subject does not give you a superiority, that is, a power over them, but only renders it the more impossible for you to make the least impression on them. Is it then an advantage to you? It may be, as it relates to your own private satisfaction, but it places a greater gulf between you and society. It throws stumbling blocks in your way at every turn. All that you take most pride and pleasure in is lost upon the vulgar eye. What they are pleased with is a matter of indifference or of distaste to you. In seeing a number of persons turn over a portfolio of prints from different masters, what a trial it is to the patience, how it jars the nerves to hear them fall into raptures at some common-place flimsy thing, and pass over some divine expression of countenance without notice, or with a remark that it is very singular-looking? How useless is it in such cases to fret or argue, or remonstrate? Is it not quite as well to be without all this hypercritical, fastidious knowledge, and to be pleased or displeased as it happens, or struck with the first fault or beauty that is pointed out by others? I would be glad almost to change my acquaintance with pictures, with books, and, certainly, what I know of mankind, for any body's ignorance of them!

It is recorded in the life of some worthy (whose name I forget) that he was one of those 'who loved hospitality and respect:' and I profess to belong to the same classification of mankind. Civility is with me a jewel. I like a little comfortable cheer, and careless, indolent, chat. I hate to be always wise, or aiming at wisdom. I have enough to do with literary cabals, questions, critics, actors, essay-writing, without taking them out with me for recreation, and into all companies. I wish at these times to pass for a good-humoured fellow; and good-will is all I ask in return to make good company. I do not desire to be always posing myself or others with the questions of fate, free-will, fore-knowledge absolute, &c. I must unbend sometimes. I must occasionally lie fallow. The kind of conversation that I affect most is what sort of a day it is, and whether it is likely to rain or hold up fine for to-morrow. This I consider as enjoying the *otium cum dignitate*, as the end and privilege of a life of study. I would resign myself to this state of easy indifference, but I find I cannot. I must maintain a certain pretension, which is far enough from my wish. I must be put on my defence, I must take up the gauntlet continually, or I find I lose ground. 'I am nothing, if not critical.' While I am thinking what o'clock it is, or how I came to blunder in quoting a well-known passage, as if I had done it on purpose, others are thinking whether I am not really as dull a fellow as I am sometimes said to be. If a drizzling shower patters against the windows, it puts me in mind of a mild spring rain, from which I retired twenty years ago, into a little public house near Wem in Shropshire, and while I saw the plants and shrubs before the door imbibe the dewy moisture, quaffed a glass of sparkling ale, and walked home in the dusk of evening, brighter to me than noon-day suns at present are! Would I indulge this feeling? In vain. They ask me what news there is, and stare if I say I don't know. If a new actress has come out, why must I have seen her? If a new novel has appeared, why must I have read it? I, at one time, used to go and take a hand of cribbage with a friend, and afterwards discuss a cold sirloin of beef, and throw out a few lack-a-daisical remarks, in a way to please myself, but it would not do long. I set up little pretension, and therefore the little that I did set up was taken from me. As I said nothing on that subject myself, it was continually thrown in my teeth that I was *an author*. From having me at this disadvantage, my friend wanted to peg on a hole or two in the game, and was displeased if I would not let him. If I won of him, it was hard he should be beat by an author. If he won, it would be strange if he did not understand the game better than I did. If I mentioned my favourite game of rackets, there was a general silence, as if this was my weak point. If I complained of being ill, it was asked why I made myself so? If I said such an actor had played a part well, the answer was, there was a different account in one of the newspapers. If any allusion was made to men of letters, there was a suppressed smile. If I told a humorous story, it was difficult to say whether the laugh was at me or at the narrative. The wife hated me for my ugly face: the servants because I could not always get them tickets for the play, and because they could not tell exactly what an author meant. If a paragraph appeared against any thing I had written, I found it was ready there before me, and I was to undergo a regular *roasting*. I submitted to all this till I was tired, and then I gave it up.

One of the miseries of intellectual pretensions is, that nine-tenths of those you come in contact with do not know whether you are an impostor or not. I dread that certain anonymous criticisms should get into the hands of servants where I go, or that my hatter or shoemaker should happen to read them, who cannot possibly tell whether they are well or ill founded. The ignorance of the world leaves one at the mercy of its malice. There are people whose good opinion or good will you want, setting aside all literary pretensions; and it is hard to lose by an ill report (which you have no means of rectifying) what you cannot gain by a good one. After a *diatribe* in the —,[2] (which is taken in by a gentleman who occupies my old apartments on the first floor) my landlord brings me up his bill (of some standing), and on my offering to give him so much in money, and a note of hand for the rest, shakes his head, and says, he is afraid he could make no use of it. Soon after, the daughter comes in, and on my mentioning the circumstance carelessly to her, replies gravely, 'that indeed her father has been almost ruined by bills.' *This is the unkindest cut of all.* It is in vain for me to endeavour to explain that the publication in which I am abused is a mere government engine – an organ of a political faction. They know nothing about that. They only know such and such imputations are thrown out; and the more I try to remove them, the more they think there is some truth in them. Perhaps the people of the house are strong Tories – government-agents of some sort. Is it for me to enlighten their ignorance? If I say, I once wrote a thing called Prince Maurice's Parrot, and an Essay on the Regal Character,[3] in the former of which allusion is made to a noble marquis, and in the latter to a great personage (so at least, I am told, it has been construed), and that Mr Croker has peremptory instructions to retaliate; they cannot conceive what connection there can be between me and such distinguished characters. I can get no farther. Such is the misery of pretensions beyond your situation, and which are not backed by any external symbols of wealth or rank, intelligible to all mankind!

The importance of admiration is scarcely more tolerable than the demonstrations of contempt. I have known a person, whom I had never seen before, besiege me all dinner-time with asking, what articles I had written in the Edinburgh Review? I was at last ashamed to answer to my splendid sins in that way. Others will pick out something not yours, and say, they are sure no one else could write it. By the first sentence they can always tell your style. Now I hate my style to be known; as I hate all *idiosyncrasy*. These obsequious flatterers could not pay me a worse compliment. Then there are those who make a point of reading every thing you write (which is fulsome); while others, more provoking, regularly lend your works to a friend as soon as they receive them. They pretty well know your notions on the different subjects, from having heard you talk about them. Besides, they have a greater value for your personal character than they have for your writings. You explain things better in a common way, when you are not aiming at effect. Others tell you of the faults they have heard found with your last book, and that they defend your style in general from a charge of obscurity. A friend once told me of a quarrel he had had with a near relation, who denied that I knew how to spell the commonest words. These are comfortable confidential communications, to which authors, who have their friends and excusers, are subject. A gentleman told me, that a lady had objected to my use of the word *learneder*, as bad grammar. He said, that he thought it a pity that I did not take more care, but that the lady was perhaps prejudiced, as her husband held a government-office. I looked for the word, and found it in a motto from Butler. I was piqued, and desired him to tell the fair critic, that the fault was not in me, but in one who had far more wit, more learning, and loyalty than I could pretend to. Then, again, some will pick out the flattest thing of yours they can find, to load it with panegyrics; and others tell you (by way of letting you see how high they rank your capacity), that your best passages are failures. L—[4] has a knack of tasting (or as he would say, *palating*) the insipid: L. H.[5] has a trick of turning away from the relishing morsels you put on his plate. There is no getting the start of some people. Do what you will, they can do it better; meet with what success you may, their own good opinion stands them in better stead, and runs before the applause of the world. I once shewed a person of this over-weening turn (with no small triumph I confess) a letter of a very flattering description I had received from the celebrated Count Stendhal,[6] dated Rome. He returned it with a smile of indifference, and said, he had had a letter from Rome himself the day before, from his friend S—! I did not think this 'germane to the matter.' G—dw—n pretends I never wrote any thing worth a farthing but my answers to Vetus, and that I fail altogether when I attempt to write an essay, or any thing in a short compass.

What can one do in such cases? Shall I confess a weakness? The only set-off I know to these rebuffs and mortifications, is sometimes in an accidental notice or involuntary mark of distinction from a stranger. I feel the force of Horace's *digito monstrari* – I like to be pointed out in the street, or to hear people ask in Mr Powell's court,[7] *which is Mr H*—? This is to me a pleasing extension of one's personal identity. Your name so repeated leaves an echo like music on the ear: it stirs the blood like the sound of a trumpet. It shews that other people are curious to see you: that they think of you, and feel an interest in you without your knowing it. This is a bolster to lean upon; a lining to your poor, shivering, threadbare opinion of yourself. You want some such cordial to exhausted spirits, and relief to the dreariness of abstract speculation. You are something; and, from occupying a place in the thoughts of others, think less contemptuously of yourself. You are the better able to run the gauntlet of prejudice and vulgar abuse. It is pleasant in this way to have your opinion quoted against yourself, and your own sayings repeated to you as good things. I was once talking with an intelligent man in the pit, and criticising Mr Knight's performance of Filch. 'Ah!' he said, 'little Simmons was the fellow to play that character.' He added, 'There was a most excellent remark made upon his acting it in the EXAMINER (I think it was) – *That he looked as if he had the gallows in one eye and a pretty girl in the other.*' I said nothing, but he was in remarkably good humour the rest of the evening. I have seldom been in a company where fives-playing has been talked of, but some one has asked, in the course of it, 'Pray did any one ever see an account of one Cavanagh, that appeared some time back in most of the papers? Is it known who wrote it?' These are trying moments. I had a triumph over a person, whose name I will not mention, on the following occasion. I happened to be saying something about Burke, and was expressing my opinion of his talents in no measured terms, when this gentleman interrupted me by saying, he thought, for his part, that Burke had been greatly over-rated, and then added, in a careless way, 'Pray did you read a character of him in the last number of the ——?' 'I wrote it!' – I could not resist the antithesis, but was afterwards ashamed of my momentary petulance. Yet no one, that I find, ever spares me.

Some persons seek out and obtrude themselves on public characters, in order, as it might seem, to pick out their failings, and afterwards betray them. Appearances are for it, but truth and a better knowledge of nature are against this interpretation of the matter. Sycophants and flatterers are undesignedly treacherous and fickle. They are prone to admire inordinately at first, and not finding a constant supply of food for this kind of sickly appetite, take a distaste to the object of their idolatry. To be even with themselves for their credulity, they sharpen their wits to spy out faults, and are delighted to find that this answers better than their first employment. It is a course of study, 'lively, audible, and full of vent.' They have the organ of wonder and the organ of fear in a prominent degree. The first requires new objects of admiration to satisfy its uneasy cravings: the second makes them crouch to power wherever its shifting standard appears, and willing to curry favour with all parties, and ready to betray any out of sheer weakness and servility. I do not think they mean any harm. At least, I can look at this obliquity with indifference in my own particular case. I have been more disposed to resent it as I have seen it practised upon others, where I have been better able to judge of the extent of the mischief, and the heartlessness and idiot folly it discovered.

I do not think great intellectual attainments are any recommendation to the women. They puzzle them, and are a diversion to the main question. If scholars talk to ladies of what they understand, their hearers are none the wiser: if they talk of other things, they only prove themselves fools. The conversation between Angelica and Foresight, in Love for Love, is a receipt in full for all such overstrained nonsense: while he is wandering among the signs of the zodiac, she is standing a tip-toe on the earth. It has been remarked that poets do not choose mistresses very wisely. I believe it is not choice, but necessity. If they could throw the handkerchief like the Grand Turk, I imagine we should see scarce mortals, but rather goddesses, surrounding their steps, and each exclaiming, with Lord Byron's own Ionian maid —

> 'So shalt thou find me ever at thy side,
> Here and hereafter, if the last may be!'

Ah! no, these are bespoke, carried off by men of mortal, not ethereal mould, and thenceforth the poet, from whose mind the ideas of love and beauty are inseparable as dreams from sleep, goes on the forlorn hope of the passion, and dresses up the first Dulcinea that will take compassion on him, in all the colours of fancy. What boots it to complain if the delusion lasts for life, and the rainbow still paints its form in the cloud?

There is one mistake I would wish, if possible, to correct. Men of letters, artists, and others, not succeeding with women in a certain rank of life, think the objection is to their want of fortune, and that they shall stand a better chance by descending lower, where only their good qualities or talents will be thought of. Oh! worse and worse. The objection is to themselves, not to their fortune – to their abstraction, to their absence of mind, to their unintelligible and romantic notions. Women of education may have a glimpse of their meaning, may get a clue to their character, but to all others they are thick darkness. If the mistress smiles at their *ideal* advances, the maid will laugh outright; she will throw water over you, get her little sister to listen, send her sweetheart to ask you what you mean, will set the village or the house upon your back; it will be a farce, a comedy, a standing jest for a year, and then the murder will out. Scholars should be sworn at Highgate.[8] They are no match for chamber maids, or wenches at lodging-houses. They had better try their hands on heiresses or ladies of quality. These last have high notions of themselves that may fit some of your epithets! They are above mortality, so are your thoughts! But with low life, trick, ignorance, and cunning, you have nothing in common. Whoever you are, that think you can make a compromise or a conquest there by good nature, or good sense, be warned by a friendly voice, and retreat in time from the unequal contest.

If, as I have said above, scholars are no match for chambermaids, on the other hand, gentlemen are no match for blackguards. The former are on their honour, act on the square; the latter take all advantages, and have no idea of any other principle. It is astonishing how soon a fellow without education will learn to cheat. He is impervious to any ray of liberal knowledge; his understanding is

'Not pierceable by power of any star' –

but it is porous to all sorts of tricks, chicanery, stratagems, and knavery, by which any thing is to be got. Mrs Peachum, indeed, says, that 'to succeed at the gaming-table, the candidate should have the education of a nobleman.' I do not know how far this example contradicts my theory. I think it is a rule that men in business should not be taught other things. Any one will be almost sure to make money who has no other idea in his head. A college-education, or intense study of abstract truth, will not enable a man to drive a bargain, to over-reach another, or even to guard himself from being over-reached. As Shakespear says, that 'to have a good face is the effect of study, but reading and writing come by nature:' so it might be argued, that to be a knave is the gift of fortune, but to play the fool to advantage it is necessary to be a learned man. The best politicians are not those who are deeply grounded in mathematical or in ethical science. Rules stand in the way of expediency. Many a man has been hindered from pushing his fortune in the world by an early cultivation of his moral sense, and has repented of it at leisure during the rest of his life. A shrewd man said of my father, that he would not send a son of his to school to him on any account, for that by teaching him to speak the truth, he would disqualify him from getting his living in the world!

It is hardly necessary to add any illustration to prove that the most original and profound thinkers are not always the most successful or popular writers. This is not merely a temporary disadvantage; but many great philosophers have not only been scouted while they were living, but forgotten as soon as they were dead. The name of Hobbes is perhaps sufficient to explain this assertion. But I do not wish to go farther into this part of the subject, which is obvious in itself. I have said, I believe, enough to take off the air of paradox which hangs over the title of this Essay.

From *Table-Talk* (1821).

ON *GUSTO*

GUSTO in art is power or passion defining any object. It is not so difficult to explain this term in what relates to expression (of which it may be said to be the highest degree) as in what relates to things without expression, to the natural appearances of objects, as mere colour or form. In one sense, however, there is hardly any object entirely devoid of expression, without some character of power belonging to it, some precise association with pleasure or pain: and it is in giving this truth of character from the truth of feeling, whether in the highest or the lowest degree, but always in the highest degree of which the subject is capable, that gusto consists.

There is a gusto in the colouring of Titian. Not only do his heads seem to think – his bodies seem to feel. This is what the Italians mean by the *morbidezza* of his flesh-colour. It seems sensitive and alive all over; not merely to have the look and texture of flesh, but the feeling in itself. For example, the limbs of his female figures have a luxurious softness and delicacy, which appears conscious of the pleasure of the beholder. As the objects themselves in nature would produce an impression on the sense, distinct from every other object, and having something divine in it, which the heart owns and the imagination consecrates, the objects in the picture preserve the same impression, absolute, unimpaired, stamped with all the truth of passion, the pride of the eye, and the charm of beauty. Rubens makes his flesh-colour like flowers; Albano's is like ivory;[1] Titian's is like flesh, and like nothing else. It is as different from that of other painters, as the skin is from a piece of white or red drapery thrown over it. The blood circulates here and there, the blue veins just appear, the rest is distinguished through-out only by that sort of tingling sensation to the eye, which the body feels within itself. This is gusto. Vandyke's flesh-colour, though it has great truth and purity, wants gusto. It has not the internal character, the living principle in it. It is a smooth surface, not a warm, moving mass. It is painted without passion, with indifference. The hand only has been concerned. The impression slides off from the eye, and does not, like the tones of Titian's pencil, leave a sting behind it in the mind of the spectator. The eye does not acquire a taste or appetite for what it sees. In a word, gusto in paint-ing is where the impression made on one sense excites by affinity those of another.

Michael Angelo's forms are full of gusto. They every-where obtrude the sense of power upon the eye. His limbs convey an idea of muscular strength, of moral grandeur, and even of intellectual dignity: they are firm, command-ing, broad, and massy, capable of executing with ease the determined purposes of the will. His faces have no other expression than his figures, conscious power and capacity. They appear only to think what they shall do, and to know that they can do it. This is what is meant by saying that his style is hard and masculine. It is the reverse of Correggio's, which is effeminate. That is, the gusto of Michael Angelo consists in expressing energy of will without proportionable sensibility, Correggio's in expressing exquisite sensibility without energy of will. In Correggio's faces as well as figures we see neither bones nor muscles, but then what a soul is there, full of sweetness and of grace – pure, playful, soft, angelical! There is sentiment enough in a hand painted by Correggio to set up a school of history painters. Whenever we look at the hands of Correggio's women or of Raphael's, we always wish to touch them.

Again, Titian's landscapes have a prodigious gusto, both in the colouring and forms. We shall never forget one

that we saw many years ago in the Orleans Gallery[2] of
Acteon hunting.[3] It had a brown, mellow, autumnal look.
The sky was of the colour of stone. The winds seemed to
sing through the rustling branches of the trees, and already
you might hear the twanging of bows resound through the
tangled mazes of the wood. Mr West,[4] we understand, has
this landscape. He will know if this description of it is just.
The landscape back-ground of the St Peter Martyr[5] is another well known instance of the power of this great painter
to give a romantic interest and an appropriate character to
the objects of his pencil, where every circumstance adds to
the effect of the scene, — the bold trunks of the tall forest
trees, the trailing ground plants, with that tall convent spire
rising in the distance, amidst the blue sapphire mountains
and the golden sky.

Rubens has a great deal of gusto in his Fauns and Satyrs,
and in all that expresses motion, but in nothing else. Rembrandt has it in everything; everything in his pictures has a
tangible character. If he puts a diamond in the ear of a
burgomaster's wife, it is of the first water; and his furs and
stuffs are proof against a Russian winter. Raphael's gusto
was only in expression; he had no idea of the character of
anything but the human form. The dryness and poverty
of his style in other respects is a phenomenon in the art. His
trees are like sprigs of grass stuck in a book of botanical
specimens. Was it that Raphael never had time to go beyond the walls of Rome? That he was always in the
streets, at church, or in the bath? He was not one of the
Society of Arcadians.*

* Raphael not only could not paint a landscape; he could not paint
people in a landscape. He could not have painted the heads or the
figures, or even the dresses, of the St Peter Martyr. His figures have
always an *in-door* look, that is, a set, determined, voluntary, dramatic
character, arising from their own expression, which is connected with
the accidents of nature and the changes of the elements. He has nothing *romantic* about him.

Claude's landscapes, perfect as they are, want gusto. This is not easy to explain. They are perfect abstractions of the visible images of things; they speak the visible language of nature truly. They resemble a mirror or a microscope. To the eye only they are more perfect than any other landscapes that ever were or will be painted; they give more of nature, as cognisable by one sense alone; but they lay an equal stress on all visible impressions. They do not interpret one sense by another; they do not distinguish the character of different objects as we are taught, and can only be taught, to distinguish them by their effect on the different senses. That is, his eye wanted imagination: it did not strongly sympathise with his other faculties. He saw the atmosphere, but he did not feel it. He painted the trunk of a tree or a rock in the foreground as smooth — with as complete an abstraction of the gross, tangible impression, as any other part of the picture. His trees are perfectly beautiful, but quite immovable; they have a look of enchantment. In short, his landscapes are unequalled imitations of nature, released from its subjection to the elements, as if all objects were become a delightful fairy vision, and the eye had rarefied and refined away the other senses.

The gusto in the Greek statues is of a very singular kind. The sense of perfect form nearly occupies the whole mind, and hardly suffers it to dwell on any other feeling. It seems enough for them *to be*, without acting or suffering. Their forms are ideal, spiritual. Their beauty is power. By their beauty they are raised above the frailties of pain or passion; by their beauty they are deified.

The infinite quantity of dramatic invention in Shakespear takes from his gusto. The power he delights to show is not intense, but discursive. He never insists on anything as much as he might, except a quibble. Milton has great gusto. He repeats his blows twice; grapples with and exhausts his subject. His imagination has a double relish of its objects,

an inveterate attachment to the things he describes, and to
the words describing them.

> – 'Or where Chineses drive'
> With sails and wind their *cany* waggons *light*.'

.   .   .   .   .

> 'Wild above rule or art, *enormous* bliss.'

There is a gusto in Pope's compliments, in Dryden's satires,
and Prior's tales; and among prose writers Boccaccio and
Rabelais had the most of it. We will only mention one other
work which appears to us to be full of gusto, and that is the
Beggar's Opera. If it is not, we are altogether mistaken in our
notions on this delicate subject.

From the *Examiner* (3 March 1816) reprinted
in *The Round Table* (1817).

ON FAMILIAR STYLE

IT is not easy to write a familiar style. Many people mistake a familiar for a vulgar style, and suppose that to write without affectation is to write at random. On the contrary, there is nothing that requires more precision, and, if I may so say, purity of expression, than the style I am speaking of. It utterly rejects not only all unmeaning pomp, but all low, cant phrases, and loose, unconnected, *slipshod* allusions. It is not to take the first word that offers, but the best word in common use; it is not to throw words together in any combinations we please, but to follow and avail ourselves of the true idiom of the language. To write a genuine familiar or truly English style, is to write as any one would speak in common conversation, who had a thorough command and choice of words, or who could discourse with ease, force, and perspicuity, setting aside all pedantic and oratorical flourishes. Or to give another illustration, to write naturally is the same thing in regard to common conversation, as to read naturally is in regard to common speech. It does not follow that it is an easy thing to give the true accent and inflection to the words you utter, because you do not attempt to rise above the level of ordinary life and colloquial speaking. You do not assume indeed the solemnity of the pulpit, or the tone of stage-declamation: neither are you at liberty to gabble on at a venture, without emphasis or discretion, or to resort to vulgar dialect or clownish pronunciation. You must steer a middle course. You are tied down to a given and appropriate articulation, which is determined by the habitual associations between sense and sound, and which you can only hit by entering into the author's meaning, as

you must find the proper words and style to express yourself
by fixing your thoughts on the subject you have to write
about. Any one may mouth out a passage with a theatrical
cadence, or get upon stilts to tell his thoughts: but to write
or speak with propriety and simplicity is a more difficult
task. Thus it is easy to affect a pompous style, to use a word
twice as big as the thing you want to express: it is not so
easy to pitch upon the very word that exactly fits it. Out of
eight or ten words equally common, equally intelligible,
with nearly equal pretensions, it is a matter of some nicety
and discrimination to pick out the very one, the preferable-
ness of which is scarcely perceptible, but decisive. The reason
why I object to Dr Johnson's style is, that there is no discrimination, no selection, no variety in it. He uses none but
'tall, opaque words,' taken from the 'first row of the rubric:'
– words with the greatest number of syllables, or Latin
phrases with merely English terminations. If a fine style
depended on this sort of arbitrary pretension, it would be
fair to judge of an author's elegance by the measurement of
his words, and the substitution of foreign circumlocutions
(with no precise associations) for the mother-tongue.* How
simple it is to be dignified without ease, to be pompous without meaning! Surely, it is but a mechanical rule for avoiding
what is low to be always pedantic and affected. It is clear you
cannot use a vulgar English word, if you never use a common English word at all. A fine tact is shewn in adhering to
those which are perfectly common, and yet never falling into
any expressions which are debased by disgusting circumstances, or which owe their signification and point to technical or professional allusions. A truly natural or familiar
style can never be quaint or vulgar, for this reason, that it is

---

* I have heard of such a thing as an author, who makes it a rule
never to admit a monosyllable into his vapid verse. Yet the charm
and sweetness of Marlow's lines depended often on their being made
up almost entirely of monosyllables.

of universal force and applicability, and that quaintness and vulgarity arise out of the immediate connection of certain words with coarse and disagreeable, or with confined ideas. The last form what we understand by *cant* or *slang* phrases. — To give an example of what is not very clear in the general statement. I should say that the phrase *To cut with a knife*, or *To cut a piece of wood*, is perfectly free from vulgarity, because it is perfectly common : but to *cut an acquaintance* is not quite unexceptionable, because it is not perfectly common or intelligible, and has hardly yet escaped out of the limits of slang phraseology. I should hardly therefore use the word in this sense without putting it in italics as a license of expression, to be received *cum grano salis*. All provincial or bye-phrases come under the same mark of reprobation — all such as the writer transfers to the page from his fire-side or a particular *coterie*, or that he invents for his own sole use and convenience. I conceive that words are like money, not the worse for being common, but that it is the stamp of custom alone that gives them circulation or value. I am fastidious in this respect, and would almost as soon coin the currency of the realm as counterfeit the King's English. I never invented or gave a new and unauthorised meaning to any word but one single one (the term *impersonal* applied to feelings) and that was in an abstruse metaphysical discussion to express a very difficult distinction. I have been (I know) loudly accused of revelling in vulgarisms and broken English.[1] I cannot speak to that point: but so far I plead guilty to the determined use of acknowledged idioms and common elliptical expressions. I am not sure that the critics in question know the one from the other, that is, can distinguish any medium between formal pedantry and the most barbarous solecism. As an author, I endeavour to employ plain words and popular modes of construction, as were I a chapman and dealer, I should common weights and measures.

The proper force of words lies not in the words themselves, but in their application. A word may be a fine-sounding word, of an unusual length, and very imposing from its learning and novelty, and yet in the connection in which it is introduced, may be quite pointless and irrelevant. It is not pomp or presentation, but the adaptation of the expression to the idea that clenches a writer's meaning: — as it is not the size or glossiness of the materials, but their being fitted each to its place, that gives strength to the arch; or as the pegs and nails are as necessary to the support of the building as the larger timbers, and more so than the mere shewy, unsubstantial ornaments. I hate any thing that occupies more space than it is worth. I hate to see a load of bandboxes go along the street, and I hate to see a parcel of big words without any thing in them. A person who does not deliberately dispose of all his thoughts alike in cumbrous draperies and flimsy disguises, may strike out twenty varieties of familiar every-day language, each coming somewhat nearer to the feeling he wants to convey, and at last not hit upon that particular and only one, which may be said to be identical with the exact impression in his mind. This would seem to shew that Mr Cobbett is hardly right[2] in saying that the first word that occurs is always the best. It may be a very good one; and yet a better may present itself on reflection or from time to time. It should be suggested naturally, however, and spontaneously, from a fresh and lively conception of the subject. We seldom succeed by trying at improvement, or by merely substituting one word for another that we are not satisfied with, as we cannot recollect the name of a place or person by merely plaguing ourselves about it. We wander farther from the point by persisting in a wrong scent but it starts up accidentally in the memory when we least expected it, by touching some link in the chain of previous association.

There are those who hoard up and make a cautious display of nothing but rich and rare phraseology; – ancient medals, obscure coins, and Spanish pieces of eight. They are very curious to inspect; but I myself would neither offer nor take them in the course of exchange. A sprinkling of archaisms is not amiss; but a tissue of obsolete expressions is more fit *for keep than wear*. I do not say I would not use any phrase that had been brought into fashion before the middle or the end of the last century; but I should be shy of using any that had not been employed by any approved author during the whole of that time. Words, like clothes, get old-fashioned, or mean and ridiculous, when they have been for some time laid aside. Mr Lamb is the only imitator of old English style I can read with pleasure; and he is so thoroughly imbued with the spirit of his authors, that the idea of imitation is almost done away. There is an inward unction, a marrowy vein both in the thought and feeling, an intuition, deep and lively, of his subject, that carries off any quaintness or awkwardness arising from an antiquated style and dress. The matter is completely his own, though the manner is assumed. Perhaps his ideas are altogether so marked and individual, as to require their point and pungency to be neutralised by the affectation of a singular but traditional form of conveyance. Tricked out in the prevailing costume, they would probably seem more startling and out of the way. The old English authors, Burton, Fuller, Coryate, Sir Thomas Brown, are a kind of mediators between us and the more eccentric and whimsical modern, reconciling us to his peculiarities. I do not however know how far this is the case or not, till he condescends to write like one of us. I must confess that what I like best of his papers under the signature of Elia (still I do not presume, amidst such excellence, to decide what is most excellent) is the account of *Mrs Battle's Opinions on Whist*, which is also the most free from obsolete allusions and turns of expression –

'A well of native English undefiled.'

To those acquainted with his admired prototypes, these Essays of the ingenious and highly gifted author have the same sort of charm and relish, that Erasmus's Colloquies[3] or a fine piece of modern Latin have to the classical scholar. Certainly, I do not know any borrowed pencil that has more power or felicity of execution than the one of which I have here been speaking.

It is as easy to write a gaudy style without ideas, as it is to spread a pallet of shewy colours, or to smear in a flaunting transparency. 'What do you read,' – 'Words, words, words.' – 'What is the matter?' – '*Nothing*,'. it might be answered. The florid style is the reverse of the familiar. The last is employed as an unvarnished medium to convey ideas; the first is resorted to as a spangled veil to conceal the want of them. When there is nothing to be set down but words, it costs little to have them fine. Look through the dictionary, and cull out a *florilegium*, rival the *tulippomania*. *Rouge* high enough, and never mind the natural complexion. The vulgar, who are not in the secret, will admire the look of preternatural health and vigour; and the fashionable, who regard only appearances, will be delighted with the imposition. Keep to your sounding generalities, your tinkling phrases, and all will be well. Swell out an unmeaning truism to a perfect tympany of style. A thought, a distinction is the rock on which all this brittle cargo of verbiage splits at once. Such writers have merely *verbal* imaginations, that retain nothing but words. Or their puny thoughts have dragon-wings, all green and gold. They soar far above the vulgar failing of the *Sermo humi obrepens* – their most ordinary speech is never short of an hyperbole, splendid, imposing, vague, incomprehensible, magniloquent, a cento of sounding common-places. If some of us, whose 'ambition is more lowly,' pry a little too narrowly into nooks and corners to pick up a number of 'unconsidered trifles,' they never once direct their eyes or lift their hands to seize on any but the most gorgeous, tarnished, thread-bare patch-work set of phrases, the left-off finery of poetic extravagance, transmitted down through successive generations of barren pretenders. If they criticise actors and actresses, a huddled phantasmagoria of feathers, spangles, floods of light, and oceans of sound float before their morbid sense, which they paint in the style of Ancient Pistol. Not a glimpse can you get of the merits or defects of the performers: they are hidden in a profusion of barbarous epithets and wilful rhodomontade. Our hypercritics are not thinking of these little fantoccini beings –

'That strut and fret their hour upon the stage' –

but of tall phantoms of words, abstractions, *genera* and *species*, sweeping clauses, periods that unite the Poles, forced alliterations, astounding antitheses –

'And on their pens *Fustian* sits plumed.'

If they describe kings and queens, it is an Eastern pageant. The Coronation at either House is nothing to it. We get at four repeated images – a curtain, a throne, a sceptre, and a foot-stool. These are with them the wardrobe of a lofty imagination; and they turn their servile strains to servile uses. Do we read a description of pictures? It is not a reflection of tones and hues which 'nature's own sweet and cunning hand laid on,' but piles of precious stones, rubies, pearls, emeralds, Golconda's mines, and all the blazonry of art. Such persons are in fact besotted with words, and their brains are turned with the glittering, but empty and sterile phantoms of things. Personifications, capital letters, seas of sunbeams, visions of glory, shining inscriptions, the figures of a transparency, Britannia with her shield, or Hope leaning on an anchor, make up their stock in trade. They may be considered as *hieroglyphical* writers. Images stand out in their minds isolated and important merely in themselves, without any ground-work of feeling – there is no context in their imaginations. Words affect them in the same way, by the mere sound, that is, by their possible, not by their actual application to the subject in hand. They are fascinated by first appearances, and have no sense of consequences. Nothing more is meant by them than meets the ear: they understand or feel nothing more than meets their eye. The web and texture of the universe, and of the heart of man, is a mystery to them: they have no faculty that strikes a chord in unison with it. They cannot get beyond the daubings of fancy, the varnish of sentiment. Objects are not linked to feelings, words to things, but images revolve in splendid mockery, words represent themselves in their strange rhapsodies. The categories of such a mind are pride and ignorance – pride in outside show, to which they sacrifice every thing, and ignorance of the true worth and hidden structure both of words and things. With a sovereign contempt for what is familiar and natural, they are the slaves of vulgar affectation – of a routine of high-flown phrases. Scorning to imitate realities, they are unable to invent any thing, to strike out one original idea. They are not copyists of nature, it is true: but they are the poorest of all plagiarists, the plagiarists of words. All is far-fetched, dear-bought, artificial, oriental in subject and allusion: all is mechanical, conventional, vapid, formal, pedantic in style and execution. They startle and confound the understanding of the reader, by the remoteness and obscurity of their illustrations: they soothe the ear by the monotony of the same everlasting round of circuitous metaphors. They are the *mock-school* in poetry and prose. They flounder about between fustian in expression, and bathos in sentiment. They tantalise the fancy, but never reach the head nor touch the heart. Their Temple of Fame is like a shadowy structure raised by

Dulness to Vanity, or like Cowper's description of the Empress of Russia's palace of ice, as 'worthless as in shew 'twas glittering' –

'It smiled, and it was cold !'

From *Table-Talk* (1821).

THE LAKE SCHOOL

MR WORDSWORTH is at the head of that which has been denominated the Lake school of poetry; a school which, with all my respect for it, I do not think sacred from criticism or exempt from faults, of some of which faults I shall speak with becoming frankness; for I do not see that the liberty of the press ought to be shackled, or freedom of speech curtailed, to screen either its revolutionary or renegado extravagances. This school of poetry had its origin in the French revolution, or rather in those sentiments and opinions which produced that revolution; and which sentiments and opinions were indirectly imported into this country in translations from the German about that period. Our poetical literature had, towards the close of the last century, degenerated into the most trite, insipid, and mechanical of all things, in the hands of the followers of Pope and the old French school of poetry. It wanted something to stir it up, and it found that something in the principles and events of the French revolution. From the impulse it thus received, it rose at once from the most servile imitation and tamest common-place, to the utmost pitch of singularity and paradox. The change in the belles-lettres was as complete, and to many persons as startling, as the change in politics, with which it went hand in hand. There was a mighty ferment in the heads of statesmen and poets, kings and people. According to the prevailing notions, all was to be natural and new. Nothing that was established was to be tolerated. All the common-place figures of poetry, tropes, allegories, personifications, with the whole heathen mythology, were instantly discarded; a classical allusion was considered as a piece of antiquated foppery; capital letters were no more allowed in print, than letters-patent of nobility were permitted in real life; kings and queens were dethroned from their rank and station in legitimate tragedy or epic poetry, as they were decapitated elsewhere; rhyme was looked upon as a relic of the feudal system, and regular metre was abolished along with regular government. Authority and fashion, elegance or arrangement, were hooted out of countenance, as pedantry and prejudice. Every one did that which was good in his own eyes. The object was to reduce all things to an absolute level; and a singularly affected and outrageous simplicity prevailed in dress and manners, in style and sentiment. A striking effect produced where it was least expected, something new and original, no matter whether good, bad, or indifferent, whether mean or lofty, extravagant or childish, was all that was aimed at, or considered as compatible with sound philosophy and an age of reason. The licentiousness grew extreme: Coryate's Crudities were nothing to it. The world was to be turned topsy-turvy; and poetry, by the good will of our Adamwits, was to share its fate and begin *de novo*. It was a time of promise, a renewal of the world and of letters; and the Deucalions,[1] who were to perform this feat of regeneration, were the present poet-laureat and the two authors of the Lyrical Ballads. The Germans, who made heroes of robbers, and honest women of cast-off mistresses, had already exhausted the extravagant and marvellous in sentiment and situation: our native writers adopted a wonderful simplicity of style and matter. The paradox they set out with was, that all things are by nature equally fit subjects for poetry; or that if there is any preference to be given, those that are the meanest and most unpromising are the best, as they leave the greatest scope for the unbounded stores of thought and fancy in the writer's own mind. Poetry had with them 'neither buttress nor coigne of vantage to make its pendant bed and procreant cradle.' It was not 'born so high: its aiery buildeth in the cedar's top, and dallies with the wind, and scorns the sun.' It grew like a mushroom out of the ground; or was hidden in it like a truffle, which it required a particular sagacity and industry to find out and dig up. They founded the new school on a principle of sheer humanity, on pure nature void of art. It could not be said of these sweeping reformers and dictators in the republic of letters, that 'in their train walked crowns and crownets; that realms and islands, like plates, dropt from their pockets': but they were surrounded, in company with Muses, by a mixed rabble of idle appentices and Botany Bay convicts, female vagrants, gipsies, meek daughters in the family of Christ, of ideot boys and mad mothers, and after them 'owls and night-ravens flew.' They scorned 'degrees, priority, and place, insisture, course, proportion, season, form, office, and custom in all line of order': – the distinctions of birth, the vicissitudes of fortune, did not enter into their abstracted, lofty, and levelling calculation of human nature. He who was more than man, with them was none. They claimed kindred only with the commonest of the people: peasants, pedlars, and village-barbers were their oracles and bosom friends. Their poetry, in the extreme to which it professedly tended, and was in effect carried, levels all distinctions of nature and society; has 'no figures nor no fantasies,' which the prejudices of superstition or the customs of the world draw in the brains of men; 'no trivial fond records' of all that has existed in the history of past ages; it has no adventitious pride, pomp, or circumstance, to set it off; 'the marshal's truncheon, nor the judge's robe'; neither tradition, reverence, nor ceremony, 'that to great ones 'longs': it breaks in pieces the golden images of poetry, and defaces its armorial bearings, to melt them down in the mould of common humanity or of its own upstart self-sufficiency. They took the same method in their new-fangled 'metre ballad-mongering' scheme, which Rousseau did in his prose paradoxes – of exciting attention by reversing the established standards of opinion and estimation in the world. They were for bringing poetry back to its primitive simplicity and state of nature, as he was for bringing society back to the savage state: so that the only thing remarkable left in the world by this change, would be the persons who had produced it. A thorough adept in this school of poetry and philanthropy is jealous of all excellence but his own. He does not even like to share his reputation with his subject; for he would have it all proceed from his own power and originality of mind. Such a one is slow to admire any thing that is admirable; feels no interest in what is most interesting to others, no grandeur in any thing grand, no beauty in anything beautiful. He tolerates only what he himself creates; he sympathizes only with what can enter into no competition with him, with 'the bare trees and mountains bare, and grass in the green field.' He sees nothing but himself and the universe.

From 'On the Living Poets' in *Lectures on the English Poets* (1818), reprinted in *The Spirit of the Age* or *Contemporary Portraits* (1825).

MR WORDSWORTH

MR WORDSWORTH's genius is a pure emanation of the Spirit of the Age. Had he lived in any other period of the world, he would never have been heard of. As it is, he has some difficulty to contend with the hebetude of his intellect, and the meanness of his subject. With him 'lowliness is young ambition's ladder': but he finds it a toil to climb in this way the steep of Fame. His homely Muse can hardly raise her wing from the ground, nor spread her hidden glories to the sun. He has 'no figures nor no fantasies, which busy *passion* draws in the brains of men:' neither the gorgeous machinery of mythologic lore, nor the splendid colours of poetic diction. His style is vernacular: he delivers household truths. He sees nothing loftier than human hopes; nothing deeper than the human heart. This he probes, this he tampers with, this he poises, with all its incalculable weight of thought and feeling, in his hands; and at the same time calms the throbbing pulses of his own heart, by keeping his eye ever fixed on the face of nature. If he can make the life-blood flow from the wounded breast, this is the living colouring with which he paints his verse: if he can assuage the pain or close up the wound with the balm of solitary musing, or the healing power of plants and herbs and 'skyey influences,' this is the sole triumph of his art. He takes the simplest elements of nature and of the human mind, the mere abstract conditions inseparable from our being, and tries to compound a new system of poetry from them; and has perhaps succeeded as well as any one could. 'Nihil humani a me alienum puto' – is the motto of his works. He thinks nothing low or indifferent of which this can be affirmed: every thing that professes to be more than this, that is not an absolute essence of truth and feeling, he holds to be vitiated, false, and spurious. In a word, his poetry is founded on setting up an opposition (and pushing it to the utmost length) between the natural and the artificial; between the spirit of humanity, and the spirit of fashion and of the world!

It is one of the innovations of the time. It partakes of, and is carried along with, the revolutionary movement of our age: the political changes of the day were the model on which he formed and conducted his poetical experiments. His Muse (it cannot be denied, and without this we cannot explain its character at all) is a levelling one. It proceeds on a principle of equality, and strives to reduce all things to the same standard. It is distinguished by a proud humility. It relies upon its own resources, and disdains external show and relief. It takes the commonest events and objects, as a test to prove that nature is always interesting from its inherent truth and beauty, without any of the ornaments of dress or pomp of circumstances to set it off. Hence the unaccountable mixture of seeming simplicity and real abstruseness in the *Lyrical Ballads*. Fools have laughed at, wise men scarcely understand them. He takes a subject or a story merely as pegs or loops to hang thought and feeling on; the incidents are trifling, in proportion to his contempt for imposing appearances; the reflections are profound, according to the gravity and the aspiring pretensions of his mind.

His popular, inartificial style gets rid (at a blow) of all the trappings of verse, of all the high places of poetry: 'the cloud-capt towers, the solemn temples, the gorgeous palaces,' are swept to the ground, and 'like the baseless fabric of a vision, leave not a wreck behind.' All the traditions of learning, all the superstitions of age, are obliterated and effaced. We begin *de novo*, on a *tabula rasa* of poetry. The purple pall, the nodding plume of tragedy are exploded as mere pantomime and trick, to return to the simplicity of

truth and nature. Kings, queens, priests, nobles, the altar
and the throne, the distinctions of rank, birth, wealth,
power, 'the judge's robe, the marshal's truncheon, the ceremony that to great ones 'longs,' are not to be found here.
The author tramples on the pride of art with greater pride.
The Ode and Epode, the Strophe and the Antistrophe, he
laughs to scorn. The harp of Homer, the trump of Pindar
and of Alcæus are still. The decencies of costume, the
decorations of vanity are stripped off without mercy as barbarous, idle, and Gothic. The jewels in the crisped hair, the
diadem on the polished brow are thought meretricious, theatrical, vulgar; and nothing contents his fastidious taste
beyond a simple garland of flowers. Neither does he avail
himself of the advantages which nature or accident holds out
to him. He chooses to have his subject a foil to his invention,
to owe nothing but to himself. He gathers manna in the wilderness, he strikes the barren rock for the gushing moisture.
He elevates the mean by the strength of his own aspirations;
he clothes the naked with beauty and grandeur from the
stores of his own recollections. No cypress grove loads his
verse with funeral pomp: but his imagination lends 'a sense
of joy

> 'To the bare trees and mountains bare,
> And grass in the green field.'

No storm, no shipwreck startles us by its horrors: but the
rainbow lifts it head in the cloud, and the breeze sighs
through the withered fern. No sad vicissitude of fate, no
overwhelming catastrophe in nature deforms his page: but
the dew-drop glitters on the bending flower, the tear collects
in the glistening eye.

> 'Beneath the hills, along the flowery vales,
> The generations are prepared; the pangs,
> The internal pangs are ready; the dread strife
> Of poor humanity's afflicted will,
> Struggling in vain with ruthless destiny.'

As the lark ascends from its low bed on fluttering wing, and salutes the morning skies; so Mr Wordsworth's unpretending Muse, in russet guise, scales the summits of reflection, while it makes the round earth its footstool, and its home!

Possibly a good deal of this may be regarded as the effect of disappointed views and an inverted ambition. Prevented by native pride and indolence from climbing the ascent of learning or greatness, taught by political opinions to say to the vain pomp and glory of the world, 'I hate ye,' seeing the path of classical and artificial poetry blocked up by the cumbrous ornaments of style and turgid *common-places*, so that nothing more could be achieved in that direction but by the most ridiculous bombast or the tamest servility; he has turned back partly from the bias of his mind, partly perhaps from a judicious policy – has struck into the sequestered vale of humble life, sought out the Muse among sheep-cotes and hamlets and the peasant's mountain-haunts, has discarded all the tinsel pageantry of verse, and endeavoured (not in vain) to aggrandise the trivial and add the charm of novelty to the familiar. No one has shown the same imagination in raising trifles into importance: no one has displayed the same pathos in treating of the simplest feelings of the heart. Reserved, yet haughty, having no unruly or violent passions, (or those passions having been early suppressed,) Mr Wordsworth has passed his life in solitary musing, or in daily converse with the face of nature. He exemplifies in an eminent degree the power of *association*; for his poetry has no other source or character. He has dwelt among pastoral scenes, till each object has become connected with a thousand feelings, a link in the chain of thought, a fibre of his own heart. Every one is by habit and familiarity strongly attached to the place of his birth, or to objects that recal the most pleasing and eventful circumstances of his life. But to the author of the *Lyrical Ballads*, nature is a kind of home; and he may be said to take a personal interest in the universe. There is no image so insignificant that it has not in some mood or other found the way into his heart: no sound that does not awaken the memory of other years. –

> 'To him the meanest flower that blows can give
> Thoughts that do often lie too deep for tears.'

The daisy looks up to him with sparkling eye as an old acquaintance: the cuckoo haunts him with sounds of early youth not to be expressed: a linnet's nest startles him with boyish delight: an old withered thorn is weighed down with a heap of recollections: a grey cloak, seen on some wild moor, torn by the wind, or drenched in the rain, afterwards becomes an object of imagination to him: even the lichens on the rock have a life and being in his thoughts. He has described all these objects in a way and with an intensity of feeling that no one else had done before him, and has given a new view or aspect of nature. He is in this sense the most original poet now living, and the one whose writings could the least be spared: for they have no substitute elsewhere. The vulgar do not read them, the learned, who see all things through books, do not understand them, the great despise, the fashionable may ridicule them: but the author has created himself an interest in the heart of the retired and lonely student of nature, which can never die. Persons of this class will still continue to feel what he has felt: he has expressed what they might in vain wish to express, except with glistening eye and faultering tongue! There is a lofty philosophic tone, a thoughtful humanity, infused into his pastoral vein. Remote from the passions and events of the great world, he has communicated interest and dignity to the primal movements of the heart of man, and ingrafted his own conscious reflections on the casual thoughts of hinds and shepherds. Nursed amidst the grandeur of mountain scenery, he has stooped to have a nearer view of the daisy under his feet, or plucked a branch of white-thorn from the spray: but in describing it, his mind seems imbued with the majesty and solemnity of the objects around him – the tall rock lifts its head in the erectness of his spirit; the cataract roars in the sound of his verse; and in its dim and mysterious meaning, the mists seem to gather in the hollows of Helvellyn, and the forked Skiddaw hovers in the distance. There is little mention of mountainous scenery in Mr Wordsworth's poetry; but by internal evidence one might be almost sure that it was written in a mountainous country, from its bareness, its simplicity, its loftiness and its depth!

His later philosophic productions have a somewhat different character. They are a departure from, a dereliction of his first principles. They are classical and courtly. They are polished in style, without being gaudy; dignified in subject, without affectation. They seem to have been composed not in a cottage at Grasmere, but among the half-inspired groves and stately recollections of Cole-Orton.[1] We might allude in particular, for examples of what we mean, to the lines on a Picture by Claude Lorraine, and to the exquisite poem, entitled *Laodamia*. The last of these breathes the pure spirit of the finest fragments of antiquity – the sweetness, the gravity, the strength, the beauty and the languor of death –

'Calm contemplation and majestic pains.'

Its glossy brilliancy arises from the perfection of the finishing, like that of careful sculpture, not from gaudy colouring – the texture of the thoughts has the smoothness and solidity of marble. It is a poem that might be read aloud in Elysium, and the spirits of departed heroes and sages would gather round to listen to it! Mr Wordsworth's philosophic poetry, with a less glowing aspect and less tumult in the veins than Lord Byron's on similar occasions, bends a calmer and keener eye on morality; the impression, if less vivid, is more pleasing and permanent; and we confess it

(perhaps it is a want of taste and proper feeling) that there
are lines and poems of our author's, that we think of ten
times for once that we recur to any of Lord Byron's. Or if
there are any of the latter's writings, that we can dwell upon
in the same way, that is, as lasting and heart-felt sentiments,
it is when laying aside his usual pomp and pretension, he
descends with Mr Wordsworth to the common ground of a
disinterested humanity. It may be considered as characteristic of our poet's writings, that they either make no impression on the mind at all, seem mere *nonsense-verses*, or that
they leave a mark behind them that never wears out. They
either

'Fall blunted from the indurated breast' –

without any perceptible result, or they absorb it like a passion. To one class of readers he appears sublime, to another
(and we fear the largest) ridiculous. He has probably realised
Milton's wish,[2] – 'and fit audience found, though few'; but
we suspect he is not reconciled to the alternative. There are
delightful passages in the EXCURSION, both of natural
description and of inspired reflection (passages of the latter
kind that in the sound of the thoughts and of the swelling language resemble heavenly symphonies, mournful
requiems over the grave of human hopes); but we must add,
in justice and in sincerity, that we think it impossible that
this work should ever become popular, even in the same
degree as the *Lyrical Ballads*. It affects a system without
having any intelligible clue to one; and instead of unfolding
a principle in various and striking lights, repeats the same
conclusions till they become flat and insipid. Mr Wordsworth's mind is obtuse, except as it is the organ and the
receptacle of accumulated feelings; it is not analytic, but syn-
thetic; it is reflecting, rather than theoretical. The EXCUR-
SION, we believe, fell still-born from the press. There was
something abortive, and clumsy, and ill-judged in the

attempt. It was long and laboured. The personages, for the most part, were low, the fare rustic: the plan raised expectations which were not fulfilled, and the effect was like being ushered into a stately hall and invited to sit down to a splendid banquet in the company of clowns, and with nothing but successive courses of apple-dumplings served up. It was not even *toujours perdrix*!

Mr Wordsworth, in his person, is above the middle size, with marked features, and an air somewhat stately and Quixotic. He reminds one of some of Holbein's heads, grave, saturnine, with a slight indication of sly humour, kept under by the manners of the age or by the pretensions of the person. He has a peculiar sweetness in his smile, and great depth and manliness and a rugged harmony, in the tones of his voice. His manner of reading his own poetry is particularly imposing; and in his favourite passages his eye beams with preternatural lustre, and the meaning labours slowly up from his swelling breast. No one who has seen him at these moments could go away with an impression that he was a 'man of no mark or likelihood.' Perhaps the comment of his face and voice is necessary to convey a full idea of his poetry. His language may not be intelligible, but his manner is not to be mistaken. It is clear that he is either mad or inspired. In company, even in a *tête-à-tête*, Mr Wordsworth is often silent, indolent, and reserved. If he is become verbose and oracular of late years, he was not so in his better days. He threw out a bold or an indifferent remark without either effort or pretension, and relapsed into musing again. He shone most (because he seemed most roused and animated) in reciting his own poetry, or in talking about it. He sometimes gave striking views of his feelings and trains of association in composing certain passages; or if one did not always understand his distinctions, still there was no want of interest — there was a latent meaning worth inquiring into, like a vein of ore that one cannot exactly hit upon at the moment, but of which there are sure indications. His standard of poetry is high and severe, almost to exclusiveness. He admits of nothing below, scarcely of any thing above himself. It is fine to hear him talk of the way in which certain subjects should have been treated by eminent poets, according to his notions of the art. Thus he finds fault with Dryden's description of Bacchus in the *Alexander's Feast*, as if he were a mere good-looking youth, or boon companion –

> 'Flushed with a purple grace,
> He shows his honest face' –

instead of representing the God returning from the conquest of India, crowned with vine-leaves, and drawn by panthers, and followed by troops of satyrs, of wild men and animals that he had tamed. You would think, in hearing him speak on this subject, that you saw Titian's picture of the meeting of *Bacchus and Ariadne* – so classic were his conceptions, so glowing his style. Milton is his great idol, and he sometimes dares to compare himself with him. His Sonnets, indeed, have something of the same high-raised tone and prophetic spirit. Chaucer is another prime favourite of his, and he has been at the pains to modernize some of the Canterbury Tales.[3] Those persons who look upon Mr Wordsworth as a merely puerile writer, must be rather at a loss to account for his strong predilection for such geniuses as Dante and Michael Angelo. We do not think our author has any very cordial sympathy with Shakespear. How should he? Shakespear was the least of an egotist of any body in the world. He does not much relish the variety and scope of dramatic composition. 'He hates those interlocutions between Lucius and Caius.' Yet Mr Wordsworth himself wrote a tragedy[4] when he was young; and we have heard the following energetic lines quoted from it, as put into the mouth of a person smit with remorse for some rash crime:

– 'Action is momentary,
The motion of a muscle this way or that;
Suffering is long, obscure, and infinite!'

Perhaps for want of light and shade, and the unshackled spirit of the drama, this performance was never brought forward. Our critic has a great dislike to Gray, and a fondness for Thomson and Collins. It is mortifying to hear him speak of Pope and Dryden, whom, because they have been supposed to have all the possible excellences of poetry, he will allow to have none. Nothing, however, can be fairer, or more amusing, than the way in which he sometimes exposes the unmeaning verbiage of modern poetry. Thus, in the beginning of Dr Johnson's *Vanity of Human Wishes* –

'Let observation with extensive view
Survey mankind from China to Peru'

he says there is a total want of imagination accompanying the words, the same idea is repeated three times under the disguise of a different phraseology: it comes to this – 'let *observation*, with extensive *observation*, *observe mankind*'; or take away the first line, and the second,

'Survey mankind from China to Peru.'

literally conveys the whole. Mr Wordsworth is, we must say, a perfect Drawcansir⁵ as to prose writers. He complains of the dry reasoners and matter-of-fact people for their want of *passion*; and he is jealous of the rhetorical declaimers and rhapsodists as trenching on the province of poetry. He condemns all French writers (as well of poetry as prose) in the lump. His list in this way is indeed small. He approves of Walton's Angler, Paley, and some other writers of an inoffensive modesty of pretension. He also likes books of voyages and travels, and Robinson Crusoe. In art, he greatly esteems Bewick's woodcuts, and Waterloo's sylvan etchings.[6] But he sometimes takes a higher tone, and gives his mind fair play. We have known him enlarge with a noble intelligence and enthusiasm on Nicolas Poussin's fine landscape-compositions, pointing out the unity of design that pervades them, the superintending mind, the imaginative principle that brings all to bear on the same end; and declaring he would not give a rush for any landscape that did not express the time of day, the climate, the period of the world it was meant to illustrate, or had not this character of *wholeness* in it. His eye also does justice to Rembrandt's fine and masterly effects. In the way in which that artist works something out of nothing, and transforms the stump of a tree, a common figure into an *ideal* object, by the gorgeous light and shade thrown upon it, he perceives an analogy to his own mode of investing the minute details of nature with an atmosphere of sentiment; and in pronouncing Rembrandt to be a man of genius, feels that he strengthens his own claim to the title. It has been said of Mr Wordsworth, that 'he hates conchology, that he hates the Venus of Medicis.' But these, we hope, are mere epigrams and *jeux-d'esprit*, as far from truth as they are free from malice; a sort of running satire or critical clenches –

> 'Where one for sense and one for rhyme
> Is quite sufficient at one time.'

We think, however, that if Mr Wordsworth had been a more liberal and candid critic, he would have been a more sterling writer. If a greater number of sources of pleasure had been open to him, he would have communicated pleasure to the world more frequently. Had he been less fastidious in pronouncing sentence on the works of others, his own would have been received more favourably, and treated more leniently. The current of his feelings is deep, but narrow; the range of his understanding is lofty and aspiring rather than discursive. The force, the originality, the absolute truth and identity with which he feels some things, makes him indifferent to so many others. The simplicity and enthusiasm of his feelings, with respect to nature, renders him bigotted and intolerant in his judgments of men and things. But it happens to him, as to others, that his strength lies in his weakness; and perhaps we have no right to complain. We might get rid of the cynic and the egotist, and find in his stead a common place man. We should 'take the good the Gods provide us': a fine and original vein of poetry is not one of their most contemptible gifts, and the rest is scarcely worth thinking of, except as it may be a mortification to those who expect perfection from human nature; or who have been idle enough at some period of their lives, to deify men of genius as possessing claims above it. But this is a chord that jars, and we shall not dwell upon it.

Lord Byron we have called, according to the old proverb, 'the spoiled child of fortune': Mr Wordsworth might plead, in mitigation of some peculiarities, that he is 'the spoiled child of disappointment.' We are convinced, if he had been early a popular poet, he would have borne his honours meekly, and would have been a person of great *bonhommie* and frankness of disposition. But the sense of injustice and of undeserved ridicule sours the temper and narrows the views. To have produced works of genius, and to find them neglected or treated with scorn, is one of the heaviest trials of human patience. We exaggerate our own merits when they are denied by others, and are apt to grudge and cavil at every particle of praise bestowed on those to whom we feel a conscious superiority. In mere self-defence we turn against the world, when it turns against us; brood over the undeserved slights we receive; and thus the genial current of the soul is stopped, or vents itself in effusions of petulance and self-conceit. Mr Wordsworth has thought too much of contemporary critics and criticism; and less than he ought of the award of posterity, and of the opinion, we do not say of private friends, but of those who were made so by their admiration of his genius. He did not court popularity by a conformity to established models, and he ought not to have been surprised that his originality was not understood as a matter of course. He has *gnawed too much on the bridle*; and has often thrown out crusts to the critics, in mere defiance or as a point of honour when he was challenged, which otherwise his own good sense would have withheld. We suspect that Mr Wordsworth's feelings are a little morbid in this respect, or that he resents censure more than he is gratified by praise. Otherwise, the tide has turned much in his favour of late years – he has a large body of determined partisans – and is at present sufficiently in request with the public to save or relieve him from the last necessity to which a man of genius can be reduced – that of becoming the God of his own idolatry!

From *On the Living Poets* (1818), reprinted in *The Spirit of the Age* (1825).

MR COLERIDGE

THE present is an age of talkers, and not of doers; and the reason is, that the world is growing old. We are so far advanced in the Arts and Sciences, that we live in retrospect, and doat on past achievements. The accumulation of knowledge has been so great, that we are lost in wonder at the height it has reached, instead of attempting to climb or add to it; while the variety of objects distracts and dazzles the looker-on. What *niche* remains unoccupied? What path untried? What is the use of doing anything, unless we could do better than all those who have gone before us? What hope is there of this? We are like those who have been to see some noble monument of art, who are content to admire without thinking of rivalling it; or like guests after a feast, who praise the hospitality of the donor 'and thank the bounteous Pan' – perhaps carrying away some trifling fragments; or like the spectators of a mighty battle, who still hear its sound afar off, and the clashing of armour and the neighing of the war-horse and the shout of victory is in their ears, like the rushing of innumerable waters!

Mr Coleridge has 'a mind reflecting ages past'; his voice is like the echo of the congregated roar of the 'dark rearward and abyss' of thought. He who has seen a mouldering tower by the side of a chrystal lake, hid by the mist, but glittering in the wave below, may conceive the dim, gleaming, uncertain intelligence of his eye: he who has marked the evening clouds unrolled (a world of vapours), has seen the picture of his mind, unearthly, unsubstantial, with gorgeous tints and ever-varying forms –

'That which was now a horse, even with a thought
The rack dislimns, and makes it indistinct
As water is in water.'

Our author's mind is (as he himself might express it) *tangential*. There is no subject on which he has not touched, none on which he has rested. With an understanding fertile, subtle, expansive, 'quick, forgetive, apprehensive,' beyond all living precedent, few traces of it will perhaps remain. He lends himself to all impressions alike; he gives up his mind and liberty of thought to none. He is a general lover of art and science, and wedded to no one in particular. He pursues knowledge as a mistress, with outstretched hands and winged speed; but as he is about to embrace her, his Daphne turns – alas! not to a laurel! Hardly a speculation has been left on record from the earliest time, but it is loosely folded up in Mr Coleridge's memory, like a rich, but somewhat tattered piece of tapestry: we might add (with more seeming than real extravagance), that scarce a thought can pass through the mind of man, but its sound has at some time or other passed over his head with rustling pinions. On whatever question or author you speak, he is prepared to take up the theme with advantage – from Peter Abelard down to Thomas Moore, from the subtlest metaphysics to the politics of the *Courier*. There is no man of genius, in whose praise, he descants, but the critic seems to stand above the author, and 'what in him is weak, to strengthen, what is low, to raise and support': nor is there any work of genius that does not come out of his hands like an illuminated Missal, sparkling even in its defects. If Mr Coleridge had not been the most impressive talker of his age, he would probably have been the finest writer; but he lays down his pen to make sure of an auditor, and mortgages the admiration of posterity for the stare of an idler. If he had not been a poet, he would have been a powerful logician; if he had not dipped his wing in the Unitarian controversy, he might

have soared to the very summit of fancy. But in writing
verse, he is trying to subject the Muse to *transcendental*
theories: in his abstract reasoning, he misses his way by
strewing it with flowers. All that he has done of moment,
he had done twenty years ago: since then, he may be said
to have lived on the sound of his own voice. Mr Coleridge
is too rich in intellectual wealth, to need to task himself to
any drudgery: he has only to draw the sliders of his imagination, and a thousand subjects expand before him, startling
him with their brilliancy, or losing themselves in endless
obscurity –

> 'And by the force of blear illusion,
> They draw him on to his confusion.'

What is the little he could add to the stock, compared with
the countless stores that lie about him, that he should stoop
to pick up a name, or to polish an idle fancy? He walks
abroad in the majesty of an universal understanding, eyeing
the 'rich strond,' or golden sky above him, and 'goes sounding on his way,' in eloquent accents, uncompelled and free!

Persons of the greatest capacity are often those, who for
this reason do the least; for surveying themselves from the
highest point of view, amidst the infinite variety of the universe, their own share in it seems trifling, and scarce worth
a thought, and they prefer the contemplation of all that is,
or has been, or can be, to the making a coil about doing
what, when done, is no better than vanity. It is hard to con-
centrate all our attention and efforts on one pursuit, except
from ignorance of others; and without this concentration of
our faculties, no great progress can be made in any one
effort; it does not think the effort worth making. Action is
one; but thought is manifold. He whose restless eye glances
through the wide compass of nature and art, will not consent to have 'his own nothings monstered'; but he must do
this, before he can give his whole soul to them. The mind,
after 'letting contemplation have its fill,' or

'Sailing with supreme dominion,
Through the azure deep of air,'

sinks down on the ground, breathless, exhausted, power-
less, inactive; or if it must have some vent to its feelings,
seeks the most easy and obvious; is soothed by friendly flattery, lulled by the murmur of immediate applause, thinks
as it were aloud, and babbles in its dreams! A scholar (so to
speak) is a more disinterested and abstracted character than
a mere author. The first looks at the numberless volumes of
a library, and says, 'All these are mine': the other points to
a single volume (perhaps it may be an immortal one) and
says, 'My name is written on the back of it.' This is a puny
and groveling ambition, beneath the lofty amplitude of Mr
Coleridge's mind. No, he revolves in his wayward soul, or
utters to the passing wind, or discourses to his own shadow,
things mightier and more various! – Let us draw the curtain, and unlock the shrine.

Learning rocked him in his cradle, and while yet a child,

'He lisped in numbers, for the numbers came.'

At sixteen he wrote his *Ode on Chatterton*,[1] and he still re-
verts to that period with delight, not so much as it relates
to himself (for that string of his own early promise of fame
rather jars than otherwise) but as exemplifying the youth of
a poet. Mr Coleridge talks of himself, without being an
egotist, for in him the individual is always merged in the
abstract and general. He distinguished himself at school and
at the University by his knowledge of the classics, and
gained several prizes for Greek epigrams. How many men
are there (great scholars, celebrated names in literature) who
having done the same thing in their youth, have no other
idea all the rest of their lives but of this achievement, of a
fellowship and dinner, and who, installed in academic
honours, would look down on our author as a mere strolling bard! At Christ's Hospital, where he was brought up,

he was the idol of those among his schoolfellows, who mingled with their bookish studies the music of thought and of humanity; and he was usually attended round the cloisters by a group of these (inspiring and inspired) whose hearts, even then, burnt within them as he talked, and where the sounds yet linger to mock ELIA on his way, still turning pensive to the past! One of the finest and rarest parts of Mr Coleridge's conversation, is when he expatiates on the Greek tragedians (not that he is not well acquainted, when he pleases, with the epic poets, or the philosophers, or orators, or historians of antiquity) – on the subtle reasonings and melting pathos of Euripides, on the harmonious gracefulness of Sophocles, tuning his love-laboured song, like sweetest warblings from a sacred grove; on the high-wrought trumpet-tongued eloquence of Æschylus, whose Prometheus, above all, is like an Ode to Fate, and a pleading with Providence, his thoughts being let loose as his body is chained on his solitary rock, and his afflicted will (the emblem of mortality)

'Struggling in vain with ruthless destiny.'

As the impassioned critic speaks and rises in his theme, you would think you heard the voice of the Man hated by the Gods, contending with the wild winds as they roar, and his eye glitters with the spirit of Antiquity!

Next, he was engaged with Hartley's tribes of mind, 'etherial braid, thought-woven,' – and he busied himself for a year or two with vibrations and vibratiuncles and the great law of association that binds all things in its mystic chain, and the doctrine of Necessity (the mild teacher of Charity) and the Millennium, anticipative of a life to come – and he plunged deep into the controversy on Matter and Spirit, and, as an escape from Dr Priestley's Materialism, where he felt himself imprisoned by the logician's spell, like Ariel in the cloven pine-tree, he became suddenly enamoured of Bishop Berkeley's fairy-world,* and used in all companies to build the universe, like a brave poetical fiction, of fine words – and he was deep-read in Malebranche, and in Cudworth's Intellectual System (a huge pile of learning, unwieldy, enormous) and in Lord Brook's hieroglyphic theories, and in Bishop Butler's Sermons, and in the Duchess of Newcastle's fantastic folios, and in Clark and South and Tillotson, and all the fine thinkers and masculine reasoners of that age – and Leibnitz's *Pre-Established Harmony* reared its arch above his head, like the rainbow in the cloud, convenanting with the hopes of man – and then he fell plump, ten thousand fathoms down (but his wings saved him harmless) into the *hortus siccus* of Dissent, where he pared religion down to the standard of reason and stripped faith of mystery, and preached Christ crucified and the Unity of the Godhead, and so dwelt for a while in the spirit with John Huss and Jerome of Prague and Socinus and old John Zisca, and ran through Neal's History of the Puritans, and Calamy's Non-Conformists' Memorial, having like thoughts and passions with them – but then Spinoza became his God, and he took up the vast chain of being in his hand, and the round world became the centre and the soul of all things in some shadowy sense, forlorn of meaning, and around him he beheld the living traces and the sky-pointing proportions of the mighty Pan – but poetry redeemed him from this spectral philosophy, and he bathed his heart in beauty, and gazed at the golden light of heaven, and drank

---

* Mr Coleridge named his eldest son (the writer of some beautiful Sonnets) after Hartley, and the second after Berkeley. The third was called Derwent, after the river of that name. Nothing can be more characteristic of his mind than this circumstance. All his ideas indeed are like a river, flowing on for ever, and still murmuring as it flows, discharging its waters and still replenished –

> 'And so by many winding nooks it strays,
> With willing sport to the wild ocean!'

of the spirit of the universe, and wandered at eve by fairy-
stream or fountain,

> '– When he saw nought but beauty,
> When he heard the voice of that Almighty One
> In every breeze that blew, or wave that murmured' –

and wedded with truth in Plato's shade, and in the writings
of Proclus and Plotinus saw the ideas of things in the eternal
mind, and unfolded all mysteries with the Schoolmen and
fathomed the depths of Duns Scotus and Thomas Aquinas,
and entered the third heaven with Jacob Behmen, and
walked hand in hand with Swedenborg through the pavi-
lions of the New Jerusalem, and sung his faith in the
promise and in the word in his *Religious Musings* – and
lowering himself from that dizzy height, poised himself on
Milton's wings, and spread out his thoughts in charity with
the glad prose of Jeremy Taylor, and wept over Bowles's
Sonnets, and studied Cowper's blank verse, and betook himself to Thomson's Castle of Indolence, and sported with the
wits of Charles the Second's days and of Queen Anne, and
relished Swift's style and that of the John Bull[2] (Arbuthnot's
we mean, not Mr Croker's), and dallied with the British
Essayists and Novelists, and knew all qualities of more
modern writers with a learned spirit, Johnson, and Goldsmith, and Junius, and Burke, and Godwin, and the Sorrows of Werter, and Jean Jacques Rousseau, and Voltaire,
and Marivaux, and Crebillon, and thousands more – now
'laughed with Rabelais in his easy chair' or pointed to
Hogarth, or afterwards dwelt on Claude's classic scenes, or
spoke with rapture of Raphael, and compared the women
at Rome to figures that had walked out of his pictures, or
visited the Oratory of Pisa, and described the works of
Giotto and Ghirlandaio and Massaccio, and gave the moral
of the picture of the Triumph of Death,[3] where the beggars
and the wretched invoke his dreadful dart, but the rich and

mighty of the earth quail and shrink before it; and in that land of siren sights and sounds, saw a dance of peasant girls, and was charmed with lutes and gondolas, – or wandered into Germany and lost himself in the labyrinths of the Hartz Forest and of the Kantean philosophy, and amongst the cabalistic names of Fichtè and Schelling and Lessing, and God knows who – this was long after, but all the former while, he had nerved his heart and filled his eyes with tears, as he hailed the rising orb of liberty, since quenched in darkness and in blood, and had kindled his affections at the blaze of the French Revolution, and sang for joy when the towers of the Bastile [4] and the proud places of the insolent and the oppressor fell, and would have floated his bark, freighted with fondest fancies, across the Atlantic wave with Southey and others to seek for peace and freedom –

'In Philarmonia's undivided dale!'

Alas! 'Frailty, thy name is *Genius*!' – What is become of all this mighty heap of hope, of thought, of learning, and humanity? It has ended in swallowing doses of oblivion [5] and in writing paragraphs in the *Courier*. – Such, and so little is the mind of man!

It was not to be supposed that Mr Coleridge could keep on at the rate he set off; he could not realize all he knew or thought, and less could not fix his desultory ambition; other stimulants supplied the place, and kept up the intoxicating dream, the fever and the madness of his early impressions. Liberty (the philosopher's and the poet's bride) had fallen a victim, meanwhile, to the murderous practices of the hag, Legitimacy. Proscribed by court-hirelings, too romantic for the herd of vulgar politicians, our enthusiast stood at bay, and at last turned on the pivot of a subtle casuistry to the *unclean side*: but his discursive reason would not let him trammel himself into a poet-laureate or stamp-distributor, [6] and he stopped, ere he had quite passed that well-known 'bourne from whence no traveller returns' – and so has sunk into torpid, uneasy repose, tantalized by useless resources, haunted by vain imaginings, his lips idly moving, but his heart for ever still, or, as the shattered chords vibrate of themselves, making melancholy music to the ear of memory! Such is the fate of genius in an age, when in the unequal contest with sovereign wrong, every man is ground to powder who is not either a born slave, or who does not willingly and at once offer up the yearnings of humanity and the dictates of reason as a welcome sacrifice to besotted prejudice and loathsome power.

Of all Mr Coleridge's productions, the *Ancient Mariner* is the only one that we could with confidence put into any person's hands, on whom we wished to impress a favourable idea of his extraordinary powers. Let whatever other objections be made to it, it is unquestionably a work of genius – of wild, irregular, overwhelming imagination, and has that rich, varied movement in the verse, which gives a distant idea of the lofty or changeful tones of Mr Coleridge's voice. In the *Christabel*, there is one splendid passage on divided friendship. The *Translation of Schiller's Wallenstein* is also a masterly production in its kind, faithful and spirited. Among his smaller pieces there are occasional bursts of pathos and fancy, equal to what we might expect from him; but these form the exception, and not the rule. Such, for instance, is his affecting Sonnet to the author of the Robbers.

'Schiller! that hour I would have wish'd to die,
  If through the shudd'ring midnight I had sent
  From the dark dungeon of the tower time-rent,
That fearful voice, a famish'd father's cry –
That in no after-moment aught less vast
  Might stamp me mortal! A triumphant shout
  Black horror scream'd, and all her goblin rout
From the more with'ring scene diminsh'd pass'd.

Ah ! Bard tremendous in sublimity !
  Could I behold thee in thy loftier mood,
Wand'ring at eve, with finely frenzied eye,
  Beneath some vast old tempest-swinging wood !
  Awhile, with mute awe gazing, I would brood,
Then weep aloud in a wild ecstacy.'

His Tragedy, entitled *Remorse*, is full of beautiful and striking passages, but it does not place the author in the first rank of dramatic writers. But if Mr Coleridge's works do not place him in that rank, they injure instead of conveying a just idea of the man, for he himself is certainly in the first class of general intellect.

If our author's poetry is inferior to his conversation, his prose is utterly abortive. Hardly a gleam is to be found in it of the brilliancy and richness of those stores of thought and language that he pours out incessantly, when they are lost like drops of water in the ground. The principal work, in which he has attempted to embody his general views of things, is the FRIEND, of which, though it contains some noble passages and fine trains of thought, prolixity and obscurity are the most frequent characteristics.

No two persons can be conceived more opposite in character or genius than the subject of the present and of the preceding sketch. Mr Godwin, with less natural capacity, and with fewer acquired advantages, by concentrating his mind on some given object, and doing what he had to do with all his might, has accomplished much, and will leave more than one monument of a powerful intellect behind him; Mr Coleridge, by dissipating his, and dallying with every subject by turns, has done little or nothing to justify to the world or to posterity, the high opinion which all who have ever heard him converse, or known him intimately, with one accord entertain of him. Mr Godwin's faculties have kept at home, and plied their task in the workshop of the brain, diligently and effectually: Mr Coleridge's have gossipped their time away, and gadded about from house to house, as if life's business were to melt the hours in listless talk. Mr Godwin is intent on a subject, only as it concerns himself and his reputation; he works it out as a matter of duty, and discards from his mind whatever does not forward his main object as impertinent and vain. Mr Coleridge, on the other hand, delights in nothing but episodes and digressions, neglects whatever he undertakes to perform, and can act only on spontaneous impulses, without object or method. 'He cannot be constrained by mastery.' While he should be occupied with a given pursuit, he is thinking of a thousand other things; a thousand tastes, a thousand objects tempt him, and distract his mind, which keeps open house, and entertains all comers; and after being fatigued and amused with morning calls from idle visitors, finds the day consumed and its business unconcluded. Mr Godwin, on the contrary, is somewhat exclusive and unsocial in his habits of mind, entertains no company but what he gives his whole time and attention to, and wisely writes over the doors of his understanding, his fancy, and his senses – 'No admittance except on business.' He has none of that fastidious refinement and false delicacy, which might lead him to balance between the endless variety of modern attainments. He does not throw away his life (nor a single half-hour of it) in adjusting the claims of different accomplishments, and in choosing between them or making himself master of them all. He sets about his task, (whatever it may be) and goes through it with spirit and fortitude. He has the happiness to think an author the greatest character in the world, and himself the greatest author in it. Mr Coleridge, in writing an harmonious stanza, would stop to consider whether there was not more grace and beauty in a *Pas de trois*, and would not proceed till he had resolved this question by a chain of metaphysical reasoning without end. Not so Mr Godwin. That is best to him, which he can do best. He does not waste himself in vain aspirations and effeminate sympathies. He is blind, deaf, insensible to all but the trump of Fame. Plays, operas, painting, music, ball-rooms, wealth, fashion, titles, lords, ladies, touch him not — all these are no more to him than to the magician in his cell, and he writes on to the end of the chapter, through good report and evil report. *Pingo in eternitatem* — is his motto. He neither envies nor admires what others are, but is contented to be what he is, and strives to do the utmost he can. Mr Coleridge has flirted with the Muses as with a set of mistresses: Mr Godwin has been married twice, to Reason and to Fancy, and has to boast no short-lived progeny by each. So to speak, he has *valves* belonging to his mind, to regulate the quantity of gas admitted into it, so that like the bare, unsightly, but well-compacted steam-vessel, it cuts its liquid way, and arrives at its promised end: while Mr Coleridge's bark, 'taught with the little nautilus to sail,' the sport of every breath, dancing to every wave,

'Youth at its prow, and Pleasure at its helm,'

flutters its gaudy pennons in the air, glitters in the sun, but we wait in vain to hear of its arrival in the destined harbour. Mr Godwin, with less variety and vividness, with less subtlety and susceptibility both of thought and feeling, has had firmer nerves, a more determined purpose, a more comprehensive grasp of his subject, and the results are as we find them. Each has met with his reward: for justice has, after all, been done to the pretensions of each; and we must, in all cases, use means to ends!

It was a misfortune to any man of talent to be born in the latter end of the last century. Genius stopped the way of Legitimacy, and therefore it was to be abated, crushed, or set aside as a nuisance. The spirit of the monarchy was at variance with the spirit of the age. The flame of liberty, the light of intellect was to be extinguished with the sword — or with slander, whose edge is sharper than the sword. The war between power and reason was carried on by the first of these abroad – by the last at home. No quarter was given (then or now) by the Government-critics, the authorised censors of the press, to those who followed the dictates of independence, who listened to the voice of the tempter, Fancy. Instead of gathering fruits and flowers, immortal fruits and amaranthine flowers, they soon found themselves beset not only by a host of prejudices, but assailed with all the engines of power, by nicknames, by lies, by all the arts of malice, interest and hypocrisy, without the possibility of their defending themselves 'from the pelting of the pitiless storm,' that poured down upon them from the strong-holds of corruption and authority. The philosophers, the dry abstract reasoners, submitted to this reverse pretty well, and armed themselves with patience 'as with triple steel' to bear discomfiture, persecution, and disgrace. But the poets, the creatures of sympathy, could not stand the frowns both of king and people. They did not like to be shut out when places and pensions, when the critic's praises, and the laurel-wreath were about to be distributed. They did not stomach being *sent to Coventry*, and Mr Coleridge sounded a retreat for them by the help of casuistry, and a musical voice. – 'His words were hollow, but they pleased the ear' of his friends of the Lake School, who turned back disgusted and panic-struck from the dry desert of unpopularity, like Hassan the camel driver,

> 'And curs'd the hour, and curs'd the luckless day,
> When first from Shiraz' walls they bent their way.'

They are safely inclosed there, but Mr Coleridge did not enter with them; pitching his tent upon the barren waste without, and having no abiding place nor city of refuge.

From 'To Know a Man Well Were To Know Himself in *The Spirit of the Age, or Contemporary Portraits* (1825).

MR SOUTHEY

WE know no other person in whom 'fierce extremes' meet
with such mutual self-complacency: whose opinions change
so much without any change in the author's mind; who
lives so entirely in the 'present ignorant thought,' without
the smallest 'discourse of reason looking before or after.' Mr
Southey is a man incapable of reasoning connectedly on any
subject. He has not strength of mind to see the whole of any
question; he has not modesty to suspend his judgment till
he has examined the grounds of it. He can comprehend but
one idea at a time, and that is always an extreme one; because he will neither listen to, nor tolerate any thing that
can disturb or moderate the petulance of his self-opinion
The woman that deliberates is lost. So it is with the effeminate soul of Mr Southey. Any concession is fatal to his consistency; and he can only keep out of one absurdity by the
tenaciousness with which he stickles for another. He calls to
the aid of his disjointed opinions a proportionate quantity of
spleen; and regularly makes up for the weakness of his own
reasons, by charging others with *bad motives*. The terms
knave and fool, wise and good, have undergone a total
change in the last twenty years: the former he applies to all
those who agreed with him formerly – the latter to all those
who agree with him now. His public spirit was then a prude
and a scold; and 'his poor virtue,' turned into a literary
prostitute, is grown more abusive than ever. Wat Tyler and
the Quarterly Review are an illustration of these remarks.
The author of Wat Tyler was an Ultra-jacobin; the author
of Parliamentary Reform is an Ultra-royalist;[1] the one was a
frantic demagogue; the other is a servile court-tool: the
one maintained second-hand paradoxes; the other repeats

second-hand common-places: the one vented those opinions which gratified the vanity of youth; the other adopts those prejudices which are most conducive to the convenience of age: the one saw nothing but the abuses of power; the other sees nothing but the horrors of resistance to those abuses: the one did not stop short of general anarchy; the other goes the whole length of despotism; the one vilified kings, priests, and nobles; the other vilifies the people: the one was for universal suffrage and perfect equality; the other is for seat-selling, and the increasing influence of the Crown: the one admired the preaching of John Ball; the other recommends the Suspension of the Habeas Corpus, and the putting down of the *Examiner* [2] by the sword, the dagger, or the thumb-screw; for the pen, Mr Southey tells us, is not sufficient. We wonder that in all this contempt which our prose-poet has felt at different times for different persons and things, he has never felt any dissatisfaction with himself, or distrust of his own infallibility. Our differing from others sometimes staggers our confidence in our own conclusions: if we had been chargeable with as many contradictions as Mr Southey, we suppose we should have had the same senseless self-sufficiency. A changeling is your only oracle. Those who have undergone a total change of sentiment on important questions, ought certainly to learn modesty in themselves, and moderation towards others; on the contrary, they are generally the most violent in their own opinions, and the most intolerant towards others. . .

From 'Wat Tyler and the Quarterly Review'
in *Political Essays* (1819).

MR CRABBE

MR CRABBE presents an entire contrast to Mr Campbell: – The one is the most ambitious and aspiring of living poets, the other the most humble and prosaic. If the poetry of the one is like the arch of the rainbow, spanning and adorning the earth, that of the other is like a dull, leaden cloud hanging over it. Mr Crabbe's style might be cited as an answer to Audrey's question – 'Is poetry a true thing?' There are here no ornaments, no flights of fancy, no illusions of sentiment, no tinsel of words. His song is one sad reality, one unraised, unvaried note of unavailing woe. Literal fidelity serves him in the place of invention; he assumes importance by a number of petty details; he rivets attention by being tedious. He not only deals in incessant matters of fact, but in matters of fact of the most familiar, the least animating, and the most unpleasant kind; but he relies for the effect of novelty on the microscopic minuteness with which he dissects the most trivial objects – and for the interest he excites, on the unshrinking determination with which he handles the most painful. His poetry has an official and professional air. He is called in to cases of difficult births, of fractured limbs, or breaches of the peace; and makes out a parochial list of accidents and offences. He takes the most trite, the most gross and obvious and revolting part of nature, for the subject of his elaborate descriptions; but it is Nature still, and Nature is a great and mighty Goddess! It is well for the Reverend Author that it is so. Individuality is, in his theory, the only definition of poetry. Whatever *is*, he hitches into rhyme. Whoever makes an exact image of any thing on the earth, however deformed or insignificant, according to him, must succeed – and he himself has succeeded. Mr Crabbe is one of the most popular and admired of our living authors. That he is so, can be accounted for on no other principle than the strong ties that bind us to the world about us, and our involuntary yearnings after whatever in any manner powerfully and directly reminds us of it. His Muse is not one of *the Daughters of Memory*, but the old toothless, mumbling, dame herself, doling out the gossip and scandal of the neighbourhood, recounting *totidem verbis et literis*, what happens in every place of the kingdom every hour in the year, and fastening always on the worst as the most palatable morsels. But she is a circumstantial old lady, communicative, scrupulous, leaving nothing to the imagination, harping on the smallest grievances, a village oracle and critic, most veritable, most identical, bringing us acquainted with persons and things just as they chanced to exist, and giving us a local interest in all she knows and tells. Mr Crabbe's Helicon is choked up with weeds and corruption; it reflects no light from heaven, it emits no cheerful sound: no flowers of love, of hope, or joy spring up near it, or they bloom only to wither in a moment. Our poet's verse does not put a spirit of youth in every thing, but a spirit of fear, despondency, and decay: it is not an electric spark to kindle or expand, but acts like the torpedo's touch to deaden or contract. It lends no dazzling tints to fancy, it aids no soothing feelings in the heart, it gladdens no prospect, it stirs no wish; in its view the current of life runs slow, dull, cold, dispirited, half under ground, muddy, and clogged with all creeping things. The world is one vast infirmary; the hill of Parnassus is a penitentiary, of which our author is the overseer: to read him is a penance, yet we read on! Mr Crabbe, it must be confessed, is a repulsive writer. He contrives to 'turn diseases to commodities,' and makes a virtue of necessity. He puts us out of conceit with this world, which perhaps a severe divine should do; yet does not, as a charitable divine ought, point to another.

His morbid feelings droop and cling to the earth, grovel where they should soar; and throw a dead weight on every aspiration of the soul after the good or beautiful. By degrees we submit, and are reconciled to our fate, like patients to the physician, or prisoners in the condemned cell. We can only explain this by saying, as we said before, that Mr Crabbe gives us one part of nature, the mean, the little, the disgusting, the distressing; that he does this thoroughly and like a master, and we forgive all the rest.

Mr Crabbe's first poems were published so long ago as the year 1782, and received the approbation of Dr Johnson only a little before he died. This was the testimony from an enemy; for Dr Johnson was not an admirer of the simple in style or minute in description. Still he was an acute, strong-minded man, and could see truth when it was presented to him, even through the mist of his prejudices and his foibles. There was something in Mr Crabbe's intricate points that did not, after all, so ill accord with the Doctor's purblind vision; and he knew quite enough of the petty ills of life to judge of the merit of our poet's descriptions, though he himself chose to slur them over in high-sounding dogmas or general invectives. Mr Crabbe's earliest poem of the *Village*[1] was recommended to the notice of Dr Johnson by Sir Joshua Reynolds; and we cannot help thinking that a taste for that sort of poetry, which leans for support on the truth and fidelity of its imitations of nature, began to display itself much about that time, and, in a good measure, in consequence of the direction of the public taste to the subject of painting. Book-learning, the accumulation of wordy common-places, the gaudy pretensions of poetical fiction, had enfeebled and perverted our eye for nature. The study of the fine arts, which came into fashion about forty years ago, and was then first considered as a polite accomplishment, would tend imperceptibly to restore it. Painting is essentially an imitative art; it cannot subsist for a moment on empty

generalities: the critic, therefore, who had been used to this
sort of substantial entertainment, would be disposed to read
poetry with the eye of a connoisseur, would be little capti-
vated with smooth, polished, unmeaning periods, and
would turn with double eagerness and relish to the force
and precision of individual details, transferred, as it were,
to the page from the canvas. Thus an admirer of Teniers or
Hobbima might think little of the pastoral sketches of Pope
or Goldsmith; even Thomson describes not so much the
naked object as what he sees in his mind's eye, surrounded
and glowing with the mild, bland, genial vapours of his
brain: – but the adept in Dutch interiors, hovels, and pig-
styes must find in Mr Crabbe a man after his own heart. He
is the very thing itself; he paints in words, instead of
colours: there is no other difference. As Mr Crabbe is not a
painter, only because he does not use a brush and colours,
so he is for the most part a poet, only because he writes in
lines of ten syllables. All the rest might be found in a newspaper, an old magazine, or a county-register. Our author is
himself a little jealous of the prudish fidelity of his homely
Muse, and tries to justify himself by precedents. He brings
as a parallel instance of merely literal description, Pope's
lines on the gay Duke of Buckingham, beginning 'In the
worst inn's worst room see Villiers lies!' But surely nothing can be more dissimilar. Pope describes what is striking,
Crabbe would have described merely what was there. The
objects in Pope stand out to the fancy from the mixture of
the mean with the gaudy, from the contrast of the scene and
the character. There is an appeal to the imagination; you see
what is passing in a poetical point of view. In Crabbe there
is no foil, no contrast, no impulse given to the mind. It is
all on a level and of a piece. In fact, there is so little connection between the subject-matter of Mr Crabbe's lines and
the ornament of rhyme which is tacked to them, that many
of his verses read like serious burlesque, and the parodies

which have been made upon them are hardly so quaint as the originals.

Mr Crabbe's great fault is certainly that he is a sickly, a querulous, a uniformly dissatisfied poet. He sings the country; and he sings it in a pitiful tone. He chooses this subject only to take the charm out of it, and to dispel the illusion, the glory, and the dream, which had hovered over it in golden verse from Theocritus to Cowper. He sets out with professing to overturn the theory which had hallowed a shepherd's life, and made the names of grove and valley music to our ears, in order to give us truth in its stead; but why not lay aside the fool's cap and bells at once? Why not insist on the unwelcome reality in plain prose? If our author is a poet, why trouble himself with statistics? If he is a statistic writer, why set his ill news to harsh and grating verse? The philosopher in painting the dark side of human nature may have reason on his side, and a moral lesson or remedy in view. The tragic poet, who shows the sad vicissitudes of things and the disappointments of the passions, at least strengthens our yearnings after imaginary good, and lends wings to our desires, by which we, 'at one bound, high overleap all bound' of actual suffering. But Mr Crabbe does neither. He gives us discoloured paintings of life; helpless, repining, unprofitable, unedifying distress. He is not a philosopher, but a sophist, a misanthrope in verse; a *namby-pamby* Mandeville, a Malthus turned metrical romancer. He professes historical fidelity; but his vein is not dramatic; nor does he give us the *pros* and *cons* of that versatile gipsey, Nature. He does not indulge his fancy or sympathise with us, or tell us how the poor feel; but how he should feel in their situation, which we do not want to know. He does not weave the web of their lives of a mingled yarn, good and ill together, but clothes them all in the same dingy linsey-woolsey, or tinges them with a green and yellow melancholy. He blocks out all possibility of good, cancels the hope,

or even the wish for it as a weakness; checkmates Tityrus [2]
and Virgil at the game of pastoral cross-purposes, disables
all his adversary's white pieces, and leaves none but black
ones on the board. The situation of a country clergyman is
not necessarily favourable to the cultivation of the Muse. He
is set down, perhaps, as he thinks, in a small curacy for life,
and he takes his revenge by imprisoning the reader's imagination in luckless verse. Shut out from social converse, from
learned colleges and halls, where he passed his youth, he
has no cordial fellow-feeling with the unlettered manners of
the *Village* or the *Borough*; and he describes his neighbours
as more uncomfortable and discontented than himself. All
this while he dedicates successive volumes to rising generations of noble patrons; and while he desolates a line of coast
with sterile, blighting lines, the only leaf of his books where
honour, beauty, worth, or pleasure bloom, is that inscribed
to the Rutland family! [3] We might adduce instances of
what we have said from every page of his works: let one
suffice —

'Thus by himself compelled to live each day,
To wait for certain hours the tide's delay;
At the same times the same dull views to see,
The bounding marsh-bank and the blighted tree;
The water only when the tides were high,
When low, the mud half-covered and half-dry;
The sun-burnt tar that blisters on the planks,
And bank-side stakes in their uneven ranks;
Heaps of entangled weeds that slowly float,
As the tide rolls by the impeded boat.
When tides were neap, and in the sultry day,
Through the tall bounding mud-banks made their way,
Which on each side rose swelling, and below
The dark warm flood ran silently and slow;
There anchoring, Peter chose from man to hide,
There hang his head, and view the lazy tide
In its hot slimy channel slowly glide;

Where the small eels, that left the deeper way
For the warm shore, within the shallows play;
Where gaping muscles, left upon the mud,
Slope their slow passage to the fall'n flood :
Here dull and hopeless he'd lie down and trace
How side-long crabs had crawled their crooked race;
Or sadly listen to the tuneless cry
Of fishing-gull or clanging golden-eye;
What time the sea-birds to the marsh would come,
And the loud bittern, from the bull-rush home,
Gave from the salt-ditch-side the bellowing boom :
He nursed the feelings these dull scenes produce
And loved to stop beside the opening sluice;
Where the small stream, confined in narrow bound,
Ran with a dull, unvaried, saddening sound;
Where all, presented to the eye or ear,
Oppressed the soul with misery, grief, and fear.'[4]

This is an exact *fac-simile* of some of the most unlovely parts of the creation. Indeed the whole of Mr Crabbe's *Borough*, from which the above passage is taken, is done so to the life, that it seems almost like some sea-monster, crawled out of the neighbouring slime, and harbouring a breed of strange vermin, with a strong local scent of tar and bulge-water. Mr Crabbe's *Tales* are more readable than his *Poems*; but in proportion as the interest increases, they become more oppressive. They turn, one and all, upon the same sort of teazing, helpless, mechanical, unimaginative distress; – and though it is not easy to lay them down, you never wish to take them up again. Still in this way, they are highly finished, striking, and original portraits, worked out with an eye to nature, and an intimate knowledge of the small and intricate folds of the human heart. Some of the best are the *Confidant*, the story of *Silly Shore*, the *Young Poet*, the *Painter*. The episode of *Phœbe Dawson* in the *Village*, is one of the most tender and pensive; and the character of the methodist parson who persecutes the sailor's widow with his godly, selfish love is one of the most profound. In a word, if Mr Crabbe's writings do not add greatly to the store of entertaining and delightful fiction, yet they will remain, 'as a thorn in the side of poetry,' perhaps for a century to come!

From 'Mr Campbell and Mr Crabbe'
in *The Spirit of the Age* (1825).

MR LAMB

MR LAMB has a distaste to new faces, to new books, to new buildings, to new customs. He is shy of all imposing appearances, of all assumptions of self-importance, of all adventitious ornaments, of all mechanical advantages, even to a nervous excess. It is not merely that he does not rely upon, or ordinarily avail himself of them; he holds them in abhorrence, he utterly abjures and discards them, and places a great gulph between him and them. He disdains all the vulgar artifices of authorship, all the cant of criticism, and helps to notoriety. He has no grand swelling theories to attract the visionary and the enthusiast, no passing topics to allure the thoughtless and the vain. He evades the present, he mocks the future. His affections revert to, and settle on the past, but then, even this must have something personal and local in it to interest him deeply and thoroughly; he pitches his tent in the suburbs of existing manners; brings down the account of character to the few straggling remains of the last generation; seldom ventures beyond the bills of mortality, and occupies that nice point between egotism and disinterested humanity. No one makes the tour of our southern metropolis, or describes the manners of the last age, so well as Mr Lamb – with so fine, and yet so formal an air – with such vivid obscurity, with such arch piquancy, such picturesque quaintness, such smiling pathos. How admirably he has sketched the former inmates of the South-Sea House; what 'fine fretwork he makes of their double and single entries!' With what a firm, yet subtle pencil he has embodied *Mrs Battle's Opinions on Whist*! How notably he embalms a battered *beau*; how delightfully an amour, that was cold forty years ago, revives in his pages!

With what well-disguised humour, he introduces us to his relations, and how freely he serves up his friends! Certainly, some of his portraits are *fixtures*, and will do to hang up as lasting and lively emblems of human infirmity. Then there is no one who has so sure an ear for 'the chimes at midnight,' not even excepting Mr Justice Shallow; nor could Master Silence himself take his 'cheese and pippins' with a more significant and satisfactory air. With what a gusto Mr Lamb describes the inns and courts of law, the Temple and Gray's-Inn, as if he had been a student there for the last two hundred years, and had been as well acquainted with the person of Sir Francis Bacon as he is with his portrait or writings! It is hard to say whether St John's Gate is connected with more intense and authentic associations in his mind, as a part of old London Wall, or as the frontispiece (time out of mind) of the Gentleman's Magazine. He haunts Watling-street like a gentle spirit; the avenues to the playhouses are thick with panting recollections, and Christ's-Hospital still breathes the balmy breath of infancy in his description of it! Whittington and his Cat are a fine hallucination for Mr Lamb's historic Muse, and we believe he never heartily forgave a certain writer who took the subject of Guy Faux out of his hands.[1] The streets of London are his fairy-land, teeming with wonder, with life and interest to his retrospective glance, as it did to the eager eye of childhood; he has contrived to weave its tritest traditions into a bright and endless romance!

Mr Lamb's taste in books is also fine, and it is peculiar. It is not the worse for a little *idiosyncrasy*. He does not go deep into the Scotch novels,[2] but he is at home in Smollet or Fielding. He is little read in Junius or Gibbon, but no man can give a better account of Burton's Anatomy of Melancholy, or Sir Thomas Brown's Urn-Burial, or Fuller's Worthies, or John Bunyan's Holy War. No one is more unimpressible to a specious declamation; no one relishes a recondite beauty more. His admiration of Shakespear and Milton does not make him despise Pope; and he can read Parnell with patience, and Gay with delight. His taste in French and German literature is somewhat defective; nor has he made much progress in the science of Political Economy or other abstruse studies, though he has read vast folios of controversial divinity, merely for the sake of the intricacy of style, and to save himself the pain of thinking. Mr Lamb is a good judge of prints and pictures. His admiration of Hogarth does credit to both, particularly when it is considered that Leonardo da Vinci is his next greatest favourite, and that his love of the *actual* does not proceed from a want of taste for the *ideal*. His worst fault is a over-eagerness of enthusiasm, which occasionally makes him take a surfeit of his highest favourites. – Mr Lamb excels in familiar conversation almost as much as in writing, when his modesty does not overpower his self-possession. He is as little of a proser as possible; but he *blurts* out the finest wit and sense in the world. He keeps a good deal in the background at first, till some excellent conceit pushes him forward, and then he abounds in whim and pleasantry. There is a primitive simplicity and self-denial about his manners; and a Quakerism in his personal appearance, which is, however, relieved by a fine Titian head,[3] full of dumb eloquence! Mr Lamb is a general favourite with those who know him. His character is equally singular and amiable. He is endeared to his friends not less by his foibles than his virtues; he insures their esteeem by the one, and does not wound their self-love by the other. He gains ground in the opinion of others, by making no advances in his own. We easily admire genius where the diffidence of the possessor makes our acknowledgment of merit seem like a sort of patronage, or act of condescension, as we willingly extend our good offices where they are not exacted as obligations, or repaid with sullen indifference. – The style of the Essays of Elia is liable to the charge of a certain *mannerism*. His sentences are cast in the mould of old authors; his expressions are borrowed from them; but his feelings and observations are genuine and original, taken from actual life, or from his own breast; and he may be said (if any one can) 'to have coined his heart for *jests*,' and to have split his brain for fine distinctions! Mr Lamb, from the peculiarity of his exterior and address as an author, would probably never have made his way by detached and independent efforts; but, fortunately for himself and others, he has taken advantage of the Periodical Press, where he has been stuck into notice, and the texture of his compositions is assuredly fine enough to bear the broadest glare of popularity that has hitherto shone upon them. Mr Lamb's literary efforts have procured him civic honours (a thing unheard of in our times), and he has been invited, in his character of ELIA, to dine at a select party with the Lord Mayor.[4] We should prefer this distinction to that of being poet-laureat. We would recommend to Mr Waithman's perusal (if Mr Lamb has not anticipated us) the *Rosamond Gray* and the *John Woodvil* of the same author, as an agreeable relief to the noise of a City feast, and the heat of City elections. A friend, a short time ago, quoted some lines * from the last-mentioned of these works, which meeting Mr Godwin's eye, he was so struck with the beauty of the passage, and with a consciousness of having seen it before, that he was uneasy till he could recollect where, and after hunting in vain for it in Ben Jonson, Beaumont and Fletcher, and other not unlikely places, sent to Mr Lamb to know if he could help him to the author!

From 'Elia, and Geoffrey Crayon'
in *The Spirit of the Age* (1825).

* The description of sports in the forest:
     'To see the sun to bed and to arise,
      Like some hot amourist with glowing eyes,' &c.

THE TIMES NEWSPAPER

THE TIMES NEWSPAPER is, we suppose, entitled to the character it gives itself, of being the 'Leading Journal of Europe,' and is perhaps the greatest engine of temporary opinion in the world. Still it is not to our taste – either in matter or manner. It is elaborate, but heavy; full, but not readable: it is stuffed up with official documents, with matter-of-fact details. It seems intended to be deposited in the office of the Keeper of the Records, and might be imagined to be composed as well as printed with a steam-engine. It is pompous, dogmatical, and full of pretensions, but neither light, various, nor agreeable. It sells more, and contains more, than any other paper; and when you have said this, you have said all. It presents a most formidable front to the inexperienced reader. It makes a toil of pleasure. It is said to be calculated for persons in business, and yet it is the business of a whole morning to get through it. Bating voluminous details of what had better be omitted, the same things are better done in the Chronicle. To say nothing of poetry (which may be thought too frivolous and attenuated for the atmosphere of the city), the prose is inferior. No equally sterling articles can be referred to in it, either for argument or wit. More, in short, is effected in the Morning Chronicle, without the formality and without the effort. The Times is not a *classical* paper. It is a commercial paper, a paper of business, and it is conducted on principles of trade and business. It floats with the tide: it sails with the stream. It has no other principle, as we take it. It is not ministerial; it is not patriotic; but it is *civic*. It is the lungs of the British metropolis; the mouthpiece, oracle, and echo of the Stock Exchange; the representative of the mercantile interest. One would think so much gravity of style might be accompanied with more steadiness and weight of opinion. But *the* TIMES conforms to the changes of the time. It bears down upon a question, like a first-rate man of war, with streamers flying and all hands on deck; but if the first broadside does not answer, turns short upon it, like a triremed galley, firing off a few paltry squibs to cover its retreat. It takes up no falling cause; fights no up-hill battle; advocates no great principle; holds out a helping hand to no oppressed or obscure individual. It is 'ever strong upon the stronger side.' Its style is magniloquent; its spirit is not magnanimous. It is valiant, swaggering, insolent, with a hundred thousand readers at its heels; but the instant the rascal rout turn round with the 'whiff and wind' of some fell circumstance, the Times, the renegade, inconstant Times, turns with them! Let the mob shout, let the city roar, and the voice of the Times is heard above them all, with outrageous deafening clamour; but let the vulgar hubbub cease, and no whisper, no echo of it is ever after heard of in the Times. Like Bully Bottom in the play, it then 'aggravates its voice so, as if it were a singing dove, an it were any nightingale.' Its coarse ribaldry is turned to a harmless jest; its swelling rhodomontade sinks to a vapid commonplace; and the editor amuses himself in the interval, before another great explosion, by collecting and publishing from time to time, Affidavits of the number of his paper sold in the last stormy period of the press.

The Times rose into notice through its diligence and promptitude in furnishing Continental intelligence, at a time when foreign news was the most interesting commodity in the market; but at present it engrosses every other department. It grew obscene and furious during the revolutionary war; and the nicknames which Mr Walter[1] bestowed on the French Ruler were the counters with which he made his fortune. When the game of war and madness was over, and the proprietor wished to pocket his dear-bought gains quietly, he happened to have a writer in his employ[2] who wanted to roar on, as if any thing more was to be got by his continued war-whoop, and who scandalized the whole body of disinterested Jews, contractors, and stock-jobbers, by the din and smithery with which, in the piping times of peace, he was for rivetting on the chains of foreign nations. It was found, or thought at least, that this could not go on. The tide of gold no longer flowed up the river, and the tide of Billingsgate and blood could no longer flow down it, with any pretence to decency, morality, or religion. There is a cant of patriotism in the city: there is a cant of humanity among hackneyed politicians. The *writer* of the LEADING ARTICLE, it is true, was a fanatic; but the *proprietor* of the LEADING JOURNAL was neither a martyr nor confessor. The principles gave way to the policy of the paper; and this was the origin of the NEW TIMES.

This new Morning paper is one which every Tory ought to encourage. If the friend of the people cannot *away with* it, the friend of power ought not to be without it. Nay, it may be of use to the liberal or the wavering; for it goes all lengths, boggles at no consequences, and unmasks the features of despotism fearlessly and shamelessly, without remorse and without pity. The Editor deals in no half measures, in no half principles; but is a thorough-paced stickler for the modernized doctrines of passive obedience and non-resistance. Dr Sacheverel,[3] in his day, could not go beyond him. He is no flincher, no trimmer; he 'champions *Legitimacy* to the outrance.'

From 'The Periodical Press' in *Contributions to The Edinburgh Review* (1823).

DR JOHNSON

What most distinguishes Dr Johnson from other writers is the pomp and uniformity of his style. All his periods are cast in the same mould, are of the same size and shape, and consequently have little fitness to the variety of things he professes to treat of. His subjects are familiar, but the author is always upon stilts. He has neither ease nor simplicity, and his efforts at playfulness, in part, remind one of the lines in Milton:—

> '— The elephant
> To make them sport wreath'd his proboscis lithe.'

His Letters from Correspondents, in particular, are more pompous and unwieldy than what he writes in his own person. This want of relaxation and variety of manner has, I think, after the first effects of novelty and surprise were over, been prejudicial to the matter. It takes from the general power, not only to please, but to instruct. The monotony of style produces an apparent monotony of ideas. What is really striking and valuable, is lost in the vain ostentation and circumlocution of the expression; for when we find the same pains and pomp of diction bestowed upon the most trifling as upon the most important parts of a sentence or discourse, we grow tired of distinguishing between pretension and reality, and are disposed to confound the tinsel and bombast of the phraseology with want of weight in the thoughts. Thus, from the imposing and oracular nature of the style, people are tempted at first to imagine that our author's speculations are all wisdom and profundity: till having found out their mistake in some instances, they suppose that there is nothing but common-place in them, con-

cealed under verbiage and pedantry; and in both they are
wrong. The fault of Dr Johnson's style is, that it reduces all
things to the same artificial and unmeaning level. It destroys all shades of difference, the association between words
and things. It is a perpetual paradox and innovation. He
condescends to the familiar till we are ashamed of our interest in it: he expands the little till it looks big. 'If he were
to write a fable of little fishes,' as Goldsmith said of him, 'he
would make them speak like great whales.' We can no more
distinguish the most familiar objects in his descriptions of
them, than we can a well-known face under a huge painted
mask. The structure of his sentences, which was his own
invention, and which has been generally imitated since his
time, is a species rhyming in prose, where one clause answers to another in measure and quantity, like the tagging of
syllables at the end of a verse; the close of the period follows as mechanically as the oscillation of a pendulum, the
sense is balanced with the sound; each sentence, revolving
round its centre of gravity, is contained with itself like a
couplet, and each paragraph forms itself into a stanza. Dr
Johnson is also a complete balance-master in the topics of
morality. He never encourages hope, but he counteracts it by
fear; he never elicits a truth, but he suggests some objection
in answer to it. He seizes and alternately quits the clue of
reason, lest it should involve him in the labyrinths of endless error: he wants confidence in himself and his fellows.
He dares not trust himself with the immediate impressions
of things, for fear of compromising his dignity; or follow
them into their consequences, for fear of committing his
prejudices. His timidity is the result, not of ignorance, but of
morbid apprehension. 'He runs the great circle, and is still at
home.' No advance is made by his writings in any sentiment, or mode of reasoning. Out of the pale of established
authority and received dogmas, all is sceptical, loose, and
desultory: he seems in imagination to strengthen the

dominion of prejudice, as he weakens and dissipates that of reason; and round the rock of faith and power, on the edge of which he slumbers blindfold and uneasy, the waves and billows of uncertain and dangerous opinion roar and heave for evermore. His Rasselas is the most melancholy and debilitating moral speculation that ever was put forth. Doubtful of the faculties of his mind, as of his organs of vision, Johnson trusted only to his feelings and his fears. He cultivated a belief in witches as an out-guard to the evidences of religion; and abused Milton, and patronised Lauder,[1] in spite of his aversion to his countrymen, as a step to secure the existing establishment in church and state. This was neither right feeling nor sound logic.

The most triumphant record of the talents and character of Johnson is to be found in Boswell's Life of him. The man was superior to the author. When he threw aside his pen, which he regarded as an incumbrance, he became not only learned and thoughtful, but acute, witty, humorous, natural, honest; hearty and determined, 'the king of good fellows and wale of old men.' There are as many smart repartees, profound remarks, and keen invectives to be found in Boswell's 'inventory of all he said,' as are recorded of any celebrated man. The life and dramatic play of his conversation forms a contrast to his written works. His natural powers and undisguised opinions were called out in convivial intercourse. In public, he practised with the foils on: in private, he unsheathed the sword of controversy, and it was 'the Ebro's temper.'[2] The eagerness of opposition roused him from his natural sluggishness and acquired timidity; he returned blow for blow; and whether the trial were of argument or wit, none of his rivals could boast much of the encounter. Burke seems to have been the only person who had a chance with him: and it is the unpardonable sin of Boswell's work, that he has purposely omitted their combats of strength and skill. Goldsmith asked, 'Does he wind into a subject like a serpent, as Burke does?' And when exhausted with sickness, he himself said, 'If that fellow Burke were here now, he would kill me.' It is to be observed, that Johnson's colloquial style was as blunt, direct, and downright, as his style of studied composition was involved and circuitous. As when Topham Beauclerc and Langton knocked him up at his chambers, at three in the morning, and he came to the door with the poker in his hand, but seeing them, exclaimed, 'What is it you, my lads? then I'll have a frisk with you!' and he afterwards reproaches Langton, who was a literary milksop, for leaving them to go to an engagement 'with some *un-idead* girls.' What words to come from the mouth of the great moralist and lexicographer! His good deeds were as many as his good sayings. His domestic habits, his tenderness to servants, and readiness to oblige his friends; the quantity of strong tea that he drank to keep down sad thoughts; his many labours reluctantly begun, and irresolutely laid aside; his honest acknowledgement of his own, and indulgence to the weaknesses of others; his throwing himself back in the post-chaise with Boswell, and saying, 'Now I think I am a good-humoured fellow,' though nobody thought him so, and yet he was; his quitting the society of Garrick and his actresses, and his reason for it; his dining with Wilkes, and his kindness to Goldsmith; his sitting with the young ladies on his knee at the Mitre, to give them good advice, in which situation, if not explained, he might be taken for Falstaff; and last and noblest, his carrying the unfortunate victim of disease and dissipation on his back up through Fleet Street, (an act which realises the parable of the good Samaritan) – all these, and innumerable others, endear him to the reader, and must be remembered to his lasting honour. He had faults, but they lie buried with him. He had his prejudices and his intolerant feelings; but he suffered enough in the conflict of his own mind with them. For if no man can be happy in the free exercise of his reason, no wise man can be happy without it. His were not time-serving, heartless, hypocritical prejudices; but deep, inwoven, not to be rooted out but with life and hope, which he found from old habit necessary to his own peace of mind, and thought so to the peace of mankind. I do not hate, but love him for them. They were between himself and his conscience; and should be left to that higher tribunal, 'where they in trembling hope repose, the bosom of his Father and his God.' In a word, he has left behind him few wiser or better men.

> From 'On the Periodical Essayists' in *Lectures on the English Comic Writers* (1819).

DR JOHNSON AND SHAKESPEARE

DR JOHNSON's Preface to his edition of Shakespear looks like a laborious attempt to bury the characteristic merits of his author under a load of cumbrous phraseology, and to weigh his excellences and defects in equal scales, stuffed full of 'swelling figures and sonorous epithets.' Nor could it well be otherwise; Dr Johnson's general powers of reasoning overlaid his critical susceptibility. All his ideas were cast in a given mould, in a set form: they were made out by rule and system, by climax, inference, and antithesis: – Shakespear's were the reverse. Johnson's understanding dealt only in round numbers: the fractions were lost upon him. He reduced everything to the common standard of conventional propriety; and the most exquisite refinement or sublimity produced an effect on his mind, only as they could be translated into the language of measured prose. To him an excess of beauty was a fault; for it appeared to him like an excrescence; and his imagination was dazzled by the blaze of light. His writings neither shone with the beams of native genius, nor reflected them. The shifting shapes of fancy, the rainbow hues of things, made no impression on him: he seized only on the permanent and tangible. He had no idea of natural objects but 'such as he could measure with a two-foot rule, or tell upon ten fingers': he judged of human nature in the same way, by mood and figure: he saw only the definite, the positive, and the practical, the average forms of things, not their striking differences – their classes, not their degrees. He was a man of strong common sense and practical wisdom, rather than of genius or feeling. He retained the regular, habitual impressions of actual objects, but he could not follow the rapid flights of fancy, or the strong movements of passion. That is, he was to the poet what the painter of still life is to the painter of history. Common sense sympathises with the impressions of things on ordinary minds in ordinary circumstances: genius catches the glancing combinations presented to the eye of fancy, under the influence of passion. It is the province of the didactic reasoner to take cognizance of those results of human nature which are constantly repeated and always the same, which follow one another in regular succession, which are acted upon by large classes of men, and embodied in received customs, laws, language, and institutions; and it was in arranging, comparing, and arguing on these kind of general results, that Johnson's excellence lay. But he could not quit his hold of the common-place and mechanical, and apply the general rule to the particular exception, or shew how the nature of man was modified by the workings of passion, or the infinite fluctuations of thought and accident. Hence he could judge neither of the heights nor depths of poetry. Nor is this all; for being conscious of great powers in himself, and those powers of an adverse tendency to those of his author, he would be for setting up a foreign jurisdiction over poetry, and making criticism a kind of Procrustes' bed of genius, where he might cut down imagination to matter-of-fact, regulate the passions according to reason, and translate the whole into logical diagrams and rhetorical declamation. Thus he says of Shakespear's characters, in contradiction to what Pope had observed, and to what every one else feels, that each character is a species, instead of being an individual. He in fact found the general species or *didactic* form in Shakespear's characters, which was all he sought or cared for; he did not find the individual traits, or the *dramatic* distinctions which Shakespear has engrafted on this general nature, because he felt no interest in them. Shakespear's bold and happy flights of imagination were equally thrown away upon our author. He was not only without any particular fineness of organic sensibility, alive to all the 'mighty world of ear and eye,' which is necessary to the painter or musician, but without that intenseness of passion, which, seeking to exaggerate whatever excites the feelings of pleasure or power in the mind, and moulding the impressions of natural objects according to the impulses of imagination, produces a genius and a taste for poetry. According to Dr Johnson, a mountain is sublime, or a rose is beautiful; for that their name and definition imply. But he would no more be able to give the description of Dover cliff in *Lear*, or the description of flowers in *The Winter's Tale*, than to describe the objects of a sixth sense; nor do we think he would have any very profound feeling of the beauty of the passages here referred to. A stately common-place, such as Congreve's description of a ruin in the *Mourning Bride*, would have answered Johnson's purpose just as well, or better than the first; and an indiscriminate profusion of scents and hues would have interfered less with the ordinary routine of his imagination than Perdita's lines, which seem enamoured of their own sweetness –

> – 'Daffodils
> That come before the swallow dares, and take
> The winds of March with beauty; violets dim,
> But sweeter than the lids of Juno's eyes,
> Or Cytherea's breath.' –

From Preface to *Characters of Shakespear's Plays* (1817).

MONTAIGNE[1]

THE great merit of Montaigne was, that he may be said to have been the first who had the courage to say as an author what he felt as a man. And as courage is generally the effect of conscious strength, he was probably led to do so by the richness, truth, and force of his own observations on books and men. He was, in the truest sense, a man of original mind, that is, he had the power of looking at things for himself, or as they really were, instead of blindly trusting to, and fondly repeating what others told him that they were. He got rid of the go-cart of prejudice and affectation, with the learned lumber that follows at their heels, because he could do without them. In taking up his pen he did not set up for a philosopher, wit, orator, or moralist, but he became all these by merely daring to tell us whatever passed through his mind, in its naked simplicity and force, that he thought any ways worth communicating. He did not, in the abstract character of an author, undertake to say all that could be said upon a subject, but what in his capacity as an inquirer after truth he happened to know about it. He was neither a pedant nor a bigot. He neither supposed that he was bound to know all things, nor that all things were bound to conform to what he had fancied or would have them to be. In treating of men and manners, he spoke of them as he found them, not according to preconceived notions and abstract dogmas; and he began by teaching us what he himself was. In criticising books he did not compare them with rules and systems, but told us what he saw to like or dislike in them. He did not take his standard of excellence 'according to an exact scale' of Aristotle, or fall out with a work that was good for any thing, because 'not one of the angles at the four corners was a right one.' He was, in a word, the first author who was not a book-maker, and who wrote not to make converts of others to established creeds and prejudices, but to satisfy his own mind of the truth of things. In this respect we know not which to be most charmed with, the author or the man. There is an inexpressible frankness and sincerity, as well as power, in what he writes. There is no attempt at imposition or concealment, no juggling tricks or solemn mouthing, no laboured attempts at proving himself always in the right, and every body else in the wrong; he says what is uppermost, lays open what floats at the top or the bottom of his mind, and deserves Pope's character of him, where he professes to

> '– pour out all as plain
> As downright Shippen, or as old Montaigne.'

He does not converse with us like a pedagogue with his pupil, whom he wishes to make as great a blockhead as himself, but like a philosopher and friend who has passed through life with thought and observation, and is willing to enable others to pass through it with pleasure and profit. A writer of this stamp, I confess, appears to me as much superior to a common bookworm, as a library of real books is superior to a mere book-case, painted and lettered on the outside with the names of celebrated works. As he was the first to attempt this new way of writing, so the same strong natural impulse which prompted the undertaking, carried him to the end of his career. The same force and honesty of mind which urged him to throw off the shackles of custom and prejudice, would enable him to complete his triumph over them. He has left little for his successors to achieve in the way of just and original speculation on human life. Nearly all the thinking of the two last centuries of that kind which the French denominate *morale observatrice*, is to be found in Montaigne's Essays: there is the germ, at least, and generally much more. He sowed the seed and cleared away the rubbish, even where others have reaped the fruit, or cultivated and decorated the soil to a greater degree of nicety and perfection. There is no one to whom the old Latin adage is more applicable than to Montaigne, *'Pereant isti qui ante nostra dixerunt.'* There has been no new impulse given to thought since his time. Among the specimens of criticisms on authors which he has left us, are those on Virgil, Ovid, and Boccaccio, in the account of books which he thinks worth reading, or (which is the same thing) which he finds he can read in his old age, and which may be reckoned among the few criticisms which are worth reading at any age.

From 'On the Periodical Essayists' in *Lectures on the English Comic Writers* (1819).

WILLIAM SHAKESPEARE

IT has been said by some critic, that Shakespear was distinguished from the other dramatic writers of his day only by his wit; that they had all his other qualities but that; one writer had as much sense, another as much fancy, another as much knowledge of character, another the same depth of passion, and another as great a power of language. This statement is not true; nor is the inference from it well-founded, even if it were. This person does not seem to have been aware that, upon his own shewing, the great distinction of Shakespear's genius was its virtually including the genius of all the great men of his age, and not his differing from them in one accidental particular. But to have done with such minute and literal trifling.

The striking peculiarity of Shakespear's mind was its generic quality, its power of communication with all other minds – so that it contained a universe of thought and feeling within itself, and had no one peculiar bias, or exclusive excellence more than another. He was just like any other man, but that he was like all other men. He was the least of an egotist that it was possible to be. He was nothing in himself; but he was all that others were, or that they could become. He not only had in himself the germs of every faculty and feeling, but he could follow them by anticipation, intuitively, into all their conceivable ramifications, through every change of fortune or conflict of passion, or turn of thought. He had 'a mind reflecting ages past,'[1] and present: – all the people that ever lived are there. There was no respect of persons with him. His genius shone equally on the evil and on the good, on the wise and the foolish, the monarch and the beggar: 'All corners of the earth, kings, queens, and states, maids, matrons, nay, the secrets of the grave,' are hardly hid from his searching glance. He was like the genius of humanity, changing places with all of us at pleasure, and playing with our purposes as with his own. He turned the globe round for his amusement, and surveyed the generations of men, and the individuals as they passed, with their different concerns, passions, follies, vices, virtues, actions, and motives – as well those that they knew, as those which they did not know, or acknowledge to themselves. The dreams of childhood, the ravings of despair, were the toys of his fancy. Airy beings waited at his call, and came at his bidding. Harmless fairies 'nodded to him, and did him curtesies': and the night-hag bestrode the blast at the command of 'his so potent art.' The world of spirits lay open to him, like the world of real men and women: and there is the same truth in his delineations of the one as of the other; for if the preternatural characters he describes could be supposed to exist, they would speak, and feel, and act, as he makes them. He had only to think of any thing in order to become that thing, with all the circumstances belonging to it. When he conceived of a character, whether real or imaginary, he not only entered into all its thoughts and feelings, but seemed instantly, and as if by touching a secret spring, to be surrounded with all the same objects, 'subject to the same skyey influences,' the same local, outward, and unforeseen accidents which would occur in reality. Thus the character of Caliban not only stands before us with a language and manners of its own, but the scenery and situation of the enchanted island he inhabits, the traditions of the place, its strange noises, its hidden recesses, 'his frequent haunts and ancient neighbourhood,' are given with a miraculous truth of nature, and with all the familiarity of an old recollection. The whole 'coheres semblably together' in time, place, and circumstance. In reading this author, you do not merely learn what his characters say, – you see their persons. By something expressed or understood, you are at no loss to decypher their peculiar physiognomy, the meaning of a look, the grouping, the bye-play, as we might see it on the stage. A word, an epithet paints a whole scene, or throws us back whole years in the history of the person represented.

From 'On Shakespear and Milton' in *Lectures on the English Poets* (1818).

HAMLET

THIS is that Hamlet the Dane, whom we read of in our youth, and whom we may be said almost to remember in our after-years; he who made that famous soliloquy on life, who gave the advice to the players, who thought 'this goodly frame, the earth, a steril promontory, and this brave o'er-hanging firmament, the air, this majestical roof fretted with golden fire, a foul and pestilent congregation of vapours'; whom 'man delighted not, nor woman neither'; he who talked with the grave-diggers, and moralised on Yorick's skull; the school-fellow of Rosencranz and Guilderstern at Wittenberg; the friend of Horatio; the lover of Ophelia; he that was mad and sent to England; the slow avenger of his father's death; who lived at the court of Horwendillus five hundred years before we were born, but all whose thoughts we seem to know as well as we do our own, because we have read them in Shakespear.

Hamlet is a name; his speeches and sayings but the idle coinage of the poet's brain. What then, are they not real? They are as real as our own thoughts. Their reality is in the reader's mind. It is *we* who are Hamlet. This play has a prophetic truth, which is above that of history. Whoever has become thoughtful and melancholy through his own mis-haps or those of others; whoever has borne about with him the clouded brow of reflection, and thought himself 'too much i' th' sun'; whoever has seen the golden lamp of day dimmed by envious mists rising in his own breast, and could find in the world before him only a dull blank with nothing left remarkable in it; whoever has known 'the pangs of despised love, the insolence of office, or the spurns which patient merit of the unworthy takes'; he who has felt his mind sink within him, and sadness cling to his heart like a malady, who has had his hopes blighted and his youth staggered by the apparitions of strange things; who cannot be well at ease, while he sees evil hovering near him like a spectre; whose powers of action have been eaten up by thought, he to whom the universe seems infinite, and himself nothing; whose bitterness of soul makes him careless of consequences, and who goes to a play as his best resource to shove off, to a second remove, the evils of life by a mock representation of them – this is the true Hamlet.

We have been so used to this tragedy that we hardly know how to criticise it any more than we should know how to describe our own faces. But we must make such observations as we can. It is the one of Shakespear's plays that we think of the oftenest, because it abounds most in striking reflections on human life, and because the distresses of Hamlet are transferred, by the turn of his mind, to the general account of humanity. Whatever happens to him we apply to ourselves, because he applies it so himself as a means of general reasoning. He is a great moraliser; and what makes him worth attending to is, that he moralises on his own feelings and experience. He is not a common-place pedant. If *Lear* is distinguished by the greatest depth of passion, HAMLET is the most remarkable for the ingenuity, originality, and unstudied developement of character. Shakespear had more magnanimity than any other poet, and he has shewn more of it in this play than in any other. There is no attempt to force an interest: every thing is left for time and circumstances to unfold. The attention is excited without effort, the incidents succeed each other as matters of course, the characters think and speak and act just as they might do, if left entirely to themselves. There is no set purpose, no straining at a point. The observations are suggested by the passing scene – the gusts of passion come and go like sounds of music borne on the wind. The whole play is an exact transcript of what might be supposed to have taken place at the court of Denmark, at the remote period of time fixed upon, before the modern refinements in morals and manners were heard of. It would have been interesting enough to have been admitted as a by-stander in such a scene, at such a time, to have heard and witnessed something of what was going on. But here we are more than spectators. We have not only 'the outward pageants and the signs of grief'; but 'we have that within which passes shew.' We read the thoughts of the heart, we catch the passions living as they rise. Other dramatic writers give us very fine versions and paraphrases of nature; but Shakespear, together with his own comments, gives us the original text, that we may judge for ourselves. This is a very great advantage.

From *Characters of Shakespear's Plays* (1817).

ROMEO AND JULIET

ROMEO AND JULIET is the only tragedy which Shakespear has written entirely on a love-story. It is supposed to have been his first play, and it deserves to stand in that proud rank. There is the buoyant spirit of youth in every line, in the rapturous intoxication of hope, and in the bitterness of despair. It has been said of ROMEO AND JULIET by a great critic, that 'whatever is most intoxicating in the odour of a southern spring, languishing in the song of the nightingale, or voluptuous in the first opening of the rose, is to be found in this poem.' The description is true; and yet it does not answer to our idea of the play. For if it has the sweetness of the rose, it has its freshness too; if it has the languor of the nightingale's song, it has also its giddy transport; if it has the softness of a southern spring, it is as glowing and as bright. There is nothing of a sickly and sentimental cast. Romeo and Juliet are in love, but they are not love-sick. Every thing speaks the very soul of pleasure, the high and healthy pulse of the passions: the heart beats, the blood circulates and mantles throughout. Their courtship is not an insipid interchange of sentiments lip-deep, learnt at second-hand from poems and plays, – made up of beauties of the most shadowy kind, of 'fancies wan that hang the pensive head,' of evanescent smiles, and sighs that breathe not, of delicacy that shrinks from the touch, and feebleness that scarce supports itself, an elaborate vacuity of thought, and an artificial dearth of sense, spirit, truth, and nature! It is the reverse of all this. It is Shakespear all over, and Shakespear when he was young.

We have heard it objected to ROMEO AND JULIET, that it is founded on an idle passion between a boy and a girl, who have scarcely seen and can have but little sympathy or rational esteem for one another, who have had no experience of the good or ills of life, and whose raptures or despair must be therefore equally groundless and fantastical. Whoever objects to the youth of the parties in this play as 'too unripe and crude' to pluck the sweets of love, and wishes to see a first-love carried on into a good old age, and the passions taken at the rebound, when their force is spent, may find all this done in the *Stranger* and in other German plays,[1] where they do things by contraries, and transpose nature to inspire sentiment and create philosophy. Shakespear proceeded in a more strait-forward, and, we think, effectual way. He did not endeavour to extract beauty from wrinkles, or the wild throb of passion from the last expiring sigh of indifference. He did not 'gather grapes of thorns nor figs of thistles.' It was not his way. But he has given a picture of human life, such as it is in the order of nature. He has founded the passion of the two lovers not on the pleasures they had experienced, but on all the pleasures they had *not* experienced. All that was to come of life was theirs. At that untried source of promised happiness they slaked their thirst, and the first eager draught made them drunk with love and joy. They were in full possession of their senses and their affections. Their hopes were of air, their desires of fire. Youth is the season of love, because the heart is then first melted in tenderness from the touch of novelty, and kindled to rapture, for it knows no end of its enjoyments or its wishes. Desire has no limit but itself. Passion, the love and expectation of pleasure, is infinite, extravagant, inexhaustible, till experience comes to check and kill it. Juliet exclaims on her first interview with Romeo —

> 'My bounty is as boundless as the sea,
> My love as deep.'

And why should it not? What was to hinder the thrilling

tide of pleasure, which had just gushed from her heart, from flowing on without stint or measure, but experience which she was yet without? What was to abate the transport of the first sweet sense of pleasure, which her heart and her senses had just tasted, but indifference which she was yet a stranger to? What was there to check the ardour of hope, of faith, of constancy, just rising in her breast, but disappointment which she had not yet felt! As are the desires and the hopes of youthful passion, such is the keenness of its disappointments, and their baleful effect. Such is the transition in this play from the highest bliss to the lowest despair, from the nuptial couch to an untimely grave. The only evil that even in apprehension befalls the two lovers is the loss of the greatest possible felicity; yet this loss is fatal to both, for they had rather part with life than bear the thought of surviving all that had made life dear to them. In all this, Shakespear has but followed nature, which existed in his time, as well as now. The modern philosophy, which reduces the whole theory of the mind to habitual impressions, and leaves the natural impulses of passion and imagination out of the account, had not then been discovered; or if it had, would have been little calculated for the uses of poetry.

It is the inadequacy of the same false system of philosophy to account for the strength of our earliest attachments, which has led Mr Wordsworth to indulge in the mystical visions of Platonism in his Ode on the Progress of Life.[2] He has very admirably described the vividness of our impressions in youth and childhood, and how 'they fade by degrees into the light of common day,' and he ascribes the change to the supposition of a pre-existent state, as if our early thoughts were nearer heaven, reflections of former trails of glory, shadows of our past being. This is idle. It is not from the knowledge of the past that the first impressions of things derive their gloss and splendour, but from our ignorance of the future, which fills the void to come with the warmth of our desires, with our gayest hopes, and brightest fancies. It is the obscurity spread before it that colours the prospect of life with hope, as it is the cloud which reflects the rainbow. There is no occasion to resort to any mystical union and transmission of feeling through different states of being to account for the romantic enthusiasm of youth; nor to plant the root of hope in the grave, nor to derive it from the skies. Its root is in the heart of man: it lifts its head above the stars. Desire and imagination are inmates of the human breast. The heaven 'that lies about us in our infancy' is only a new world, of which we know nothing but what we wish it to be, and believe all that we wish. In youth and boyhood, the world we live in is the world of desire, and of fancy: it is experience that brings us down to the world of reality. What is it that in youth sheds a dewy light round the evening star? That makes the daisy look so bright? That perfumes the hyacinth? That embalms the first kiss of love? It is the delight of novelty, and the seeing no end to the pleasure that we fondly believe is still in store for us. The heart revels in the luxury of its own thoughts, and is unable to sustain the weight of hope and love that presses upon it. – The effects of the passion of love alone might have dissipated Mr Wordsworth's theory, if he means any thing more by it than an ingenious and poetical allegory. *That* at least is not a link in the chain let down from other worlds; 'the purple light of love' is not a dim reflection of the smiles of celestial bliss. It does not appear till the middle of life, and then seems like 'another morn risen on mid-day.' In this respect the soul comes into the world 'in utter nakedness.' Love waits for the ripening of the youthful blood. The sense of pleasure precedes the love of pleasure, but with the sense of pleasure, as soon as it is felt, come thronging infinite desires and hopes of pleasure, and love is mature as soon as born. It withers and it dies almost as soon!

This play presents a beautiful *coup-d'œil* of the progress

of human life. In thought it occupies years, and embraces the circle of the affections from childhood to old age. Juliet has become a great girl, a young woman since we first remember her a little thing in the idle prattle of the nurse. Lady Capulet was about her age when she became a mother, and old Capulet somewhat impatiently tells his younger visitors,

> – 'I've seen the day
> That I have worn a visor, and could tell
> A whispering tale in a fair lady's ear,
> Such as would please: 'tis gone, 'tis gone, 'tis gone.'

Thus one period of life makes way for the following, and one generation pushes another off the stage. One of the most striking passages to show the intense feeling of youth in this play is Capulet's invitation to Paris to visit his entertainment.

> 'At my poor house, look to behold this night
> Earth-treading stars that make dark heav'n light;
> Such comfort as do lusty young men feel
> When well-apparel'd April on the heel
> Of limping winter treads, even such delight
> Among fresh female-buds shall you this night
> Inherit at my house.'

The feelings of youth and of the spring are here blended together like the breath of opening flowers.

From *Characters of Shakespear's Plays* (1817).

CORIOLANUS[1]

SHAKESPEAR has in this play shewn himself well versed in history and state-affairs. CORIOLANUS is a store-house of political common-places. Any one who studies it may save himself the trouble of reading Burke's Reflections, or Paine's Rights of Man, or the Debates in both Houses of Parliament since the French Revolution or our own. The arguments for and against aristocracy or democracy, on the privileges of the few and the claims of the many, on liberty and slavery, power and the abuse of it, peace and war, are here very ably handled, with the spirit of a poet and the acuteness of a philosopher. Shakespear himself seems to have had a leaning to the arbitrary side of the question, perhaps from some feeling of contempt for his own origin; and to have spared no occasion of baiting the rabble. What he says of them is very true: what he says of their betters is also very true, though he dwells less upon it. – The cause of the people is indeed but little calculated as a subject for poetry: it admits of rhetoric, which goes into argument and explanation, but it presents no immediate or distinct images to the mind, 'no jutting frieze, buttress, or coigne of vantage' for poetry 'to make its pendant bed and procreant cradle in.' The language of poetry naturally falls in with the language of power. The imagination is an exaggerating and exclusive faculty: it takes from one thing to add to another: it accumulates circumstances together to give the greatest possible effect to a favourite object. The understanding is a dividing and measuring faculty: it judges of things not according to their immediate impression on the mind, but according to their relations to one another. The one is a monopolising faculty,

which seeks the greatest quantity of present excitement by
inequality and disproportion; the other is a distributive
faculty, which seeks the greatest quantity of ultimate good,
by justice and proportion. The one is an aristocratical, the
other a republican faculty. The principle of poetry is a very
anti-levelling principle. It aims at effect, it exists by contrast.
It admits of no medium. It is every thing by excess. It
rises above the ordinary standard of sufferings and crimes. It
presents a dazzling appearance. It shows its head turretted,
crowned, and crested. Its front is gilt and blood-stained.
Before it 'it carries noise, and behind it leaves tears.' It has
its altars and its victims, sacrifices, human sacrifices. Kings,
priests, nobles, are its train-bearers, tyrants and slaves its
executioners. – 'Carnage is its daughter.' [2] – Poetry is right-
royal. It puts the individual for the species, the one above
the infinite many, might before right. A lion hunting a flock
of sheep or a herd of wild asses is a more poetical object than
they; and we even take part with the lordly beast, because
our vanity or some other feeling makes us disposed to place
ourselves in the situation of the strongest party. So we feel
some concern for the poor citizens of Rome when they
meet together to compare their wants and grievances, till
Coriolanus comes in and with blows and big words drives
this set of 'poor rats,' this rascal scum, to their homes and
beggary before him. There is nothing heroical in a multitude of miserable rogues not wishing to be starved, or complaining that they are like to be so: but when a single man
comes forward to brave their cries and to make them submit
to the last indignities, from mere pride and self-will, our
admiration of his prowess is immediately converted into contempt for their pusillanimity. The insolence of power is
stronger than the plea of necessity. The tame submission to
usurped authority or even the natural resistance to it has
nothing to excite or flatter the imagination: it is the assumption of a right to insult or oppress others that carries an

imposing air of superiority with it. We had rather be the oppressor than the oppressed. The love of power in ourselves and the admiration of it in others are both natural to man: the one makes him a tyrant, the other a slave. Wrong dressed out in pride, pomp, and circumstance, has more attraction than abstract right. – Coriolanus complains of the fickleness of the people: yet, the instant he cannot gratify his pride and obstinacy at their expense, he turns his arms against his country. If his country was not worth defending, why did he build his pride on its defence? He is a conqueror and a hero; he conquers other countries, and makes this a plea for enslaving his own; and when he is prevented from doing so, he leagues with its enemies to destroy his country. He rates the people 'as if he were a God to punish, and not a man of their infirmity.' He scoffs at one of their tribunes for maintaining their rights and franchises: 'Mark you his absolute *shall*?' not marking his own absolute *will* to take every thing from them, his impatience of the slightest opposition to his own pretensions being in proportion to their arrogance and absurdity. If the great and powerful had the beneficence and wisdom of Gods, then all this would have been well: if with a greater knowledge of what is good for the people, they had as great a care for their interest as they have themselves, if they were seated above the world, sympathising with the welfare, but not feeling the passions of men, receiving neither good nor hurt from them, but bestowing their benefits as free gifts on them, they might then rule over them like another Providence. But this is not the case. Coriolanus is unwilling that the senate should shew their 'cares' for the people, lest their 'cares' should be construed into 'fears,' to the subversion of all due authority; and he is no sooner disappointed in his schemes to deprive the people not only of the cares of the state, but of all power to redress themselves, than Volumnia is made madly to exclaim,

'Now the red pestilence strike all trades in Rome,
And occupations perish.'

This is but natural: it is but natural for a mother to have
more regard for her son than for a whole city; but then the
city should be left to take some care of itself. The care of the
state cannot, we here see, be safely entrusted to maternal
affection, or the domestic charities of high life. The great
have private feelings of their own, to which the interests of
humanity and justice must courtesy. Their interests are so
far from being the same as those of the community, that
they are in direct and necessary opposition to them; their
power is at the expense of *our* weakness; their riches of *our*
poverty; their pride of *our* degradation; their splendour of
our wretchedness; their tyranny of *our* servitude. If they had
the superior knowledge ascribed to them (which they have
not) it would only render them so much more formidable;
and from Gods would convert them into Devils. The
whole dramatic moral of CORIOLANUS is that those who
have little shall have less, and that those who have much
shall take all that others have left. The people are poor;
therefore they ought to be starved. They are slaves; therefore they ought to be beaten. They work hard; therefore
they ought to be treated like beasts of burden. They are ignorant; therefore they ought not to be allowed to feel that
they want food, or clothing, or rest, that they are enslaved,
oppressed, and miserable. This is the logic of the imagination and the passions; which seek to aggrandize what excites admiration and to heap contempt on misery, to raise
power into tyranny, and to make tyranny absolute; to thrust
down that which is low still lower, and to make wretches
desperate: to exalt magistrates into kings, kings into gods; to
degrade subjects to the ranks of slaves, and slaves to the condition of brutes. The history of mankind is a romance, a
mask, a tragedy, constructed upon the principles of *poetical*

justice; it is a noble or royal hunt, in which what is sport to the few is death to the many,[3] and in which the spectators halloo and encourage the strong to set upon the weak, and cry havoc in the chase though they do not share in the spoil. We may depend upon it that what men delight to read in books, they will put in practice in reality.

From *Characters of Shakespear's Plays* (1817).

ON THE *BEGGAR'S OPERA*[1]

We have begun this Essay on a very coarse sheet of damaged foolscap, and we find that we are going to write it, whether for the sake of contrast, or from having a very fine pen, in a remarkably nice hand. Something of a similar process seems to have taken place in Gay's mind, when he composed his *Beggar's Opera*. He chose a very unpromising ground to work upon, and he has prided himself in adorning it with all the graces, the precision and brilliancy of style. It is a vulgar error to call this a vulgar play. So far from it, that we do not scruple to declare our opinion that it is one of the most refined productions in the language. The elegance of the composition is in exact proportion to the coarseness of the materials: by 'happy alchemy of mind,' the author has extracted an essence of refinement from the dregs of human life, and turns its very dross into gold. The scenes, characters, and incidents are, in themselves, of the lowest and most disgusting kind: but, by the sentiments and reflections which are put into the mouths of highwaymen, turnkeys, their mistresses, wives, or daughters, he has converted this motley group into a set of fine gentlemen and ladies, satirists and philosophers. He has also effected this transformation without once violating probability, or 'o'erstepping the modesty of nature.' In fact Gay has turned the tables on the critics; and by the assumed licence of the mock-heroic style, has enabled himself to *do justice to nature*, that is, to give all the force, truth, and locality of real feeling to the thoughts and expressions, without being called to the bar of false taste and affected delicacy. The extreme beauty and feeling of the song, 'Woman is like the fair flower in its lustre,' is only equalled by its characteristic propriety and *naïveté*. It may be said that this is taken from Tibullus; but there is nothing about Covent Garden in Tibullus. *Polly* describes her lover going to the gallows with the same touching simplicity, and with all the natural fondness of a young girl in her circumstances, who sees in his approaching catastrophe nothing but the misfortunes and the personal accomplishments of the object of her affections. 'I see him sweeter than the nosegay in his hand: the admiring crowd lament that so lovely a youth should come to an untimely end: – even butchers weep, and Jack Ketch refuses his fee rather than consent to tie the fatal knot.' The preservation of the character and costume is complete. It has been said by a great authority, 'There is some soul of goodness in things evil': and the *Beggar's Opera* is a goodnatured but instructive comment on this text. The poet has thrown all the gaiety and sunshine of the imagination, all the intoxication of pleasure, and the vanity of despair, round the short-lived existence of his heroes; while *Peachum* and *Lockitt* are seen in the back-ground, parcelling out their months and weeks between them. The general view exhibited of human life, is of the most masterly and abstracted kind. The author has, with great felicity, brought out the good qualities and interesting emotions almost inseparable from the lowest conditions; and with the same penetrating glance has detected the disguises which rank and circumstances lend to exalted vice. Every line in this sterling comedy sparkles with wit, and is fraught with the keenest sarcasm. The very wit, however, takes off from the offensiveness of the satire; and we have seen great statesmen, very great statesmen, heartily enjoying the joke, laughing most immoderately at the compliments paid to them as not much worse than pickpockets and cut-throats in a different line of life, and pleased, as it were, to see themselves humanised by some sort of fellowship with their kind. Indeed, it may be said that the moral of the piece is to show the *vulgarity* of vice; and that the

same violations of integrity and decorum, the same habitual
sophistry in palliating their want of principle, are common
to the great and powerful, with the lowest and most contemptible of the species. What can be more convincing than
the arguments used by these would-be politicians, to shew
that in hypocrisy, selfishness, and treachery, they do not
come up to many of their betters? The exclamation of *Mrs
Peachum*, when her daughter marries *Macheath*, 'Hussey,
hussey, you will be as ill used, and as much neglected, as if
you had married a lord,' is worth all Miss Hannah More's
laboured invectives[2] on the laxity of the manners of high
life!

From *The Round Table* (1817).

LIBER AMORIS:
or The New Pygmalion[1]

Part I

THE PICTURE

H. OH! is it you? I had something to shew you – I have got a picture here. Do you know any one it's like?

S. No, Sir.

H. Don't you think it like yourself?

S. No: it's much handsomer than I can pretend to be.

H. That's because you don't see yourself with the same eyes that others do. *I* don't think it handsomer, and the expression is hardly so fine as your's sometimes is.

S. Now you flatter me. Besides, the complexion is fair, and mine is dark.

H. Thine is pale and beautiful, my love, not dark! But if your colour were a little heightened, and you wore the same dress, and your hair were let down over your shoulders, as it is here, it might be taken for a picture of you. Look here, only see how like it is. The forehead is like, with that little obstinate protrusion in the middle; the eyebrows are like, and the eyes are just like your's, when you look up and say – 'No – never!'

S. What then, do I always say – 'No – never!' when I look up?

H. I don't know about that – I never heard you say so but once; but that was once too often for my peace. It was when you told me, 'you could never be mine.' Ah! if you are never to be mine, I shall not long be myself. I cannot go on as I am. My faculties leave me: I think of nothing, I have no feeling about any thing but thee: thy sweet image has taken possession of me, haunts me, and will drive me to distraction. Yet I could almost wish to go mad for thy sake: for then I might fancy that I had thy love in return, which I cannot live without!

s. Do not, I beg, talk in that manner, but tell me what this is a picture of.

H. I hardly know; but it is a very small and delicate copy (painted in oil on a gold ground) of some fine old Italian picture, Guido's or Raphael's, but I think Raphael's. Some say it is a Madona; others call it a Magdalen, and say you may distinguish the tear upon the cheek, though no tear is there. But it seems to me more like Raphael's St Cecilia, 'with looks commercing with the skies,' than anything else. – See, Sarah, how beautiful it is! Ah! dear girl, these are the ideas I have cherished in my heart, and in my brain; and I never found any thing to realise them on earth till I met with thee, my love! While thou didst seem sensible of my kindness, I was but too happy: but now thou hast cruelly cast me off.

s. You have no reason to say so: you are the same to me as ever.

H. That is, nothing. You are to me everything, and I am nothing to you. Is it not too true?

s. No.

H. Then kiss me, my sweetest. Oh! could you see your face now – your mouth full of suppressed sensibility, your downcast eyes, the soft blush upon that cheek, you would not say the picture is not like because it is too handsome, or because you want complexion. Thou art heavenly-fair, my love – like her from whom the picture was taken – the idol of the painter's heart, as thou art of mine! Shall I make a drawing of it, altering the dress a little, to shew you how like it is?

s. As you please.

THE INVITATION

H. But I am afraid I tire you with this prosing description of the French character and abuse of the English? You know there is but one subject on which I should ever wish to talk, if you would let me.

s. I must say, you don't seem to have a very high opinion of this country.

H. Yes, it is the place that gave you birth.

s. Do you like the French women better than the English?

H. No: though they have finer eyes, talk better, and are better made. But they none of them look like you. I like the Italian women I have seen, much better than the French: they have darker eyes, darker hair, and the accents of their native tongue are much richer and more melodious. But I will give you a better account of them when I come back from Italy, if you would like to hear it.

s. I should much. It is for that I have sometimes had a wish for travelling abroad, to understand something of the manners and characters of different people.

H. My sweet girl! I will give you the best account I can — unless you would rather go and judge for yourself.

s. I cannot.

H. Yes, you shall go with me, and you shall go *with honour* — you know what I mean.

s. You know it is not in your power to take me so.

H. But it soon may: and if you would consent to bear me company, I would swear never to think of an Italian woman while I am abroad, nor of an English one after I return home. Thou art to me more than thy whole sex.

s. I require no such sacrifices.

H. Is that what you thought I meant by *sacrifices* last night? But sacrifices are no sacrifices when they are repaid a thousand fold.

s. I have no way of doing it.

h. You have not the will. –

s. I must go now.

h. Stay, and hear me a little. I shall soon be where I can no more hear thy voice, far distant from her I love, to see what change of climate and bright skies will do for a sad heart. I shall perhaps see thee no more, but I shall still think of thee the same as ever – I shall say to myself, 'Where is she now? – what is she doing?' But I shall hardly wish you to think of me, unless you could do so more favourably than I am afraid you will. Ah! dearest creature, I shall be 'far distant from you,' as you once said of another, but you will not think of me as of him, 'with the sincerest affection.' The smallest share of thy tenderness would make me blest; but couldst thou ever love me as thou didst him, I should feel like a God! My face would change to a different expression: my whole form would undergo alteration. I was getting well, I was growing young in the sweet proofs of your friendship: you see how I droop and wither under your displeasure! Thou art divine, my love, and canst make me either more or less than mortal. Indeed I am thy creature, thy slave – I only wish to live for your sake – I would gladly die for you –

s. That would give me no pleasure. But indeed you greatly overrate my power.

h. Your power over me is that of sovereign grace and beauty. When I am near thee, nothing can harm me. Thou art an angel of light, shadowing me with thy softness. But when I let go thy hand, I stagger on a precipice: out of thy sight the world is dark to me and comfortless. There is no breathing out of this house: the air of Italy will stifle me. Go with me and lighten it. I can know no pleasure away from thee –

> 'But I will come again, my love,
> An' it were ten thousand mile!'

THE MESSAGE

s. Mrs E— has called for the book, Sir.

h. Oh! it is there. Let her wait a minute or two. I see this is a busy-day with you. How beautiful your arms look in those short sleeves!

s. I do not like to wear them.

h. Then that is because you are merciful, and would spare frail mortals who might die with gazing.

s. I have no power to kill.

h. You have, you have – Your charms are irresistible as your will is inexorable. I wish I could see you always thus. But I would have no one else see you so. I am jealous of all eyes but my own. I should almost like you to wear a veil, and to be muffled up from head to foot; but even if you were, and not a glimpse of you could be seen, it would be to no purpose – you would only have to move, and you would be admired as the most graceful creature in the world. You smile – Well, if you were to be won by fine speeches –

s. You could supply them!

h. It is however no laughing matter with me; thy beauty kills me daily, and I shall think of nothing but thy charms, till the last word trembles on my tongue, and that will be thy name, my love – the name of my Infelice! You will live by that name, you rogue, fifty years after you are dead. Don't you thank me for that?

s. I have no such ambition, Sir. But Mrs E— is waiting.

h. She is not in love, like me. You look so handsome to-day, I cannot let you go. You have got a colour.

s. But you say I look best when I am pale.

h. When you are pale, I think so; but when you have a colour, I then think you still more beautiful. It is you that I admire; and whatever you are, I like best. I like you as Miss

L—, I should like you still more as Mrs —. I once thought you were half inclined to be a prude, and I admired you as a 'pensive nun, devout and pure.' I now think you are more than half a coquet, and I like you for your roguery. The truth is, I am in love with you, my angel; and whatever you are, is to me the perfection of thy sex. I care not what thou art, while thou art still thyself. Smile but so, and turn my heart to what shape you please!

s. I am afraid, Sir, Mrs E— will think you have forgotten her.

h. I had, my charmer. But go, and make her a sweet apology, all graceful as thou art. One kiss! Ah! ought I not to think myself the happiest of men?

THE FLAGEOLET

h. Where have you been, my love!

s. I have been down to see my aunt, Sir.

h. And I hope she has been giving you good advice.

s. I did not go to ask her opinion about any thing.

h. And yet you seem anxious and agitated. You appear pale and dejected, as if your refusal of me had touched your own breast with pity. Cruel girl! you look at this moment heavenly-soft, saint-like, or resemble some graceful marble statue, in the moon's pale ray! Sadness only heightens the elegance of your features. How can I escape from you, when every new occasion, even your cruelty and scorn, brings out some new charm. Nay, your rejection of me, by the way in which you do it, is only a new link added to my chain. Raise those down-cast eyes, bend as if an angel stooped, and kiss me. . . . Ah! enchanting little trembler! if such is thy sweetness where thou dost not love, what must thy love have been? I cannot think how any man, having the heart of one, could go and leave it.

s. No one did, that I know of.

H. Yes, you told me yourself he left you (though he liked you, and though he knew – Oh! gracious God! – that you loved him) he left you because 'the pride of birth would not permit a union.' – For myself, I would leave a throne to ascend to the heaven of thy charms. I live but for thee, here – I only wish to live again to pass all eternity with thee. But even in another world, I suppose you would turn from me to seek him out who scorned you here.

S. If the proud scorn us here, in that place we shall all be equal.

H. Do not look so – do not talk so – unless you would drive me mad. I could worship you at this moment. Can I witness such perfection, and bear to think I have lost you for ever? Oh! let me hope! You see you can mould me as you like. You can lead me by the hand, like a little child; and with you my way would be like a little child's: – you could strew flowers in my path, and pour new life and hope into me. I should then indeed hail the return of spring with joy, could I indulge the faintest hope – would you but let me try to please you!

S. Nothing can alter my resolution, Sir.

H. Will you go and leave me so?

S. It is late, and my father will be getting impatient at my stopping so long.

H. You know he has nothing to fear for you – it is poor I that am alone in danger. But I wanted to ask about buying you a flageolet. Could I see that which you have? If it is a pretty one, it would hardly be worth while; but if it isn't, I thought of bespeaking an ivory one for you. Can't you bring up your own to shew me.

S. Not to-night, Sir.

H. I wish you could.

S. I cannot – but I will in the morning.

H. Whatever you determine, I must submit to. Good night, and bless thee!

*[The next morning, S. brought up the tea-kettle as usual;
and looking towards the tea-tray, she said, 'Oh! I see my
sister has forgot the tea-pot.' It was not there, sure enough;
and tripping down stairs, she came up in a minute, with the
tea-pot in one hand, and the flageolet in the other, balanced
so sweetly and gracefully. It would have been awkward to
have brought up the flageolet in the tea-tray, and she could
not have well gone down again on purpose to fetch it. Something, therefore, was to be omitted as an excuse. Exquisite
witch! But do I love her the less dearly for it? I cannot.]*

THE CONFESSION

H. You say you cannot love. Is there not a prior attachment
in the case? Was there any one else that you *did* like?

s. Yes, there was another.

H. Ah! I thought as much. Is it long ago then?

s. It is two years, Sir.

H. And has time made no alteration? Or do you still see
him sometimes?

s. No, Sir! But he is one to whom I feel the sincerest affection, and ever shall, though he is far distant.

H. And did he return your regard?

s. I had every reason to think so.

H. What then broke off your intimacy?

s. It was the pride of birth, Sir, that would not permit him
to think of a union.

H. Was he a young man of rank, then?

s. His connections were high.

H. And did he never attempt to persuade you to any other
step?

s. No – he had too great a regard for me.

H. Tell me, my angel, how was it? Was he so very handsome? Or was it the fineness of his manners?

s. It was more his manner: but I can't tell how it was. It

was chiefly my own fault. I was foolish to suppose he could ever think seriously of me. But he used to make me read with him – and I used to be with him a good deal, though not much neither – and I found my affections entangled before I was aware of it.

H. And did your mother and family know of it?

S. No – I have never told any one but you; nor I should not have mentioned it now, but I thought it might give you some satisfaction.

H. Why did he go at last?

S. We thought it better to part.

H. And do you correspond?

S. No, Sir. But perhaps I may see him again some time or other, though it will be only in the way of friendship.

H My God! what a heart is thine, to live for years upon that bare hope!

S. I did not wish to live always, Sir – I wished to die for a long time after, till I thought it not right; and since then I have endeavoured to be as resigned as I can.

H. And do you think the impression will never wear out?

S. Not if I can judge from my feelings hitherto. It is now sometime since, – and I find no difference.

H. May God for ever bless you! How can I thank you for your condescension in letting me know your sweet sentiments? You have changed my esteem into adoration. – Never can I harbour a thought of ill in thee again.

S. Indeed, Sir, I wish for your good opinion and your friendship.

H. And can you return them?

S. Yes.

H. And nothing more?

S. No, Sir.

H. You are an angel, and I will spend my life, if you will let me, in paying you the homage that my heart feels towards you.

THE QUARREL

H. You are angry with me?

S. Have I not reason?

H. I hope you have; for I would give the world to believe my suspicions unjust. But, oh! my God! after what I have thought of you and felt towards you, as little less than an angel, to have but a doubt cross my mind for an instant that you were what I dare not name – a common lodging-house decoy, a kissing convenience, that your lips were as common as the stairs –

S. Let me go, Sir!

H. Nay – prove to me that you are not so, and I will fall down and worship you. You were the only creature that ever seemed to love me; and to have my hopes, and all my fondness for you, thus turned to a mockery – it is too much! Tell me why you have deceived me, and singled me out as your victim?

S. I never have, Sir. I always said I could not love.

H. There is a difference between love and making me a laughing-stock. Yet what else could be the meaning of your little sister's running out to you, and saying 'He thought I did not see him!' when I had followed you into the other room? Is it a joke upon me that I make free with you? Or is not the joke rather against *her* sister, unless you make my courtship of you a jest to the whole house? Indeed I do not well see how you can come and stay with me as you do, by the hour together, and day after day, as openly as you do, unless you give it some such turn with your family. Or do you deceive them as well as me?

S. I deceive no one, Sir. But my sister Betsey was always watching and listening when Mr M— was courting my eldest sister, till he was obliged to complain of it.

H. That I can understand, but not the other. You may remember, when your servant Maria looked in and found you sitting in my lap one day, and I was afraid she might tell your mother, you said 'You did not care, for you had no secrets from your mother.' This seemed to me odd at the time, but I thought no more of it, till other things brought it to my mind. Am I to suppose, then, that you are acting a part, a vile part, all this time, and that you come up here, and stay as long as I like, that you sit on my knee and put your arms round my neck, and feed me with kisses, and let me take other liberties with you, and that for a year together; and that you do all this not out of love, or liking, or regard, but go through your regular task, like some young witch, without one natural feeling, to shew your cleverness, and get a few presents out of me, and go down into the kitchen to make a fine laugh of it? There is something monstrous in it, that I cannot believe of you.

s. Sir, you have no right to harass my feelings in the manner you do. I have never made a jest of you to anyone, but always felt and expressed the greatest esteem for you. You have no ground for complaint in my conduct; and I cannot help what Betsey or others do. I have always been consistent from the first. I told you my regard could amount to no more than friendship.

H. Nay, Sarah, it was more than half a year before I knew that there was an insurmountable obstacle in the way. You say your regard is merely friendship, and that you are sorry I have ever felt anything more for you. Yet the first time I ever asked you, you let me kiss you; the first time I ever saw you, as you went out of the room, you turned full round at the door, with that inimitable grace with which you do everything, and fixed your eyes full upon me, as much as to say, 'Is he caught?' – that very week you sat upon my knee, twined your arms round me, caressed me with every mark of tenderness consistent with modesty; and I have not got much farther since. Now if you did all this with me, a perfect stranger to you, and without any particular liking to me, must I not conclude you do so as a matter of course with everyone? – Or, if you do not do so with others, it was because you took a liking to me for some reason or other.

s. It was gratitude, Sir, for different obligations.

H. If you mean by obligations the presents I made you, I had given you none the first day I came. You do not consider yourself *obliged* to everyone who asks you for a kiss?

s. No, Sir.

H. I should not have thought anything of it in anyone but you. But you seemed so reserved and modest, so soft, so timid, you spoke so low, you looked so innocent – I thought it impossible you could deceive me. Whatever favors you granted must proceed from pure regard. No betrothed virgin ever gave the object of her choice kisses, caresses more modest or more bewitching than those you have given me a thousand and a thousand times. Could I have thought I should ever live to believe them an inhuman mockery of one who had the sincerest regard for you? Do you think they will not now turn to rank poison in my veins, and kill me, soul and body? You say it is friendship – but if this is friendship, I'll forswear love. Ah! Sarah! it must be something more or less than friendship. If your caresses are sincere, they shew fondness – if they are not, I must be more than indifferent to you. Indeed you once let some words drop, as if I were out of the question in such matters, and you could trifle with me with impunity. Yet you complain at other times that no one ever took such liberties with you as I have done. I remember once in particular your saying, as you went out at the door in anger – 'I had an attachment before, but that person never attempted anything of the kind.' Good God! How did I dwell on that word *before*, thinking it implied an attachment to me also; but you have since disclaimed any such meaning. You say you have never professed more than esteem. Yet once, when you were sitting in your old place, on my knee, embracing and fondly embraced, and I asked you if you could not love, you made answer, 'I could easily say so, whether I did or not – YOU SHOULD JUDGE BY MY ACTIONS!' And another time, when you were in the same posture, and I reproached you with indifference, you replied in these words, 'Do I SEEM INDIFFERENT?' Was I to blame after this to indulge my passion for the loveliest of her sex? Or what can I think?

s. I am no prude, Sir.

H. Yet you might be taken for one. So your mother said, 'It was hard if you might not indulge in a little levity.' She has strange notions of levity. But levity, my dear, is quite out of character in you. Your ordinary walk is as if you were performing some religious ceremony : you come up to my table of a morning, when you merely bring in the tea-things, as if you were advancing to the altar. You move in minuet-time : you measure every step, as if you were afraid of offending in the smallest things. I never hear your approach on the stairs, but by a sort of hushed silence. When you enter the room, the Graces wait on you, and Love waves round your person in gentle undulations, breathing balm into the soul! By Heaven, you are an angel! You look like one at this instant! Do I not adore you – and have I merited this return?

s. I have repeatedly answered that question. You sit and fancy things out of your own head, and then lay them to my charge. There is not a word of truth in your suspicions.

H. Did I not overhear the conversation down-stairs last night, to which you were a party? Shall I repeat it?

s. I had rather not hear it!

H. Or what am I to think of this story of the footman?

s. It is false, Sir, I never did anything of the sort.

H. Nay, when I told your mother I wished she wouldn't ⁎ ⁎ ⁎ ⁎ ⁎ ⁎ ⁎ ⁎ ⁎ (as I heard she did) she said 'Oh, there's nothing in that, for Sarah very often * * * * * *,' and your doing so before company, is only a trifling addition to the sport.

s. I'll call my mother, Sir, and she shall contradict you.

H. Then she'll contradict herself. But did not you boast you were 'very persevering in your resistance to gay young men,' and had been 'several times obliged to ring the bell?' Did you always ring it? Or did you get into these dilemmas that made it necessary, merely by the demureness of your looks and ways? Or had nothing else passed? Or have you two characters, one that you palm off upon me, and another, your natural one, that you resume when you get out of the room, like an actress who throws aside her artificial part behind the scenes? Did you not, when I was courting you on the staircase the first night Mr C— came, beg me to desist, for if the new lodger heard us, he'd take you for a light character? Was that all? Were you only afraid of being *taken* for a light character? Oh! Sarah!

s. I'll stay and hear this no longer.

H. Yes, one word more. Did you not love another?

s. Yes, and ever shall most sincerely.

H. Then, *that* is my only hope. If you could feel this sentiment for him, you cannot be what you seem to me of late. But there is another thing I had to say – be what you will, I love you to distraction! You are the only woman that ever made me think she loved me, and that feeling was so new to me, and so delicious, that it 'will never from my heart.' Thou wert to me a little tender flower, blooming in the wilderness of my life; and though thou should'st turn out a weed, I'll not fling thee from me, while I can help it. Wert thou all that I dread to think – wert thou a wretched wanderer in the street, covered with rags, disease, and infamy, I'd clasp thee to my bosom, and live and die with thee, my love. Kiss me, thou little sorceress!

s. Never!

H. Then go: but remember I cannot live without you — nor I will not.

THE RECONCILIATION

H. I HAVE then lost your friendship?

S. Nothing tends more to alienate friendship than insult.

H. The words I uttered hurt me more than they did you.

S. It was not words merely, but actions as well.

H. Nothing I can say or do can ever alter my fondness for you — Ah, Sarah! I am unworthy of your love: I hardly dare ask for your pity; but oh! save me — save me from your scorn: I cannot bear it — it withers me like lightning.

S. I bear no malice, Sir; but my brother, who would scorn to tell a lie for his sister, can bear witness for me that there was no truth in what you were told.

H. I believe it; or there is no truth in woman. It is enough for me to know that you do not return my regard; it would be too much for me to think that you did not deserve it. But cannot you forgive the agony of the moment?

S. I can forgive; but it is not easy to forget some things!

H. Nay, my sweet Sarah (frown if you will, I can bear your resentment for my ill behaviour, it is only your scorn and indifference that harrow up my soul) — but I was going to ask, if you had been engaged to be married to any one, and the day was fixed, and he had heard what I did, whether he could have felt any true regard for the character of his bride, his wife, if he had not been hurt and alarmed as I was?

S. I believe, actual contracts of marriage have sometimes been broken off by unjust suspicions.

H. Or had it been your old friend, what do you think he would have said in my case?

S. He would never have listened to anything of the sort.

H. He had greater reasons for confidence than I have. But it

is your repeated cruel rejection of me that drives me almost
to madness. Tell me, love, is there not, besides your attachment to him, a repugnance to me?

s. No, none whatever.

H. I fear there is an original dislike, which no efforts of mine
can overcome.

s. It is not *you* – it is my feelings with respect to another,
which are unalterable.

H. And yet you have no hope of ever being his? And yet
you accuse me of being romantic in my sentiments.

s. I have indeed long ceased to hope; but yet I sometimes
hope against hope.

H. My love! were it in my power, thy hopes should be fulfilled to-morrow. Next to my own, there is nothing that
could give me so much satisfaction as to see thine realized!
Do I not love thee, when I can feel such an interest in thy
love for another? It was that which first wedded my very
soul to you. I would give worlds for a share in a heart so rich
in pure affection!

s. And yet I did not tell you of the circumstance to raise
myself in your opinion.

H. You are a sublime little thing! And yet, as you have no
prospects there, I cannot help thinking, the best thing would
be to do as I have said.

s. I would never marry a man I did not love beyond all the
world.

H. I should be satisfied with less than that – with the love, or
regard, or whatever you call it, you have shown me before
marriage, if that has only been sincere. You would hardly
like me less afterwards.

s. Endearments would, I should think, increase regard,
where there was love beforehand; but that is not exactly my
case.

H. But I think you would be happier than you are at present.
You take pleasure in my conversation, and you say you have

an esteem for me; and it is upon this, after the honeymoon, that marriage chiefly turns.

s. Do you think there is no pleasure in a single life?

h. Do you mean on account of its liberty?

s. No, but I feel that forced duty is no duty. I have high ideas of the married state!

h. Higher than of the maiden state?

s. I understand you, Sir.

h. I meant nothing; but you have sometimes spoken of any serious attachment as a tie upon you. It is not that you prefer flirting with 'gay young men' to becoming a mere dull domestic wife?

s. You have no right to throw out such insinuations: for though I am but a tradesman's daughter, I have as nice a sense of honour as anyone can have.

h. Talk of a tradesman's daughter! you would ennoble any family, thou glorious girl, by true nobility of mind.

s. Oh! Sir, you flatter me. I know my own inferiority to most.

h. To none; there is no one above thee, man nor woman either. You are above your situation, which is not fit for you.

s. I am contented with my lot, and do my duty as cheerfully as I can.

h. Have you not told me your spirits grow worse every year?

s. Not on that account: but some disappointments are hard to bear up against.

h. If you talk about that, you'll unman me. But tell me, my love, – I have thought of it as something that might account for some circumstances; that is, as a mere possibility. But tell me, there was not a likeness between me and your old lover that struck you at first sight? Was there?

s. No, Sir, none.

h. Well, I didn't think it likely there should.

s. But there was a likeness.

h. To whom?

s. To that little image! [*looking intently on a small bronze figure of Buonaparte on the mantlepiece*].

h. What, do you mean to Buonaparte?

s. Yes, all but the nose was just like.

h. And was his figure the same?

s. He was taller!

[*I got up and gave her the image, and told her it was her's by every right that was sacred. She refused at first to take so valuable a curiosity, and said she would keep it for me. But I pressed it eagerly, and she took it. She immediately came and sat down, and put her arm round my neck, and kissed me, and I said, 'Is it not plain we are the best friends in the world, since we are always so glad to make it up?' And then I added 'How odd it was that the God of my idolatry should turn out to be like her Idol, and said it was no wonder that the same face which awed the world should conquer the sweetest creature in it!' How I loved her at that moment! Is it possible that the wretch who writes this could ever have been so blest! Heavenly delicious creature! Can I live without her? Oh! no – never – never.*

'What is this world? What asken men to have,
Now with his love, now in the cold grave,
Alone, withouten any compagnie!'

Let me but see her again! She cannot hate the man who loves her as I do.]

LETTERS TO THE SAME

Feb., 1822.

– You will scold me for this, and ask me if this is keeping my promise to mind my work. One half of it was to think of Sarah: and besides, I do not neglect my work either, I assure you. I regularly do ten pages a day, which mounts up to thirty guineas' worth a week, so that you see I should grow rich at this rate, if I could keep on so; *and I could keep*

on so, if I had you with me to encourage me with your
sweet smiles, and share my lot. The Berwick smacks sail
twice a week, and the wind sits fair. When I think of the
thousand endearing caresses that have passed between us, I
do not wonder at the strong attachment that draws me to
you; but I am sorry for my own want of power to please. I
hear the wind sigh through the lattice, and keep repeating
over and over to myself two lines of Lord Byron's Tragedy –

> 'So shalt thou find me ever at thy side
> Here and hereafter, if the last may be.' –

applying them to thee, my love, and thinking whether I
shall ever see thee again. Perhaps not – for some years at
least – till both thou and I are old – and then, when all else
have forsaken thee, I will creep to thee, and die in thine
arms. You once made me believe I was not hated by her I
loved; and for that sensation, so delicious was it, though but
a mockery and a dream, I owe you more than I can ever pay.
I thought to have dried up my tears for ever, the day I left
you; but as I write this, they stream again. If they did not, I
think my heart would burst. I walk out here of an afternoon, and hear the notes of the thrush, that come up from
a sheltered valley below, welcome in the spring; but
they do not melt my heart as they used: it is grown cold
and dead. As you say, it will one day be colder.　Forgive
what I have written above; I did not intend it: but you were
once my little all, and I cannot bear the thought of having
lost you for ever, I fear through my own fault. Has any one
called? Do not send any letters that come. I should like you
and your mother (if agreeable) to go and see Mr Kean in
Othello, and Miss Stephens in Love in a Village. If you will,
I will write to Mr T—, to send you tickets. Has Mr P—
called? I think I must send to him for the picture to kiss and
talk to. Kiss me, my best beloved. Ah! if you can never be
mine, still let me be your proud and happy slave.　H.

TO THE SAME

March, 1822.

– You will be glad to learn I have done my work – a volume in less than a month. This is one reason why I am better than when I came, and another is, I have had two letters from Sarah. I am pleased I have got through this job, as I was afraid I might lose reputation by it (which I can little afford to lose) – and besides, I am more anxious to do well now, as I wish you to hear me well spoken of. I walk out of an afternoon, and hear the birds sing as I told you, and think, if I had you hanging on my arm, *and that for life*, how happy I should be – happier than I ever hoped to be, or had any conception of till I knew you. '*But that can never be*' – I hear you answer in a soft, low murmur. Well, let me dream of it sometimes – I am not happy too often, except when that favourite note, the harbinger of spring, recalling the hopes of my youth, whispers thy name and peace together in my ear. I was reading something about Mr Macready to-day, and this put me in mind of that delicious night, when I went with your mother and you to see Romeo and Juliet. Can I forget it for a moment – your sweet modest looks, your infinite propriety of behaviour, all your sweet winning ways – your hesitating about taking my arm as we came out till your mother did – your laughing about nearly losing your cloak – your stepping into the coach without my being able to make the slightest discovery – and oh! my sitting down beside you there, you whom I had loved so long, so well, and your assuring me I had not lessened your pleasure at the play by being with you, and giving me your dear hand to press in mine! I thought I was in heaven – that slender exquisitely-turned form contained my all of heaven upon earth; and as I folded you – yes, you, my own best Sarah, to my bosom, there was, as you say, *a tie between us* – you did seem to me, for those few short moments, to be mine in all truth and honour and sacredness – Oh! that we could be always so – Do not mock me, for I am a very child in love. I ought to beg pardon for behaving so ill afterwards, but I hope the *little image* made it up between us, &c.

[*To this letter I have received no answer, not a line. The rolling years of eternity will never fill up that blank. Where shall I be? What am I? Or where have I been?*]

WRITTEN IN A BLANK LEAF OF ENDYMION

I WANT a hand to guide me, an eye to cheer me, a bosom to repose on; all which I shall never have, but shall stagger into my grave, old before my time, unloved and unlovely, unless S. L. keeps her faith with me.

– But by her dove's eyes ånd serpent-shape, I think she does not hate me; by her smooth forehead and her crested hair, I own I love her; by her soft looks and queen-like grace (which men might fall down and worship) I swear to live and die for her!

A PROPOSAL OF LOVE

[*Given to her in our early acquaintance*]

'OH! if I thought it could be in a woman
(As, if it can, I will presume in you)
To feed for aye her lamp and flames of love,
To keep her constancy in plight and youth,
Outliving beauties outward with a mind
That doth renew swifter than blood decays:
Or that persuasion could but thus convince me,
That my integrity and truth to you
Might be confronted with the match and weight
Of such a winnowed purity in love –

How were I then uplifted! But, alas,
I am as true as truth's simplicity,
And simpler than the infancy of truth.'

TROILUS AND CRESSIDA

LIBER AMORIS

Part II

LETTERS TO C.P——,[2] ESQ.

Bees-Inn.

MY GOOD FRIEND, Here I am in Scotland (and shall have been here three weeks, next Monday) as I may say, *on my probation*. This is a lone inn, but on a great scale, thirty miles from Edinburgh. It is situated on a rising ground (a mark for all the winds, which blow here incessantly) – there is a woody hill opposite, with a winding valley below, and the London road stretches out on either side. You may guess which way I oftenest walk. I have written two letters to S. L. and got one cold, prudish answer, beginning *Sir*, and ending *From your's truly*, with *Best respects from herself and relations*. I was going to give in, but have returned an answer, which I think is a touch-stone. I send it you on the other side to keep as a curiosity, in case she kills me by her exquisite rejoinder. I am convinced from the profound contemplations I have had on the subject here and coming along, that I am on a wrong scent. We had a famous parting-scene, a complete quarrel and then a reconciliation, in which she did beguile me of my tears, but the deuce of a one did she shed. What do you think? She cajoled me out of my little Buonaparte as cleverly as possible, in manner and form following. She was shy the Saturday and Sunday (the day of my departure) so I got in dudgeon, and began to rip up grievances. I asked her how she came to admit me to such extreme familiarities, the first week I entered the

house. 'If she had no particular regard for me, she must do
so (or more) with everyone: if she had a liking to me from
the first, why refuse me with scorn and wilfulness?' If you
had seen how she flounced, and looked, and went to the
door, saying 'She was obliged to me for letting her know the
opinion I had always entertained of her' – then I said,
'Sarah!' and she came back and took my hand, and fixed
her eyes on the mantle-piece – (she must have been invok-
ing her idol then – if I thought so, I could devour her, the
darling – but I doubt her) – So I said 'There is one thing that
has occurred to me sometimes as possible, to account for
your conduct to me at first – there wasn't a likeness, was
there, to your old friend?' She answered 'No, none – but
there was a likeness' – I asked, to what? She said 'to that
little image!' I said, 'Do you mean Buonaparte?' – She said,
'Yes, all but the nose.' – 'And the figure?' – 'He was
taller.' – I could not stand this. So I got up and took it, and
gave it her, and after some reluctance, she consented to
'keep it for me.' What will you bet me that it wasn't all a
trick? I'll tell you why I suspect it, besides being fairly out
of my wits about her. I had told her mother half an hour
before, that I should take this image and leave it at Mrs
B.'s, for that I didn't wish to leave anything behind me that
must bring me back again. Then up she comes and starts a
likeness to her lover: she knew I should give it her on the
spot – 'No, she would keep it for me!' So I must come back
for it. Whether art or nature, it is sublime. I told her I should
write and tell you so, and that I parted from her, confiding,
adoring! – She is beyond me, that's certain. Do go and see
her, and desire her not to give my present address to a single
soul, and learn if the lodging is let, and to whom. My letter
to her is as follows. If she shews the least remorse at it, I'll
be hanged, though it might move a stone, I modestly think.
(*See before, Part I. page* 309)

N.B. – I have begun a book of our conversations (I mean

mine and the statue's) which I call LIBER AMORIS. I was detained at Stamford and found myself dull, and could hit upon no other way of employing my time so agreeably.

LETTER II

DEAR P—, Here, without loss of time, in order that I may have your opinion upon it, is little YES and No's answer to my last.

'SIR, I should not have disregarded your injunction not to send you any more letters that might come to you, had I not promised the Gentleman who left the enclosed to forward it the earliest opportunity, as he said it was *of consequence*. Mr P— called the day after you left town. My mother and myself are much obliged by your kind offer of tickets to the play, but must decline accepting it. My family send their best respects, in which they are joined by

Your's, truly,

S. L.'

The deuce a bit more is there of it. If you can make anything out of it (or any body else) I'll be hanged. You are to understand, this comes in a frank, the second I have received from her, with a name I can't make out, and she won't tell me, though I asked her, where she got franks, as also whether the lodgings were let to neither of which a word of answer. * * * * is the name on the frank: see if you can decypher it by a Red-book. I suspect her grievously of being an arrant jilt, to say no more – yet I love her dearly. Do you know I'm going to write to that sweet rogue presently, having a whole evening to myself in advance of my work? Now mark, before you set about your exposition of the new Apocalypse of the new Calypso, the only thing to be endured in the above letter is the date. It was written the very day after she received mine. By this she seems willing to lose no time in receiving these letters 'of such sweet breath composed.' If I thought so – but I wait for your reply. After all, what is there in her but a pretty figure, and that you can't get a word out of her? Her's is the Fabian method of making love and conquests. What do you suppose she said the night before I left her?

H. Could you not come and live with me as a friend?

S. I don't know: and yet it would be of no use if I did, you would always be hankering after what could never be!'

I asked her if she would do so at once – the very next day? And what do you guess was her answer – 'Do you think it would be prudent?' As I didn't proceed to extremities on the spot, she began to look grave, and declare off. 'Would she live with me in her own house – to be with me all day as dear friends, if nothing more, to sit and read and talk with me?' – 'She would make no promises, but I should find her the same.' – 'Would she go to the play with me sometimes, and let it be understood that I was paying my addresses to her?' – 'She could not, as a habit – her father was rather strict, and would object.' – Now what am I to think of all this? Am I mad or a fool? Answer me to that, Master Brook! You are a philosopher.

LETTER III

DEAR FRIEND, I ought to have written to you before; but since I received your letter, I have been in a sort of purgatory, and what is worse, I see no prospect of getting out of it. I would put an end to my torments at once; but I am as great a coward as I have been a dupe. Do you know I have not had a word of answer from her since! What can be the reason? Is she offended at my letting you know she wrote to me, or is it some new affair? I wrote to her in the tenderest, most respectful manner, poured my soul at her feet, and this is the return she makes me! Can you account for it, except on the admission of my worst doubts concerning her? Oh God! can I bear after all to think of her so, or that I am scorned and made a sport of by the creature to whom I had given my whole heart? – Thus has it been with me all my life; and so will it be to the end of it! – If you should learn anything, good or bad, tell me, I conjure you: I can bear anything but this cruel suspense. If I knew she was a mere abandoned creature, I should try to forget her; but till I do know this, nothing can tear me from her, I have drank in poison from her lips too long – alas! mine do not poison again. I sit and indulge my grief by the hour together; my weakness grows upon me; and I have no hope left, unless I could lose my senses quite. Do you know I think I should like this? To forget, ah! to forget – there would be something in that – to change to an ideot for some few years, and then to wake up a poor wretched old man, to recollect my misery as past, and die! Yet, oh! with her, only a little while ago, I had different hopes, forfeited for nothing that I know of! * * * * * * If you can give me any consolation on the subject of my tormentor, pray do. The pain I suffer wears me out daily. I write this on the supposition that Mrs — may still come here, and that I may be detained some weeks longer. Direct to me at the Post office; and if I return to town directly as I fear, I will leave word for them to forward the letter to me in London – not at my old lodgings. I will not go back there: yet how can I breathe away from her? Her hatred of me must be great, since my love of her could not overcome it! I have finished the book of my conversations with her, which I told you of: if I am not mistaken, you will think it very nice reading.

Your's ever.

Have you read Sardanapalus? How like the little Greek slave, Myrrha, is to *her*!

LETTER IV
(*Written in the Winter*)

MY GOOD FRIEND, I received your letter this morning, and I kiss the rod not only with submission, but gratitude. Your reproofs of me and your defences of her are the only things that save my soul from perdition. She is my heart's idol; and believe me those words of yours applied to the dear saint – 'To lip a chaste one and suppose her wanton' – were balm and rapture to me. I have *lipped her*, God knows how often, and oh! is it even possible that she is chaste, and that she has bestowed her loved 'endearments' on me (her own sweet word) out of true regard? That thought, out of the lowest depths of despair, would at any time make me strike my forehead against the stars. Could I but think the love 'honest,' I am proof against all hazards. She by her silence makes my *dark hour*; and you by your encouragements dissipate it for twenty-four hours. Another thing has brought me to life. Mrs — is actually on her way here about the divorce. Should this unpleasant business (which has been so long talked of) succeed, and I should become free, do you think S. L. will agree to change her name to —? If she *will*, she *shall*; and to call her so to you, or to hear her called so by others, would be music to my ears, such as they never drank in. Do you think if she knew how I love her, my depressions and my altitudes, my wanderings and my constancy, it would not move her? She knows it all; and if she is not an *incorrigible*, she loves me, or regards me with a feeling next to love. I don't believe that any woman was ever courted more passionately than she has been by me. As Rousseau said of Madame d'Houptot (forgive the allusion) my heart has found a tongue in speaking to her, and I have talked to her the divine language of love. Yet she says, she is insensible to it. Am I to believe her or you? You – for I wish it and wish it to madness, now that I am like to be free, and to have it in my power to say to her without a possibility of suspicion, 'Sarah, will you be mine?' When I sometimes think of the time I first saw the sweet apparition, August 16, 1820, and that possibly she may be my bride before that day two years, it makes me dizzy with incredible joy and love of her. Write soon.

LETTER V

MY DEAR FRIEND, I read your answer this morning with gratitude. I have felt somewhat easier since. It shewed your interest in my vexations, and also that you know nothing worse than I do. I cannot describe the weakness of mind to which she has reduced me. This state of suspense is like hanging in the air by a single thread that exhausts all your strength to keep hold of it; and yet if that fails you, you have nothing in the world else left to trust to. I am come back to Edinburgh about this cursed business, and Mrs — is coming from Montrose next week. How it will end, I can't say; and don't care, except as it regards the other affair. I should, I confess, like to have it in my power to make her the offer direct and unequivocal, to see how she'd receive it. It would be worth something at any rate to see her superfine airs upon the occasion; and if she should take it into her head to turn round her sweet neck, drop her eye-lids, and say — 'Yes, I will be yours!' — why then, 'treason domestic, foreign levy, nothing could touch me further.' By Heaven! I doat on her. The truth is, I never had any pleasure, like love, with any one but her. Then how can I bear to part with her? Do you know I like to think of her best in her morning-gown and mob-cap — it is so she has oftenest come into my room and enchanted me! She was once ill, pale, and had lost all her freshness. I only adored her the more for it, and fell in love with the decay of her beauty. I could devour the little witch. If she had a plague-spot on her, I could touch the infection: if she was in a burning fever, I could kiss her, and drink death as I have drank life from her lips. When I press her hand, I enjoy perfect happiness and contentment of soul. It is not what she says or what she does – it is herself that I love. To be with her is to be at peace. I have no other wish or desire. The air about her is serene, blissful; and he who breathes it is like one of the Gods! So that I can but have her with me always, I care for nothing more. I never could tire of her sweetness; I feel that I could grow to her, body and soul? My heart, my heart is her's.

LETTER VI
(*Written in May*)

DEAR P—, What have I suffered since I parted with you! A raging fire is in my heart and in my brain, that never quits me. The steam-boat (which I foolishly ventured on board) seems a prison-house, a sort of spectre-ship, moving on through an infernal lake, without wind or tide, by some necromantic power – the splashing of the waves, the noise of the engine gives me no rest, night or day – no tree, no natural object varies the scene – but the abyss is before me, and all my peace lies weltering in it! I feel the eternity of punishment in this life; for I see no end of my woes. The people about me are ill, uncomfortable, wretched enough, many of them – but to-morrow or next day, they reach the place of their destination, and all will be new and delightful. To me it will be the same. I can neither escape from her, nor from myself. All is endurable where there is a limit: but I have nothing but the blackness and the fiendishness of scorn around me – mocked by her (the false one) in whom I placed my hope, and who hardens herself against me! – I believe you thought me quite gay, vain, insolent, half mad, the night I left the house – no tongue can tell the heaviness of heart I felt at that moment. No footsteps ever fell more slow, more sad than mine; for every step bore me farther from her, with whom my soul and every thought lingered. I had parted with her in anger, and each had spoken words of high disdain, not soon to be forgiven. Should I ever behold her again? Where go to live and die far from her? In her sight there was Elysium; her smile was heaven; her voice was enchantment; the air of love waved round her, breathing balm into my heart: for a little while I had sat with the Gods at their golden tables, I had tasted of all earth's bliss, 'both living and loving!' But now Paradise barred its doors against me; I was driven from her presence, where rosy blushes and delicious sighs and all soft wishes dwelt, the outcast of nature and the scoff of love! I thought of the time when I was a little happy careless child, of my father's house, of my early lessons, of my brother's picture of me when a boy, of all that had since happened to me, and of the waste of years to come – I stopped, faultered, and was going to turn back once more to make a longer truce with wretchedness and patch up a hollow league with love, when the recollection of her words – 'I always told you I had no affection for you' – steeled my resolution, and I determined to proceed. You see by this she always hated me, and only played with my credulity till she could find some one to supply the place of her unalterable attachment to *the little image*. * * * * * I am a little, a very little better to-day. Would it were quietly over; and that this misshapen form (made to be mocked) were hid out of the sight of cold, sullen eyes! The people about me even take notice of my dumb despair, and pity me. What is to be done? I cannot forget *her*; and I can find no other like what *she seemed*. I should wish you to call, if you can make an excuse, and see whether or no she is quite marble – whether I may go back again at my return, and whether she will see me and talk to me sometimes as an old friend. Suppose you were to call on

M— from me, and ask him what his impression is that I ought to do. But do as you think best. Pardon, pardon.

p.s. – I send this from Scarborough, where the vessel stops for a few minutes. I scarcely know what I should have done, but for this relief to my feelings.

LETTER VII

MY DEAR FRIEND, The important step is taken, and I am virtually a free man. * * * What had I better do in these circumstances? I dare not write to her, I dare not write to her father, or else I would. She has shot me through with poisoned arrows, and I think another 'winged wound' would finish me. It is a pleasant sort of balm (as you express it) she has left in my heart! One thing I agree with you in, it will remain there for ever; but yet not very long. It festers, and consumes me. If it were not for my little boy, whose face I see struck blank at the news, looking through the world for pity and meeting with contempt instead, I should soon, I fear, settle the question by my death. That recollection is the only thought that brings my wandering reason to an anchor; that stirs the smallest interest in me; or gives me fortitude to bear up against what I am doomed to feel for the *ungrateful*. Otherwise, I am dead to every thing but the sense of what I have lost. She was my life – it is gone from me, and I am grown spectral! If I find myself in a place I am acquainted with, it reminds me of her, of the way in which I thought of her,

> – 'and carved on every tree
> The soft, the fair, the inexpressive she!'

If it is a place that is new to me, it is desolate, barren of all interest; for nothing touches me but what has a reference to her. If the clock strikes, the sound jars me; a million hours will not bring back peace to my breast. The light startles me; the darkness terrifies me. I seem falling into a pit, without a hand to help me. She has deceived me, and the earth fails from under my feet; no object in nature is substantial, real, but false and hollow, like her faith on which I built my trust. She came (I knew not how) and sat by my side and was folded in my arms, a vision of love and joy, as if she had dropped from the Heavens to bless me by some especial dispensation of a favouring Providence, and make me amends for all; and now without any fault of mine but too much fondness, she has vanished from me, and I am left to perish. My heart is torn out of me, with every feeling for which I wished to live. The whole is like a dream, an effect of enchantment; it torments me, and it drives me mad. I lie down with it; I rise up with it! and see no chance of repose. I grasp at a shadow, I try to undo the past, and weep with rage and pity over my own weakness and misery. I spared her again and again (fool that I was) thinking what she allowed from me was love, friendship, sweetness, not wantonness. How could I doubt it, looking in her face, and hearing her words, like sighs breathed from the gentlest of all bosoms? I had hopes, I had prospects to come, the flattery of something like fame, a pleasure in writing, health even would have come back with her smile – she has blighted all, turned all to poison and childish tears. Yet the barbed arrow is in my heart – I can neither endure it, nor draw it out; for with it flows my life's-blood. I had conversed too long with abstracted truth to trust myself with the immortal thoughts of love. *That S. L. might have been mine, and now never can* – these are the two sole propositions that for ever stare me in the face, and look ghastly in at my poor brain. I am in some sense proud that I can feel this dreadful passion – it gives me a kind of rank in the kingdom of love – but I could have wished it had been for an object that at least could have understood its value and pitied its excess. You say her not coming to the door when you went is a proof – yes, that her complement is at present full! That is the reason she doesn't want me there, lest I should discover the new affair – wretch that I am! Another has possession of her, oh Hell! I'm satisfied of it from her manner, which had a wanton insolence in it. Well might I run wild when I received no letters from her. I foresaw, I felt my fate. The gates of Paradise were once open to me too, and I blushed to enter but with the golden keys of love! I would die; but her lover – my love of her – ought not to die. When I am dead, who will love her as I have done? If she should be in misfortune, who will comfort her? when she is old, who will look in her face, and bless her? Would there be any harm in calling upon M—, to know confidentially if he thinks it worth my while to make her an offer the instant it is in my power? Let me have an answer, and save me, if possible, *for* her and *from* myself.

LETTER VIII

MY DEAR FRIEND, Your letter raised me for a moment from the depths of despair; but not hearing from you yesterday or to-day (as I hoped) I have had a relapse. You say I want to get rid of her. I hope you are more right in your conjectures about her than in this about me. Oh no! believe it, I love her as I do my own soul; my very heart is wedded to her (be she what she may) and I would not hesitate a moment between her and 'an angel from Heaven.' I grant all you say about my self-tormenting folly: but has it been without cause? Has she not refused me again and again with a mixture of scorn and resentment, after going the utmost lengths with a man for whom she now disclaims all affection; and what security can I have for her reserve with others, who will not be restrained by feelings of delicacy towards her, and whom she has probably preferred to me for their want of it. '*She can make no more confidences*' – these words ring for ever in my ears, and will be my death-watch.

They can have but one meaning, be sure of it – she always expressed herself with the exactest propriety. That was one of the things for which I loved her – shall I live to hate her for it? My poor fond heart, that brooded over her and the remains of her affections as my only hope of comfort upon earth, cannot brook this new degradation. Who is there so low as me? Who is there besides (I ask) after the homage I have paid her and the caresses she has lavished on me, so vile, so abhorrent to love, to whom such an indignity could have happened? When I think of this (and I think of nothing else) it stifles me. I am pent up in burning, fruitless desires, which can find no vent or object. Am I not hated, repulsed, derided by her whom alone I love or ever did love? I cannot stay in any place, and seek in vain for relief from the sense of her contempt and her ingratitude. I can settle to nothing: what is the use of all I have done? Is it not that very circumstance (my thinking beyond my strength, my feeling more than I need about so many things) that has withered me up, and made me a thing for Love to shrink from and wonder at? Who could ever feel that peace from the touch of her dear hand that I have done; and is it not torn from me for ever? My state is this, that I shall never lie down again at night nor rise up in the morning in peace, nor ever behold my little boy's face with pleasure while I live – unless I am restored to her favour. Instead of that delicious feeling I had when she was heavenly-kind to me, and my heart softened and melted in its own tenderness and her sweetness, I am now inclosed in a dungeon of despair. The sky is marble to my thoughts; nature is dead around me, as hope is within me; no object can give me one gleam of satisfaction now, nor the prospect of it in time to come. I wander by the sea-side; and the eternal ocean and lasting despair and her face are before me. Slighted by her, on whom my heart by its last fibre hung, where shall I turn? I wake with her by my side, not as my sweet bedfellow, but as the corpse of my love, without a heart in her bosom, cold, insensible, or struggling from me; and the worm gnaws me, and the sting of unrequited love, and the canker of a hopeless, endless sorrow. I have lost the taste of my food by feverish anxiety; and my favourite beverage,[3] which used to refresh me when I got up, has no moisture in it. Oh! cold, solitary, sepulchral breakfasts, compared with those which I promised myself with her; or which I made when she had been standing an hour by my side, my guardian-angel, my wife, my sister, my sweet friend, my Eve, my all; and had blest me with her seraph kisses! Ah! what I suffer at present only shews what I have enjoyed. But 'the girl is a good girl, if there is goodness in human nature.' I thank you for those words; and I will fall down and worship you, if you can prove them true: and I would not do much less for him that proves her a demon. She is one or the other, that's certain: but I fear the worst. Do let me know if anything has passed: suspense is my greatest punishment. I am going into the country to see if I can work a little in the three weeks I have yet to stay here. Write on the receipt of this, and believe me ever your unspeakably obliged friend.

TO EDINBURGH

– 'STONYHEARTED' Edinburgh! What art thou to me? The dust of thy streets mingles with my tears and blinds me. City of palaces, or of tombs – a quarry, rather than the habitation of men! Art thou like London, that populous hive, with its sunburnt, well-baked, brick-built houses – its public edifices, its theatres, its bridges, its squares, its ladies, and its pomp, its throng of wealth, its oustretched magnitude, and its mighty heart that never lies still? Thy cold grey walls reflect back the leaden melancholy of the soul. The square, hard-edged, unyielding faces of thy inhabitants have no sympathy to impart. What is it to me that I look

along the level line of thy tenantless streets, and meet perhaps a lawyer like a grasshopper chirping and skipping, or
the daughter of a Highland laird, haughty, fair, and
freckled? Or why should I look down your boasted Prince's
Street, with the beetle-browed Castle on one side, and the
Calton Hill with its proud monument at the further end,
and the ridgy steep of Salisbury Crag, cut off abruptly by
Nature's boldest hand, and Arthur's Seat overlooking all,
like a lioness watching her cubs? Or shall I turn to the far-
off Pentland Hills, with Craig-Crook nestling beneath them,
where lives the prince of critics [4] and the king of men? Or
cast my eye unsated over the Firth of Forth, that from my
window of an evening (as I read of Amy and her love) glitters like a broad golden mirror in the sun, and kisses the
winding shores of kingly Fife? Oh no! But to thee, to thee I
turn, North Berwick-Law, with thy blue cone rising out of
summer seas; for thou art the beacon of my banished
thoughts, and dost point my way to her, who is my heart's
true home. The air is too thin for me, that has not the breath
of Love in it; that is not embalmed by her sighs!

A THOUGHT

I AM not mad, but my heart is so; and raves within me, fierce
and untameable, like a panther in its den, and tries to get
loose to its lost mate, and fawn on her hand, and bend lowly
at her feet.

Another

Oh! thou dumb heart, lonely, sad, shut up in the prison-
house of this rude form, that hast never found a fellow but
for an instant, and in very mockery of thy misery, speak,
find bleeding words to express thy thoughts, break thy
dungeon-gloom, or die pronouncing thy Infelice's name!

Another

Within my heart is lurking suspicion, and base fear, and shame and hate; but above all, tyrannous love sits throned, crowned with her graces, silent and in tears.

LETTER IX

MY DEAR P—, You have been very kind to me in this business; but I fear even your indulgence for my infirmities is beginning to fail. To what a state am I reduced, and for what? For fancying a little artful vixen to be an angel and a saint, because she affected to look like one, to hide her rank thoughts and deadly purposes. Has she not murdered me under the mask of the tenderest friendship? And why? Be-. cause I have loved her with unutterable love, and sought to make her my wife. You say it is my own 'outrageous conduct' that has estranged her: nay, I have been *too gentle* with her. I ask you first in candour whether the ambiguity of her behaviour with respect to me, sitting and fondling a man (circumstanced as I was) sometimes for half a day together, and then declaring she had no love for him beyond a common regard, and professing never to marry, was not enough to excite my suspicions, which the different exposures from the conversations below-stairs were not calculated to allay? I ask you what you yourself would have felt or done, if loving her as I did, you had heard what I did, time after time? Did not her mother own to one of the grossest charges (which I shall not repeat) — and is such indelicacy to be reconciled with her pretended character (that character with which I fell in love, and to which I *made love*) without supposing her to be the greatest hypocrite in the world? My unpardonable offence has been that I took her at her word, and was willing to believe her the precise little puritanical person she set up for. After exciting her wayward desires by the fondest embraces and the purest kisses, as if she had been 'made my wedded wife yestreen,' or was to become so to-morrow (for that was always my feeling with respect to her) — I did not proceed to gratify them, or to follow up my advantage by any action which should declare, 'I think you a common adventurer, and will see whether you are so or not!' Yet any one but a credulous fool like me would have made the experiment, with whatever violence to himself, as a matter of life and death; for I had every reason to distrust appearances. Her conduct has been of a piece from the beginning. In the midst of her closest and falsest endearments, she has always (with one or two exceptions) disclaimed the natural inference to be drawn from them, and made a verbal reservation, by which she might lead me on in a Fool's Paradise, and make me the tool of her levity, her avarice, and her love of intrigue as long as she liked, and dismiss me whenever it suited her. This, you see, she has done, because my intentions grew serious, and if complied with, would deprive her of *the pleasures of a single life*! Offer marriage to this 'tradesman's daughter, who has as nice a sense of honour as any one can have;' and like Lady Bellaston in *Tom Jones*, she *cuts* you immediately in a fit of abhorrence and alarm. Yet she seemed to be of a different mind formerly, when struggling from me in the height of our first intimacy, she exclaimed — 'However I might agree to my own ruin, I never will consent to bring disgrace upon my family!' That I should have spared the traitress after expressions like this, astonishes me when I look back upon it. Yet if it were all to do over again, I know I should act just the same part. Such is her power over me! I cannot run the least risk of offending her — I love her so. When I look in her face, I cannot doubt her truth! Wretched being that I am! I have thrown away my heart and soul upon an unfeeling girl; and my life (that might have been so happy, had she been what I thought her) will soon follow either voluntarily, or by the force of grief, remorse, and disappointment. I cannot get rid of the reflection for an instant, nor even seek relief from its galling pressure. Ah! what a heart she has lost! All the love and affection of my whole life were centred in her, who alone, I thought, of all women had found out my true character, and knew how to value my tenderness. Alas! alas! that this, the only hope, joy, or comfort I ever had, should turn to a mockery, and hang like an ugly film over the remainder of my days! – I was at Roslin Castle yesterday. It lies low in a rude, but sheltered valley, hid from the vulgar gaze, and powerfully reminds one of the old song. The straggling fragments of the russet ruins, suspended smiling and graceful in the air as if they would linger out another century to please the curious beholder, the green larch-trees trembling between with the blue sky and white silver clouds, the wild mountain plants starting out here and there, the date of the year on an old low door-way, but still more, the beds of flowers in orderly decay, that seem to have no hand to tend them, but keep up a sort of traditional remembrance of civilization in former ages, present altogether a delightful and amiable subject for contemplation. The exquisite beauty of the scene, with the thought of what I should feel, should I ever be restored to her, and have to lead her through such places as my adored, my angel-wife, almost drove me beside myself. For this picture, this ecstatic vision, what have I of late instead as the image of the reality? Demoniacal possessions. I see the young witch seated in another's lap, twining her serpent arms round him, her eye glancing and her cheeks on fire – why does not the hideous thought choke me? Or why do I not go and find out the truth at once? The moonlight streams over the silver waters: the bark is in the bay that might waft me to her, almost with a wish. The mountain-breeze sighs out her name: old ocean with a world of tears murmurs back my woes! Does not my heart yearn to be with her; and shall I not follow its bidding? No, I must wait till I am free; and then I will take my Freedom (a glad prize) and lay it at her feet and tell her my proud love of her that would not brook a rival in her dishonour, and that would have her all or none, and gain her or lose myself for ever! —

You see by this letter the way I am in, and I hope you will excuse it as the picture of a half-disordered mind. The least respite from my uneasiness (such as I had yesterday) only brings the contrary reflection back upon me, like a flood; and by letting me see the happiness I have lost, makes me feel, by contrast, more acutely what I am doomed to bear.

LETTER X

DEAR FRIEND, Here I am at St Bees once more, amid the scenes which I greeted in their barrenness in winter; but which have now put on their full green attire that shews luxuriant to the eye, but speaks a tale of sadness to this heart widowed of its last, its dearest, its only hope! Oh! lovely Bees-Inn! here I composed a volume of law-cases, here I wrote my enamoured follies to her, thinking her human, and that 'all below was not the fiend's' — here I got two cold, sullen answers from the little witch, and here I was — and I was damned. I thought the revisiting the old haunts would have soothed me for a time, but it only brings back the sense of what I have suffered for her and of her unkindness the more strongly, till I cannot endure the recollection. I eye the Heavens in dumb despair or vent my sorrows in the desart air. 'To the winds, to the waves, to the rocks I complain' — you may suppose with what effect! I fear I shall be obliged to return. I am tossed about (backwards and for-wards) by my passion, so as to become ridiculous. I can now understand how it is that mad people never remain in the same place — they are moving on for ever, *from themselves!*

Do you know, you would have been delighted with the effect of the Northern twilight on this romantic country as I rode along last night? The hills and groves and herds of cattle were seen reposing in the grey dawn of midnight, as in a moonlight without shadow. The whole wide canopy of Heaven shed its reflex light upon them, like a pure crystal mirror. No sharp points, no petty details, no hard contrasts – every object was seen softened yet distinct, in its simple outline and natural tones, transparent with an inward light, breathing its own mild lustre. The landscape altogether was like an airy piece of mosaic-work, or like one of Poussin's broad massy landscapes or Titian's lovely pastoral scenes. Is it not so, that poets see nature, veiled to the sight, but revealed to the soul in visionary grace and grandeur! I confess the sight touched me; and might have removed all sadness except mine. So (I thought) the light of her celestial face once shone into my soul, and wrapt me in a heavenly trance. The sense I have of beauty raises me for a moment above myself, but depresses me the more afterwards, when I recollect how it is thrown away in vain admiration, and that it only makes me more susceptible of pain from the mortifications I meet with. Would I had never seen her! I might then not indeed have been happy, but at least I might have passed my life in peace, and have sunk into forgetfulness without a pang. – The noble scenery in this country mixes with my passion, and refines, but does not relieve it. I was at Stirling Castle not long ago. It gave me no pleasure. The declivity seemed to me abrupt, not sublime; for in truth I did not shrink back from it with terror. The weather-beaten towers were stiff and formal: the air was damp and chill: the river winded its dull, slimy way like a snake along the marshy grounds: and the dim misty tops of Ben Leddi, and the lovely Highlands (woven fantastically of thin air) mocked my embraces and tempted my longing eyes like her, the sole queen and mistress of my thoughts! I never found my contemplations on this subject so subtilised and at the same time so desponding as on that occasion. I wept myself almost blind, and I gazed at the broad golden sun-set through my tears that fell in showers. As I trod the green mountain turf, oh! how I wished to be laid beneath it – in one grave with her – that I might sleep with her in that cold bed, my hand in hers, and my heart for ever still – while worms should taste her sweet body, that I had never tasted! There was a time when I could bear solitude; but it is too much for me at present. Now I am no sooner left to myself than I am lost in infinite space, and look round me in vain for support or comfort. She was my stay, my hope: without her hand to cling to, I stagger like an infant on the edge of a precipice. The universe without her is one wide, hollow abyss, in which my harassed thoughts can find no resting-place. I must break off here; for the *hysterica passio* comes upon me, and threatens to unhinge my reason.

LETTER XI

MY DEAR AND GOOD FRIEND, I am afraid I trouble you with my querulous epistles, but this is probably the last. To-morrow or the next day decides my fate with respect to the divorce, when I expect to be a free man. In vain! Was it not for her and to lay my freedom at her feet, that I consented to this step which has cost me infinite perplexity, and now to be discarded for the first pretender that came in her way! If so, I hardly think I can survive it. You who have been a favourite with women, do not know what it is to be deprived of one's only hope, and to have it turned to shame and disappointment. There is nothing in the world left that can afford me one drop of comfort – *this* I feel more and more. Everything is to me a mockery of pleasure, like her love. The breeze does not cool me: the blue sky does not cheer me. I gaze only on her face averted from me – alas!

the only face that ever was turned fondly to me! And why am I thus treated? Because I wanted her to be mine for ever in love or friendship, and did not push my gross familiarities as far as I might. 'Why can you not go on as we have done, and say nothing about the word, *forever*?' Was it not plain from this that she even then meditated an escape from me to some less sentimental lover? 'Do you allow anyone else to do so?' I said to her once, as I was toying with her. 'No, not now!' was her answer; that is, because there was nobody else in the house to take freedoms with her. I was very well as a stopgap, but I was to be nothing more. While the coast was clear, I had it all my own way; but the instant C—came, she flung herself at his head in the most barefaced way, ran breathless up stairs before him, blushed when his foot was heard, watched for him in the passage, and was sure to be in close conference with him when he went down again. It was then my mad proceedings commenced. No wonder. Had I not reason to be jealous of every appearance of familiarity with others, knowing how easy she had been with me at first, and that she only grew shy when I did not take farther liberties? What has her character to rest upon but her attachment to me, which she now denies, not modestly, but impudently? Will you yourself say that if she had all along no particular regard for me, she will not do as much or more with other more likely men? 'She has had,' she says, 'enough of my conversation,' so it could not be that! Ah! my friend, it was not to be supposed I should ever meet even with the outward demonstrations of regard from any woman but a common trader in the endearments of love! I have tasted the sweets of the well practised illusion, and now feel the bitterness of knowing what a bliss I am deprived of, and must ever be deprived of. Intolerable conviction! Yet I might, I believe, have won her by other methods; but some demon held my hand. How indeed could I offer her the least insult when I worshipped her very footsteps; and even now pay her divine honours from my inmost heart, whenever I think of her, abased and brutalised as I have been by that Circean cup of kisses, of enchantments, of which I have drunk! I am choked, withered, dried up with chagrin, remorse, despair, from which I have not a moment's respite, day or night. I have always some horrid dream about her, and wake wondering what is the matter that 'she is no longer the same to me as ever?' I thought at least we should always remain dear friends, if nothing more – did she not talk of coming to live with me only the day before I left her in the winter? But 'she's gone, I am abused, and my revenge must be to *love* her!' – Yet she knows that one line, one word would save me, the cruel, heartless destroyer! I see nothing for it but madness, unless Friday brings a change, or unless she is willing to let me go back. You must know I wrote to her to that purpose, but it was a very quiet, sober letter, begging pardon, and professing reform for the future, and all that. What effect it will have, I know not. I was forced to get out of the way of her answer, till Friday came.

Ever your's.

TO S. L.

MY DEAR MISS L—, *Evil to them that evil think*, is an old saying; and I have found it a true one. I have ruined myself by my unjust suspicions of you. Your sweet friendship was the balm of my life; and I have lost it, I fear for ever, by one fault and folly after another. What would I give to be restored to the place in your esteem, which, you assured me, I held only a few months ago! Yet I was not contented, but did all I could to torment myself and harass you by endless doubts and jealousy. Can you not forget and forgive the past, and judge of me by my conduct in future? Can you not take all my follies in the lump, and say like a good, generous girl, 'Well, I'll think no more of them?' In a word, may I come back, and try to behave better? A line to say so would be an additional favour to so many already received by

Your obliged friend,
And sincere well-wisher.

LETTER XII. TO C.P—

I HAVE no answer from her. I'm mad. I wish you to call on M— in confidence, to say I intend to make her an offer of my hand, and that I will write to her father to that effect the instant I am free, and ask him whether he thinks it will be to any purpose, and what he would advise me to do.

UNALTERED LOVE

'Love is not love that alteration finds:
Oh no! it is an ever-fixed mark,
That looks on tempests and is never shaken.'

SHALL I not love her for herself alone, in spite of fickleness and folly? To love her for her regard to me, is not to love her, but myself. She has robbed me of herself: shall she also rob me of my love of her? Did I not live on her smile? Is it less sweet because it is withdrawn from me? Did I not adore her every grace? Does she bend less enchantingly, because she has turned from me to another? Is my love then in the power of fortune, or of her caprice? No, I will have it lasting as it is pure; and I will make a Goddess of her, and build a temple to her in my heart, and worship her on indestructible altars, and raise statues to her: and my homage shall be unblemished as her unrivalled symmetry of form; and when that fails, the memory of it shall survive; and my bosom shall be proof to scorn, as her's has been to pity; and I will pursue her with an unrelenting love, and sue to be her slave, and tend her steps without notice and without reward; and serve her living, and mourn for her when dead. And thus my love will have shewn itself superior to her hate; and I shall triumph and then die. This is my idea of the only true and heroic love! Such is mine for her.

PERFECT LOVE

PERFECT love has this advantage in it, that it leaves the possessor of it nothing farther to desire. There is one object (at least) in which the soul finds absolute content, for which it seeks to live, or dares to die. The heart has as it were filled up the moulds of the imagination. The truth of passion keeps pace with and outvies the extravagance of mere language. There are no words so fine, no flattery so soft, that there is not a sentiment beyond them, that it is impossible to express, at the bottom of the heart where true love is. What idle sounds the common phrases, *adorable creature*, *angel*, *divinity*, are? What a proud reflection it is to have a feeling answering to all these, rooted in the breast, unalterable, unutterable, to which all other feelings are light and vain! Perfect love reposes on the object of its choice, like the halcyon on the wave; and the air of heaven is around it.

FROM C.P., ESQ.

London, July 4th, 1822.

I HAVE seen M—! Now, my dear H—, let me entreat and adjure you to take what I have to tell you, *for what it is worth* – neither for less, nor more. In the first place, I have learned nothing decisive from him. This, as you will at once see, is, as far as it goes, good. I am either to hear from him, or see him again in a day or two ; but I thought you would like to know what passed inconclusive as it was – so

I write without delay, and in great haste to save a post. I
found him frank, and even friendly in his manner to me,
and in his views respecting you. I think that he is sincerely
sorry for your situation; and he feels that the person who has
placed you in that situation is not much less awkwardly situated herself; and he professes that he would willingly do
what he can for the good of both. But he sees great difficulties attending the affair – which he frankly professes to consider as an altogether unfortunate one. With respect to the
marriage, he seems to see the most formidable objections to
it, on both sides; but yet he by no means decidedly says that
it cannot, or that it ought not to take place. These, mind
you, are his own feelings on the subject: but the most important point I learn from him is this, that he is not prepared
to use his influence either way – that the rest of the family
are of the same way of feeling; and that, in fact, the thing
must and does entirely rest with herself. To learn this was,
as you see, gaining a great point. – When I then endeavoured to ascertain whether he knew anything decisive
as to what are her views on the subject, I found that he did
not. He has an opinion on the subject, and he didn't scruple
to tell me what it was; but he has no positive knowledge.
In short, he believes, from what he learns from herself
(and he had purposely seen her on the subject, in consequence of my application to him) that she is at present
indisposed to the marriage; but he is not prepared to say
positively that she will not consent to it. Now all this, coming from him in the most frank and unaffected manner, and
without any appearance of cant, caution, or reserve, I take
to be most important as it respects your views, whatever they
may be; and certainly much more favorable to them (I confess it) than I was prepared to expect, supposing them to
remain as they were. In fact, as I said before, the affair rests
entirely with herself. They are none of them disposed either
to further the marriage, or throw any insurmountable ob-

stacles in the way of it; and what is more important than all, they are evidently by no means *certain* that SHE may not, at some future period, consent to it; or they would, for her sake as well as their own, let you know as much flatly, and put an end to the affair at once.

Seeing in how frank and straitforward a manner he received what I had to say to him, and replied to it, I proceeded to ask him what were *his* views, and what were likely to be *her's* (in case she did not consent) as to whether you should return to live in the house; – but I added, without waiting for his answer, that if she intended to persist in treating you as she had done for some time past, it would be worse than madness for you to think of returning. I added that, in case you did return, all you would expect from her would be that she would treat you with civility and kindness – that she would continue to evince that friendly feeling towards you, that she had done for a great length of time, &c. To this, he said, he could really give no decisive reply, but that he should be most happy if, by any intervention of his, he could conduce to your comfort; but he seemed to think that for you to return on any express understanding that she should behave to you in any particular manner, would be to place her in a most awkward situation. He went somewhat at length into this point, and talked very reasonably about it; the result, however, was that he would not throw any obstacles in the way of your return, or of her treating you as a friend, &c., nor did it appear that he believed she would refuse to do so. And, finally, we parted on the understanding that he would see them on the subject, and ascertain what could be done for the comfort of all parties: though he was of opinion that if you could make up your mind to break off the acquaintance altogether, it would be the best plan of all. I am to hear from him again in a day or two. – Well, what do you say to all this? Can you turn it to any thing but good – comparative good? If you would know what *I* say to it, it is this: – She is still to be won by wise and prudent conduct on your part; she was always to have been won by such; – and if she is lost, it has been (not, as you sometimes suppose, because you have not carried that unwise, may I not say *unworthy?* conduct still farther, but) because you gave way to it at all. Of course I use the terms 'wise' and 'prudent' with reference to your object. Whether the pursuit of that object is wise, only yourself can judge. I say she has all along been to be won, and she still is to be won; and all that stands in the way of your views at this moment is your past conduct. They are all of them, every soul, frightened at you; they have *seen* enough of you to make them so; and they have doubtless heard ten times more than they have seen, or than anyone else has seen. They are all of them, including M— (and particularly she herself) frightened out of their wits, as to what might be your treatment of her if she were your's; and they dare not trust you – they will not trust you, at present. I do not say that they will trust you, or rather that *she* will, for it all depends on her, when you have gone through a probation, but I am sure that she will not trust you till you have. You will, I hope, not be angry with me when I say that she would be a fool if she did. If she were to accept you at present, and without knowing more of you, even *I* should begin to suspect that she had an unworthy motive for doing it. Let me not forget to mention what is perhaps as important a point as any, as it regards the marriage. I of course stated to M— that when you are free, you are prepared to make her a formal offer of your hand; but I begged him, if he was certain that such an offer would be refused, to tell me so plainly at once, that I might endeavour, in that case, to dissuade you from subjecting yourself to the pain of such a refusal. *He would not tell me that he was certain*. He said his opinion was that she would not accept your offer, but still he seemed to think that there would be no harm in making it! – One word more, and

a very important one. He once, and without my referring in
the slightest manner to that part of the subject, spoke of her
as a *good girl*, and *likely to make any man a excellent
wife!* Do you think if she were a bad girl (and if she were,
he must know her to be so) he would have dared to do this,
under these circumstances? – And once, in speaking of *his*
not being a fit person to set his face against 'marrying for
love,' he added 'I did so myself, and out of that house; and
I have had reason to rejoice at it ever since.' And mind (for
I anticipate your cursed suspicions) I'm certain, at least, if
manner can entitle one to be certain of any thing, that he
said all this spontaneously, and without any understood
motive; and I'm certain, too, that he knows you to be a person that it would not do to play any tricks of this kind with.
I believe – (and all this would never have entered my
thoughts, but that I know it will enter your's) I believe that
even if they thought (as you have sometimes supposed they
do) that she needs whitewashing, or making an honest
woman of, *you* would be the last person they would think
of using for such a purpose, for they know (as well as I do)
that you couldn't fail to find out the trick in a month, and
would turn her into the street the next moment, though
she were twenty times your wife – and that, as to the consequences of doing so, you would laugh at them, even if
you cou'dn't escape from them. – I shall lose the post if I
say more.

> Believe me,
> Ever truly your friend,
> C. P.

LETTER XIII

MY DEAR P—, You have saved my life. If I do not keep
friends with her now, I deserve to be hanged, drawn, and
quartered. She is an angel from Heaven, and you cannot

pretend I ever said a word to the contrary! The little rogue
must have liked me from the first, or she never could have
stood all these hurricanes without slipping her cable. What
could she find in me? 'I have mistook my person all this
while,' &c. Do you know I saw a picture, the very pattern
of her, the other day, at Dalkeith Palace (Hope finding
Fortune in the Sea), just before this blessed news came, and
the resemblance drove me almost out of my senses. Such
delicacy, such fulness, such perfect softness, such buoyancy,
such grace! If it is not the very image of her, I am no judge.
– You have the face to doubt my making the best husband
in the world; you might as well doubt it if I was married to
one of the Houris of Paradise. She is a saint, an angel, a
love. If she deceives me again, she kills me. But I will have
such a kiss when I get back, as shall last me twenty years.
May God bless her for not utterly disowning and destroying
me! What an exquisite little creature it is, and now she
holds out to the last in her system of consistent contradictions! Since I wrote to you about making a formal proposal,
I have had her face constantly before me, looking so like
some faultless marble statue, as cold, as fixed and graceful as
ever statue did; the expression (nothing was ever like *that*!)
seemed to say – 'I wish I could love you better than I do, but
still I will be your's.' No, I'll never believe again that she
will not be mine; for I think she was made on purpose for
me. If there's anyone else that understands that turn of her
head as I do, I'll give her up without scruple. I have made
up my mind to this, never to dream of another woman,
while she even thinks it worth her while to *refuse to have
me*. You see I am not hard to please, after all. Did M—
know of the intimacy that had subsisted between us? Or did
you hint at it? I think it would be a *clencher*, if he did. How
ought I to behave when I go back? Advise a fool, who had
nearly lost a Goddess by his folly. The thing was, I could
not think it possible she would ever like *me*. Her taste is

singular, but not the worse for that. I'd rather have her love, or liking (call it what you will) than empires. I deserve to call her mine; for nothing else *can* atone for what I've gone through for her. I hope your next letter will not reverse all, and then I shall be happy till I see her, – one of the blest when I do see her, if she looks like my own beautiful love. I may perhaps write a line when I come to my right wits. – Farewel at present, and thank you a thousand times for what you have done for your poor friend.

p.s. – I like what M— said about her sister, much. There are good people in the world: I begin to see it, and believe it.

LETTER THE LAST

DEAR P—, To-morrow is the decisive day that makes me or mars me. I will let you know the result by a line added to this. Yet what signifies it, since either way I have little hope there, 'whence alone my hope cometh!' You must know I am strangely in the dumps at this present writing. My reception with her is doubtful, and my fate is then certain. The hearing of your happiness has, I own, made me thoughtful. It is just what I proposed to her to do – to have crossed the Alps with me, to sail on sunny seas, to bask in Italian skies, to have visited Vevai and the rocks of Meillerie, and to have repeated to her on the spot the story of Julia and St Preux, and to have shewn her all that my heart had stored up for her – but on my forehead alone is written – REJECTED! Yet I too could have adored as fervently, and loved as tenderly as others, had I been permitted. You are going abroad, you say, happy in making happy. Where shall I be? In the grave, I hope, or else in her arms. To me, alas! there is no sweetness out of her sight, and that sweetness has turned to bitterness, I fear; that gentleness to sullen scorn! Still I hope for the best. If she will but *have* me, I'll make her *love* me: and I think her not giving a positive answer looks like it, and also shews that there is no one else. Her holding out to the last also, I think, proves that she was never to have been gained but with honour. She's a strange, almost an inscrutable girl: but if I once win her consent, I shall kill her with kindness. – Will you let me have a sight of *somebody* before you go? I should be most proud. I was in hopes to have got away by the Steam-boat to-morrow, but owing to the business not coming on till then, I cannot; and may not be in town for another week, unless I come by the Mail, which I am strongly tempted to do. In the latter case I shall be *there*, and visible on Saturday evening. Will you look in and see, about eight o'clock? I wish much to see you and her and J. H. and my little boy once more; and then, if she is not what she once was to me, I care not if I die that instant. I will conclude here till to-morrow, as I am getting into my old melancholy. –

It is all over, I am my own man, and your's ever –

LIBER AMORIS

Part III
ADDRESSED TO J.S.K.[5]

My dear K—, It is all over, and I know my fate. I told you I would send you word, if anything decisive happened; but an impenetrable mystery hung over the affair till lately. It is at last (by the merest accident in the world) dissipated; and I keep my promise, both for your satisfaction, and for the ease of my own mind.

You remember the morning when I said 'I will go and repose my sorrows at the foot of Ben Lomond' – and when from Dumbarton Bridge its giant-shadow, clad in air and sunshine, appeared in view. We had a pleasant day's walk. We passed Smollett's monument on the road (somehow these poets touch one in reflection more than most military heroes) – talked of old times; you repeated Logan's beautiful verses to the cuckoo,* which I wanted to compare with Wordsworth's, but my courage failed me; you then told me some passages of an early attachment which was suddenly broken off; we considered together which was the most to be pitied, a disappointment in love where the attachment was mutual or one where there has been no return, and we both agreed, I think, that the former was best to be endured, and that to have the consciousness of it a companion for life was the least evil of the two, as there was a secret sweetness that took off the bitterness and the sting of regret, and 'the

---

* 'Sweet bird, thy bower is ever green,
    Thy sky is ever clear;

memory of what once had been' atoned, in some measure, and at intervals, for what 'never more could be.' In the other case, there was nothing to look back to with tender satisfaction, no redeeming trait, not even a possibility of turning it to good. It left behind it not cherished sighs, but stifled pangs. The galling sense of it did not bring moisture into the eyes, but dried up the heart ever after. One had been my fate, the other had been yours! –

You startled me every now and then from my reverie by the robust voice, in which you asked the country people (by no means prodigal of their answers) – 'If there was any trout-fishing in those streams?' – and our dinner at Luss set us up for the rest of our day's march. The sky now became overcast; but this, I think, added to the effect of the scene. The road to Tarbet is superb. It is on the very verge of the lake – hard, level, rocky, with low stone bridges constantly flung across it, and fringed with birch trees, just then budding into spring, behind which, as through a slight veil, you saw the huge shadowy form of Ben Lomond. It lifts its enormous but graceful bulk direct from the edge of the water without any projecting lowlands, and has in this respect much the advantage of Skiddaw. Loch Lomond comes upon you by degrees as you advance, unfolding and then withdrawing its conscious beauties like an accomplished coquet. You are struck with the point of a rock, the arch of a bridge, the Highland huts (like the first rude habitations of men) dug out of the soil, built of turf, and covered with

---

Thou hast no sorrow in thy song,
No winter in thy year.'

So they begin. It was the month of May; the cuckoo sang shrouded in some woody copse; the showers fell between whiles; my friend repeated the lines with native enthusiasm in a clear manly voice, still resonant of youth and hope. Mr Wordsworth will excuse me, if in these circumstances I declined entering the field with his profounder metaphysical strain, and kept my preference to myself.

brown heather, a sheep-cote, some straggling cattle feeding half-way down a precipice; but as you advance farther on, the view expands into the perfection of lake scenery. It is nothing (or your eye is caught by nothing) but water, earth, and sky. Ben Lomond waves to the right, in its simple majesty, cloud-capt or bare, and descending to a point at the head of the lake, shews the Trossacs beyond, tumbling about their blue ridges like woods waving; to the left is the Cobler, whose top is like a castle shattered in pieces and nodding to its ruin; and at your side rise the shapes of round pastoral hills, green, fleeced with herds, and retiring into mountainous bays and upland valleys, where solitude and peace might make their lasting home, if peace were to be found in solitude! That it was not always so, I was a sufficient proof; for there was one image that alone haunted me in the midst of all this sublimity and beauty, and turned it to a mockery and a dream!

The snow on the mountain would not let us ascend; and being weary of waiting and of being visited by the guide every two hours to let us know that the weather would not do, we returned, you homewards, and I to London –

'Italiam, Italiam!'

You know the anxious expectations with which I set out: – now hear the result. –

As the vessel sailed up the Thames, the air thickened with the consciousness of being near her, and I 'heaved her name pantingly forth.' As I approached the house, I could not help thinking of the lines –

> 'How near am I to happiness,
> That earth exceeds not; Not another like it.
> The treasures of the deep are not so precious
> As are the conceal'd comforts of a man
> Lock'd up in woman's love. I scent the air
> Of blessings when I come but near the house.

What a delicious breath true love sends forth !
The violet-beds not sweeter. Now for a welcome
Able to draw men's envies upon man :
A kiss now that will hang upon my lip,
As sweet as morning dew upon a rose,
And full as long !'

I saw her, but I saw at the first glance that there was something amiss. It was with much difficulty and after several pressing intreaties that she was prevailed on to come up into the room; and when she did, she stood at the door, cold, distant, averse; and when at length she was persuaded by my repeated remonstrances to come and take my hand, and I offered to touch her lips, she turned her head and shrunk from my embraces, as if quite alienated or mortally offended. I asked what it could mean? What had I done in her absence to have incurred her displeasure? Why had she not written to me? I could get only short, sullen, disconnected answers, as if there was something labouring in her mind which she either could not or would not impart. I hardly knew how to bear this first reception after so long an absence, and so different from the one my sentiments towards her merited; but I thought it possible it might be prudery (as I had returned without having actually accomplished what I went about) or that she had taken offence at something in my letters. She saw how much I was hurt. I asked her, 'If she was altered since I went away?' – 'No.' 'If there was any one else who had been so fortunate as to gain her favourable opinion?' – 'No, there was no one else.' 'What was it then? Was it any thing in my letters? Or had I displeased her by letting Mr P— know she wrote to me?' – 'No, not at all; but she did not apprehend my last letter required any answer, or she would have replied to it.' All this appeared to me very unsatisfactory and evasive; but I could get no more from her, and was obliged to let her go with a heavy, foreboding heart. I however found that C— was gone, and no one else had been there, of whom I had cause to be jealous. – 'Should I see her on the morrow?' – 'She believed so, but she could not promise.' The next morning she did not appear with the breakfast as usual. At this I grew somewhat uneasy. The little Buonaparte, however, was placed in its old position on the mantle-piece, which I considered as a sort of recognition of old times. I saw her once or twice casually; nothing particular happened till the next day, which was Sunday. I took occasion to go into the parlour for the newspaper, which she gave me with a gracious smile, and seemed tolerably frank and cordial. This of course acted as a spell upon me. I walked out with my little boy,[6] intending to go and dine out at one or two places, but I found that I still contrived to bend my steps towards her, and I went back to take tea at home. While we were out, I talked to William about Sarah, saying that she too was unhappy, and asking him to make it up with her. He said, if she was unhappy, he would not bear her malice any more. When she came up with the tea-things, I said to her, 'William has something to say to you – I believe he wants to be friends.' On which he said in his abrupt, hearty manner, 'Sarah, I'm sorry if I've ever said anything to vex you' – so they shook hands, and she said, smiling affably – '*Then* I'll think no more of it!' I added – 'I see you've brought me back my little Buonaparte' – She answered with tremulous softness – 'I told you I'd keep it safe for you!' – as if her pride and pleasure in doing so had been equal, and she had, as it were, thought of nothing during my absence but how to greet me with this proof of her fidelity on my return. I cannot describe her manner. Her words are few and simple; but you can have no idea of the exquisite, unstudied, irresistible graces with which she accompanies them, unless you can suppose a Greek statue to smile, move, and speak. Those lines in Tibullus seem to have been written on purpose for her –

Quicquid agit quoquo vestigià vertit,
Componit furtim, subsequiturque decor.

Or what do you think of those in a modern play, which might actually have been composed with an eye to this little trifler –

– 'See with what a waving air she goes
Along the corridor. How like a fawn!
Yet statelier. No sound (however soft)
Nor gentlest echo telleth when she treads,
But every motion of her shape doth seem
Hallowed by silence. So did Hebe grow
Among the gods a paragon! Away, I'm grown
The very fool of Love!'

The truth is, I never saw anything like her, nor I never shall again. How then do I console myself for the loss of her? Shall I tell you, but you will not mention it again? I am foolish enough to believe that she and I, in spite of every thing, shall be sitting together over a sea-coal fire, a comfortable good old couple, twenty years hence! But to my narrative. –

I was delighted with the alteration in her manner, and said, referring to the bust – 'You know it is not mine, but your's; I gave it you; nay, I have given you all – my heart, and whatever I possess, is your's!' She seemed good-humouredly to decline this *carte blanche* offer, and waved, like a thing of enchantment, out of the room. False calm! – Deceitful smiles! – Short interval of peace, followed by lasting woe! I sought an interview with her that same evening. I could not get her to come any farther than the door. 'She was busy – she could hear what I had to say there.' 'Why do you seem to avoid me as you do? Not one five minutes' conversation, for the sake of old acquaintance? Well, then, for the sake of *the little image!*' The appeal seemed to have lost its efficacy; the charm was broken; she remained immoveable. 'Well, then I must come to you, if

you will not run away.' I went and sat down in a chair near
the door, and took her hand, and talked to her for three
quarters of an hour; and she listened patiently, thought-
fully, and seemed a good deal affected by what I said. I told
her how much I had felt, how much I had suffered for her
in my absence, and how much I had been hurt by her sudden silence, for which I knew not how to account. I could
have done nothing to offend her while I was away; and
my letters were, I hoped, tender and respectful. I had had
but one thought ever present with me; her image never
quitted my side, alone or in company, to delight or distract
me. Without her I could have no peace, nor ever should
again, unless she would behave to me as she had done
formerly. There was no abatement of my regard to her; why
was she so changed? I said to her, 'Ah! Sarah, when I think
that it is only a year ago that you were everything to me I
could wish, and that now you seem lost to me for ever, the
month of May (the name of which ought to be a signal for
joy and hope) strikes chill to my heart. – How different is
this meeting from that delicious parting, when you seemed
never weary of repeating the proofs of your regard and
tenderness, and it was with difficulty we tore ourselves
asunder at last! I am ten thousand times fonder of you than
I was then, and ten thousand times more unhappy.' 'You
have no reason to be so; my feelings towards you are the
same as they ever were.' I told her 'She was my all of hope
or comfort: my passion for her grew stronger every time I
saw her.' She answered, 'She was sorry for it; for *that* she
never could return.' I said something about looking ill: she
said in her pretty, mincing, emphatic way, 'I despise looks!'
So, thought I, it is not that; and she says there's no one
else: it must be some strange air she gives herself, in consequence of the approaching change in my circumstances. She
has been probably advised not to give up till all is fairly over,
and then she will be my own sweet girl again. All this

time she was standing just outside the door, my hand in hers (would that they could have grown together!) she was dressed in a loose morning-gown, her hair curled beautifully; she stood with her profile to me, and looked down the whole time. No expression was ever more soft or perfect. Her whole attitude, her whole form, was dignity and bewitching grace. I said to her, 'You look like a queen, my love, adorned with your own graces!' I grew idolatrous, and would have kneeled to her. She made a movement, as if she was displeased. I tried to draw her towards me. She wouldn't. I then got up, and offered to kiss her at parting. I found she obstinately refused. This stung me to the quick. It was the first time in her life she had ever done so. There must be some new bar between us to produce these continued denials; and she had not even esteem enough left to tell me so. I followed her half-way down-stairs, but to no purpose, and returned into my room, confirmed in my most dreadful surmises. I could bear it no longer. I gave way to all the fury of disappointed hope and jealous passion. I was made the dupe of trick and cunning, killed with cold, sullen scorn; and, after all the agony I had suffered, could obtain no explanation why I was subjected to it. I was still to be tantalized, tortured, made the cruel sport of one, for whom I would have sacrificed all. I tore the locket which contained her hair (and which I used to wear continually in my bosom, as the precious token of her dear regard) from my neck, and trampled it in pieces. I then dashed the little Buonaparte on the ground, and stamped upon it, as one of her instruments of mockery. I could not stay in the room; I could not leave it; my rage, my despair were uncontrollable. I shrieked curses on her name, and on her false love; and the scream I uttered (so pitiful and so piercing was it, that the sound of it terrified me) instantly brought the whole house, father, mother, lodgers and all, into the room. They thought I was destroying her and myself. I had gone into the bedroom, merely to hide away from myself, and as I came out of it, raging-mad with the new sense of present shame and lasting misery, Mrs F— said, 'She's in there! He has got her in there!' thinking the cries had proceeded from her, and that I had been offering her violence. 'Oh! no,' I said, 'She's in no danger from me; I am not the person;' and tried to burst from this scene of degradation. The mother endeavoured to stop me, and said, 'For God's sake, don't go out, Mr —! for God's sake, don't!' Her father, who was not, I believe, in the secret, and was therefore justly scandalised at such outrageous conduct, said angrily, 'Let him go! Why should he stay?' I however sprang down stairs, and as they called out to me, 'What is it? – What has she done to you?' I answered, 'She has murdered me! – She has destroyed me for ever! – She has doomed my soul to perdition!' I rushed out of the house, thinking to quit it forever; but I was no sooner in the street, than the desolation and the darkness became greater, more intolerable; and the eddying violence of my passion drove me back to the source, from whence it sprung. This unexpected explosion, with the conjectures to which it would give rise, could not be very agreeable to the *précieuse* or her family; and when I went back, the father was waiting at the door, as if anticipating this sudden turn of my feelings, with no friendly aspect. I said, 'I have to beg pardon, Sir; but my mad fit is over, and I wish to say a few words to you in private.' He seemed to hesitate, but some uneasy forebodings on his own account, probably, prevailed over his resentment; or, perhaps (as philosophers have a desire to know the cause of thunder) it was a natural curiosity to know what circumstances of provocation had given rise to such an extraordinary scene of confusion. When we reached my room, I requested him to be seated. I said, 'It is true, Sir, I have lost my peace of mind for ever, but at present I am quite calm and collected, and I wish to explain to you why I have behaved in so extravagant a way, and to ask for your advice and intercession.' He appeared satisfied, and I went on. I had no chance either of exculpating myself, or of probing the question to the bottom, but by stating the naked truth, and therefore I said at once, 'Sarah told me, Sir (and I never shall forget the way in which she told me, fixing her dove's eyes upon me, and looking a thousand tender reproaches for the loss of that good opinion, which she held dearer than all the world) she told me, Sir, that as you one day passed the door, which stood a-jar, you saw her in an attitude which a good deal startled you; I mean sitting in my lap, with her arms round my neck, and mine twined round her in the fondest manner. What I wished to ask was, whether this was actually the case, or whether it was a mere invention of her own, to enhance the sense of my obligations to her; for I begin to doubt everything?' – 'Indeed, it was so; and very much surprised and hurt I was to see it.' 'Well then, Sir, I can only say, that as you saw her sitting then, so she had been sitting for the last year and a half, almost every day of her life, by the hour together; and you may judge yourself, knowing what a nice modest-looking girl she is, whether, after having been admitted to such intimacy with so sweet a creature, and for so long a time, it is not enough to make any one frantic to be received by her as I have been since my return, without any provocation given or cause assigned for it.' The old man answered very seriously, and, as I think, sincerely, 'What you now tell me, Sir, mortifies and shocks me as much as it can do yourself. I had no idea such a thing was possible. I was much pained at what I saw; but I thought it an accident, and that it would never happen again.' – 'It was a constant habit; it has happened a hundred times since, and a thousand before. I lived on her caresses as my daily food, nor can I live without them.' So I told him the whole story, 'what conjurations, and what mighty magic I won his daughter with,' to be anything but *mine for life*.

Nothing could well exceed his astonishment and apparent mortification. 'What I had said,' he owned, 'had left a weight upon his mind that he should not easily get rid of.' I told him, 'For myself, I never could recover the blow I had received. I thought, however, for her own sake, she ought to alter her present behaviour. Her marked neglect and dislike, so far from justifying, left her former intimacies without excuse; for nothing could reconcile them to propriety, or even a pretence to common decency, but either love, or friendship so strong and pure that it could put on the guise of love. She was certainly a singular girl. Did she think it right and becoming to be free with strangers, and strange to old friends?' I frankly declared, 'I did not see how it was in human nature for any one who was not rendered callous to such familiarities by bestowing them indiscriminately on every one, to grant the extreme and continued indulgences she had done to me, without either liking the man at first, or coming to like him in the end, in spite of herself. When my addresses had nothing, and could have nothing honourable in them, she gave them every encouragement; when I wished to make them honourable, she treated them with the utmost contempt. The terms we had been all along on were such as if she had been to be my bride next day. It was only when I wished her actually to become so, to ensure her own character and my happiness, that she shrunk back with precipitation and panic-fear. There seemed to me something wrong in all this; a want both of common propriety, and I might say, of natural feeling; yet, with all her faults, I loved her, and ever should, beyond any other human being. I had drank in the poison of her sweetness too long ever to be cured of it; and though I might find it to be poison in the end, it was still in my veins. My only ambition was to be permitted to live with her, and to die in her arms. Be she what she would, treat me how she would, I felt that my soul was wedded to hers; and were she a mere lost creature, I would try to snatch her from perdition, and marry her to-morrow if she would have me. That was the question – 'Would she have me, or would she not?' He said he could not tell; but should not attempt to put any constraint upon her inclinations, one way or other. I acquiesced, and added, that 'I had brought all this upon myself, by acting contrary to the suggestions of my friend, Mr —, who had desired me to take no notice whether she came near me or kept away, whether she smiled or frowned, was kind or contemptuous – all you have to do, is to wait patiently for a month till you are your own man, as you will be in all probability; then make her an offer of your hand, and if she refuses, there's an end of the matter.' Mr L. said, 'Well, Sir, and I don't think you can follow a better advice!' I took this as at least a sort of negative encouragement, and so we parted.

TO THE SAME
(in continuation).

My dear Friend, The next day I felt almost as sailors must do after a violent storm over-night, that has subsided towards day-break. The morning was a dull and stupid calm, and I found she was unwell, in consequence of what had happened. In the evening I grew more uneasy, and determined on going into the country for a week or two. I gathered up the fragments of the locket of her hair, and the little bronze statue, which were strewed about the floor, kissed them, folded them up in a sheet of paper, and sent them to her, with these lines written in pencil on the outside – *'Pieces of a broken heart, to be kept in remembrance of the unhappy. Farewell.'* No notice was taken; nor did I expect any. The following morning I requested Betsey to pack up my box for me, as I should go out of town the next day, and at the same time wrote a note to her sister to say, I should take it as a favour if she would please to accept of the enclosed copies of the *Vicar of Wakefield*, *The Man of Feeling*, and *Nature and Art*, in lieu of three volumes of my own writings, which I had given her on different occasions, in the course of our acquaintance. I was piqued, in fact, that she should have these to shew as proofs of my weakness, and as if I thought the way to win her was by plaguing her with my own performances. She sent me word back that the books I had sent were of no use to her, and that I should have those I wished for in the afternoon; but that she could not before, as she had lent them to her sister, Mrs M—. I said, 'very well;' but observed (laughing) to Betsey, 'It's a bad rule to give and take; so, if Sarah won't have these books, you must; they are very pretty ones, I assure you.' She curtsied and took them, according to the family custom. In the afternoon, when I came back to tea, I found the little girl on her knees, busy in packing up my things, and a large paper parcel on the table, which I could not at first tell what to make of. On opening it, however, I soon found what it was. It contained a number of volumes which I had given her at different times (among others, a little Prayer-Book, bound in crimson velvet, with green silk linings; she kissed it twenty times when she received it, and said it was the prettiest present in the world, and that she would shew it to her aunt, who would be proud of it) – and all these she had returned together. Her name in the title-page was cut out of them all. I doubted at the instant whether she had done this before or after I had sent for them back, and I have doubted of it since; but there is no occasion to suppose her *ugly all over with hypocrisy*. Poor little thing! She has enough to answer for, as it is. I asked Betsey if she could carry a message for me, and she said '*Yes*.' 'Will you tell your sister, then, that I did not want all these books; and give my love to her, and say that I shall be obliged if she will still keep these that I have sent back, and tell her that it

is only those of my own writing that I think unworthy of
her.' What do you think the little imp made answer? She
raised herself on the other side of the table where she stood,
as if inspired by the genius of the place, and said – 'AND
THOSE ARE THE ONES THAT SHE PRIZES THE MOST!'
If there were ever words spoken that could revive the dead,
those were the words. Let me kiss them, and forget that my
ears have heard aught else! I said, 'Are you sure of that?'
and she said, 'Yes, quite sure.' I told her, 'If I could be, I
should be very different from what I was.' And I became so
that instant, for these casual words carried assurance to my
heart of her esteem – that once implied, I had proofs enough
of her fondness. Oh! how I felt at that moment! Restored
to love, hope, and joy, by a breath which I had caught by
the merest accident, and which I might have pined in absence and mute despair for want of hearing! I did not know
how to contain myself; I was childish, wanton, drunk with
pleasure. I gave Betsey a twenty-shilling note which I happened to have in my hand, and on her asking 'What's this
for, Sir?' I said, 'It's for you. Don't you think it worth that
to be made happy? You once made me very wretched by
some words I heard you drop, and now you have made me as
happy; and all I wish you is, when you grow up, that you
may find some one to love you as well as I do your sister, and
that you may love better than she does me!' I continued in
this state of delirium or dotage all that day and the next,
talked incessantly, laughed at every thing, and was so extravagant, nobody could tell what was the matter with me. I
murmured her name; I blest her; I folded her to my heart
in delicious fondness; I called her by my own name; I worshipped her: I was mad for her. I told P— I should laugh in
her face, if ever she pretended not to like me again. Her
mother came in and said, she hoped I should excuse Sarah's
coming up. 'Oh, Ma'am,' I said, 'I have no wish to see her;
I feel her at my heart; she does not hate me after all, and I

wish for nothing. Let her come when she will, she is to me welcomer than light, than life; but let it be in her own sweet time, and at her own dear pleasure.' Betsey also told me she was 'so glad to get the books back.' I, however, sobered and wavered (by degrees) from seeing nothing of her, day after day; and in less than a week I was devoted to the Infernal Gods. I could hold out no longer than the Monday evening following. I sent a message to her; she returned an ambiguous answer; but she came up. Pity me, my friend, for the shame of this recital. Pity me for the pain of having ever had to make it! If the spirits of mortal creatures, purified by faith and hope, can (according to the highest assurances) ever, during thousands of years of smooth-rolling eternity and balmy, sainted repose, forget the pain, the toil, the anguish, the helplessness, and the despair they have suffered here, in this frail being, then may I forget that withering hour, and her, that fair, pale form that entered, my inhuman betrayer, and my only earthly love! She said, 'Did you wish to speak to me, Sir?' I said, 'Yes, may I not speak to you? I wanted to see you and be friends.' I rose up, offered her an arm-chair which stood facing, bowed on it, and knelt to her adoring. She said (going) 'If that's all, I have nothing to say.' I replied, 'Why do you treat me thus? What have I done to become thus hateful to you?' *Answer*, 'I always told you I had no affection for you.' You may suppose this was a blow, after the imaginary honey-moon in which I had passed the preceding week. I was stunned by it; my heart sunk within me. I contrived to say, 'Nay, my dear girl, not always neither; for did you not once (if I might presume to look back to those happy, happy times), when you were sitting on my knee as usual, embracing and embraced, and I asked if you could not love me at last, did you not make answer, in the softest tones that ever man heard, *'I could easily say so, whether I did or not; you should judge by my actions!'* Was I to blame in taking you at your word, when every hope I had depended on your sincerity? And did you not say since I came back, '*Your feelings to me were the same as ever*?' Why then is your behaviour so different?' s. 'Is it nothing, your exposing me to the whole house in the way you did the other evening?' H. 'Nay, that was the consequence of your cruel reception of me, not the cause of it. I had better have gone away last year, as I proposed to do, unless you would give some pledge of your fidelity; but it was your own offer that I should remain. "Why should I go?" you said, "Why could we not go on the same as we had done, and say nothing about the word *forever*?"' s. 'And how did you behave when you returned?' H. 'That was all forgiven when we last parted, and your last words were, "I should find you the same as ever" when I came home? Did you not that very day enchant and madden me over again by the purest kisses and embraces, and did I not go from you (as I said) adoring, confiding, with every assurance of mutual esteem and friendship?' s. 'Yes, and in your absence I found that you had told my aunt what had passed between us.' H. 'It was to induce her to extort your real sentiments from you, that you might no longer make a secret of your true regard for me, which your actions (but not your words) confessed.' s. 'I own I have been guilty of improprieties, which you have gone and repeated, not only in the house, but out of it; so that it has come to my ears from various quarters, as if I was a light character. And I am determined in future to be guided by the advice of my relations, and particularly of my aunt, whom I consider as my best friend, and keep every lodger at a proper distance.' You will find hereafter that her favourite lodger, whom she visits daily, had left the house; so that she might easily make and keep this vow of extraordinary self-denial. Precious little dissembler! Yet her aunt, her best friend, says, 'No, Sir, no; Sarah's no hypocrite!' which I was fool enough to believe; and yet my great and unpardonable offence is to have entertained passing doubts on this delicate point. I said, Whatever errors I had committed, arose from my anxiety to have everything explained to her honour: my conduct shewed that I had that at heart, and that I built on the purity of her character as on a rock. My esteem for her amounted to adoration. 'She did not want adoration.' It was only when any thing happened to imply that I had been mistaken, that I committed any extravagance, because I could not bear to think her short of perfection. 'She was far from perfection,' she replied, with an air and manner (oh, my God!) as near it as possible. 'How could she accuse me of a want of regard to her? It was but the other day, Sarah,' I said to her, 'when that little circumstance of the books happened, and I fancied the expressions your sister dropped proved the sincerity of all your kindness to me – you don't know how my heart melted within me at the thought, that after all, I might be dear to you. New hopes sprung up in my heart, and I felt as Adam must have done when his Eve was created for him!' 'She had heard enough of that sort of conversation,' (moving towards the door). This, I own, was the unkindest cut of all. I had, in that case, no hopes whatever. I felt that I had expended words in vain, and that the conversation below stairs (which I told you of when I saw you) had spoiled her taste for mine. If the allusion had been classical I should have been to blame; but it was scriptural, it was a sort of religious courtship, and Miss L. is religious!

> 'At once he took his Muse and dipt her
> Right in the middle of the Scripture.'

It would not do – the lady could make neither head nor tail of it. This is a poor attempt at levity. Alas! I am sad enough. 'Would she go and leave me so? If it was only my own behaviour, I still did not doubt of success. I knew the sincerity of my love, and she would be convinced of it in time. If

that was all, I did not care: but tell me true, is there not a
new attachment that is the real cause of your estrangement?
Tell me, my sweet friend, and before you tell me, give me
your hand (nay, both hands) that I may have something to
support me under the dreadful conviction.' She let me take
her hands in mine, saying, 'She supposed there could be no
objection to that,' – as if she acted on the suggestions of
others, instead of following her own will – but still avoided
giving me any answer. I conjured her to tell me the worst,
and kill me on the spot. Any thing was better than my present state. I said, 'Is it Mr C—?' She smiled, and said with
gay indifference. 'Mr C— was here a very short time.' 'Well,
then, was it Mr —?' She hesitated, and then replied faintly,
'No.' This was a mere trick to mislead; one of the profound-
nesses of Satan, in which she is an adept. 'But,' she added
hastily, 'she could make no more confidences.' 'Then,' said
I, 'you have something to communicate.' 'No; but she had
once mentioned a thing of the sort, which I had hinted to
her mother, though it signified little.' All this while I was in
tortures. Every word, every half-denial, stabbed me. 'Had
she any tie?' 'No, I have no tie?' 'You are not going to be
married soon?' 'I don't intend ever to marry at all!' 'Can't
you be friends with me as of old?' 'She could give no promises.' 'Would she make her own terms?' 'She would make
none.' – 'I was sadly afraid the *little image* was dethroned
from her heart, as I had dashed it to the ground the other
night.' – 'She was neither desperate nor violent.' I did not
answer – 'But deliberate and deadly,' – though I might; and
so she vanished in this running fight of question and
answer, in spite of my vain efforts to detain her. The cocka-
trice, I said, mocks me: so she has always done. The thought
was a dagger to me. My head reeled, my heart recoiled within me. I was stung with scorpions; my flesh crawled; I was
choked with rage; her scorn scorched me like flames; her air
(her heavenly air) withdrawn from me, stifled me, and left

me gasping for breath and being. It was a fable. She started up in her own likeness, a serpent in place of a woman. She had fascinated, she had stung me, and had returned to her proper shape, gliding from me after inflicting the mortal wound, and instilling deadly poison into every pore; but her form lost none of its original brightness by the change of character, but was all glittering, beauteous, voluptuous grace. Seed of the serpent or of the woman, she was divine! I felt that she was a witch, and had bewitched me. Fate had enclosed me round about. *I* was transformed too, no longer human (any more than she, to whom I had knit myself) my feelings were marble; my blood was of molten lead; my thoughts on fire. I was taken out of myself, wrapt into another sphere, far from the light of day, of hope, of love. I had no natural affection left; she had slain me, but no other thing had power over me. Her arms embraced another; but her mock-embrace, the phantom of her love, still bound me, and I had not a wish to escape. So I felt then, and so perhaps shall feel till I grow old and die, nor have any desire that my years should last longer than they are linked in the chain of those amorous folds, or than her enchantments steep my soul in oblivion of all other things! I started to find myself alone – for ever alone, without a creature to love me. I looked round the room for help; I saw the tables, the chairs, the places where she stood or sat, empty, deserted, dead. I could not stay where I was; I had no one to go to but to the parent-mischief, the preternatural hag, that had 'drugged this posset' of her daughter's charms and falsehood for me, and I went down and (such was my weakness and helplessness) sat with her for an hour, and talked with her of her daughter, and the sweet days we had passed together, and said I thought her a good girl, and believed that if there was no rival, she still had a regard for me at the bottom of her heart; and how I liked her all the better for her coy, maiden airs: and I received the assurance over and over that there was no one else; and that Sarah (they all knew) never staid five minutes with any other lodger, while with me she would stay by the hour together, in spite of all her father could say to her (what were her motives, was best known to herself!) and while we were talking of her, she came bounding into the room, smiling with smothered delight at the consummation of my folly and her own art; and I asked her mother whether she thought she looked as if she hated me, and I took her wrinkled, withered, cadaverous, clammy hand at parting, and kissed it. Faugh! —

I will make an end of this story; there is something in it discordant to honest ears. I left the house the next day, and returned to Scotland in a state so near to phrenzy that I take it the shades sometimes ran into one another. R—[7] met me the day after I arrived, and will tell you the way I was in. I was like a person in a high fever; only mine was in the mind instead of the body. It had the same irritating, uncomfortable effect on the bye-standers. I was incapable of any application, and don't know what I should have done, had it not been for the kindness of —. I came to see you, to 'bestow some of my tediousness upon you,' but you were gone from home. Everything went on well as to the law business; and as it approached to a conclusion, I wrote to my good friend P— to go to M—, who had married her sister, and ask him if it would be worth my while to make her a formal offer, as soon as I was free, as, with the least encouragement, I was ready to throw myself at her feet; and to know, in case of refusal, whether I might go back there and be treated as an old friend. Not a word of answer could be got from her on either point, notwithstanding every importunity and intreaty; but it was the opinion of M— that I might go and try my fortune. I did so with joy, with something like confidence. I thought her giving no positive answer implied a chance, at least, of the reversion of her favour, in case I behaved well. All was false, hollow, insidious. The first night after I got home, I slept on down. In Scotland, the flint had been my pillow. But now I slept under the same roof with her. What softness, what balmy repose in the very thought! I saw her that same day and shook hands with her, and told her how glad I was to see her; and she was kind and comfortable, though still cold and distant. Her manner was altered from what it was the last time. She still absented herself from the room, but was mild and affable when she did come. She was pale, dejected, evidently uneasy about something, and had been ill. I thought it was perhaps her reluctance to yield to my wishes, her pity for what I suffered; and that in the struggle between both, she did not know what to do. How I worshipped her at these moments! We had a long interview the third day, and I thought all was doing well. I found her sitting at work in the window-seat of the front parlour; and on my asking if I might come in, she made no objection. I sat down by her; she let me take her hand; I talked to her of indifferent things, and of old times. I asked her if she would put some new frills on my shirts? – 'With the greatest pleasure.' If she could get *the little image* mended? 'It was broken in three pieces, and the sword was gone, but she would try.' I then asked her to make up a plaid silk which I had given her in the winter, and which she said would make a pretty summer gown. I so longed to see her in it! – 'She had little time to spare, but perhaps might!' Think what I felt, talking peaceably, kindly, tenderly with my love, – not passionately, not violently. I tried to take pattern by her patient meekness, as I thought it, and to subdue my desires to her will. I then sued to her, but respectfully, to be admitted to her friendship – she must know I was as true a friend as ever a woman had – or if there was a bar to our intimacy from a dearer attachment, to let me know it frankly, as I shewed her all my heart. She drew out her handkerchief and wiped her eyes 'of tears which sacred pity had engendered there.' Was it so or not? I cannot tell. But so she stood (while I pleaded my cause to her with all the earnestness, and fondness in the world) with the tears trickling from her eye-lashes, her head stooping, her attitude fixed, with the finest expression that ever was seen of mixed regret, pity, and stubborn resolution; but without speaking a word, without altering a feature. It was like a petrifaction of a human face in the softest moment of passion. 'Ah!' I said, 'how you look! I have prayed again and again while I was away from you, in the agony of my spirit, that I might but live to see you look so again, and then breathe my last!' I intreated her to give me some explanation. In vain! At length she said she must go, and disappeared like a spirit. That week she did all the little trifling favours I had asked of her. The frills were put on, and she sent up to know if I wanted any more done. She got the Buonaparte mended. This was like healing old wounds indeed! How? As follows, for thereby hangs the conclusion of my tale. Listen.

I had sent a message one evening to speak to her about some special affairs of the house, and received no answer. I waited an hour expecting her, and then went out in great vexation at my disappointment. I complained to her mother a day or two after, saying I thought it so unlike Sarah's usual propriety of behaviour, that she must mean it as a mark of disrespect. Mrs L— said, 'La! Sir, you're always fancying things. Why, she was dressing to go out, and she was only going to get the little image you're both so fond of mended; and it's to be done this evening. She has been to two or three places to see about it, before she could get anyone to undertake it.' My heart, my poor heart, almost melted within me at this news. I answered, 'Ah! Madam, that's always the way with the dear creature. I am finding fault with her and thinking the hardest things of her; and at that very time she's doing something to shew the most delicate attention, and that she has no greater satisfaction than in

gratifying my wishes!' On this we had some farther talk,
and I took nearly the whole of the lodgings at a hundred
guineas a year, – that (as I said) she might have a little leisure
to sit at her needle of an evening, or to read if she chose, or
to walk out when it was fine. She was not in good health,
and it would do her good to be less confined. I would be the
drudge and she should no longer be the slave. I asked nothing in return. To see her happy, to make her so, was to be
so myself. – This was agreed to. I went over to Blackheath
that evening, delighted as I could be after all I had suffered,
and lay the whole of the next morning on the heath under
the open sky, dreaming of my earthly Goddess. This was
Sunday. That evening I returned, for I could hardly bear
to be for a moment out of the house where she was, and the
next morning she tapped at the door – it was opened – it was
she – she hesitated and then came forward: she had got the
little image in her hand, I took it, and blest her from my
heart. She said 'They had been obliged to put some new
pieces to it.' I said 'I didn't care how it was done, so that I
had it restored to me safe, and by her.' I thanked her and
begged to shake hands with her. She did so, and as I held
the only hand in the world that I never wished to let go, I
looked up in her face, and said 'Have pity on me, have pity
on me, and save me if you can!' Not a word of answer, but
she looked full in my eyes, as much as to say, 'Well I'll
think of it; and if I can, I will save you!' We talked about
the expense of repairing the figure. 'Was the man waiting?'
– 'No, she had fetched it on Saturday evening.' I said I'd
give her the money in the course of the day, and then shook
hands with her again in token of reconciliation; and she
went waving out of the room, but at the door turned round
and looked full at me, as she did the first time she beguiled
me of my heart. This was the last. –

All that day I longed to go down stairs to ask her and her
mother to set out with me for Scotland on Wednesday, and

on Saturday I would make her my wife. Something with-held me. In the evening, however, I could not rest without seeing her, and I said to her younger sister, 'Betsey, if Sarah will come up now, I'll pay her what she laid out for me the other day.' – 'My sister's gone out, Sir,' was the answer. What again! thought I, that's somewhat sudden. I told P— her sitting in the window-seat of the front parlour boded me no good. It was not in her old character. She did not use to know there were doors or windows in the house – and now she goes out three times in a week. It is to meet some one, I'll lay my life on 't. 'Where is she gone?' – 'To my grandmother's, Sir.' 'Where does your grandmother live now?' – 'At Somers' Town.' I immediately set out to Somers' Town. I passed one or two streets, and at last turned up King Street, thinking it most likely she would return that way home. I passed a house in King Street where I had once lived, and had not proceeded many paces, rumi-nating on chance and change and old times, when I saw her coming towards me. I felt a strange pang at the sight, but I thought her alone. Some people before me moved on, and I saw another person with her. *The murder was out.* It was a tall, rather well-looking young man, but I did not at first recollect him. We passed at the crossing of the street with-out speaking. Will you believe it, after all that had passed between us for two years, after what had passed in the last half-year, after what had passed that very morning, she went by me without even changing countenance, without express-ing the slightest emotion, without betraying either shame or pity or remorse or any other feeling that any other human being but herself must have shewn in the same situation. She had no time to prepare for acting a part, to suppress her feelings – the truth is, she has not one natural feeling in her bosom to suppress. 1 turned and looked – they also turned and looked – and as if by mutual consent, we both retrod our steps and passed again, in the same way. I went home. I was stifled. I could not stay in the house, walked into the street and met them coming towards home. As soon as he had left her at the door (I fancy she had prevailed with him to accompany her, dreading some violence) I returned, went up stairs, and requested an interview. Tell her, I said, I'm in excellent temper and good spirits, but I must see her! She came smiling, and I said 'Come in, my dear girl, and sit down, and tell me all about it, how it is and who it is.' – 'What,' she said, 'do you mean Mr C—?' 'Oh,' said I, 'then it is he! Ah! you rogue, I always suspected there was something between you, but you know you denied it lustily: why did you not tell me all about it at the time, instead of letting me suffer as I have done? But, however, no reproaches. I only wish it may all end happily and honourably for you, and I am satisfied. But,' I said, 'you know you used to tell me, you despised looks.' – 'She didn't think Mr C— was so particularly handsome.' 'No, but he's very well to pass, and a well-grown youth into the bargain.' Pshaw! let me put an end to the fulsome detail. I found he had lived over the way, that he had been lured thence, no doubt, almost a year before, that they had first spoken in the street, and that he had never once hinted at marriage, and had gone away, because (as he said) they were too much together, and that it was better for her to meet him occasionally out of doors. 'There could be no harm in them walking together.' 'No, but you may go some where afterwards.' – 'One must trust to one's principle for that.' Consummate hypocrite! * * * * * * I told her Mr M—, who had married her sister, did not wish to leave the house. I, who would have married her, did not wish to leave it. I told her I hoped I should not live to see her come to shame, after all my love for her; but put her on her guard as well as I could, and said, after the lengths she had permitted herself with me, I could not help being alarmed at the influence of one over her, whom she could hardly herself suppose to have a tenth part of my esteem for her!! She made no answer to this, but thanked me coldly for my good advice, and rose to go. I begged her to sit a few minutes, that I might try to recollect if there was anything else I wished to say to her, perhaps for the last time; and then, not finding anything, I bade her good night, and asked for a farewell kiss. Do you know she refused; so little does she understand what is due to friendship, or love, or honour! We parted friends, however, and I felt deep grief, but no enmity against her. I thought C— had pressed his suit after I went, and had prevailed. There was no harm in that – a little fickleness or so, a little over-pretension to unalterable attachment – but that was all. She liked him better than me – it was my hard hap, but I must bear it. I went out to roam the desert streets, when, turning a corner, whom should I meet but her very lover? I went up to him and asked for a few minutes' conversation on a subject that was highly interesting to me and I believed not indifferent to him: and in the course of four hours' talk, it came out that for three months previous to my quitting London for Scotland, she had been playing the same game with him as with me – that he breakfasted first, and enjoyed an hour of her society, and then I took my turn, so that we never jostled; and this explained why, when he came back some-times and passed my door, as she was sitting in my lap, she coloured violently, thinking if her lover looked in, what a *dénouement* there would be. He could not help again and again expressing his astonishment at finding that our inti-macy had continued unimpaired up to so late a period after he came, and when they were on the most intimate footing. She used to deny positively to him that there was anything between us, just as she used to assure me with impenetrable effrontery that 'Mr C— was nothing to her, but merely a lodger.' All this while she kept up the farce of her romantic attachment to her old lover, vowed that she never could alter in that respect, let me go to Scotland on the solemn and repeated assurance that there was no new flame, that there was no bar between us but this shadowy love – I leave her on this understanding, she becomes more fond or more intimate with her new lover; he quitting the house (whether tired out or not, I can't say) – in revenge she ceases to write to me, keeps me in wretched suspense, treats me like something loathsome to her when I return to enquire the cause, denies it with scorn and impudence, destroys me and shews no pity, no desire to soothe or shorten the pangs she has occasioned by her wantonness and hypocrisy, and wishes to linger the affair on to the last moment, going out to keep an appointment with another while she pretends to be obliging me in the tenderest point (which C— himself said was too much). . . . What do you think of all this? Shall I tell you my opinion? But I must try to do it in another letter.

TO THE SAME
(in conclusion)

I DID not sleep a wink all that night; nor did I know till the next day the full meaning of what had happened to me. With the morning's light, conviction glared in upon me that I had not only lost her for ever – but every feeling I had ever had towards her – respect, tenderness, pity – all but my fatal passion, was gone. The whole was a mockery, a frightful illusion. I had embraced the false Florimel instead of the true; or was like the man in the Arabian Nights who had married a *goul*. How different was the idea I once had of her? Was this she,

> – 'Who had been beguiled – she who was made
> Within a gentle bosom to be laid –
> To bless and to be blessed – to be heart-bare
> To one who found his bettered likeness there –
> To think for ever with him, like a bride –
> To haunt his eye, like taste personified –

To double his delight, to share his sorrow,
And like a morning beam, wake to him every morrow?'

I saw her pale, cold form glide silent by me, dead to shame as to pity. Still I seemed to clasp this piece of witch-craft to my bosom; this lifeless image, which was all that was left of my love, was the only thing to which my sad heart clung. Were she dead, should I not wish to gaze once more upon her pallid features? She is dead to me; but what she once was to me, can never die! The agony, the conflict of hope and fear, of adoration and jealousy is over; or it would, ere long, have ended with my life. I am no more lifted now to Heaven, and then plunged in the abyss; but I seem to have been thrown from the top of a precipice, and to lie groveling, stunned, and stupefied. I am melancholy, lone-some, and weaker than a child. The worst is, I have no pros-pect of any alteration for the better: she has cut off all possi-bility of a reconcilement at any future period. Were she even to return to her former pretended fondness and endear-ments, I could have no pleasure, no confidence in them. I can scarce make out the contradiction to myself. I strive to think she always was what I now know she is; but I have great difficulty in it, and can hardly believe but she still *is* what she so long *seemed*. Poor thing! I am afraid she is little better off herself; nor do I see what is to become of her, unless she throws off the mask at once, and *runs a-muck* at infamy. She is exposed and laid bare to all those whose opinion she set a value upon. Yet she held her head very high, and must feel (if she feels any thing) proportionately mortified. – A more complete experiment on character was never made. If I had not met her lover immediately after I parted with her, it would have been nothing. I might have supposed she had changed her mind in my absence, and had given him the preference as soon as she felt it, and even shewn her delicacy in declining any farther intimacy with me. But it comes out that she had gone on in the most for-

ward and familiar way with both at once – (she could not
change her mind in passing from one room to another) –
told both the same bare-faced and unblushing falsehoods,
like the commonest creature; received presents from me to
the very last, and wished to keep up the game still longer,
either to gratify her humour, her avarice, or her vanity in
playing with my passion, or to have me as a *dernier résort*, in
case of accidents. Again, it would have been nothing, if she
had not come up with her demure, well-composed, wheed-
ling looks that morning, and then met me in the evening in
a situation, which (she believed) might kill me on the spot,
with no more feeling than a common courtesan shews, who
bilks a customer, and passes him, leering up at her bully, the
moment after. If there had been the frailty of passion, it
would have been excusable; but it is evident she is a practised, callous jilt, a regular lodging-house decoy, played off
by her mother upon the lodgers, one after another, applying
them to her different purposes, laughing at them in turns,
and herself the probable dupe and victim of some favourite
gallant in the end. I know all this; but what do I gain by it,
unless I could find some one with her shape and air, to supply the place of the lovely apparition? That a professed
wanton should come and sit on a man's knee, and put her
arms round his neck, and caress him, and seem fond of him,
means nothing, proves nothing, no one concludes anything
from it; but that a pretty, reserved, modest, delicate-looking
girl should do this, from the first hour to the last of your
being in the house, without intending anything by it, is
new, and, I think, worth explaining. It was, I confess, out of
my calculation, and may be out of that of others. Her un-
moved indifference and self-possession all the while, shew
that it is her constant practice. Her look even, if closely
examined, bears this interpretation. It is that of studied
hypocrisy or startled guilt, rather than of refined sensibility
or conscious innocence. 'She defied anyone to read her

thoughts,' she once told me. 'Do they then require conceal-ing?' I imprudently asked her. The command over herself is surprising. She never once betrays herself by any momen-tary forgetfulness, by any appearance of triumph or superiority to the person who is her dupe, by any levity of manner in the plenitude of her success; it is one faultless, undeviating, consistent, consummate piece of acting. Were she a saint on earth, she could not seem more like one. Her hypocritical high-flown pretensions, indeed, make her the worse: but still the ascendancy of her will, her determined perseverance in what she undertakes to do, has something admirable in it, approaching to the heroic. She is certainly an extraordinary girl! Her retired manner, and invariable propriety of behaviour made me think it next to impossible she could grant the same favours indiscriminately to every one that she did to me. Yet this now appears to be the fact. She must have done the very same with C—, invited him in-to the house to carry on a closer intrigue with her, and then commenced the double game with both together. She always 'despised looks.' This was a favourite phrase with her, and one of the hooks which she baited for me. Nothing could win her but a man's behaviour and sentiments. Besides, she could never like another – she was a martyr to disappointed affection – and friendship was all she could even extend to any other man. All the time, she was making signals, play-ing off her pretty person, and having occasional interviews in the street with this very man, whom she could only have taken so sudden and violent a liking to from his looks, his personal appearance, and what she probably conjectured of his circumstances. Her sister had married a counsellor – the Miss F—'s, who kept the house before, had done so too – and so would she. 'There was a precedent for it.' Yet if she was so desperately enamoured of this new acquaintance, if he had displaced *the little image* from her breast, if he was become her *second* 'unalterable attachment' (which I would

have given my life to have been) why continue the same unwarrantable familiarities with me to the last, and promise
that they should be renewed on my return (if I had not unfortunately stumbled upon the truth to her aunt) and yet
keep up the same refined cant about her old attachment all
the time, as if it was that which stood in the way of my pretensions, and not her faithlessness to it? 'If one swerves
from one, one shall swerve from another' – was her excuse
for not returning my regard. Yet that which I thought a
prophecy, was I suspect a history. She had swerved twice
from her vowed engagements, first to me, and then from me
to another. If she made a fool of me, what did she make of
her lover? I fancy he has put that question to himself. I said
nothing to him about the amount of the presents; which is
another damning circumstance, that might have opened my
eyes long before; but they were shut by my fond affection,
which 'turned all to favour and to prettiness.' She cannot
be supposed to have kept up an appearance of old regard
to me, from a fear of hurting my feelings by her desertion;
for she not only shewed herself indifferent to, but evidently
triumphed in my sufferings, and heaped every kind of insult and indignity upon them. I must have incurred her
contempt and resentment by my mistaken delicacy at different times; and her manner, when I have hinted at becoming a reformed man in this respect, convinces me of it.
'She hated it!' She always hated whatever she liked most.
She 'hated Mr C—'s red slippers,' when he first came! One
more count finishes the indictment. She not only discovered
the most hardened indifference to the feelings of others; she
has not shewn the least regard to her own character, or
shame when she was detected. When found out, she
seemed to say, 'Well, what if I am? I have played the game
as long as I could; and if I could keep it up no longer, it
was not for want of good will!' Her colouring once or twice
is the only sign of grace she has exhibited. Such is the crea-

ture on whom I had thrown away my heart and soul – one who was incapable of feeling the commonest emotions of human nature, as they regarded herself or any one else. 'She had no feelings with respect to herself,' she often said. She in fact knows what she is, and recoils from the good opinion or sympathy of others, which she feels to be founded on a deception; so that my overweening opinion of her must have appeared like irony, or direct insult. My seeing her in the street has gone a good way to satisfy me. Her manner there explains her manner in-doors to be conscious and overdone; and besides, she looks but indifferently. She is diminutive in stature, and her measured step and timid air do not suit these public airings. I am afraid she will soon grow common to my imagination, as well as worthless in herself. Her image seems fast 'going into the wastes of time,' like a weed that the wave bears farther and farther from me. Alas! thou poor hapless weed, when I entirely lose sight of thee, and for ever, no flower will ever bloom on earth to glad my heart again!

THE END.

Published anonymously in 1823. Reprinted in 1884 and again in 1893, with an introduction by Richard Le Gallienne.

MAN IS A TOAD-EATING ANIMAL

MAN is a toad-eating animal. The admiration of power in others is as common to man as the love of it in himself: the one makes him a tyrant, the other a slave. It is not he alone, who wears the golden crown, that is proud of it: the wretch who pines in a dungeon, and in chains, is dazzled with it; and if he could but shake off his own fetters, would care little about the wretches whom he left behind him, so that he might have an opportunity, on being set free himself, of gazing at this glittering gew-gaw 'on some high holiday of once a year.' The slave, who has no other hope of consolation, clings to the apparition of royal magnificence, which insults his misery and his despair; stares through the hollow eyes of famine at the insolence of pride and luxury which has occasioned it, and hugs his chains the closer, because he has nothing else left. The French, under the old regime, made the glory of their *Grand Monarque* a set-off against rags and hunger, equally satisfied with *shows or bread*; and the poor Spaniard, delivered from temporary to permanent oppression, looks up once more with pious awe, to the time-hallowed towers of the Holy Inquisition. As the herd of mankind are stripped of every thing, in body and mind, so are they thankful for what is left; as is the desolation of their hearts and the wreck of their little all, so is the pomp and pride which is built upon their ruin, and their fawning admiration of it.

> 'I've heard of hearts unkind, kind deeds
> With coldness still returning:
> Alas! the gratitude of men
> Has oftener set me mourning.'

There is something in the human mind, which requires

an object for it to repose on; and, driven from all other sources of pride or pleasure, it falls in love with misery, and grows enamoured of oppression. It gazes after the liberty, the happiness, the comfort, the knowledge, which have been torn from it by the unfeeling gripe of wealth and power, as the poor debtor gazes with envy and wonder at the Lord Mayor's show. Thus is the world by degrees reduced to a spital or lazar-house, where the people waste away with want and disease, and are thankful if they are only suffered to crawl forgotten to their graves. Just in proportion to the systematic tyranny exercised over a nation, to its loss of a sense of freedom and the spirit of resistance, will be its loyalty; the most abject submission will always be rendered to the most confirmed despotism. The most wretched slaves are the veriest sycophants. The lacquey, mounted behind his master's coach, looks down with contempt upon the mob, forgetting his own origin and his actual situation, and comparing them only with that standard of gentility which he has perpetually in his eye. The hireling of the press (a still meaner slave) wears his livery, and is proud of it. He measures the greatness of others by his own meanness; their lofty pretensions indemnify him for his servility; he magnifies the sacredness of their persons to cover the laxity of his own principles. He offers up his own humanity, and that of all men, at the shrine of royalty. He sneaks to court; and the bland accents of power close his ears to the voice of freedom ever after; its velvet touch makes his heart marble to a people's sufferings. He is the intellectual pimp of power, as others are the practical ones of the pleasures of the great, and often on the same disinterested principle. For one tyrant, there are a thousand ready slaves. Man is naturally a worshipper of idols and a lover of kings. It is the excess of individual power, that strikes and gains over his imagination: the general misery and degradation which are the necessary consequences of it, are spread too wide, they lie too deep, their weight and import are too great, to appeal to any but the slow, inert, speculative, imperfect faculty of reason. The cause of liberty is lost in its own truth and magnitude; while the cause of despotism flourishes, triumphs, and is irresistible in the gross mixture, the *Belle Alliance*, of pride and ignorance.

Power is the grim idol that the world adore; that arms itself with destruction, and reigns by terror in the coward heart of man; that dazzles the senses, haunts the imagination, confounds the understanding, and tames the will, by the vastness of its pretensions, and the very hopelessness of resistance to them. Nay more, the more mischievous and extensive the tyranny – the longer it has lasted, and the longer it is likely to last – the stronger is the hold it takes of the minds of its victims, the devotion to it increasing with the dread. It does not satisfy the enormity of the appetite for servility, till it has slain the mind of a nation, and becomes like the evil principle of the universe, from which there is no escape. So in some countries, the most destructive animals are held sacred, despair and terror completely overpowering reason. The prejudices of superstition (religion is another name for fear) are always the strongest in favour of those forms of worship which require the most bloody sacrifices; the foulest idols are those which are approached with the greatest awe; for it should seem that those objects are the most sacred to passion and imagination, which are the most revolting to reason and common sense. No wonder that the Editor of *The Times* bows his head before the idol of Divine Right, or of Legitimacy, (as he calls it) which has had more lives sacrificed to its ridiculous and unintelligible pretensions, in the last twenty-five years, than were ever sacrificed to any other idol in all preceding ages. Never was there any thing so well contrived as this fiction of Legitimacy, to suit the fastidious delicacy of modern sycophants. It hits their grovelling servility and petulant egotism exactly between

wind and water. The contrivers or re-modellers of this idol,
beat all other idol-mongers, whether Jews, Gentiles or Chris-
tians, hollow. The principle of an idolatry is the same: it is
the want of something to admire, without knowing what or
why: it is the love of an effect without a cause; it is a voluntary tribute of admiration which does not compromise our
vanity: it is setting something up over all the rest of the
world, to which we feel ourselves to be superior, for it is
our own handy-work; so that the more perverse the homage
we pay to it, the more it pampers our self-will: the meaner
the object, the more magnificent and pompous the attributes
we bestow upon it; the greater the lie, the more enthusiasti-
cally it is believed and greedily swallowed: –

> 'Of whatsoever race his godhead be,
> Stock, stone, or other homely pedigree,
> In his defence his servants are as bold
> As if he had been made of beaten gold.'

In this inverted ratio, the bungling impostors of former
times, and less refined countries, got no further than stocks
and stones: their utmost stretch of refinement in absurdity
went no further than to select the most mischievous animals
or the most worthless objects for the adoration of their besotted votaries: but the framers of the new law-fiction of
legitimacy have started a nonentity. The ancients sometimes
worshipped the sun or stars, or deified heroes and great
men: the moderns have found out the image of the divinity
in Louis XVIII.! They have set up an object for their
idolatry, which they themselves must laugh at, if hypocrisy
were not with them the most serious thing in the world.
They offer up thirty millions of men to it as its victims, and
yet they know that it is nothing but a scare-crow to keep
the world in subjection to their renegado whimsies and pre-
posterous hatred of the liberty and happiness of mankind.
They do not think kings gods, but they make believe that

they do so, to degrade their fellows to the rank of brutes. Legitimacy answers every object of their meanness and malice – *omne tulit punctum*. – This mock-doctrine, this little Hunchback, which our resurrection-men, the Humane Society of Divine Right, have foisted on the altar of Liberty, is not only a phantom of the imagination, but a contradiction in terms; it is a prejudice, but an exploded prejudice; it is an imposture, that imposes on nobody; it is powerful only in impotence, safe in absurdity, courted from fear and hatred, a dead prejudice linked to the living mind; the sink of honour, the grave of liberty, a palsy in the heart of a nation; it claims the species as its property, and derives its right neither from God nor man; not from the authority of the Church, which it treats cavalierly, and yet in contempt of the will of the people, which it scouts as opposed to its own : its two chief supporters are, the sword of the Duke of Wellington and the pen of the Editor of *The Times*! The last of these props has, we understand, just failed it.

We formerly gave the Editor of *The Times* a definition of a true Jacobin, as one 'who had seen the evening star set over a poor man's cottage, and connected it with the hope of human happiness.' The city-politician laughed this pastoral definition to scorn, and nicknamed the person who had very innocently laid it down, 'the true Jacobin who writes in the Chronicle,' – a nickname by which we profited as little as he has by our Illustrations. Since that time our imagination has grown a little less romantic: so we will give him another, which he may chew the cud upon at his leisure. A true Jacobin, then, is one who does not believe in the divine right of kings, or in any other *alias* for it, which implies that they reign 'in contempt of the will of the people;' and he holds all such kings to be tyrants, and their subjects slaves. To be a true Jacobin, a man must be a good hater; but this is the most difficult and the least amiable of all the virtues : the most trying and the most thankless of all tasks. The love

of liberty consists in the hatred of tyrants. The true Jacobin
hates the enemies of liberty as they hate liberty, with all his
strength and with all his might, and with all his heart and
with all his soul. His memory is as long, and his will as
strong as theirs, though his hands are shorter. He never forgets or forgives an injury done to the people, for tyrants
never forget or forgive one done to themselves. There is no
love lost between them. He does not leave them the sole
benefit of their old motto, *Odia in longum jaciens quæ con-
deret auctaque promeret.* He makes neither peace nor truce
with them. His hatred of wrong only ceases with the wrong.
The sense of it, and of the barefaced assumption of the right
to inflict it, deprives him of his rest. It stagnates in his
blood. It loads his heart with aspics' tongues, deadly to venal
pens. It settles in his brain – it puts him beside himself. Who
will not feel all this for a girl, a toy, a turn of the dice, a
word, a blow, for any thing relating to himself; and will not
the friend of liberty feel as much for mankind? The love of
truth is a passion in his mind, as the love of power is a passion in the minds of others. Abstract reason, unassisted
by passion, is no match for power and prejudice, armed with
force and cunning. The love of liberty is the love of others;
the love of power is the love of ourselves. The one is real;
the other often but an empty dream. Hence the defection of
modern apostates. While they are looking about, wavering
and distracted, in pursuit of universal good or universal
fame, the eye of power is upon them, like the eye of Providence, that neither slumbers nor sleeps, and that watches but
for one object, its own good. They take no notice of it at
first, but it is still upon them, and never off them. It at
length catches theirs, and they bow to its sacred light; and
like the poor fluttering bird, quail beneath it, are seized with
a vertigo, and drop senseless into its jaws, that close upon
them for ever, and so we see no more of them, which is well.

'And we saw three poets in a dream,'[1] walking up and

down on the face of the earth, and holding in their hands a human heart, which, as they raised their eyes to heaven, they kissed and worshipped; and a mighty shout arose and shook the air, for the towers of the Bastile had fallen, and a nation had become, of slaves, freemen; and the three poets, as they heard the sound, leaped and shouted, and made merry, and their voice was choked with tears of joy, which they shed over the human heart, which they kissed and worshipped. And not long after, we saw the same three poets, the one with a receipt-stamp in his hand, the other with a laurel on his head, and the third with a symbol which we could make nothing of, for it was neither literal nor allegorical, following in the train of the Pope and the Inquisition and the Bourbons, and worshipping the mark of the Beast, with the emblem of the human heart thrown beneath their feet, which they trampled and spit upon!' – This apologue is not worth finishing, nor are the people to whom it relates worth talking of. We have done with them.

From 'The Times Newspaper' in
Political Essays (1819).

CHARACTER OF THE LATE MR PITT*

THE character of Mr Pitt was, perhaps, one of the most singular that ever existed. With few talents, and fewer virtues, he acquired and preserved, in one of the most trying situations, and in spite of all opposition, the highest reputation for the possession of every moral excellence, and as having carried the attainments of eloquence and wisdom as far as human abilities could go. This he did (strange as it may appear) by a negation (together with the common virtues) of the common vices of human nature, and by the complete negation of every other talent that might interfere with the only ones which he possessed in a supreme degree, and which, indeed, may be made to include the appearance of all others, – an artful use of words, and a certain dexterity of logical arrangement. In these alone his power consisted; and the defect of all other qualities, which usually constitute greatness, contributed to the more complete success of these. Having no strong feelings, no distinct perceptions, – his mind having no link, as it were, to connect it with the world of external nature, every subject presented to him nothing more than a *tabula rasa*, on which he was at liberty to lay whatever colouring of language he pleased; having no general principles, no comprehensive views of things, no moral habits of thinking, no system of action, there was nothing to hinder him from pursuing any particular purpose by any means that offered; having never any plan, he could not be convicted of inconsistency, and his own pride and obstinacy were the only rules of his conduct. Without insight into human nature, without sympathy with the passions of men, or apprehension of their real designs, he

*Written in 1806.

seemed perfectly insensible to the consequences of things, and would believe nothing till it actually happened. The fog and haze in which he saw every thing communicated itself to others; and the total indistinctness and uncertainty of his own ideas tended to confound the perceptions of his hearers more effectually than the most ingenious misrepresentation could have done. Indeed, in defending his conduct, he never seemed to consider himself as at all responsible for the success of his measures, or to suppose that future events were in our own power; but that, as the best-laid schemes might fail, and there was no providing against all possible contingencies, this was sufficient excuse for our plunging at once into any dangerous or absurd enterprise without the least regard to consequences. His reserved logic confined itself solely to the *possible* and the *impossible*, and he appeared to regard the *probable* and *improbable*, the only foundation of moral prudence or political wisdom, as beneath the notice of a profound statesman; as if the pride of the human intellect were concerned in never entrusting itself with subjects, where it may be compelled to acknowledge its weakness. Nothing could ever drive him out of his dull forms, and naked generalities; which, as they are susceptible neither of degree nor variation, are therefore equally applicable to every emergency that can happen : and in the most critical aspect of affairs, he saw nothing but the same flimsy web of remote possibilities and metaphysical uncertainty. In his mind, the wholesome pulp of practical wisdom and salutary advice was immediately converted into the dry chaff and husks of a miserable logic. From his manner of reasoning, he seemed not to have believed that the truth of his statements depended on the reality of the facts, but that the facts themselves depended on the order in which he arranged them in words : you would not suppose him to be agitating a serious question, which had real grounds to go upon, but to be declaiming upon an imaginary thesis, proposed as an exercise in the schools. He never set himself to examine the force of the objections that were brought against him, or attempted to defend his measures upon clear, solid grounds of his own; but constantly contented himself with first gravely stating the logical form, or dilemma to which the question reduced itself; and then, after having declared his opinion, proceeded to amuse his hearers by a series of rhetorical common-places, connected together in grave, sonorous, and elaborately constructed periods, without ever shewing their real application to the subject in dispute. Thus, if any member of the opposition disapproved of any measure, and enforced his objections by pointing out the many evils with which it was fraught, or the difficulties attending its execution, his only answer was, 'that it was true there might be inconveniences attending the measure proposed, but we were to remember, that every expedient that could be devised might be said to be nothing more than a choice of difficulties, and that all that human prudence could do, was to consider on which side the advantages lay; that, for his part, he conceived that the present measure was attended with more advantages and fewer disadvantages than any other that could be adopted; that if we were diverted from our object by every appearance of difficulty, the wheels of government would be clogged by endless delays and imaginary grievances; that most of the objections made to the measure appeared to him to be trivial, others of them unfounded and improbable; or that, if a scheme, free from all these objections, could be proposed, it might, after all, prove inefficient; while, in the meantime, a material object remained unprovided for, or the opportunity of action was lost.' This mode of reasoning is admirably described by Hobbes,[1] in speaking of the writings of some of the schoolmen,[2] of whom he says that 'they had learned the trick of imposing what they list upon their readers, and declining the force of true reason by verbal forks, that is, distinctions, which signify nothing, but serve only to astonish the multitude of ignorant men.' That what we have here stated comprehends the whole force of his mind, which consisted solely in this evasive dexterity and perplexing formality, assisted by a copiousness of words and common-place topics, will, we think, be evident to any one who carefully looks over his speeches, undazzled by the reputation or personal influence of the speaker. It will be in vain to look in them for any of the common proofs of human genius or wisdom. He has not left behind him a single memorable saying, – not one profound maxim, – one solid observation, – one forcible description, – one beautiful thought, – one humorous picture, – one affecting sentiment. He has made no addition whatever to the stock of human knowledge. He did not possess any one of those faculties which contribute to the instruction and delight of mankind, – depth of understanding, imagination, sensibility, wit, vivacity, clear and solid judgment. But it may be asked, If these qualities are not to be found in him, where are we to look for them? and we may be required to point out instances of them. We shall answer then, that he had none of the abstract, legislative wisdom, refined sagacity, or rich, impetuous, high-wrought imagination of Burke; the manly eloquence, exact knowledge, vehemence, and natural simplicity of Fox;[3] the ease, brilliancy, and acuteness of Sheridan.[4] It is not merely that he had not all these qualities in the degree that they were severally possessed by his rivals, but he had not any of them in any remarkable degree. His reasoning is a technical arrangement of unmeaning common-places, his eloquence rhetorical, his style monotonous and artificial. If he could pretend to any one excellence more than another, it was to taste in composition. There is certainly nothing low, nothing puerile, nothing far-fetched or abrupt in his speeches; there is a kind of faultless regularity pervading them throughout; but in the confined, formal, passive mode of eloquence which he adopted, it seemed rather more difficult to commit errors than to avoid them. A man who is determined never to move out of the beaten road cannot lose his way. However, habit, joined to the peculiar mechanical memory which he possessed, carried this correctness to a degree which, in an extemporaneous speaker, was almost miraculous; he, perhaps, hardly ever uttered a sentence that was not perfectly regular and connected. In this respect, he not only had the advantage over his own contemporaries, but perhaps no one that ever lived equalled him in this singular faculty. But for this, he would always have passed for a common man; and to this the constant sameness, and, if we may so say, vulgarity of his ideas, must have contributed not a little, as there was nothing to distract his mind from this one object of his unintermitted attention; and as, even in his choice of words, he never aimed at any thing more than a certain general propriety and stately uniformity of style. His talents were exactly fitted for the situation in which he was placed; where it was his business not to overcome others, but to avoid being overcome. He was able to baffle opposition, not from strength or firmness, but from the evasive ambiguity and impalpable nature of his resistance, which gave no hold to the rude grasp of his opponents: no force could bind the loose phantom, and his mind (though 'not matchless, and his pride humbled by such rebuke') soon rose from defeat unhurt,

'And in its liquid texture, mortal wound
Receiv'd no more than can the fluid air.'

From *The Round Table* (1817).

FROM A LETTER TO WILLIAM GIFFORD[1]

S IR , – You have an ugly trick of saying what is not true of
any one you do not like; and it will be the object of this letter to cure you of it. You say what you please of others : it is
time you were told what you are. In doing this, give me leave
to borrow the familiarity of your style : – for the fidelity of
the picture I shall be answerable.

You are a little person, but a considerable cat's-paw; and
so far worthy of notice. Your clandestine connexion with
persons high in office constantly influences your opinions,
and alone gives importance to them. You are the *Government Critic*, a character nicely differing from that of a government spy – the invisible link, that connects literature
with the police. It is your business to keep a strict eye over
all writers who differ in opinion with his Majesty's Ministers, and to measure their talents and attainments by the
standard of their servility and meanness. For this office you
are well qualified. Besides being the Editor of the Quarterly
Review, you are also paymaster of the band of Gentlemen
Pensioners; and when an author comes before you in the
one capacity, with whom you are not acquainted in the
other, you know how to deal with him. You have your cue
beforehand. The distinction between truth and falsehood
you make no account of : you mind only the distinction between Whig and Tory. Accustomed to the indulgence of
your mercenary virulence and party-spite, you have lost all
relish as well as capacity for the unperverted exercises of the
understanding, and make up for the obvious want of ability
by a bare-faced want of principle. The same set of thread-
bare common-places, the same second-hand assortment of
abusive nick-names, the same assumption of little magis-

terial airs of superiority, are regularly repeated; and the ready convenient lie comes in aid of the dearth of other resources, and passes off, with impunity, in the garb of religion and loyalty. If no one finds it out, why then there is no harm done, *snug's the word*; or if it should be detected, it is a good joke, shews spirit and invention in proportion to its grossness and impudence, and it is only a pity that what was so well meant in so good a cause, should miscarry! The end sanctifies the means; and you keep no faith with heretics in religion or government. You are under the protection of the *Court*; and your zeal for your king and country entitles you to say what you chuse of every public writer who does not do all in his power to pamper the one into a tyrant, and to trample the other into a herd of slaves. You derive your weight with the great and powerful from the very circumstance that takes away all real weight from your authority, *viz.* that it is avowedly, and upon every occasion, exerted for no one purpose but to hold up to hatred and contempt what ever opposes in the slightest degree and in the most flagrant instances of abuse their pride and passions. You dictate your opinions to a party, because not one of your opinions is formed upon an honest conviction of the truth or justice of the case, but by collusion with the prejudices, caprice, interest or vanity of your employers. The mob of well-dressed readers who consult the Quarterly Review, know that *there is no offence in it*. They put faith in it because they are aware that it is 'false and hollow, but will please the ear'; that it will tell them nothing but what they would wish to believe. Your reasoning comes under the head of Court-news; your taste is a standard of the prevailing *ton* in certain circles, like Ackerman's dresses for May. When you damn an author, one knows that he is not a favourite at Carlton House. When you say that an author cannot write common sense or English, you mean that he does not believe in the doctrine of *divine right*. Of course, the clergy and gentry will not read such an author. Your praise or blame has nothing to do with the merits of a work, but with the party to which the writer belongs, or is in the inverse *ratio* of its merits. The dingy cover that wraps the pages of the Quarterly Review does not contain a concentrated essence of taste and knowledge, but is a receptacle for the scum and sediment of all the prejudice, bigotry, ill-will, ignorance, and rancour, afloat in the kingdom. This the fools and knaves who pin their faith on you know, and it is on this account they pin their faith on you. They come to you for a scale not of literary talent but of political subserviency. They want you to set your mark of approbation on a writer as a thorough-paced tool, or of reprobation as an honest man. Your fashionable readers, Sir, are hypocrites as well as knaves and fools; and the watch-word, the practical intelligence they want, must be conveyed to them without implied offence to their candour and liberality, in the *patois* and gibberish of fraud of which you are a master. When you begin to jabber about common sense and English, they know what to be at, shut up the book, and wonder that any respectable publisher can be found to let it lie on his counter, as much as if it were a Petition for Reform. Do you suppose, Sir, that such persons as the Rev. Gerard Valerian Wellesley[2] and the Rev. Weeden Butler[3] would not be glad to ruin what they call a Jacobin author as well as a Jacobin stationer? Or that they will not thank you for persuading them that their doing so in the former case is a proof of their taste and good sense, as well as loyalty and religion? You know very well that if a particle of truth or fairness were to find its way into a single number of your publication, another Quarterly Review would be set up to-morrow for the express purpose of depriving every author, in prose or verse, of his reputation and livelihood, who is not a regular hack of the vilest cabal that ever disgraced this or any other country.

There is something in your nature and habits that fits you for the situation into which your good fortune has thrown you. In the first place, you are in no danger of exciting the jealousy of your patrons by a mortifying display of extra-ordinary talents, while your sordid devotion to their will and to your own interest at once ensures their gratitude and contempt. To crawl and lick the dust is all they expect of you, and all you can do. Otherwise they might fear your power, for they could have no dependence on your fidelity: but they take you with safety and fondness to their bosoms; for they know if you cease to be a tool, you cease to be anything. If you had an exuberance of wit, the unguarded use of it might sometimes glance at your employers; if you were sincere yourself, you might respect the motives of others; if you had sufficient understanding, you might attempt an argument, and fail in it. But luckily for yourself and your admirers, you are but the dull echo, 'the tenth transmitter' of some hackneyed jest: the want of all manly and candid feeling in yourself only excites your suspicion and antipathy to it in others, as something at which your nature recoils: your slowness to understand makes you quick to misrepresent; and you infallibly make nonsense of what you cannot possibly conceive. What seem your wilful blunders are often the felicity of natural parts, and your want of penetration has all the appearance of an affected petulance!

Again, of an humble origin yourself, you recommend your performances to persons of fashion by always abusing *low people*, with the smartness of a lady's waiting woman, and the independent spirit of a travelling tutor. Raised from the lowest rank to your present despicable eminence in the world of letters, you are indignant that any one should attempt to rise into notice, except by the same regular trammels and servile gradations, or should go about to separate the stamp of merit from the badge of sycophancy. The silent listener in select circles, and menial tool of noble families, you have become the oracle of Church and State. The purveyor to the prejudices or passions of a private patron succeeds, by no other title, to regulate the public taste. You have felt the inconveniences of poverty, and look up with base and groveling admiration to the advantages of wealth and power: you have had to contend with the mechanical difficulties of a want of education, and you see nothing in learning but its mechanical uses. A self-taught man naturally becomes a pedant, and mistakes the means of knowledge for the end, unless he is a man of genius; and you, Sir, are not a man of genius. From having known nothing originally, you think it a great acquisition to know anything now, no matter what or how small it is – nay, the smaller and more insignificant it is, the more curious you seem to think it, as it is farther removed from common sense and human nature. The collating of points and commas is the highest game your literary ambition can reach to, and the squabbles of editors are to you infinitely more important than the meaning of an author. You think more of the letter than the spirit of a passage; and in your eagerness to show your minute superiority over those who have gone before you, generally miss both. In comparing yourself with others, you make a considerable mistake. You suppose the common advantages of a liberal education to be something peculiar to yourself, and calculate your progress beyond the rest of the world from the obscure point at which you first set out. Yet your overweening self-complacency is never easy but in the expression of your contempt for others; like a conceited mechanic in a village ale-house, you would set down every one who differs from you as an ignorant blockhead; and very fairly infer that any one who is beneath yourself must be nothing. You have been well called an Ultra-Crepidarian critic. From the difficulty you yourself have in constructing a sentence of common grammar, and your frequent failures, you instinctively presume that no author who comes under the lash of your pen can understand his mother-tongue: and again, you suspect every one who is not your 'very good friend' of knowing nothing of the Greek or Latin, because you are surprised to think how you came by your own knowledge of them. There is an innate littleness and vulgarity in all you do. In combating an opinion, you never take a broad and liberal ground, state it fairly, allow what there is of truth or an appearance of truth, and then assert your own judgment by exposing what is deficient in it, and giving a more masterly view of the subject. No: this would be committing your powers and pretensions where you dare not trust them. You know yourself better. You deny the meaning altogether, misquote or misapply, and then plume yourself on your own superiority to the absurdity you have created. Your triumph over your antagonists is the triumph of your cunning and mean-spiritedness over some nonentity of your own making; and your wary self-knowledge shrinks from a comparison with any but the most puny pretensions, as the spider retreats from the caterpillar into its web.

There cannot be a greater nuisance than a dull, envious, pragmatical, low-bred man, who is placed as you are in the situation of the Editor of such a work as the Quarterly Review. Conscious that his reputation stands on very slender and narrow grounds, he is naturally jealous of that of others. He insults over unsuccessful authors; he hates successful ones. He is angry at the faults of a work; more angry at its excellences. If an opinion is old, he treats it with supercilious indifference; if it is new, it provokes his rage. Everything beyond his limited range of inquiry, appears to him a paradox and an absurdity: and he resents every suggestion of the kind as an imposition on the public, and an imputation on his own sagacity. He cavils at what he does not comprehend, and misrepresents what he knows to be true. Bound to go through the nauseous task of abusing all those who are not like himself the abject tools of power, his irritation increases with the number of obstacles he encounters, and the number of sacrifices he is obliged to make of common sense and decency to his interest and self-conceit. Every instance of prevarication he wilfully commits makes him more in love with hypocrisy, and every indulgence of his hired malignity makes him more disposed to repeat the insult and the injury. His understanding becomes daily more distorted, and his feelings more and more callous. Grown old in the service of corruption, he drivels on to the last with prostituted impotence and shameless effrontery; salves a meagre reputation for wit, by venting the driblets of his spleen and impertinence on others; answers their arguments by confuting himself; mistakes habitual obtuseness of intellect for a particular acuteness, not to be imposed upon by shallow appearances; unprincipled rancour for zealous loyalty; and the irritable, discontented, vindictive, peevish effusions of bodily pain and mental imbecility for proofs of refinement of taste and strength of understanding.

Such, Sir, is the picture of which you have sat for the outline.

From *A Letter to William Gifford, Esq.* (1819).

ON THE PLEASURE OF HATING

THERE is a spider crawling along the matted floor of the room where I sit (not the one which has been so well allegorised in the admirable *Lines to a Spider*,[1] but another of the same edifying breed) – he runs with heedless, hurried haste, he hobbles awkwardly towards me, he stops – he sees the giant shadow before him, and, at a loss whether to retreat or proceed, meditates his huge foe – but as I do not start up and seize upon the struggling caitiff, as he would upon a helpless fly within his toils, he takes heart, and ventures on, with mingled cunning, impudence, and fear. As he passes me, I lift up the matting to assist his escape, am glad to get rid of the unwelcome intruder, and shudder at the recollection after he is gone. A child, a woman, a clown, or a moralist a century ago, would have crushed the little reptile to death – my philosophy has got beyond that – I bear the creature no ill-will, but still I hate the very sight of it. The spirit of malevolence survives the practical exertion of it. We learn to curb our will and keep our overt actions within the bounds of humanity, long before we can subdue our sentiments and imaginations to the same mild tone. We give up the external demonstration, the *brute* violence, but cannot part with the essence or principle of hostility. We do not tread upon the poor little animal in question (that seems barbarous and pitiful!) but we regard it with a sort of mystic horror and superstitious loathing. It will ask another hundred years of fine writing and hard thinking to cure us of the prejudice, and make us feel towards this ill-omened tribe with something of 'the milk of human kindness,' instead of their own shyness and venom.

Nature seems (the more we look into it) made up of antipathies: without something to hate, we should lose the very spring of thought and action. Life would turn to a stagnant pool, were it not ruffled by the jarring interests, the unruly passions of men. The white streak in our own fortunes is brightened (or just rendered visible) by making all round it as dark as possible, so the rainbow paints its form upon the cloud. Is it pride? Is it envy? Is it the force of contrast? Is it weakness or malice? But so it is, that there is a secret affinity, a *hankering* after evil in the human mind, and that it takes a perverse, but a fortunate delight in mischief, since it is a never-failing source of satisfaction. Pure good soon grows insipid, wants variety and spirit. Pain is a bitter-sweet which never surfeits. Love turns, with a little indulgence, to indifference or disgust: hatred alone is immortal. Do we not see this principle at work everywhere? Animals torment and worry one another without mercy: children kill flies for sport: everyone reads the accidents and offences in a news-paper, as the cream of the jest: a whole town runs to be present at a fire, and the spectator by no means exults to see it extinguished. It is better to have it so, but it diminishes the interest; and our feelings take part with our passions, rather than with our understandings. Men assemble in crowds, with eager enthusiasms, to witness a tragedy: but if there were an execution going forward in the next street, as Mr Burke observes, the theatre would be left empty. A strange cur in a village, an ideot, a crazy woman, are set upon and baited by the whole community. Public nuisances are in the nature of public benefits. How long did the Pope, the Bourbons, and the Inquisition keep the people of Eng-land in breath, and supply them with nick-names to vent their spleen upon! Had they done us any harm of late? No: but we have always a quantity of superfluous bile upon the stomach, and we want an object to let it out upon. How loth were we to give up our pious belief in ghosts and witches, because we liked to persecute the one, and frighten ourselves to death with the other! It is not so much the quality as the quantity of excitement that we are anxious about: we cannot bear a state of indifference and *ennui*: the mind seems to abhor a *vacuum* as much as ever matter was supposed to do. Even when the spirit of the age (that is, the progress of intellectual refinement, warring with our natural infirmities) no longer allows us to carry our vindictive and headstrong humours into effect, we try to revive them in description, and keep up the old bugbears, the phantoms of our terror and our hate, in imagination. We burn Guy Faux in effigy, and the hooting and buffeting and maltreating that poor tattered figure of rags and straw makes a festival in every village in England once a year. Protestants and Papists do not now burn one another at the stake: but we subscribe to new editions of *Fox's Book of Martyrs*; and the secret of the success of the *Scotch Novels* is much the same – they carry us back to the feuds, the heart-burnings, the havoc, the dismay, the wrongs and the revenge of a barbarous age and people – to the rooted prejudices and deadly animosities of sects and parties in politics and religion, and of contending chiefs and clans in war and intrigue. We feel the full force of the spirit of hatred with all of them in turn. As we read, we throw aside the trammels of civilisation, the flimsy veil of humanity. 'Off, you lendings!' The wild beast resumes its sway within us, we feel like hunting-animals, and as the hound starts in his sleep and rushes on the chase in fancy, the heart rouses itself in its native lair, and utters a wild cry of joy, at being restored once more to freedom and lawless, unrestrained impulses. Every one has his full swing, or goes to the Devil his own way. Here are no Jeremy Bentham Panopticons,[2] none of Mr Owen's impassable Parallelograms, (Rob Roy would have spurned and poured a thousand curses on them), no long calculations of self-interest – the will takes its instant way to its object; as the mountain-torrent flings itself over the precipice, the greatest possible good of each individual consists in doing all the mischief he can to his neighbour: that is charming, and finds a sure and sympathetic chord in every breast! So Mr Irving, the celebrated preacher,[3] has rekindled the old, original, almost exploded hell-fire in the aisles of the Caledonian Chapel, as they introduce the real water of the New River at Sadler's Wells, to the delight and astonishment of his fair audience. *'Tis pretty, though a plague*, to sit and peep into the pit of Tophet, to play at *snap-dragon* with flames and brimstone (it gives a smart electrical shock, a lively fillip to delicate constitutions), and to see Mr Irving, like a huge Titan, looking as grim and swarthy as if he had to forge tortures for all the damned! What a strange being man is! Not content with doing all he can to vex and hurt his fellows here, 'upon this bank and shoal of time,' where one would think there were heartaches, pain, disappointment, anguish, tears, sighs, and groans enough, the bigoted maniac takes him to the top of the high peak of school divinity to hurl him down the yawning gulf of penal fire; his speculative malice asks eternity to wreak its infinite spite and calls on the Almighty to execute its relentless doom! The cannibals burn their enemies and eat them, in good fellowship with one another: meek Christian divines cast those who differ from them but a hair's breadth, body and soul, into hell-fire, for the glory of God and the good of his creatures! It is well that the power of such persons is not co-ordinate with their wills: indeed, it is from the sense of their weakness and inability to control the opinions of others, that they thus 'outdo termagant,' and endeavour to frighten them into conformity by big words and denunciations.

The pleasure of hating, like a poisonous mineral, eats into the heart of religion, and turns it to rankling spleen and bigotry; it makes patriotism an excuse for carrying fire, pestilence, and famine into other lands: it leaves to virtue nothing but the spirit of censoriousness, and a narrow, jealous, inquisitorial watchfulness over the actions and motives of others. What have the different sects, creeds, doctrines in religion been but so many pretexts set up for men to wrangle, to quarrel, to tear one another in pieces about, like a target as a mark to shoot at? Does any one suppose that the love of country in an Englishman implies any friendly feeling or disposition to serve another, bearing the same name? No, it means only hatred to the French, or the inhabitants of any other country that we happen to be at war with for the time. Does the love of any virtue denote the wish to discover or amend our own faults? No, but it atones for an obstinate adherence to our own vices by the most virulent intolerance to human frailties. This principle is of a most universal application. It extends to good as well as evil: if it makes us hate folly, it makes us no less dissatisfied with distinguished merit. If it inclines us to resent the wrongs of others, it impels us to be as impatient of their prosperity. We revenge injuries: we repay benefits with ingratitude. Even our strongest partialities and likings soon take their turn. 'That which was luscious as locusts, anon becomes bitter as colonquintida:' and love and friendship melt in their own fires. We hate old friends: we hate old books: we hate old opinions; and at last we come to hate ourselves.

I have observed that few of those, whom I have formerly known most intimate, continue on the same friendly footing, or combine the steadiness with the warmth of attachment. I have been acquainted with two or three knots of inseparable companions who saw each other 'six days in the week,' that have broken up and dispersed. I have quarrelled with almost all my old friends, (they might say this is owing to my bad temper, but) they have also quarrelled with one another. What is become of 'that set of whist-players', celebrated by Elia in his notable *Epistle To Robert*

Southey, Esq. (and now I think of it – that I myself have celebrated in this very volume) 'that for so many years called Admiral Burney friend?' They are scattered, like last year's snow. Some of them are dead – or gone to live at a distance – or pass one another in the street like strangers; or if they stop to speak, do it coolly and try to *cut* one another as soon as possible. Some of us have grown rich – others poor. Some have got places under Government – others a *niche* in the Quarterly Review. Some of us have dearly earned a name in the world; while others remain in their original privacy. We despise the one; and envy and are glad to mortify the other. Times are changed; we cannot revive old feelings; and we avoid the sight and are uneasy in the presence of those, who remind us of our infirmity, and put us upon an effort of seeming cordiality, which embarrasses ourselves and does not impose upon our *quondam* associates. Old friendships are like meats served up repeatedly, cold, comfortless and distasteful. The stomach turns against them. Either constant intercourse and familiarity breed weariness and contempt; or if we meet again after an interval of absence, we appear no longer the same. One is too wise, another too foolish for us; and we wonder we did not find this out before. We are disconcerted and kept in a state of continual alarm by the wit of one, or tired to death of the dullness of the other. The *good things* of the first (besides leaving stings behind them) by repetition grow stale, and lose their startling effect; and the insipidity of the last becomes intolerable. The most amusing or instructive companion is at best like a favourite volume, that we wish after a time to *lay upon the shelf*; but as our friends are not willing to be laid there, this produces a misunderstanding and ill-blood between us. – Or if the zeal and integrity of friendship is not abated, or its career interrupted by any obstacle arising out of its own nature, we look out for other objects of complaint and sources of dissatisfaction. We begin to criticise each other's dress, looks and general character. 'Such a one is a pleasant fellow, but it is a pity he sits so late!' Another fails to keep his appointments, and that is a sore that never heals. We get acquainted with some fashionable young men or with a mistress, and wish to introduce our friend; but he is awkward and sloven, the interview does not answer, and this throws cold water on our intercourse. Or he makes himself obnoxious to opinion – and we shrink from our own convictions on the subject as an excuse for not defending him. All or any of these causes mount up in time to a ground of coolness or irritation – and at last they break out into open violence as the only amends we can make ourselves for suppressing them so long, or the readiest means of banishing recollections of former kindness, so little compatible with our present feelings. We may try to tamper with the wounds or patch up the carcase of departed friendship, but the one will hardly bear the handling, and the other is not worth the trouble of embalming! The only way to be reconciled with old friends is to part with them for good: at a distance we may chance to be thrown back (in a waking dream) upon old times and old feelings: or at any rate, we should not think of renewing our intimacy, till we have fairly *spit our spite*, or said, thought, and felt all the ill we can of each other. Or if we can pick a quarrel with someone else, and make him the scape-goat, this is an excellent contrivance to heal a broken bone. I think I must be friends with Lamb again, since he has written that magnanimous Letter to Southey, and told him a piece of his mind! – I don't know what it is that attaches me to H(aydon) so much, except that he and I, whenever we meet, sit in judgment on another set of old friends, and 'carve them as a dish fit for the Gods.' There was L(eigh) H(unt), John Scott,[4] Mrs. (Novello), whose dark raven locks made a picturesque background to our discourse, B(arnes), who is grown fat, and is, they say, married, R(ickman); these had all separated long

ago, and their foibles are the common link that holds us together. We do not affect to condole or whine over their
follies; we enjoy, we laugh at them until we are ready to
burst our sides, '*sans* intermission, for hours by the dial.'
We serve up a course of anecdotes, *traits*, master-strokes of
character, and cut and hack at them until we are weary. Perhaps some of them are even with us. For my own part, as I
once said, I like a friend the better for having faults that I
can talk about. 'Then,' said Mrs (Montagu), 'you will never
cease to be a philanthropist!' Those in question were some
of the choice-spirits of the age, not 'fellows of no mark or
likelihood;' and we so far did them justice: but it is well
that they did not hear what we sometimes said of them. I
care little what anyone says of me, particularly behind my
back, and in the way of critical and analytical discussion – it
is looks of dislike and scorn, that I answer with the worst
venom of my pen. The expression of the face wounds me
more than the expression of the tongue. If I have in one
instance mistaken this expression, or resorted to this remedy
where I ought not, I am sorry for it. . . . But the face was too
fine over which it mantled, and I am too old to have misunderstood it! . . . I sometimes go up to [Montagu's?]; and
as often as I do, resolve never to go again. I do not find the
old homely welcome. The ghost of friendship meets me at
the door, and sits with me all dinner-time. They have got a
set of fine notions and new acquaintance. Allusions to past
occurrences are thought trivial, nor is it always safe to touch
upon more general subjects. M(ontagu) does not begin as he
formerly did every five minutes, 'Fawcett used to say,' &c.
That topic is something worn. The girls are grown up, and
have a thousand accomplishments. I perceive there is a
jealousy on both sides. They think I give myself airs, and I
fancy the same of them. Every time I am asked, 'If I do not
think Mr Washington Irving[5] a very fine writer?' I shall
not go again until I receive an invitation for Christmas-day

in company with Mr Liston. The only intimacy I never found to flinch or fade was a purely intellectual one. There was none of the cant of candour in it, none of the whine of mawkish sensibility. Our mutual acquaintance were considered merely as objects of conversation and knowledge, not at all of affection. We regarded them no more in our experiments than 'mice in an air-pump:' or like malefactors, they were regularly cut down and given over to the dissecting-knife. We spared neither friend nor foe. We sacrificed human infirmities at the shrine of truth. The skeletons of character might be seen, after the juice was extracted, dangling in the air like flies in cobwebs: or they were kept for future inspection in some refined acid. The demonstration was as beautiful as it was new. There is no surfeiting on gall: nothing keeps so well as a decoction of spleen. We grow tired of everything but turning others into ridicule, and congratulating ourselves on their defects.

We take a dislike to our favourite books, after a time, for the same reason. We cannot read the same works for ever. Our honey-moon, even though we wed the Muse, must come to an end; and is followed by indifference, if not by disgust. There are some works, those indeed that produce the most striking effect at first by novelty and boldness of outline, that will not bear reading twice: others of a less extravagant character, and that excite and repay attention by a greater nicety of details, have hardly interest enough to keep alive our continued enthusiasm. The popularity of the most successful writers operates to wean us from them by the cant and fuss that is made about them, by hearing their names everlastingly repeated, and by the number of ignorant and indiscriminate admirers they draw after them: – we as little like to have to drag others from their unmerited obscurity, lest we should be exposed to the charge of affectation and singularity of taste. There is nothing to be said respecting an author that all the world have made up their minds about: it is a thankless as well as hopeless task to recommend one that nobody has ever heard of. To cry up Shakespear as the God of our idolatory, seems like a vulgar, national prejudice: to take down a volume of Chaucer, or Spenser, or Beaumont and Fletcher, or Ford, or Marlowe, has very much the look of pedantry and egotism. I confess it makes me hate the very name of Fame and Genius when works like these are 'gone into the wastes of time,' while each successive generation of fools is busily employed in reading the trash of the day, and women of fashion gravely join with their waiting-maids in discussing the preference between Paradise Lost and Mr Moore's Loves of the Angels.[6] I was pleased the other day on going into a shop to ask, If they had any of the *Scotch Novels*?' to be told – 'That they have just sent out the last, Sir Andrew Wylie!' – Mr Galt will also be pleased with this answer! The reputation of some books is raw and *unaired*: that of others is worm-eaten and mouldy. Why fix our affections on that which we cannot bring ourselves to have faith in, or which others have long ceased to trouble themselves about? I am half afraid to look into Tom Jones, lest it should not answer my expectations at this time of day; and if it did not, I should certainly be disposed to fling it into the fire, and never look into another novel while I lived. But surely, it may be said, there are some works, that, like nature, can never grow old; and that must always touch the imagination and passions alike! Or there are passages that seem as if we might brood over them all our lives, and not exhaust the sentiments of love and admiration they excite: they become favourites, and we are fond of them to a sort of dotage. Here is one:

> '– Sitting in my window
> Printing my thoughts in lawn, I saw a God,
> I thought (but it was you), enter our gates;
> My blood flew out and back again, as fast

As I had puffed it forth and sucked it in
Like breath; then was I called away in haste
To entertain you: never was a man
Thrust from a sheepcote to a sceptre, raised
So high in thoughts as I; you left a kiss
Upon these lips then, which I mean to keep
From you for ever. I hear you talk
Far above singing!'[7]

A passage like this indeed leaves a taste on the palate like
nectar, and we seem in reading it to sit with the Gods at
their golden tables: but if we repeat it often in ordinary
moods, it loses its flavour, becomes vapid, 'the wine of
poetry is drank, and but the lees remain.' Or, on the other
hand, if we call in the aid of extraordinary circumstances to
set it off to advantage, as the reciting it to a friend, or after
having our feelings excited by a long walk in some romantic
situation, or while we have

'– play with Amaryllis in the shade,
Or with the tangle of Neaera's hair' –[8]

we afterwards miss the accompanying circumstances, and
instead of transferring the recollection of them to the favourable side, regret what we have lost, and strive in vain to
bring back 'the irrevocable hour' – wondering in some instances how we survive it, and at the melancholy blank that
is left behind! The pleasure rises to its height in some moments of calm solitude or intoxicating sympathy, declines
ever after, and from the comparison and a conscious falling-
off, leaves rather a sense of satiety and irksomeness behind it.
... 'Is it the same in pictures?' I confess it is, with all but
those from Titian's hand. I don't know why, but an air
breathes from his landscapes, pure, refreshing as if it came
from other years; there is a look in his faces that never passes
away. I saw one the other day. Amidst the heartless desolation and finery of Fonthill,[9] there is a portfolio of the

Dresden Gallery. It opens, and a young female head looks from it;[10] a child, yet woman grown; with an air of rustic innocence and the graces of a princess, her eyes like those of doves, the lips about to open, a smile of pleasure dimpling the whole face, the jewels sparkling in her crisped hair, her youthful shape compressed in a rich antique dress, as the bursting leaves contain the April buds! Why do I not call up this image of gentle sweetness, and place it as a perpetual barrier between mischance and me? — it is because pleasure asks a greater effort of the mind to support it than pain; and we turn, after a little idle dalliance, from what we love to what we hate!

As to my old opinions, I am heartily sick of them. I have reason, for they deceived me sadly. I was taught to think, and I was willing to believe, that genius was not a bawd — that virtue was not a mask — that liberty was not a name — that love had its seat in the human heart. Now I would care little if these words were struck out of my dictionary, or if I had never heard them. They are become to my ears a mockery and a dream. Instead of patriots and friends of freedom, I see nothing but the tyrant and the slave, the people linked with kings to rivet on the chains of despotism and superstition. I see folly join with knavery, and together make up public spirit and public opinions. I see the insolent Tory, the blind Reformer, the coward Whig! If mankind had wished for what is right, they might have had it long ago. The theory is plain enough; but they are prone to mischief, 'to every good work reprobate.' I have seen all that had been done by the mighty yearnings of the spirit and intellect of men, 'of whom the world was not worthy,' and that promised a proud opening to truth and good through the vista of future years, undone by one man, with just glimmering of understanding enough to feel that he was a king, but not to comprehend how he could be king of a free people! I have seen this triumph celebrated by poets, the

friends of my youth and the friends of man, but who were
carried away by the infuriate tide that, setting in from a
throne, bore down every distinction of right reason before
it; and I have seen all those who did not join in applauding
this insult and outrage on humanity proscribed, hunted
down (they and their friends made a by-word of), so that it
has become an understood thing that no one can live by his
talents and knowledge who is not ready to prostitute those
talents and that knowledge to betray his species, and prey
upon his fellow-man. 'This was some time a mystery : but
the time gives evidence of it.' The echoes of liberty had
awakened once more in Spain, and the morning of human
hope dawned again : but that dawn has been overcast by the
foul breath of bigotry, and those reviving sounds stifled by
fresh cries from the time-rent towers of the Inquisition —
man yielding (as it is fit he should) first to brute force, but
more to the innate perversity and dastard spirit of his own
nature, which leaves no room for farther hope or disappointment. And England, that arch-reformer, that heroic de-
liverer, that mouther about liberty and tool of power, stands
gaping by, not feeling the blight and mildew coming over
it, nor its very bones crack and turn to a paste under the
grasp and circling folds of this new monster, Legitimacy!
In private life do we not see hypocrisy, servility, selfishness,
folly and impudence succeed, while modesty shrinks from
the encounter, and merit is trodden under foot? How often
is 'the rose plucked from the forehead of a virtuous love to
plant a blister there!' What chance is there of the success of
real passion? What certainty of its continuance? Seeing all
this as I do, and unravelling the web of human life into its
various threads of meanness, spite, cowardice, want of feeling, and want of understanding, of indifference towards
others and ignorance of ourselves — seeing custom prevail
over all excellence, itself giving way to infamy — mistaken as
I have been in my public and private hopes, calculating

others from myself, and calculating wrong; always disappointed where I placed most reliance; the dupe of friendship, and the fool of love; have I not reason to hate and to despise myself? Indeed I do; and chiefly for not having hated and despised the world enough.

From *The Plain Speaker* (1826).

JESUS CHRIST

THERE is something in the character of Christ too (leaving religious faith quite out of the question) of more sweetness and majesty, and more likely to work a change in the mind of man, by the contemplation of its idea alone, than any to be found in history, whether actual or feigned. This character is that of a sublime humanity, such as was never seen on earth before, nor since. This shone manifestly both in his words and actions. We see it in his washing the Disciples' feet the night before his death, that unspeakable instance of humility and love, above all art, all meanness, and all pride, and in the leave he took of them on that occasion, 'My peace I give unto you, that peace which the world cannot give, give I unto you'; and in his last commandment, that 'they should love one another.' Who can read the account of his behaviour on the cross, when turning to his mother he said, 'Woman, behold thy son,' and to the Disciple John, 'Behold thy mother,' and 'from that hour that Disciple took her to his own home,' without having his heart smote within him! We see it in his treatment of the woman taken in adultery, and in his excuse for the woman who poured precious ointment on his garment as an offering of devotion and love, which is here all in all. His religion was the religion of the heart. We see it in his discourse with the Disciples as they walked together towards Emmaus, when their hearts burned within them; in his sermon from the Mount, in his parable of the good Samaritan, and in that of the Prodigal Son – in every act and word of his life, a grace, a mildness, a dignity and love, a patience and wisdom worthy of the Son of God. His whole life and being were imbued, steeped in this word, *charity*; it was the spring, the well-head from which every thought and feeling gushed into act; and it was this that breathed a mild glory from his face in that last agony upon the cross, 'when the meek Saviour bowed his head and died,' praying for his enemies. He was the first true teacher of morality; for he alone conceived the idea of a pure humanity. He redeemed man from the worship of that idol, self, and instructed him by precept and example to love his neighbour as himself, to forgive our enemies, to do good to those that curse us and despitefully use us. He taught the love of good for the sake of good, without regard to personal or sinister views, and made the affections of the heart the sole seat of morality, instead of the pride of the understanding or the sternness of the will. In answering the question, 'who is our neighbour?' as one who stands in need of our assistance, and whose wounds we can bind up, he has done more to humanize the thoughts and tame the unruly passions, than all who have tried to reform and benefit mankind. The very idea of abstract benevolence, of the desire to do good because another wants our services, and of regarding the human race as one family, the offspring of one common parent, is hardly to be found in any other code or system. It was 'to the Jews a stumbling block, and to the Greeks foolishness.' The Greeks and Romans never thought of considering others, but as they were Greeks or Romans, as they were bound to them by certain positive ties, or, on the other hand, as separated from them by fiercer antipathies. Their virtues were the virtues of political machines, their vices were the vices of demons, ready to inflict or to endure pain with obdurate and remorseless inflexibility of purpose. But in the Christian religion, 'we perceive a softness coming over the heart of a nation, and the iron scales that fence and harden it, melt and drop off.' It becomes malleable, capable of pity, of forgiveness, of relaxing in its claims, and remitting its power.

From 'General View of the Subject' in *Lectures on the Age of Elizabeth* (1820).

METHODISTS

METHODISM, by its leading doctrines, has a peculiar charm for all those, who have an equal facility in sinning and repenting, – in whom the spirit is willing but the flesh is weak, – who have neither fortitude to withstand temptation, nor to silence the admonitions of conscience, – who like the theory of religion better than the practice, and who are willing to indulge in all the raptures of speculative devotion, without being tied down to the dull, literal performance of its duties. There is a general propensity in the human mind (even in the most vicious) to pay virtue a distant homage; and this desire is only checked by the fear of condemning ourselves by our own acknowledgments. What an admirable expedient then in 'that burning and shining light,' Whitefield, and his associates, to make this very disposition to admire and extol the highest patterns of goodness, a substitute for, instead of an obligation to, the practice of virtue, to allow us to be quit for 'the vice that most easily besets us,' by canting lamentations over the depravity of human nature, and loud hosannahs to the Son of David! How comfortably this doctrine must sit on those who are loth to give up old habits of vice, or are just tasting the sweets of new ones; or the withered hag who looks back on a life of dissipation, or the young devotee who looks forward to a life of pleasure; the knavish tradesman retiring from business or entering on it; the battered rake; the sneaking politician, who trims between his place and his conscience, wriggling between heaven and earth, a miserable two-legged creature, with sanctified face and fawning gestures; the maudling sentimentalist, the religious prostitute, the disinterested poet-laureate, the humane war-contractor, or the Society for the Suppression of Vice! This scheme happily turns morality into a sinecure, takes all the practical drudgery and trouble off your hands, 'and sweet religion makes a rhapsody of words.' Its proselytes besiege the gates of heaven, like sturdy beggars about the doors of the great, lie and bask in the sunshine of divine grace, sigh and groan and bawl out for mercy, expose their sores and blotches to excite commiseration, and cover the deformities of their nature with a garb of borrowed righteousness!

The jargon and nonsense which are so studiously inculcated in the system, are another powerful recommendation of it to the vulgar. It does not impose any tax on the understanding. Its essence is to be unintelligible. It is *carte blanche* for ignorance and folly! Those, 'numbers without number,' who are either unable or unwilling to think connectedly or rationally on any subject, are at once released from every obligation of the kind, by being told that faith and reason are opposed to one another, and the greater the impossibility, the greater the merit of the faith. A set of phrases which, without conveying any distinct idea, excite our wonder, our fear, our curiosity and desires, which let loose the imagination of the gaping multitude, and confound and baffle common sense, are the common stock-in-trade of the conventicle. They never stop for the distinctions of the understanding, and have thus got the start of other sects. ... 'Vital Christianity' is no other than an attempt to lower all religion to the level of the capacities of the lowest of the people. ... Religion, without superstition, will not answer the purposes of fanaticism, and we may safely say, that almost every sect of Christianity is a perversion of its essence, to accommodate it to the prejudices of the world. The Methodists have greased the boots of the Presbyterians, and they have done well. While the latter are weighing their doubts and scruples to the division of a hair, and shivering on the narrow brink that divides philosophy from religion, the former plunge without remorse into hell-flames, soar on the wings of divine love, are carried away with the motions of the spirit, are lost in the abyss of unfathomable mysteries – election, reprobation, predestination, – and revel in a sea of boundless nonsense. It is a gulf that swallows up everything. The cold, the calculating, and the dry, are not to the taste of the many; religion is an anticipation of the preternatural world, and it in general requires preternatural excitements to keep it alive. If it takes a definite consistent form, it loses its interest: to produce its effect it must come in the shape of an apparition. Our quacks treat grown people as the nurses do children; – terrify them with what they have no idea of, or take them to a puppet-show.

From *On the Causes of Methodism* (1817).

QUAKERS

A MOST respectable sect among ourselves (we mean the Quakers) have carried this system of negative qualities nearly to perfection. They labour diligently, and with great success, to exclude all ideas from their minds which they might have in common with others. On the principle that evil communications corrupt good manners, they retain a virgin purity of understanding, and laudable ignorance of all liberal arts and sciences; they take every precaution, and keep up a perpetual quarantine against the infection of other people's vices — or virtues; they pass through the world like figures cut out of pasteboard or wood, turning neither to the right nor the left; and their minds are no more affected by the example of the follies, the pursuits, the pleasures, or the passions of mankind, than the clothes which they wear. Their ideas want *airing*; they are the worse for not being used: for fear of soiling them, they keep them folded up and laid by in a sort of mental clothes-press, through the whole of their lives. They take their notions on trust from one generation to another, (like the scanty cut of their coats), and are so wrapped up in these traditional maxims, and so pin their faith on them, that one of the most intelligent of this class of people, not long ago, assured us that 'war was a thing that was quite going out of fashion'! This abstract sort of existence may have its advantages, but it takes away all the sources of a moral imagination, as well as strength of intellect. Interest is the only link that connects them with the world. We can understand the high enthusiasm and religious devotion of monks and anchorites, who gave up the world and its pleasures to devote themselves to a sublime contemplation of a future state. But the sect of the Quakers, who have transplanted the maxims of the desert into manufacturing towns and populous cities, who have converted the solitary cells of the religious orders into counting houses, their beads into ledgers, and keep a regular debtor and creditor account between this world and the next, puzzle us mightily! The Dissenter is not in vain, but conceited: that is, he makes up by his own good opinion for the want of the cordial admiration of others. But this often stands their self-love in so good stead that they need not envy their dignified opponents who repose on lawn sleeves and ermine. The unmerited obloquy and dislike to which they are exposed has made them cold and reserved in their intercourse with society. The same cause will account for the dryness and general homeliness of their style. They labour under a sense of the want of public sympathy. They pursue truth, for its own sake, into its private recesses and obscure corners. They have to dig their way along a narrow underground passage. It is not their object to shine; they have none of the usual incentives of vanity, light, airy, and ostentatious. Archiepiscopal Sees and mitres do not glitter in their distant horizon. They are not wafted on the wings of fancy, fanned by the breath of popular applause. The voice of the world, the tide of opinion, is not with them. They do not therefore aim at *éclat*, at outward pomp and show. They have a plain ground to work upon, and they do not attempt to embellish it with idle ornaments. It would be vain to strew the flowers of poetry round the borders of the Unitarian controversy.

There is one quality common to all sectaries, and that is, a principle of strong fidelity. They are the safest partisans, and the steadiest friends. Indeed, they are almost the only people who have any idea of an abstract attachment either to a cause or to individuals, from a sense of duty, independently of prosperous or adverse circumstances, and in spite of opposition.

From *On the Tendency of Sects* (1817).

LETTERS OF HORACE WALPOLE

HORACE WALPOLE was by no means a venerable or lofty character: — But he has here left us another volume of gay and graceful letters, which, though they indicate no peculiar originality of mind, or depth of thought, and are continually at variance with good taste and right feeling, still give a lively and amusing view of the time in which he lived. He was indeed a garrulous *old* man nearly all his days; and, luckily for his gossipping propensities, he was on familiar terms with the gay world, and set down as a man of genius by the Princess Amelia,[1] George Selwyn,[2] Mr Chute,[3] and all persons of the like talents and importance. His descriptions of court dresses, court revels, and court beauties, are in the highest style of perfection, — sprightly, fantastic and elegant: And the zeal with which he hunts after an old portrait or a piece of broken glass, is ten times more entertaining than if it were lavished on a worthier object. He is indeed the very prince of Gossips, — and it is impossible to question his supremacy, when he floats us along in a stream of bright talk, or shoots with us the rapids of polite conversation. He delights in the small squabbles of great politicians and the puns of George Selwyn, — enjoys to madness the strife of loo with half a dozen bitter old women of quality, — revels in a world of chests, cabinets, commodes, tables, boxes, turrets, stands, old printing, and old china, — and indeed lets us loose at once amongst all the frippery and folly of the last two centuries, with an ease and a courtesy equally amazing and delightful. His mind, as well as his house, was piled up with Dresden china, and illuminated through painted glass; and we look upon his heart to have been little better than a case full of enamels, painted eggs, ambers, lapis-lazuli, cameos, vases and rock-crystals. This may in some degree account for his odd and quaint manner of thinking, and his utter poverty of feeling: – he could not get a plain thought out of that cabinet of curiosities, his mind; – and he had no room for feeling, – no place to plant it in, or leisure to cultivate it. He was at all times the slave of elegant trifles; and could no more screw himself up into a decided and solid personage, than he could divest himself of petty jealousies and miniature animosities. In one word, every thing about him was in little; and the smaller the object, and the less its importance, the higher did his estimation and his praises of it ascend. He piled up trifles to a colossal height – and made a pyramid of nothings 'most marvellous to see.'

His political character was a heap of confusion: but the key to it is easy enough to find. He united an insufferable deal of aristocratical pretension with Whig professions, – and, under an assumed carelessness and liberality, he nourished a petty anxiety about court movements and a degree of rancour towards those who profited by them, which we should only look for in the most acknowledged sycophants of Government. He held out austere and barren principles, in short, to the admiration of the world, – but indemnified himself in practice by the indulgence of all the opposite ones. He wore his horse-hair shirt as an *outer* garment; and glimpses might always be caught of a silken garment within. He was truly 'of outward show elaborate; of inward less exact.' But, setting his political character – or rather the want of it – and some few private failings, and a good many other questionable peculiarities, aside, – we find Walpole an amusing companion, and should like to have such a chronicler of small matters every fifty or sixty years; – or it might be better, perhaps, if, like the aloe, they should blossom but once in a century. With what spirit does he speak of the gay and noble visitors at Strawberry Hill! How finely does he group, in his letters, the high-born and celebrated beauties of the court, with whom it was his fortune and his fancy to associate!

'Strawberry Hill is grown a perfect Paphos; it is the land of beauties. On Wednesday, the Dutchesses of Hamilton and Richmond, and Lady Ailesbury, dined there; the two latter staid all night. There never was so pretty a sight as to see them all sitting in the shell. A thousand years hence, when I begin to grow old, if that can ever be, I shall talk of that event, and tell young people how much handsomer the women of my time were than they will be. Then I shall say, "Women alter now: I remember Lady Ailesbury looking handsomer than her daughter the pretty Dutchess of Richmond, as they were sitting in the shell on my terrace, with the Dutchess of Richmond, one of the famous Gunnings," &c. &c. Yesterday, t'other famous Gunning dined there. She has made a friendship with my charming niece, to disguise her jealousy of the new Countess's beauty: there were they too, their Lords, Lord Buckingham, and Charlotte. You will think that I did not choose men for my parties so well as women. I don't include Lord Waldegrave in this bad election.'

All the rest is in the same style: and lords and ladies are shuffled about the whole work as freely as court cards in a party at loo. Horace Walpole,[4] to be sure, is always Pam: but this only makes the interest greater, and the garrulity more splendid. He is equally sprightly and facetious, whether he describes a King's death and funeral, or a quirk of George Selwyn; and is nearly as amusing when he recounts the follies and the fashions of the day, as when he affects to be patriotic, or solemnizes into the sentimental. His style is not a bit less airy when he deals with 'the horrid story of Lord Ferrers's murdering his steward,' than when it informs us that 'Miss Chudleigh has called for the council books of the subscription concert, and has struck off the name of Mrs Naylor.' He is equally amusing whether he records the death of the brave Balmerino,[5] or informs us that 'old Dunch is dead.'

The letters of eminent men make, to our taste, very choice and curious reading; and, except when their publication becomes a breach of honour or decorum, we are always rejoiced to meet with them in print. We should except, perhaps, the letters of celebrated warriors; which, for the most part, should only be published in the Gazette. But, setting these heroes aside, whose wits, Pope has informed us, 'are kept in ponderous vases,' letters are certainly the honestest records of great minds, that we can become acquainted with; and we like them the more, for letting us into the follies and treacheries of high life, the secrets of the gay and the learned world, and the mysteries of authorship. We are ushered, as it were, behind the scenes of life; and see gay ladies and learned men, the wise, the witty, and the ambitious, in all the nakedness, or undress at least, of their spirits. A poet, in his private letters, seldom thinks it necessary to keep up the farce of feeling; but casts off the trickery of sentiment, and glides into the unaffected wit, or sobers quietly into the honest man. By his published works, we know that an author becomes a 'Sir John with all Europe;' and it can only be by his letters that we discover him to be 'Jack with his brothers and sisters, and John with his familiars.' This it is that makes the private letters of a literary person so generally entertaining. He is glad to escape from the austerity of composition, and the orthodoxy of thought; and feels a relief in easy speculations or ludicrous expressions. The finest, perhaps, in our language, are eminently of this description – we mean those of Gray to his friends or literary associates. His poetry is too scholastic and elaborate, and is too visibly the result of laborious and anxious study. But, in his letters, he at once becomes an easy, and graceful, and feeling writer. The composition of familiar letters just suited his indolence, his taste, and his humour. His remarks on poetry are nearly as good as poetry itself; – his observations on life are full of sagacity and fine understanding; and his descriptions of natural scenery, or Gothic antiquities, are worth their weight in gold. Pope's letters, though extremely elegant, are failures as letters. He wrote them to the world, not to his friends; and they have therefore very much the air of universal secrets. Swift has recorded his own sour mind in many a bitter epistle; and his correspondence remains a stern and brief chronicle of the time in which he lived. Cowper hath unwittingly beguiled us of many a long hour, by his letters to Lady Hesketh; and in them we see the fluctuations of his melancholy nature more plainly, than in all the biographical dissertations of his affectionate editor. – But we must not make catalogues, – nor indulge longer in this eulogy on letter-writing. We take a particular interest, we confess, in what is thus spoken aside, as it were, and without a consciousness of being overheard; – and think there is a spirit and freedom in the tone of works written for the post, which is scarcely ever to be found in those written for the press. We are much more edified by one letter of Cowper, than we should be by a week's confinement and hard labour in the metaphysical Bridewell of Mr Coleridge; and a single letter from the pen of Gray, is worth all the pedlar-reasoning of Mr Wordsworth's Eternal Recluse, from the hour he first squats himself down in the sun to the end of his preaching. In the first we have the light unstudied pleasantries of a wit, and a man of feeling; – in the last we are talked to death by an arrogant old proser, and buried in a heap of the most perilous stuff and the most dusty philosophy.

But to come back to the work before us. – Walpole evidently formed his style upon that of Gray, with whom he travelled; and, with his own fund of pleasantry and sarcasm, we know of no other writer whom he could so successfully have studied. There are some odd passages on Gray, scattered up and down the present volume, which speak more for the poet than for the justice or friendship of Walpole. In one letter he says,

'The first volume of Spencer is published with prints designed by Kent; – but the most execrable performance you ever beheld. The graving not worse than the drawing; awkward knights, scrambling Unas, hills tumbling down themselves, no variety of prospect, and three or four perpetual spruce firs. – Our charming Mr Bentley is doing Mr Gray as much more honour as he deserves than Spencer!'

This is indeed a lordly criticism. We really never saw so much bad taste condensed into so small a portion of prose. But he next shows us what ladies of the court think of men of letters, and how lords defend them.

'My Lady Ailesbury has been much diverted, and so will you too. Gray is in their neighbourhood. My Lady Carlisle says *he is extremely like me in his manner.* They went a party to dine on a cold loaf, and passed the day. Lady A. protests he never opened his lips but once, and then only said, "Yes, my Lady, I believe so."

'I agree with you most absolutely in your opinion about Gray; he is the worst company in the world. From a melancholy turn, from living reclusely, and from a little too much dignity, he never converses easily. All his words are measured and chosen, and formed into sentences. His writings are admirable. He himself is not agreeable.'

But it is not only to his particular friends that he is thus amiably candid. Two other great names are dealt with in the same spirit in the following short sentence.

'Dr Young has published a new book, on purpose, he says himself, to have an opportunity of telling a story that he has known these forty years. Mr Addison sent for the young Lord Warwick, as he was dying, to show him in what peace a Christian could die. Unluckily he died of brandy. Nothing makes a Christian die in peace like being maudlin! But don't say this in Gath, where you are.'

It is worthy of remark, indeed, that Walpole never speaks with respect of any man of genius or talent, and, least of all, of those master spirits who 'have got the start of this majestic world.' He envied all great minds; and shrunk from encountering them, lest his own should suffer by the comparison. He contrived indeed to quarrel with all his better-spirited friends. Even the gentleman to whom these epistles were addressed, a correspondent of three score years' standing, fell at last under his displeasure, and was dismissed his friendship. He turned out the domestics of the heart as easily as those of the house; with little or no notice, and with threats of giving them a bad character as a return for their past services. He wished to have genius to wait upon him; but was always surprised that it would not submit to be a servant of all work. Poor Bentley, of whom we hear praises 'high fantastical' in the early letters, meets with but scurvy treatment the moment he gets out of fashion with his half-patron and half-friend. He is all spirit, goodness and genius, till it falls to his turn to be disliked; and then the altered patron sneers at his domestic misfortunes, depreciates his talents, and even chuckles at the failure of a play which the artist's necessities required should be successful. The following is the ill-natured passage to which we allude.

'No, I shall never cease being a dupe, till I have been undeceived round by every thing that calls itself a virtue. I came to town yesterday, through clouds of dust, to see The Wishes, and went actually feeling for Mr Bentley, and full of the emotions he must be suffering. What do you think, in a house crowded, was the first thing I saw? Mr and Madame Bentley perched up in the front boxes, and acting audience at his own play! No, all the impudence of false patriotism never came up to it. Did one ever hear of an author that had courage to see his own first night in public? I don't believe

Fielding or Foote himself ever did; and this was the modest, bashful Mr Bentley, that died at the thought of being known for an author even by his own acquaintance! In the stage-box was Lady Bute, Lord Halifax, and Lord Melcombe. I must say, the two last entertained the house as much as the play. Your King was prompter, and called out to the actors every minute to speak louder. The other went backwards and forwards behind the scenes, fetched the actors into the box, and was busier than Harlequin. The *curious* prologue was not spoken – the whole very ill acted. It turned out just what I remembered it: the good parts extremely good; the rest very flat and vulgar, &c.'

A poor painter of the name of Müntz is worse off even than Bentley; and is abused in a very ungenerous way for want of gratitude, and unmerciful extortion. There is a sad want of feeling and dignity in all this; but the key to it is, that Walpole was a miser. He loved the arts after a fashion; but his avarice pinched his affections. He would have had 'that which he esteemed the ornament of life,' but that he 'lived a coward in his own esteem.' The following haggling passage in one of his letters would disgrace a petty merchant in Duke's Place, in a bargain for the reversion of an old pair of trowsers.

'I am disposed to prefer the younger picture of Madame Grammont by Lely; but I stumbled at the price; twelve guineas for a copy in enamel is very dear. Mrs Vesey tells me his originals cost sixteen, and are not so good as his copies. I will certainly have none of his originals. His, what is his name? I would fain resist this copy; I would more fain excuse myself for having it. I say to myself it would be rude not to have it, now Lady Kingsland and Mr Montagu have had so much trouble. Well – *I think I must have it*, as my Lady Wishfort says, *why does not the fellow take me?* Do try if he will take ten; – remember it is the younger picture.'

Thus did he coquet with his own avarice. Of poor Mason, another of his dear friends, he speaks thus spitefully –

'Mr Mason has published another drama, called Caractacus. There are some incantations poetical enough, and odes so Greek as to have very little meaning. But the whole is laboured, uninteresting, and no more resembling the manners of Britons than of Japanese. It is introduced by a piping elegy; for Mason, an imitation of Gray, *will cry and roar all night*, without the least provocation.'

Mason might have endured the paltriness of this remark, if he could have seen the following pertinent remark on the Cymbeline of Shakespeare.

'You want news. I must make it if I send it. To change the dulness of the scene, I went to the play, where I had not been this winter. They are so crowded, that though I went before six, I got no better place than a fifth row, where I heard very ill, and was pent for five hours without a soul near me that I knew. It was Cymbeline; and appeared to me as long as if every body in it went really to Italy in every act, and back again. With a few pretty passages and a scene or two, it is so absurd and tiresome, that I am persuaded Garrick * * * *'

This precious piece of criticism is cut short; whether from the sagacity of the editor or the prudence of the publishers, we cannot say. But it is much to be lamented. For it must have been very edifying to have seen Shakespear thus pleasantly put down with a dash of the Honourable Mr Walpole's pen – as if he had never written any thing better than the Mysterious Mother.

A conversation is here recorded between Hogarth and Walpole, which seems to us very curious and characteristic; though we cannot help smiling a little at the conclusion, where our author humanely refrains from erasing the line of praise which he had 'consecrated' to Hogarth; – as if the painter would infallibly have been damned into oblivion by that portentous erasure. But he is of the stuff that cannot die. With many defects, he was a person of great and original powers – a true and a terrific historian of the human heart: and his works will be remembered and *read*, as long as men and women retain their old habits, passions and vices. The following is the conversation of which we have spoken.

'*Hogarth*. – I am told you are going to entertain the town with something in our way. *Walpole*. Not very soon, Mr Hogarth.– H. I wish you would let me have it to correct; I should be very sorry to have you expose yourself to censure; we painters must know more of those things than other people. w. Do you think nobody understands painting but painters? H. Oh! so far from it, there's Reynolds who certainly has genius; why but t'other day he offered a hundred pounds for a picture that I would not hang in my cellars; and indeed, to say truth, I have generally found that persons, who had studied painting least, were the best judges of it; but what I particularly wished to say to you was about Sir James Thornhill (you know he married Sir James's daughter); I would not have you say any thing against him: there was a book published some time ago, abusing him, and it gave great offence. He was the first that attempted history in England; and I assure you, some Germans have said that he was a very great painter. w. My work will go no lower than the year one thousand seven hundred, and I really have not considered whether Sir J. Thornhill will come into my plan or not: if he does, I fear you and I shall not agree upon his merits. H. I wish you would let me correct it; besides I am writing something of the same kind myself – I should be sorry we should clash. w. I believe it is not much known what my work is; very few persons have seen it. H. Why, it is a critical history of painting, is it not? w. No, it is an antiquarian history of it in England. I bought Mr Vertue's MSS. and I believe the work will not give much offence; besides if it does I cannot help it: when I publish any thing I give it to the world to think as they please. H. Oh! if it is an antiquarian work we shall not clash; mine is a critical work; I don't know whether I shall ever publish it. It is rather an apology for painters. I think it is owing to the good sense of the English that they have not painted better. w. My dear Mr Hogarth, I must take my leave of you; you now grow too wild – and I left him. If I had staid, there remained nothing but for him to bite me. I give you my honour this conversation is literal, and perhaps as long as you have known Englishmen and painters you never met with any thing so distracted. I had consecrated a line to his genius (I mean for wit) in my preface; I shall not erase it; but I hope no one will ask me if he is not mad.'

We do not think he was mad: – but the self-idolatry of fanciful persons often exhibits similar symptoms. A man of limited genius, accustomed to contemplate his own conceptions, has long settled his ideas as to every thing, and every other person existing in the world. He thinks nothing truly bright that does not reflect his own image back upon himself; – nothing truly beautiful, that is not made so by the lustre of his own feelings. He lives in a sort of chaste singleness; and holds every approach of a stronger power as dangerous to his solitary purity. He thinks nothing so important as his own thoughts – nothing so low, that his own fancy cannot elevate into greatness. He sees only 'himself and the universe;' and will 'admit no discourse to his beauty.' He is himself – alone! If such a man had had a voice in the management of the flood, he would have suffered no creeping thing to enter the ark but himself; and would have floated about the waters for forty days in lonely magnificence.

Passages of the kind we have hitherto instanced are very plentiful in all parts of the work; and we are glad they are so numerous, – because they will set Walpole's higher pretensions at rest with posterity. Time is a disinterested personage, and does his work on dull or rash men fairly and effectually. He knows nothing of criticism but its austerity and its sarcasm. He cannot feel poetry; and has, therefore, no right to settle its laws, or imitate its language. His taste in painting was affected and dogmatical. His conduct to men of genius was a piece of insolence, which Posterity is bound to resent! The true heirs of fame are not to be disturbed in the enjoyment of their property, by every insolent pretender who steps in and affects a claim upon it. The world is called on 'to defend the right.'

To come, however, to the better side of our subject. – Walpole is, as we have said, an inimitable gossip, – a most vivacious garrulous historian of fair-haired women, and curious blue china. His garrulity, moreover, hath a genius of its own – and a transparent tea-cup lets in the light of inspiration upon it, and makes it shine with colours nigh divine. An inlaid commode is, with him, the mind's easy chair.

From *The Edinburgh Review*. Hazlitt's tempestuous association with this magazine began in 1814.

BRUMMELLIANA

WE look upon Beau Brummell[1] as the greatest of small wits. Indeed, he may in this respect he considered, as Cowley says of Pindar, as 'a species alone,' and as forming a class by himself. He has arrived at the very *minimum* of wit, and reduced it, 'by happiness or pains,' to an almost invisible point. All his *bons-mots* turn upon a single circumstance, the exaggerating of the merest trifles into matters of importance, or treating everything else with the utmost *nonchalance* and indifference, as if whatever pretended to pass beyond those limits was a *bore*, and disturbed the serene air of high life. We have heard of

'A sound so fine,
That nothing lived 'twixt it and silence.'

So we may say of Mr Brummell's jests, that they are of a meaning so attenuated that 'nothing lives 'twixt them and nonsense': – they hover on the very brink of vacancy, and are in their shadowy composition next of-kin to nonentities. It is impossible for anyone to go beyond him without falling flat into insignificance and insipidity: he has touched the *ne plus ultra* that divides the dandy from the dunce. But what a fine eye to discriminate: what a sure hand to hit this last and thinnest of all intellectual partitions! *Exempli gratiâ* – for in so new a species, the theory is unintelligible without furnishing the proofs: –

Thus, in the question addressed to a noble person (which we quoted the other day), 'Do you call that *thing* a coat?' a distinction is taken as nice as it is startling. It seems all at once a vulgar prejudice to suppose that a coat is a coat, the commonest of all common things, – it is here lifted into an ineffable essence, so that a coat is no longer a *thing*; or that it would take infinite gradations of fashion, taste, and refinement, for a *thing* to aspire to the undefined privileges, and mysterious attributes of a coat. Finer 'fooling' than this cannot be imagined. What a cut upon the Duke! The beau becomes an emperor among such insects!

The first anecdote in which Mr Brummell's wit dawned upon us – and it really rises with almost every new instance – was the following: A friend one day called upon him, and found him confined to his room from a lameness in one foot, upon which he expressed his concern at the accident. 'I am sorry for it too,' answered Brummell very gravely, 'particularly as it's *my favourite leg*!' Is not this as if a man of fashion had nothing else to do than to sit and think of which of his legs he liked best; and in the plenitude of his satisfactions, and the absence of all real wants, to pamper this fanciful distinction into a serious sort of *pet* preference? Upon the whole, among so many beauties – *ubi tot nitent*, I am inclined to give my suffrage in favour of this, as the most classical of all our contemporary's *jeux d'esprit* – there is an Horatian ease and elegance about it – a slippered negligence, a cushioned effeminacy – it would take years of careless study and languid enjoyment to strike out so quaint and ingenious a conceit –

> 'A subtler web Arachne cannot spin;
> Nor the fine nets which oft we woven see
> Of scorched dew, do not in the air more lightly flee!'

It is truly the art of making something out of nothing.

We shall not go deeply into the common story of Mr Brummell's asking his servant, as he was going out for the evening, 'Where do I dine to-day, John?' This is little more than the common cant of a multiplicity of engagements, so as to make it impossible to bear them all in mind, and of an

utter disinclination to all attention to one's own affairs; but
the following is brilliant and original. Sitting one day at
table between two other persons, Mr Brummell said to his
servant, who stood behind his chair – 'John!' 'Yes, sir.'
'Who is this at my right hand?' 'If you please, sir, it's the
Marquis of Headfort.' 'And who is this at my left hand?'
'It's my Lord Yarmouth.' 'Oh, very well!' and the Beau then
proceeded to address himself to the persons who were thus
announced to him. Now, this is surely superb, and 'high
fantastical.' No, the smallest fold of that nicely adjusted
cravat was not to be deranged, the least deviation from that
select posture was not to be supposed possible. Had his
head been fastened in a vice, it could not have been more
immovably fixed than by the 'great idea in his mind,' of how
a coxcomb should sit: the air of fashion and affectation
'bound him with Styx nine times round him'; and the Beau
preserved the perfection of an attitude – like a piece of incomprehensible *still-life*, – the whole of dinner-time. The
ideal is everything, even in frivolity and folly.

It is not one of the least characteristic of our hero's
answers to a lady, who asked him if he never tasted vegetables – 'Madam, I once ate a pea!' This was reducing the
quantity of offensive grossness to the smallest assignable
fraction: anything beyond *that* his imagination was oppressed with; and even this he seemed to confess to, with a
kind of remorse, and to hasten from the subject with a certain monosyllabic brevity of style.

I do not like the mere impudence (Mr Theodore Hook,
with his extempore dullness, might do the same thing) of
forcing himself into a lady's rout, who had not invited him
to her parties, and the gabble about Hopkinses and Tom-
kinses; but there is something piquant enough in his answer
to a city-fashionable, who asked him if he would dine with
him on a certain day – 'Yes, if you won't mention it to anyone'; and in an altercation with the same person afterwards,

about obligations, the assumption of superiority implied in the appeal – 'Do you count my having *borrowed* a thousand pounds of you for nothing?' soars immediately above commonplace.

On one occasion, Mr Brummell falling ill, accounted for it by saying, 'They put me to bed to a damp —!'[2] From what slight causes direst issues spring! So sensitive and apprehensive a constitution makes one sympathise with its delicate possessor, as much as if he had been shut up in the steam of a laundry, or 'his lodging had been on the cold ground.' Mr Brummell having been interrogated as to the choice of his present place of residence (Calais) as somewhat dull replied, 'He thought it hard if a gentleman could not pass his time agreeably between London and Paris.'

Some of Brummell's *bons-mots* have been attributed to Sir Lumley Skeffington, who is even said to have been the first in this minute and tender walk of wit. It is, for instance, reported of him that, being at table and talking of daisies, he should turn round to his valet, and say with sentimental *naïveté* and trivial fondness – 'On what day of the month did I first see a daisy, Matthew?' 'On the 1st of February, sir.' There is here a kindred vein; but whoever was the inventor, Brummell has borne away the prize, as Pope eclipsed his master Dryden, and Titian surpassed Giorgione's fame. In fine, it was said, with equal truth and spirit by one of the parties concerned, that 'the year 1815 was fatal to three great men – Byron, Buonaparte, and Brummell!'[3]

From *The London Weekly Review* (February 1828).

FASHION

Is it to be wondered at that a young raw ignorant girl, who is sent up from the country as a milliner's or mantua-maker's apprentice, and stowed into a room with eight or ten others, who snatch every moment they can spare from caps and bonnets, and sit up half the night to read all the novels they can get, and as soon they have finished one, send for another, whose heart, in the course of half a year, has been pierced through with twenty beaux on paper, who has been courted, seduced, ran away with, married and put to bed under all the fine names that the imagination can invent to as many fine gentlemen, who has sighed and wept with so many heroes and heroines that her tears and sighs have at least caused in her a defluction of the brain, and a palpitation of the heart at the sight of every man, whose fancy is love-sick, and her head quite turned, should be unable to resist the first coxcomb of real flesh and blood, who in shining boots and a velvet collar accosts her in the shape of a lover, but who has no thoughts of marrying her, because if he were to take this imprudent step, he must give up his shining boots and velvet collar, and the respect they procure him in the world? Zaleucus ordained that no woman should dress herself gorgeously, unless she was a prostitute. If I were a law-giver, and chose to meddle in such matters, I would ordain that no woman should expose her shape publicly, unless she were a prostitute. – The female form is more proper for child-bearing, than for public exhibition; this secret analogy, when coupled with modesty and reserve, is however its greatest charm. The strange fancy-dresses, the perverse disguises, the counterfeit shapes, the stiff stays, and enormous hoops worn by the women in the time of the Spec-

tator gave an agreeable scope to the imagination. The greedy
eye and rash hand of licentiousness were repressed. The
senses were never satisfied in an instant. Love was entangled
in the folds of the swelling handkerchief, and the desires
might wander for ever round the circumference of a quilted
petticoat, or find a rich lodging in the flowers of a damask
stomacher. There was room for years of patient perseverance, for a thousand thoughts, fancies, conjectures, hopes,
fears, and wishes. There seemed no end to difficulties and
delays: to overcome so many obstacles was the work of ages.
A *wife* had then some meaning in it: it was an angel con-
cealed behind whalebone, flounces, and brocade. The transition from a mistress in masquerade to a wife in wedding
sheets was worth venturing for: now it is nothing, and we
hear no more of faithful courtships, and romantic loves. A
woman can be *but* undressed. – The young ladies we at
present see with the thin muslin vest drawn tight round the
slender waist, and following with nice exactness the undulations of the shape downwards, disclosing each full swell,
each coy recess, obtruding on the eye each opening charm,
the play of the muscles, the working of the thighs, and by
the help of a walk, of which every step seems a gird, and
which keeps the limbs strained to the utmost pain, display-
ing all those graceful involutions of person, and all those
powers of fascinating motion, of which the female form is
susceptible – these moving pictures of lust and nakedness,
against which the greasy imaginations of grooms and porters
may rub themselves, running the gauntlet of the saucy
looks and indecent sarcasms of the boys in the street, staring
at every ugly fellow, leering at every handsome man, and
throwing out a lure for every fool (true Spartan girls, who if
they were metamorphosed into any thing in the manner of
Ovid, it would certainly be into valerian!) are the very same,
whose mothers or grand-mothers buried themselves under
a pile of clothes, whose timid steps hardly touched the

ground, whose eyes were constantly averted from the rude gaze of the men, and who almost blushed at their own shadows. 'Of such we in romances read.' It does not require any great spirit of divination to perceive that this change in appearance must imply some change in manners. Is this change then owing entirely to the increased pressure of the principle of population, or have not French fashions, French milliners, and French dancing masters had some hand in producing it?* – Mr Malthus[1] inveighs with great severity against squalid poverty, and the vices produced by filth and rags. I allow the justice of his remarks, and think that the condition of the poor in this respect is one of the chief nuisances of society. After giving the poor a scrubbing with a coarse towel in the manner he has done, it would not have been amiss if he had taken a clean white clerical pocket-handkerchief, and applied it to wipe off the rouge from the cheeks of painted prostitution, or thrown it as a covering over the polished neck and ivory shoulders of ladies of high quality. The bishop of London would have praised the attempt. Mr Malthus might have distinguished between the involuntary rents, and the unlucky loop-holes which sometimes appear in a poor girl's petticoat, and the elegant dishabille and studied nakedness of high life. The dirt that sticks to a wench's face in cleaning a saucepan is I think likely to have less effect on the character than the red paste daubed on the cheeks before a looking-glass, to give *animation* to the eyes. The contempt which dirt and poverty excite must destroy all moral sensibility. Must not the glare of fashion and the perpetual intoxication of personal vanity have the same effect? The poor grovel in disagreeable sensations, the rich wanton in voluptuous ones. The passions are

* Have Dryden's Fables, the New Eloise, or the Memoirs of Fanny Hill never added any thing to the pressure of the principle of population, without any reference to the parish registers of deaths and marriages?

not more likely to be inflamed by stale porter, the screams of a fiddle, and the clattering of a hornpipe at a hop in St Giles's, than by the elegant liqueurs, the soft sounds of the clarionet and hautboy, and the languishing movements of walses, allemandes, and minuets *de la cour* at a ball in St James's. A fair, or an opera may equally turn the head of any silly girl that goes to one. Of the two, a tune on the salt-box would be got over sooner than Narcissus and the Graces. The tawdry prints to be seen in garrets, and the ballads sung at the corners of streets do not much improve the morals of the people: but I put it to the conscience of our sentimental divine, whether the Wanton Wife of Bath, or the tall captain with his arm round the chambermaid's waist, or Jemmy Jessamy lolling on the sofa with his mistress, may be expected to produce more accidents than those luscious collections of the poets, or those grave scripture-pieces, or classical *chef-d'œuvres* of Venus and Adonis, of Leda with her Swan, Nymphs, Fawns, and Satyrs, which gentlemen of fortune keep in their houses for the instruction of their wives and daughters. Mr Malthus is convinced that no young woman brought up in nastiness and vulgarity, however virtuous she may seem, can be good for any thing at twenty: I confess I have the same cynical opinion of those, who have the good fortune to be brought up in the obscene refinements of fashionable life.

I never fell in love but once; and then it was with a girl who always wore her handkerchief pinned tight round her neck, with a fair face, gentle eyes, a soft smile, and cool auburn locks. I mention this, because it may in some measure account for my temperate, tractable notions of this passion, compared with Mr Malthus's. It was not a raging heat, a fever in the veins: but it was like a vision, a dream, like thoughts of childhood, an everlasting hope, a distant joy, a heaven, a world that might be. The dream is still left, and sometimes comes confusedly over me in solitude and silence, and mingles with the softness of the sky, and veils my eyes from mortal grossness. After all, Mr Malthus may be right in his opinion of human nature. Though my notions of love have been thus aerial and refined, I do not know that this was any advantage to me, or that I might not have done better with a few of our author's ungovernable transports, and sensual oozings. Perhaps the workings of the heart are best expressed by a gloating countenance, by mawkish sentiments and lively gestures. Cupid often perches on broad shoulders, or on the brawny calf of a leg, a settlement is better than a love-letter, and in love not minds, but bodies and fortunes meet. I have therefore half a mind to retract all that I have said, and prove to Mr Malthus that love is not even so intellectual a passion as he sometimes admits it to be, but altogether gross and corporal.

From *A Reply to Malthus's Essay On Population* (1807).

PRONOUNCEMENTS,
DENOUNCEMENTS AND CONFESSIONS

REASON, with most people, means their own opinion. – *The New School of Reform*

There is a link of friendship in mutual political servility. – *On Envy*

I hate the sight of the Duke of Wellington for his foolish face, as much as anything else. I cannot believe that a great general is contained under such a pasteboard vizor. – ibid.

It is hard to find one's self right at last. – *On English Writers and Speakers*

There is nothing truly contemptible, but that which is always tacking and veering before the breath of power. – *The Periodical Press*

Bodies of men seldom retract or atone for the injuries they have done to an individual. – *Life and Times of Daniel Defoe*

It was my misfortune (perhaps) to be bred among Dissenters, who look with too jaundiced an eye at others, and set too high a value on their own peculiar pretensions. From being proscribed themselves, they learn to proscribe others, and come in the end to reduce all integrity of principle and soundness of opinion within the pale of their own little communion. Those who were out of it and did not belong to the class of Rational Dissenters, I was led erroneously to look upon as hardly deserving the name of rational beings. – *On the Conduct of Life*

Whether it is fortitude or cowardice, or both, there is a strong propensity in the human mind, if its suspicions are once raised, *to know the worst.* – *On Rochefoucauld's Maxims*

The love of truth, when it predominates, produces inquisitive characters, the whole tribe of gossips, tale-bearers, harmless busybodies, your blunt honest creatures, who never conceal what they think, and who are the more sure to tell it you the less you want to know it – and now and then a philosopher. – *On Mind and Motive*

Liberty is the only true riches. Of all the rest we are at once the masters and the slaves. – *Common-Places.*

I have had nothing to do all my life but think, and I have enjoyed the objects of thought, the sense of truth and beauty, in perfect integrity of soul. No one has said to me, *Believe this, do that, say what we would have you*; no one has come between me and my free-will; I have breathed the very air of truth and independence. Compared with unbiassed, uncontrolled possession of the universe of thought and nature, what I have wanted is light in the balance, and hardly claims the tribute of a sigh. – ibid.

I never knew what it was like to feel like a footman. How many lords in waiting can say as much? – ibid.

When I consider how little difference there is in mankind (either body or mind) I cannot help being astonished at the airs some people give themselves. – ibid.

The greatest proof of superiority is to bear with impertinence. – ibid.

Abuse is an indirect species of homage. – ibid.

Those who can keep secrets have no curiosity. We only wish to gain knowledge, that we may impart it. – ibid.

Artists and other studious professions are not happy, for this reason; they cannot enjoy mental repose. A state of lassitude and languor succeeds to that of overstrained, anxious exertion. – ibid.

Women are the sport of caprice, the slaves of custom. – ibid.

The greatest crime in the eye of the world is to endeavour to instruct or amend it. – ibid.

Political truth is a libel; religious truth a blasphemy. – ibid.

To be a lord, a papist and poor, is the most enviable distinction of humanity. There is all the pride and sense of independence, irritated and strengthened by being proscribed by power, and liable to be harassed by petty daily insults from even the meanest vassal. What a situation to make the mind recoil from the world upon itself, and to sit and brood in moody grandeur and disdain of soul over fallen splendours and present indignities! It is just the life I should like to have led. – ibid.

I hate to be near the sea, and to hear it roaring and raging like a wild beast in its den. It puts me in mind of the everlasting efforts of the human mind, struggling to be free, and ending just where it began. – ibid.

If a man were refused by a woman a thousand times, and he really loved her, he would still think that at the bottom of her heart she preferred him to every one else. Nor is this wonderful, when we consider that all passion is a species of madness. ... We never can persuade ourselves that a mistress cares nothing about us, till we no longer care about her. – ibid.

The grand scenes of Nature are more adapted for occasional visits than for constant residence. ... One chief advantage of the great and magnificent objects of Nature is, that they stamp their image on the mind for ever; the blow need not be repeated to have the desired effect. – ibid.

Mankind are an incorrigible race. Give them but bugbears and idols – it is all that they ask; the distinction of right and wrong, of truth and falsehood, of good and evil, are worse than indifferent to them. – ibid.

Fiction is truth in another shape. – *The Modern Gradus ad Parnassum*

A peace-officer in this country is the only person who refuses to lift a finger, and proceeds with infinite caution and repugnance in suppressing the natural growth and glory ... of assault and battery. If a fellow in the street makes an outrageous noise and threatens to knock anyone down, the watchmen in pure sympathy and admiration of his prowess, let him pass: if a poor woman falls down in a fit through intoxication or want, they have her to the watch-house in a moment. They have no compassion for the weak and helpless; their heads are full of blows and bludgeons. – *English Characteristics*

There is ... nothing that the world likes better than originality of invention, and nothing that they hate worse than originality of thought. – *On Originality*

We talk about the cant of politics or religion, as if there were no cant but that which is common to the multitude. But whenever any two individuals agree about any one thing, they begin to cant about it, and take the echo of one another's voices as the echo of truth. Half-a-dozen persons will always make a quorum of credulity and vulgarity. – *On Prejudice*

I am not very patriotic in my notions, nor prejudiced in favour of my own countrymen; and one reason is, I wish to have as good as an opinion as I can of human nature in general. If we are the paragons that some people would make us out, what must the rest of the world be? If we monopolize all the sense and virtue on the face of the globe, we 'leave the world poor indeed'. ... Let them have a few advantages that we have not – grapes and the sun! – *Aphorisms on Man*

When the Persian ambassador was at Edinburgh, an old Presbyterian lady ... fell upon him for his idolatrous belief, and said, 'I hear you worship the sun!' – 'Faith, Madame,' he replied, 'and so would you too if you had ever seen him!' – *ibid.*

America is just setting out in the path of history, on the model of England, without a language of its own, and with a continent instead of an island to run its career in – like a novice in the art, who gets a larger canvas than his master ever had to cover with his second-hand designs. – *ibid.*

Sir Walter Scott (when all's said and done) is an inspired butler. – *Mrs Siddons*

When Mrs Siddons used to sit in parties and at drawing-rooms, the Lady Marys and the Lady Dorothys of the day came and peeped into the room to get a glance of her, with more awe and wonder than if it had been a queen. This was honour, this was power. ... We can reckon up in our time three great tragic performers; Mrs Siddons, Mr Keen, and Madame Pasta ... Of these three, Mrs Siddons seemed to command every source of terror and pity, and to rule over their wildest elements with inborn ease and dignity. Her person was made to contain her spirit; her soul to fill and animate her person. Her eye answered her voice. She wore a crown. She looked as if descended from a higher sphere, and walked the earth in majesty and pride. She sounded the full diapason, touched all chords of passion, they thrilled through her, and yet she preserved an elevation of thought and character above them, like the tall cliff round which the tempest roars, but its head reposes in the blue serene! Mrs Siddons combined the utmost grandeur and force with every variety of expression and excellence: her transitions were rapid and extreme, but were massed into unity and breadth – there was nothing warped or starting from its place – she produced the most overpowering effects without the slightest effort, by a look, a word, a gesture. – *ibid*.

... The very names of a cricket bat and ball make English fingers tingle. What happy days must Long Robinson have passed in getting ready for his wickets and mending his bats, who, even when two of the fingers of his right hand were struck off by the violence of the ball, had a screw fastened to it to hold the bat, and with the other hand still sent the ball thundering against the boards that bounded Old Lord's cricket ground! What delightful hours must have been his in looking forward to the matches that were to come, in recounting the feats he had performed in those that were past! I have myself whiled away whole mornings in seeing him strike the ball (like a countryman mowing with a scythe) to the farthest extremity of the smooth, level,

sun-burnt ground, and with long awkward strides count
the notches that made victory sure! – *Merry England*

The *comfort* on which the English lay so much stress ...
arises from the same source as their mirth. Both exist by contrast and a sort of contradiction. The English are certainly
the most uncomfortable of all people in themselves, and
therefore it is that they stand in need of every kind of comfort and accommodation. The least thing puts them out of
their way, and therefore everything must be in its place.
They are mightily offended at disagreeable tastes and smells,
and therefore they exact the utmost neatness and nicety.
They are sensible of heat and cold, and therefore they cannot
exist, unless everything is snug and warm, or else open and
airy, where they are. They must have 'all appliances and
means to boot'. They are afraid of interruption and in-
trusion, and therefore they shut themselves up in in-door
enjoyments and by their own firesides. It is not that they
require luxuries (for that implies a high degree of epicurian
indulgence and gratification), but they cannot do without
their comforts; that is, whatever tends to supply their physical wants, and ward off physical pain and annoyance. As
they have not a fund of animal spirits and enjoyments in
themselves, they cling to external objects for support, and
derive solid satisfaction from the ideas of order, cleanliness,
plenty, property, and domestic quiet, as they seek for diversion from odd accidents and grotesque surprises, and have
the highest possible relish not of voluptuous softness, but of
hard knocks and dry blows, as one means of ascertaining
their personal identity. – *ibid.*

I scarce know which I dislike the most – the patronage
that effects to bring premature genius into notice, or that
which extends its piecemeal, formal charity towards it in its
decline. I hate your Literary Funds and Funds for Decayed

Artists – they are corporations for the encouragement of meanness, pretence, and insolence. – *On the Want of Money*

You say there is a common language in nature. They see nature through their wants, while you look at it for your pleasure. Ask a country lad if he does not like to hear the birds sing in the spring? And he will laugh in your face. 'What is it, then, he does like?' – 'Good victuals and drink!' As if you had not these too; but because he has them not, he thinks of nothing else, and laughs at you and your refinements, supposing you to live upon air. To those who are deprived of every other advantage, even nature is a *book sealed*. I have made this capital mistake all my life, in imagining that those objects which lay open to all, and excited an interest merely from the *idea* of them, spoke a common language to all; and that nature was a kind of universal home, where all ages, sexes, classes met. Not so. The vital air, the sky, the woods, the streams – all these go for nothing, except with a favoured few. The poor are taken up with their bodily wants – the rich, with external acquisitions: the one, with the sense of property – the other, of its privation. Both have the same distaste for *sentiment*. The *genteel* are the slaves of appearances – the vulgar, of necessity; and neither has the smallest regard for true worth, refinement, generosity. – *On Personal Identity*

In other places I forget myself, but in France I am always an Englishman. – *Travelling Abroad*

We sometimes deceive ourselves, and think worse of human nature than it deserves, in consequence of judging character from names, and classes, and modes of life. No one is simply and absolutely any one thing, though he may be branded with it as a name. Some persons have expected to see his crimes written in the face of a murderer, and have been disappointed because they did not, as if this impeached the distinction between virtue and vice. Not at all. The circumstances only showed that the man was other things, and had other feelings besides those of a murderer. If he had nothing else, if he had dreamt of nothing else, but schemes of murder, his features would have expressed nothing else: but this perfection in vice is not to be expected from the contradictory and mixed nature of our motives. Humanity is to be met with in a den of robbers; nay, modesty in a brothel. Even among the most abandoned of the other sex, there is not unfrequently found to exist (contrary to all that is generally supposed) one strong and individual attachment, which remains unshaken to the last. Virtue may be said to steal, like a guilty thing, into the secret haunts of vice and infamy; it clings to their devoted victim, and will not be driven quite away. Nothing can destroy the human heart. – *On Cant and Hypocrisy*

The cant of sentimentality has succeeded to that of religion. There is a cant of humanity, of patriotism and loyalty – not that people do not feel these emotions, but they make too great a *fuss* about them, and draw out the expression of them until they tire themselves and others. There is a cant about Shakespear. There is a cant about *Political Economy* just now. In short, there is and must be a cant about everything that excites a considerable degree of attention and interest, and that people would be thought to know and care rather more about than they actually do. Cant is the voluntary overcharging or prolongation of a real sentiment; hypocrisy is the setting up of a pretension to a feeling you never had and have no wish for. – ibid.

It is utterly impossible to persuade an Editor that he is nobody. – *On Editors*

At Lord's-Ground there are some old hands that are famous for '*blocking out and staying in*': it would seem that some of our literary veterans had taken a lesson from their youthful exercises at Harrow and Eton. – ibid.

I do not recollect having ever repented giving a letter to the postman, or wishing to retrieve it after he had once deposited it in his bag. What I have once set my hand to, I take the consequence of, and have always been much of the same humour in this respect. – *The Letter-Bell*

JAMES NORTHCOTE: 'Tom Jones is a masterpiece, as far as regards the conduct of the fable.'

HAZLITT: 'Do you know the reason? Fielding had a hooked nose, the long chin. It is that introverted physiognomy that binds and concentrates.' – *Conversations With James Northcote*

JAMES NORTHCOTE: 'There was an awkward composer at the Opera many years ago, of the name of Boccarelli; what he did was stupid enough in general, but I remember he sung an air one day at Conway's which they said Shield had transferred into the *Flitch of Bacon*. I cannot describe the effect it had on me – it seemed as if it wound into my very soul – I would give anything to hear it sung again. So I could have listened to Dignum's singing the lines out of Shakespear – 'Come unto these yellow sands, and then take hands' – a hundred times over. But I am not sure that others would be affected in the same manner by it; there may be some quaint association of idea in the case. But at least, if I am wrong, the folly is my own.'

HAZLITT: 'There is no danger of that sort – all the real

taste and feeling in the world is made up of what people *take in their heads* in this manner ...' – ibid.,

Speaking correctly is not proper to one class more than another: if the fashionable, to distinguish themselves from the vulgar, affect a peculiar tone or a set of phrases, this is mere slang. – ibid.

A man who is determined never to move out of the beaten road cannot lose his way. – *On the Principles of Human Action*

It is always easier to quote an authority than to carry on a chain of reasoning. – *Letters in Answer to Malthus*

... The common failing of wishing to be thought satirical often runs through whole families in country places, to the great annoyance of the neighbours. – *On Wit and Humour*

[Of Sterne] – 'My Uncle Toby' is one of the finest compliments ever paid to human nature. – *On the English Novelists*

Macbeth is only tolerated in this country for the sake of the music; and in the United States of America, where the philosophical principles of government are carried still further in theory and practice, we find that the Beggar's Opera is hooted from the stage. Society, by degrees, is constructed into a machine that carries us safely and insipidly from one end of life to the other, in a very comfortable prose style. – *On Poetry in General*

Faces are the best part of a picture. – ibid.

[On Matthew Prior] – His moral muse is a Magdalen, and should not have obtruded herself on public view. – *On Swift, Young, Gray, Collins, Etc.*

[On Oliver Goldsmith] – He is the most amusing and interesting person, in one of the most amusing and interesting books in the world, Boswell's Life of Johnson. – ibid.

Burn's [poetry] is a very highly sublimated essence of animal existence.

Mr Wordsworth is 'himself alone', a recluse philosopher, or a reluctant spectator of the scenes of many-coloured life; moralising on them, not describing, not entering into them. Robert Burns has exerted all the vigour of his mind, all the happiness of his nature, in exalting the pleasures of wine, of love, and good fellowship; but in Mr Wordsworth there is total disunion and divorce of the faculties of the mind from those of the body; the banns are forbid, or a separation is austerely pronounced from bed and board. ... From the Lyrical Ballads, it does not appear that men eat or drink, marry or are given in marriage. If we lived by every sentiment that proceeds out of mouths and not by bread and wine, or if the species were continued like trees (to borrow an expression from the great Sir Thomas Browne), Mr Wordsworth's poetry would be just as good as ever. It is not so with Burns: he is 'famous for the keeping of it up' ...
– *On Burns and the Old English Ballads*

Mr Moore should not have written Lalla Rookh, even for three thousand guineas. His fame is worth more than that.
– *On the Living Poets*

It remains that I should say a few words of Mr Coleridge; and there is no one who has a better right to say what he thinks of him than I have. ... He is the only person I ever knew who answered to the idea of a man of genius. He is the only person from whom I have learnt anything. There is only one thing he could learn from me in return, but *that* he has not. He was the first poet I ever knew. His genius at that time had angelic wings, and fed on manna. He talked on for ever, and you wished him to talk on for ever. His thoughts did not seem to come with labour and effort; but as if borne on the gusts of genius, and as if the wings of his imagination lifted him off his feet. His voice rolled on the ear like a pealing organ, and its sound alone was the music of thought. His mind was clothed with wings and raised on them, he lifted philosophy to heaven. In his descriptions, you saw the progress of human happiness and liberty in bright and never-ending succession, like the steps of Jacob's ladder, with airy shapes ascending and descending, and with the voice of God at the top of the ladder. And shall I, who heard him then, listen to him now? Not I! ... That spell is broken, that time is gone for ever; that voice is heard no more: but still the recollection comes rushing by with thoughts of long-past years, and rings in my ears with never-dying sound. – *On the Living Poets*

I would ... advise anyone who has an ambition to write, and to write *his best*, in the periodical press, to get if possible 'a situation' in the *Times* newspaper, the Editor of which is a man of business, and not of letters. He may write there as long and as good articles as he can, without being turned out for it ... – *A View of the English Stage*

Life is the art of being well-deceived. – *On Pedantry*

The extreme tendency of civilization is to dissipate all intellectual energy, and dissolve all moral principle. We are sometimes inclined to regret the innovations on the Catholic religion. It was a noble charter for ignorance, dullness, and prejudice of all kinds, (perhaps, after all, 'the sovereign'st things on earth'), and put an effectual stop to the vanity and restlessness of opinion. – ibid.

A full-dressed ecclesiastic is a sort of go-cart of divinity: an ethical automaton. – *On the Clerical Character*

Death cancels everything but truth; and strips a man of everything but genius and virtue. It is a sort of natural canonization. It makes the meanest of us sacred ... – *Lord Byron*

When Mr [Benjamin] West had painted a picture, he thought it was perfect. ... When Mr West walked through his gallery, the result of fifty years' labour, he saw nothing, either on the right or the left, to be added or taken away. ... When someone spoke of his *St Paul Shaking Off the Serpent from his Arm*, he said, 'A little burst of genius, Sir.' ... He lived long in the firm persuasion of being one of the elect among the sons of fame, and went to his final rest in the arms of Immortality! Happy error! – *On the Old Age of Artists*

[On Gray] He deserved that we should think of him, for he thought of others, and turned a trembling, ever-watchful ear to 'the still sad music of humanity'. His Letters are inimitably fine. If his poems are sometimes finical and pedantic, his prose is quite free from affectation. He pours his thoughts out upon paper as they arise in his mind without pretense or constraint, from the pure impulse of learned leisure and contemplative indolence. He is not here on stilts or in buckram; but smiles in his easy chair, as he moralises through the loopholes of retreat. ... He had nothing to do but to read and to think, and to tell his friends what he read and thought. His life was a luxurious, thoughtful dream ... – *On Swift, Young, Gray, Collins, Etc.*

[On Shenstone] He withdrew from the world to be followed by the crowd. ... His Letters show him ... to have been a finished literary coquet. – *ibid.*

... The different sects in this country are, or have been, the steadiest supporters of its liberties and laws; they are checks and barriers against the insidious – or avowed encroachments of arbitrary power, as effectual and indispensible as any others in the Constitution. ... It is hard for anyone to be an honest politician who is not born and bred a Dissenter. – *On Court Influence*

He who looks at beauty to admire, to adore it, who reads of its wondrous power in novels, in poems, or in plays, is not unwise: but let no man fall in love, for from that moment he is 'the baby of a girl' – How few out of the infinite number of those that marry and are given in marriage, wed with those they would prefer to all the world: nay, how far the greatest proportion are joined together by mere motives of convenience, accident, recommendation of friends, or indeed not unfrequently, by the very fear of the event, by repugnance and by a fatal fascination ... – *On Living to One's-Self*

SIMPLE GIRLS

SOME gallants set their hearts on princesses; others descend in imagination to women of quality; others are mad after opera-singers. For my part, I am shy even of actresses, and should not think of leaving my card with Madame V—. I am for none of these *bonnes fortunes*; but for a list of humble beauties, servant-maids and shepherd-girls, with their red elbows, hard hands, black stockings and mob-caps, I could furnish out a gallery equal to Cowley's, and paint them half as well. Oh! might I but attempt a description of some of them in poetic prose, Don Juan would forget his Julia, and Mr Davison might both print and publish this volume. I agree so far with Horace, and differ with Montaigne. I admire the Clementinas and Clarissas at a distance: the Pamelas and Fannys of Richardson and Fielding make my blood tingle. I have written love-letters to such in my time, *d'un pathétique à fendre les rochers*, and with about as much effect as if they had been addressed to stone. The simpletons only laughed, and said, that 'those were not the sort of things to gain the affections.' I wish I had kept copies in my own justification. What is worse, I have an utter aversion to *blue-stockings*. I do not care a fig for any woman that knows even what *an author* means. If I know that she has read any thing I have written, I cut her acquaintance immediately. This sort of literary intercourse with me passes for nothing. Her critical and scientific acquirements are *carrying coals to Newcastle*. I do not want to be told that I have published such or such a work. I knew all this before. It makes no addition to my sense of power. I do not wish the affair to be brought about in that way. I would have her read my soul: she should understand the language of the heart: she should know what I am, as if she were another self! She should love me for myself alone. I like myself without any reason: — I would have her do so too. This is not very reasonable. I abstract from my temptations to admire all the circumstances of dress, birth, breeding, fortune; and I would not willingly put forward my own pretensions, whatever they may be. The image of some fair creature is engraven on my inmost soul; it is on that I build my claim to her regard, and expect her to see into my heart, as I see her form always before me. Wherever she treads, pale primroses, like her face, vernal hyacinths, like her brow, spring up beneath her feet, and music hangs on every bough: but all is cold, barren, and desolate without her. Thus I feel and thus I think. But have I ever told her so? No. Or if I did, would she understand it? No. I 'hunt the wind, I worship a statue, cry aloud to the desert.' To see beauty is not to be beautiful, to pine in love is not to be loved again. — I always was inclined to raise and magnify the power of Love. I thought that his sweet power should only be exerted to join together the loveliest forms and fondest hearts; that none but those in whom his Godhead shone outwardly, and was inly felt, should ever partake of his triumphs; and I stood and gazed at a distance, as unworthy to mingle in so bright a throng, and did not (even for a moment) wish to tarnish the glory of so fair a vision by being myself admitted into it. I say this was my notion once, but God knows it was one of the errors of my youth. For coming nearer to look, I saw the maimed, the blind, and the halt enter in, the crooked and the dwarf, the ugly, the old and impotent, the man of pleasure and the man of the world, the dapper and the pert, the vain and shallow boaster, the fool and the pedant, the ignorant and brutal, and all that is farthest removed from earth's fairest-born, and the pride of human life. Seeing all these enter the courts of Love, and thinking that I also might venture in under favour of the crowd, but finding myself rejected, I fancied (I might be wrong) that it was not so much because I was below, as above the common standard. I did feel, but I was ashamed to feel, mortified at my repulse, when I saw the meanest of mankind, the very scum and refuse, all creeping things and every obscene creature, enter in before me. I seemed a species by myself. I took a pride even in my disgrace: and concluded I had elsewhere my inheritance! The only thing I ever piqued myself upon was the writing the *Essay on the Principles of Human Action* – a work that no woman ever read, or would ever comprehend the meaning of. But if I do not build my claim to regard on the pretensions I have, how can I build it on those I am totally without? Or why do I complain and expect to gather grapes of thorns, or figs of thistles? Thought has in me cancelled pleasure; and this dark forehead, bent upon truth, is the rock on which all affection has split. And thus I waste my life in one long sigh; nor ever (till too late) beheld a gentle face turned gently upon mine! ... But no! not too late, if that face, pure, modest, downcast, tender, with angel sweetness, not only gladdens the prospect of the future, but sheds its radiance on the past, smiling in tears. A purple light hovers round my head. The air of love is in the room. As I look at my long-neglected copy of the Death of Clorinda, golden gleams play upon the canvas, as they used when I painted it. The flowers of Hope and Joy springing up in my mind, recal the time when they first bloomed there. The years that are fled knock at the door and enter. I am in the Louvre once more. The sun of Austerlitz has not set. It still shines here – in my heart; and he, the son of glory, is not dead, nor ever shall be, to me. I am as when my life began. The rainbow is in the sky again. I see the skirts of the departed years. All that I have thought and felt has not been in vain. I am not utterly worthless, unregarded; nor shall I die and wither of pure scorn. Now could I sit on

the tomb of Liberty, and write a Hymn to Love. Oh! if I am
deceived, let me be deceived still. Let me live in the Elysium
of those soft looks; poison me with kisses, kill me with
smiles; but still mock me with thy love!

Poets chuse mistresses who have the fewest charms, that
they may make something out of nothing. They succeed best
in fiction, and they apply this rule to love. They make a
Goddess of any dowdy. As Don Quixote said, in answer to
the matter of fact remonstrances of Sancho, that Dulcinea
del Toboso answered the purpose of signalising his valour
just as well as the 'fairest princess under sky,' so any of the
fair sex will serve them to write about just as well as another. They take some awkward thing and dress her up in
fine words, as children dress up a wooden doll in fine
clothes. Perhaps, a fine head of hair, a taper waist, or some
other circumstance strikes them, and they make the rest out
according to their fancies. They have a wonderful knack of
supplying deficiencies in the subjects of their idolatry out of
the store-house of their imaginations. They presently translate their favourites to the skies, where they figure with
Berenice's locks and Ariadne's crown. This predilection for
the unprepossessing and insignificant, I take to arise not
merely from a desire in poets to have some subject to exercise their inventive talents upon, but from their jealousy of
any pretensions (even those of beauty in the other sex) that
might interfere with the continual incense offered to their
personal vanity.

From 'On Great and Little Things' in
Table-Talk (1821).

DREAMING

THERE is ... a sort of profundity in sleep; and it may be usefully consulted as an oracle. ... It may be said, that the voluntary power is suspended, and things come upon us as unexpected revelations, which we keep out of our thoughts at other times. We may be aware of a danger, that yet we do not chuse, while we have the full command of our faculties, to acknowledge to ourselves: the impending event will then appear to us as a dream, and we shall most likely find it verified afterwards. Another thing of no small consequence is, that we may sometimes discover our tacit, and almost unconscious sentiments, with respect to persons or things in the same way. We are not hypocrites in our sleep. The curb is taken off from our passions, and our imagination wanders at will. When awake, we check these rising thoughts, and fancy we have them not. In dreams, we are off our guard, they return securely and unbidden. We may make this use of the infirmity of our sleeping metamorphosis, that we may repress any feelings of this sort that we disapprove in their incipient state, and detect, ere it be too late, an unwarrantable antipathy or fatal passion. Infants cannot disguise their thoughts from others; and in sleep we reveal the secret to ourselves.

It should appear that I have never been in love, for the same reason. I never dream of the face of anyone I am particularly attached to. I have thought almost to agony of the same person for years, nearly without ceasing, so as to have her face always before me and to be haunted by a perpetual consciousness of disappointed passion, and yet I never in all that time dreamt of this person more than once or twice, and then not vividly. I conceive, therefore, that this per-

severance of the imagination in a fruitless track must have
been owing to mortified pride, to an intense desire and hope
of good in the abstract, more than to love, which I consider
as an individual and involuntary passion, and which, therefore, when it is strong, must predominate over fancy in
sleep. I think myself into love, and dream myself out of it. I
should have made a very bad Endymion, in this sense; for
all the time the heavenly Goddess was shining over my
head, I should never have had a thought about her. If I had
waked and found her gone, I might have been in a considerable *taking*. Coleridge used to laugh at me for my want of
the faculty of dreaming; and once, on my saying that I did
not like the preternatural stories in the Arabian Nights (for
the comic parts I love dearly), he said, 'That must be because you never dream. There is a class of poetry built on
this foundation, which is surely no inconsiderable part of
our nature, since we are asleep and building up imaginations of this sort half our time.' I had nothing to say against
it: it was one of his conjectural subtleties, in which he excels
all the persons I ever knew ...

From 'On Dreams' in *The Plain Speaker* (1826).

COUNTRY PEOPLE

ALL country people hate each other. They have so little comfort, that they envy their neighbours the smallest pleasure or advantage, and nearly grudge themselves the necessaries of life. From not being accustomed to enjoyment, they become hardened and averse to it – stupid, for want of thought – selfish, for want of society. There is nothing good to be had in the country, or, if there is, they will not let you have it. They had rather injure themselves than oblige any one else. Their common mode of life is a system of wretchedness and self-denial, like what we read of among barbarous tribes. You live out of the world. You cannot get your tea and sugar without sending to the next town for it: you pay double, and have it of the worst quality. The small-beer is sure to be sour – the milk skimmed – the meat bad, or spoiled in the cooking. You cannot do a single thing you like; you cannot walk out or sit at home, or write or read, or think or look as if you did, without being subject to impertinent curiosity. The apothecary annoys you with his complaisance; the parson with his superciliousness. If you are poor, you are despised; if you are rich, you are feared and hated. If you do any one a favour, the whole neighbourhood is up in arms; the clamour is like that of a rookery; and the person himself, it is ten to one, laughs at you for your pains, and takes the first opportunity of shewing you that he labours under no uneasy sense of obligation. There is a perpetual round of mischief-making and backbiting for want of any better amusement. There are no shops, no taverns, no theatres, no opera, no concerts, no pictures, no public-buildings, no crowded streets, no noise of coaches, or of courts of law, – neither courtiers nor courtesans, no literary parties, no fashionable routs, no society, no books, or knowledge of books. Vanity and luxury are the civilisers of the world, and sweeteners of human life. Without objects either of pleasure or action, it grows harsh and crabbed: the mind becomes stagnant, the affections callous, and the eye dull. Man left to himself soon degenerates into a very disagreeable person. Ignorance is always bad enough; but rustic ignorance is intolerable. Aristotle has observed, that tragedy purifies the affections by terror and pity. If so, a company of tragedians should be established at the public expence, in every village or hundred, as a better mode of education than either Bell's or Lancaster's.[1] The benefits of knowledge are never so well understood as from seeing the effects of ignorance, in their naked, undisguised state, upon the common country people. Their selfishness and insensibility are perhaps less owing to the hardships and privations, which make them, like people out at sea in a boat, ready to devour one another, than to their having no idea of anything beyond themselves and their immediate sphere of action. They have no knowledge of, and consequently can take no interest in, anything which is not an object of their senses, and of their daily pursuits. They hate all strangers, and have generally a nick-name for the inhabitants of the next village. The two young noblemen in Guzman d'Alfarache, who went to visit their mistresses only a league out of Madrid, were set upon by the peasants, who came round them calling out, '*A wolf.*' Those who have no enlarged or liberal ideas, can have no disinterested or generous sentiments. Persons who are in the habit of reading novels and romances, are compelled to take a deep interest in, and to have their affections strongly excited by, fictitious characters and imaginary situations; their thoughts and feelings are constantly carried out of themselves, to persons they never saw, and things that never existed: history enlarges the mind, by familiarising us with the great vicissitudes of human affairs, and the catastrophes of states and kingdoms; the study of morals accustoms us to refer our actions to a general standard of right and wrong; and abstract reasoning, in general, strengthens the love of truth, and produces an inflexibility of principle which cannot stoop to low trick and cunning. Books, in Lord Bacon's phrase, are 'a discipline of humanity.' Country people have none of these advantages, nor any others to supply the place of them. Having no circulating libraries to exhaust their love of the marvellous, they amuse themselves with fancying the disasters and disgraces of their particular acquaintance. Having no hump-backed *Richard* to excite their wonder and abhorrence, they make themselves a bug-bear of their own, out of the first obnoxious person they can lay their hands on. Not having the fictitious distresses and gigantic crimes of poetry to stimulate their imagination and their passions, they vent their whole stock of spleen, malice, and invention, on their friends and next-door neighbours. They get up a little pastoral drama at home, with fancied events, but real characters. All their spare time is spent in manufacturing and propagating the lie for the day, which does its office, and expires. The next day is spent in the same manner. It is thus that they embellish the simplicity of rural life! The common people in civilised countries are a kind of domesticated savages. They have not the wild imagination, the passions, the fierce energies, or dreadful vicissitudes of the savage tribes, nor have they the leisure, the indolent enjoyments and romantic superstitions, which belonged to the pastoral life in milder climates, and more remote periods of society. They are taken out of a state of nature, without being put in possession of the refinements of art. The customs and institutions of society cramp their imaginations without giving them knowledge. If the inhabitants of the mountainous districts described by Mr Wordsworth are less gross and sensual than others, they are more selfish. Their egotism becomes more concentrated, as they are more insulated, and their purposes more inveterate, as they have less competition to struggle with. The weight of matter which surrounds them, crushes the finer sympathies. Their minds become hard and cold, like the rocks which they cultivate. The immensity of their mountains makes the human form appear little and insignificant. Men are seen crawling between Heaven and earth, like insects to their graves. Nor do they regard one another more than flies on a wall. Their physiognomy expresses the materialism of their character, which has only one principle – rigid self-will. They move on with their eyes and foreheads fixed, looking neither to the right nor to the left, with a heavy slouch in their gait, and seeming as if nothing would divert them from their path. We do not admire this plodding pertinacity, always directed to the main chance. There is nothing which excites so little sympathy in our minds, as exclusive selfishness. If our theory is wrong, at least it is taken from pretty close observation, and is, we think, confirmed by Mr Wordworth's own account.

From 'On Mr Wordsworth's Excursion' in
The Round Table (1817).

RACE AND CLASS

To begin with the first. In the Memoirs of Granville Sharp, lately published, there is an anecdote recorded of the young Prince Naimbanna, well worthy the attention of all unfledged sophists, and embryo politicians.

'The name of a person having been mentioned in his presence, who was understood by him to have publicly asserted something very degrading to the general character of Africans, he broke out into violent and vindictive language. He was immediately reminded of the Christian duty of forgiving his enemies; upon which he answered nearly in the following words: – "If a man should rob me of my money, I can forgive him; if a man should shoot at me, or try to stab me, I can forgive him; if a man should sell me and all my family to a slave-ship, so that we should pass all the rest of our days in slavery in the West Indies, I can forgive him; but" (added he, rising from his seat with much emotion) "if a man takes away the character of the people of my country, I never can forgive him." Being asked, why he would not extend his forgiveness to those who took away the character of the people of his country, he answered – "If a man should try to kill me, or should sell me and my family for slaves, he would do an injury to as many as he might kill or sell; but if any one takes away the character of Black people, that man injures Black people all over the world; and when he has once taken away their character, there is nothing that he may not do to Black people ever after. That man, for instance, will beat Black men, and say, *Oh, it is only a Black man, why should I not beat him?* That man will make slaves of Black people; for when he has taken away their character, he will say, *Oh, they are only Black people, why should I not make them slaves?* That man will take away all the people of Africa if he can catch them; and if you ask him, But why do you take away all these people? he will say, *Oh, they are only Black people – why should I not take them?* That is the reason why I cannot forgive the man who takes away the character of the people of my country," ' p. 369. – So we conceive, that if we take away the character of the people of this country, or of any large proportion of them, there is no degree of turpitude or injustice that we may not introduce into the measures and treatment which we consider as most fit for them. To legislate wisely, and for the best, it is necessary that we should think as well, and not as ill, as possible, of those for whom we legislate; or otherwise we shall soon reduce them to the level of our own theories. To treat men as brute beasts in our speculations, is to encourage ourselves to treat them as such in our practice; and that is the way to make them what we pretend to believe they are. To take it for granted that any class of the community is utterly depraved and incorrigible, is not the way either to improve our own treatment of them, or to correct their vicious qualities. And when we see the lower classes of the English people uniformly singled out as marks for the malice or servility of a certain description of writers – when we see them studiously separated, like a degraded *caste*, from the rest of the community, with scarcely the attributes and faculties of the species allowed them, – nay, when they are thrust lower in the scale of humanity than the same classes of any other nation in Europe – though it is to these very classes that we owe the valour of our naval and military heroes, the industry of our artisans and labouring mechanics, and all that we have been told, again and again, elevates us above every other nation in Europe – when we see the *redundant population* (as it is fashionably called) selected as the butt for every effusion of paltry spite, and as the last resource of vindictive penal statutes – when we see every existing evil derived from this unfortunate race, and every possible vice ascribed to them – when we are accustomed to hear the poor, the uninformed, the friendless, put, by tacit consent, out of the pale of society – when their faults and wretchedness are exaggerated with eager impatience, and still greater impatience is shown at every expression of a wish to amend them – when they are familiarly spoken of as a sort of vermin only fit to be hunted down, and exterminated at the discretion of their betters : – we know pretty well what to think, both of the disinterestedness of the motives which give currency to this jargon, and of the wisdom of the policy which should either sanction, or suffer itself to be influenced by its suggestions.

From 'Capital Punishments' in the
Edinburgh Review (July 1821).

VULGARITY

In a word . . . to say what vulgarity is. Now its essence, I imagine, consists in taking manners, actions, words, opinions on trust from others, without examining one's own feelings or weighing the merits of the case. It is coarseness or shallowness of taste arising from want of individual refinement, together with the confidence and presumption inspired by example and numbers. It may be defined to be a prostitution of the mind or body to ape the more or less obvious defects of others, because by so doing we shall secure the suffrages of those we associate with. To affect a gesture, an opinion, a phrase, because it is the rage with a large number of persons, or to hold it in abhorrence because another set of persons very little, if at all, better informed, cry it down to distinguish themselves from the former, is in either case equal vulgarity and absurdity. — A thing is not vulgar merely because it is common. 'Tis common to breathe, to see, to feel, to live. Nothing is vulgar that is natural, spontaneous, unavoidable. Grossness is not vulgarity, ignorance is not vulgarity, awkwardness is not vulgarity: but all these become vulgar when they are affected and shewn off on the authority of others, or to fall in with *the fashion* or the company we keep. Caliban is coarse enough, but surely he is not vulgar. We might as well spurn the clod under our feet, and call it vulgar. Cobbett is coarse enough, but he is not vulgar. He does not belong to the herd. Nothing real, nothing original can be vulgar: but I should think an imitator of Cobbett a vulgar man. Emery's Yorkshireman is vulgar, because he is a Yorkshireman. It is the cant and gibberish, the cunning and low life of a particular district; it has 'a stamp exclusive and provincial.' He might 'gabble most brutishly' and yet not fall under the letter of the definition: but 'his speech bewrayeth him,' his dialect (like the jargon of a Bond-street lounger) is the damning circumstance. If he were a mere blockhead, it would not signify: but he thinks himself a *knowing hand*, according to the notions and practices of those with whom he was brought up, and which he thinks *the go* every where. In a word, this character is not the offspring of untutored nature but of bad habits; it is made up of ignorance and conceit. It has a mixture of *slang* in it. All slang phrases are for the same reason vulgar; but there is nothing vulgar in the common English idiom. Simplicity is not vulgarity; but the looking to affectation of any sort for distinction is. A cockney is a vulgar character, whose imagination cannot wander beyond the suburbs of the metropolis: so is a fellow who is always thinking of the High-street, Edinburgh. We want a name for this last character. An opinion is vulgar that is stewed in the rank breath of the rabble: nor is it a bit purer or more refined for having passed through the well-cleansed teeth of a whole court. The inherent vulgarity is in having no other feeling on any subject than the crude, blind, headlong, gregarious notion acquired by sympathy with the mixed multitude or with a fastidious minority, who are just as insensible to the real truth, and as indifferent to every thing but their own frivolous and vexatious pretensions. The upper are not wiser than the lower orders, because they resolve to differ from them. The fashionable have the advantage of the unfashionable in nothing but the fashion. The true vulgar are the *servum pecus imitatorum* – the herd of pretenders to what they do not feel and to what is not natural to them, whether in high or low life. To belong to any class, to move in any rank or sphere of life, is not a very exclusive distinction or test of refinement. Refinement will in all classes be the exception, not the rule, and the exception may fall out in one class as well as another.

From 'On Vulgarity and Affectation' in
Table-Talk (1821).

ON THE FEAR OF DEATH

'And our little life is rounded with a sleep.'

PERHAPS the best cure for the fear of death is to reflect that life has a beginning as well as an end. There was a time when we were not: this gives us no concern – why then should it trouble us that a time will come when we shall cease to be? I have no wish to have been alive a hundred years ago, or in the reign of Queen Anne: why should I regret and lay it so much to heart that I shall not be alive a hundred years hence, in the reign of I cannot tell whom?

When Bickerstaff wrote his Essays,[1] I knew nothing of the subjects of them: nay, much later, and but the other day, as it were, in the beginning of the reign of George III, when Goldsmith, Johnson, Burke used to meet at the Globe, when Garrick was in his glory, and Reynolds was over head and ears with his portraits, and Sterne brought out the volumes of Tristram Shandy year by year, it was without consulting me: I had not the slightest intimation of what was going on: the debates in the House of Commons on the American war, or the firing at Bunker's Hill,[2] disturbed not me: yet I thought this no evil – I neither ate, drank, nor was merry, yet I did not complain: I had not then looked out into this breathing world, yet I was well; and the world did quite as well without me as I did without it! Why then should I make all this outcry about parting with it, and being no worse off than I was before? There is nothing in the recollection that at a certain time we were not come into the world, that 'the gorge rises at' – why should we revolt at the idea that we must one day go out of it? To die is only to be as we were before we were born; yet no one feels any remorse, or regret, or repugnance, in contemplating this last idea. It is rather a relief and disburthening of the mind: it seems to have been holiday-time with us then: we were not called to appear upon the stage of life, to wear robes or tatters, to laugh or cry, be hooted or applauded; we had lain *perdu* all this while, sung, out of harm's way; and had slept out our thousands of centuries without wanting to be waked up; at peace and free from care, in a long nonage, in a sleep deeper and calmer than that of infancy, wrapped in the softest and finest dust. And the worst that we dread is, after a short, fretful, feverish being, after vain hopes, and idle fears, to sink to final repose again, and forget the troubled dream of life! ... Ye armed men, knights templars, that sleep in the stone aisles of that old Temple Church, where all is silent above, and where a deeper silence reigns below (not broken by the pealing organ), are ye not contented where ye lie? Or would you come out of your long homes to go to the Holy War? Or do ye complain that pain no longer visits you, that sickness has done its worst, that you have paid the last debt to nature, that you hear no more of the thickening phalanx of the foe, or your lady's waning love; and that while this ball of earth rolls its eternal round, no sound shall ever pierce through to disturb your lasting repose, fixed as the marble over your tombs, breathless as the grave that holds you! And thou, oh! thou, to whom my heart turns, and will turn while it has feeling left, who didst love in vain, and whose first was thy last sigh, wilt not thou too rest in peace (or wilt thou cry to me complaining from thy clay-cold bed) when that sad heart is no longer sad, and that sorrow is dead which thou wert only called into the world to feel!

It is certain that there is nothing in the idea of a pre-existent state that excites our longing like the prospect of a posthumous existence. We are satisfied to have begun life when we did; we have no ambition to have set out on our journey sooner; and feel that we have had quite enough to do to battle our way through since. We cannot say,

> 'The wars we well remember of King Nine,
> Of old Assaracus and Inachus divine:'

neither have we any wish: we are contented to read of them in story, and to stand and gaze at the vast sea of time that separates us from them. It was early days then: the world was not *well-aired* enough for us: we have no inclination to have been up and stirring. We do not consider the six thousand years of the world before we were born as so much time lost to us: we are perfectly indifferent about the matter. We do not grieve and lament that we did not happen to be in time to see the grand mask and pageant of human life going on in all that period; though we are mortified at being obliged to quit our station before the rest of the procession passes.

It may be suggested in explanation of this difference, that we know from various records and traditions what happened in the time of Queen Anne, or even in the reigns of the Assyrian monarchs: but that we have no means of ascertaining what is to happen hereafter but by awaiting the event, and that our eagerness and curiosity are sharpened in proportion as we are in the dark about it. This is not at all the case; for at that rate we should be constantly wishing to make a voyage of discovery to Greenland or to the Moon, neither of which we have, in general, the least desire to do. Neither, in truth, have we any particular solicitude to pry into the secrets of futurity, but as a pretext for prolonging our own existence. It is not so much that we care to be alive a hundred or a thousand years hence, any more than to have been alive a hundred or a thousand years ago: but the thing lies here, that we would all of us wish the present moment to last for ever. We would be as we are, and would have the world remain just as it is, to please us.

'The present eye catches the present object' –

to have and to hold while it may; and we abhor, on any terms, to have it torn from us, and nothing left in its room. It is the pang of parting, the unloosing our grasp, the breaking asunder under some strong tie, the leaving some cherished purpose unfulfilled, that creates the repugnance to go, and 'makes calamity of so long life,' as it often is.

> – 'Oh! thou strong heart!
> There's such a covenant 'twixt the world and thee,
> Ye're loth to break!'

The love of life, then, is an habitual attachment, not an abstract principle. Simply *to be* does not 'content man's natural desire:' we long to be in a certain time, place, and circumstance. We would much rather be now, 'on this bank and shoal of time,' than have our choice of any future period, than take a slice of fifty or sixty years out of the Millennium, for instance. This shows that our attachment is not confined either to *being* or to *well-being*; but that we have an inveterate prejudice in favour of our immediate existence, such as it is. The mountaineer will not leave his rock, nor the savage his hut; neither are we willing to give up our present mode of life, with all its advantages and disadvantages, for any other that could be substituted for it. No man would, I think, exchange his existence with any other man, however fortunate. We had as lief *not be*, as *not be ourselves*. There are some persons of that reach of soul that they would like to live two hundred and fifty years hence, to see to what height of empire America will have grown up in that period, or whether the English constitution will last so long. These are points beyond me. But I confess I should like to live to see the downfall of Legitimacy. That is a vital question with me; and I shall like it the better, the sooner it happens!

No young man ever thinks he shall die. He may believe that others will, or assent to the doctrine that 'all men are mortal' as an abstract proposition, but he is far enough from bringing it home to himself individually.* Youth, buoyant activity, and animal spirits, hold absolute antipathy with old age as well as with death; nor have we, in the hey-day of life, any more than in the thoughtlessness of childhood, the remotest conception how

> 'This sensible warm motion can become
> A kneaded clod' –

nor how sanguine, florid health and vigour, shall 'turn to withered, weak, and grey.' Or if in a moment of idle speculation we indulge in this notion of the close of life as a theory, it is amazing at what a distance it seems; what a long, leisurely interval there is between; what a contrast its slow and solemn approach affords to our present gay dreams of existence! We eye the farthest verge of the horizon, and think what a way we shall have to look back upon, ere we arrive at our journey's end; and without our in the least suspecting it, the mists are at our feet, and the shadows of age encompass us. The two divisions of our lives have melted into each other: the extreme points close and meet with none of that romantic interval stretching out between them, that we had reckoned upon; and for the rich, melancholy, solemn hues of age, 'the sear, the yellow leaf,' the deepening shadows of an autumnal evening, we only feel a dank, cold mist encircling all objects, after the spirit of youth is fled. There is no inducement to look forward; and what is worse, little interest in looking back to what has become so trite and common. The pleasures of our existence have worn themselves out, are 'gone into the wastes of

* 'All men think all men mortal but themselves.' – YOUNG

time,' or have turned their indifferent side to us: the pains by their repeated blows have worn us out, and have left us neither spirit nor inclination to encounter them again in retrospect. We do not want to rip up old grievances, nor to renew our youth like the phœnix, nor to live our lives twice over. Once is enough. As the tree falls, so let it lie. We shut up the book and close the account once for all!

It has been thought by some that life is like the exploring of a passage that grows narrower and darker the farther we advance, without a possibility of ever turning back, and where we are stifled for want of breath at last. For myself, I do not complain of the greater thickness of the atmosphere as I approach the *narrow house*. I felt it more formerly,* when the idea alone seemed to suppress a thousand rising hopes, and weighed upon the pulses of the blood. At present I rather feel a thinness and want of support, I stretch out my hand to some object and find none, I am too much in a world of abstraction; the naked map of life is spread out before me, and in the emptiness and desolation I see Death coming to meet me. In my youth I could not behold him for the crowd of objects and feelings, and Hope stood always between us, saying – 'Never mind that old fellow!' If I had lived *indeed*, I should not care to die. But I do not like a contract of pleasure broken off unfulfilled, a marriage with joy unconsummated, a promise of happiness rescinded. My public and private hopes have been left a ruin, or remain only to mock me. I would wish them to be re-edified. I should like to see some prospect of good to mankind, such as my life began with. I should like to leave some sterling work behind me. I should like to have some friendly hand to consign me to the grave. On these conditions I am ready, if not willing, to depart. I could then write on my tomb –

*I remember once, in particular, having this feeling in reading Schiller's Don Carlos, where there is a description of death, in a degree that almost choaked me.

GRATEFUL AND CONTENTED.[3] But I have thought and suffered too much to be willing to have thought and suffered in vain. – In looking back, it sometimes appears to me as if I had in a manner slept out my life in a dream or trance on the side of the hill of knowledge, where I have fed on books, on thoughts, on pictures, and only heard in half-murmurs the trampling of busy feet, or the noises of the throng below. Waked out of this dim, twilight existence, and startled with the passing scene, I have felt a wish to descend to the world of realities, and join in the chase. But I fear too late, and that I had better return to my bookish chimeras and indolence once more! *Zanetto, lascia le donne, et studia la matematica.*

Is it not wonderful that the contemplation and fear of death become more familiar to us as we approach nearer to it: that life seems to ebb with the decay of blood and youthful spirits; and that as we find every thing about us subject to chance and change, as our strength and beauty die, as our hopes and passions, our friends and our affections leave us, we begin by degrees to feel ourselves mortal!

I have never seen death but once, and that was in an infant. It is years ago. The look was calm and placid, and the face was fair and firm. It was as if a waxen image had been laid out in the coffin, and strewed with innocent flowers. It was not like death, but more like an image of life! No breath moved the lips, no pulse stirred, no sight or sound would enter those eyes or ears more. While I looked at it, I saw no pain was there; it seemed to smile at the short pang of life which was over: but I could not bear the coffin-lid to be closed – it almost stifled me; and still as the nettles wave in a corner of the churchyard over his little grave, the welcome breeze helps to refresh me and ease the tightness at my breast!

An ivory or marble image, like Chantry's monument [4] of the two children, is contemplated with pure delight. Why do we not grieve and fret that the marble is not alive, or fancy that it has a shortness of breath? It never was alive; and it is the difficulty of making the transition from life to death, the struggle between the two in our imagination, that confounds their properties painfully together, and makes us conceive that the infant that is but just dead, still wants to breathe, to enjoy, and look about it, and is prevented by the icy hand of death, locking up its faculties and benumbing its senses; so that, if it could, it would complain of its own hard state. Perhaps religious considerations reconcile the mind to this change sooner than any others, by representing the spirit as fled to another sphere, and leaving the body behind it. But in reflecting on death generally, we mix up the idea of life with it, and thus make it the ghastly monster it is. We think how we should feel, not how the dead feel.

> 'Still from the tomb the voice of nature cries;
> Even in our ashes live their wonted fires!'

There is an admirable passage on this subject in TUCKER'S *Light of Nature Pursued*, which I shall transcribe, as by much the best illustration I can offer of it.

'The melancholy appearance of a lifeless body, the mansion provided for it to inhabit, dark, cold, close and solitary, are shocking to the imagination; but it is to the imagination only, not the understanding; for whoever consults this faculty will see at first glance, that there is nothing dismal in all these circumstances: if the corpse were kept wrapped up in a warm bed, with a roasting fire in the chamber, it would feel no comfortable warmth therefrom; were store of tapers lighted up as soon as day shuts in, it would see no objects to divert it; were it left at large it would have no liberty, nor if surrounded with company would be cheered thereby; neither are the distorted features expressions of pain, uneasiness, or distress. This every one knows, and will readily allow upon being suggested, yet still cannot behold, nor even cast a thought upon those objects without shuddering; for knowing that a living person must suffer grievously under such appearances, they become habitually formidable to the mind, and strike a mechanical horror, which is increased by the customs of the world around us.'

There is usually one pang added voluntarily and unnecessarily to the fear of death, by our affecting to compassionate the loss which others will have in us. If that were all, we might reasonably set our minds at rest. The pathetic exhortation on country tombstones, 'Grieve not for me, my wife and children dear,' &c. is for the most part speedily followed to the letter. We do not leave so great a void in society as we are inclined to imagine, partly to magnify our own importance, and partly to console ourselves by sympathy. Even in the same family the gap is not so great; the wound closes up sooner than we should expect. Nay, *our room* is not unfrequently thought better than *our company*. People walk along the streets the day after our deaths just as they did before, and the crowd is not diminished. While we were living, the world seemed in a manner to exist only for us, for our delight and amusement, because it contributed to them. But our hearts cease to beat, and it goes on as usual, and thinks no more about us than it did in our lifetime. The million are devoid of sentiment, and care as little for you or me as if we belonged to the moon. We live the week over in the Sunday's newspaper, or are decently interred in some obituary at the month's end. It is not surprising that we are forgotten so soon after we quit this mortal stage: we are scarcely noticed, while we are on it. It is not merely that our names are not known in China – they have hardly been heard of in the next street. We are hand and glove with the universe, and think the obligation is mutual. This is an evident fallacy. If this, however, does not trouble us now, it will not hereafter. A handful of dust can have no quarrel to pick with its neighbours, or complaint to make against Providence, and might well exclaim, if it had but an understanding and a tongue, 'Go thy ways, old world, swing round in blue ether, voluble to every age, you and I shall no more jostle!'

It is amazing how soon the rich and titled, and even some of those who have wielded great political power, are forgotten:

> 'A little rule, a little sway,
> Is all the great and mighty have
> Betwixt the cradle and the grave' –

and, after its short date, they hardly leave a name behind them. 'A great man's memory may, at the common rate, survive him half a year.' His heirs and successors take his titles, his power, and his wealth – all that made him considerable or courted by others; and he has left nothing else behind him either to flatter or benefit the world. Posterity are not by any means so disinterested as they are supposed to be. They give their gratitude and admiration only in return for benefits conferred. They cherish the memory of those to whom they are indebted for instruction and delight; and they cherish it just in proportion to the instruction and delight they are conscious of receiving. The sentiment of admiration springs immediately from this ground; and cannot be otherwise than well founded.*

The effeminate clinging to life as such, as a general or abstract idea, is the effect of a highly civilised and artificial

---

*It has been usual to raise a very unjust clamour against the enormous salaries of public singers, actors, and so on. This matter seems reducible to a *moral equation*. They are paid out of money raised by voluntary contributions in the strictest sense; and if they did not bring certain sums into the treasury, the Managers would not engage them. These sums are exactly in proportion to the number of individuals to whom their performance gives an extraordinary degree of pleasure. The talents of a singer, actor, &c. are therefore worth just as much as they will fetch.

state of society. Men formerly plunged into all the vicissitudes and dangers of war, or staked their all upon a single die, or some one passion, which if they could not have gratified, life became a burthen to them – now our strongest passion is to think, our chief amusement is to read new plays, new poems, new novels, and this we may do at our leisure, in perfect security, *ad infinitum*. If we look into the old histories and romances, before the *belles-lettres* neutralised human affairs and reduced passion to a state of mental equivocation, we find the heroes and heroines not setting their lives 'at a pin's fee,' but rather courting opportunities of throwing them away in very wantonness of spirit. They raise their fondness for some favourite pursuit to its height, to a pitch of madness, and think no price too dear to pay for its full gratification. Every thing else is dross. They go to death as to a bridal bed, and sacrifice themselves or others without remorse at the shrine of love, of honour, of religion, or any other prevailing feeling. Romeo runs his 'sea-sick, weary bark upon the rocks' of death, the instant he finds himself deprived of his Juliet; and she clasps his neck in their last agonies, and follows him to the same fatal shore. One strong idea takes possession of the mind and overrules every other; and even life itself, joyless without that, becomes an object of indifference or loathing. There is at least more of imagination in such a state of things, more vigour of feeling and promptitude to act than in our lingering, languid, protracted attachment to life for its own poor sake. It is, perhaps, also better, as well as more heroical, to strike at some daring or darling object, and if we fail in that, to take the consequences manfully, than to renew the lease of a tedious, spiritless, charmless existence, merely (as Pierre says) 'to lose it afterwards in some vile brawl' for some worthless object. Was there not a spirit of martyrdom as well as a spice of the reckless energy of barbarism in this bold defiance of death? Had not religion something to do with it; the implicit belief in another state of being, which rendered this of less value, and embodied something beyond it to the imagination; so that the rough soldier, the infatuated lover, the valorous knight, &c. could afford to throw away the present venture, and take a leap into the arms of futurity, which the modern sceptic shrinks back from, with all his boasted reason and vain philosophy, weaker than a woman! I cannot help thinking so myself; but I have endeavoured to explain this point before, and will not enlarge farther on it here.

A life of action and danger moderates the dread of death. It not only gives us fortitude to bear pain, but teaches us at every step the precarious tenure on which we hold our present being. Sedentary and studious men are the most apprehensive on this score. Dr Johnson was an instance in point. A few years seemed to him soon over, compared with those sweeping contemplations on time and infinity with which he had been used to pose himself. In the *still-life* of a man of letters, there was no obvious reason for a change. He might sit in an arm-chair and pour out cups of tea to all eternity. Would it had been possible for him to do so! The most rational cure after all for the inordinate fear of death is to set a just value on life. If we merely wish to continue on the scene to indulge our headstrong humours and tormenting passions, we had better begone at once: and if we only cherish a fondness for existence according to the benefits we reap from it, the pang we feel at parting with it will not be very severe![5]

From *Table-Talk* (1821).

A FAREWELL TO ESSAY-WRITING

'This life is best, if quiet life is best.'

FOOD, warmth, sleep, and a book; these are all I at present
ask – the *ultima thule* of my wandering desires. Do you not
then wish for

> 'A friend in your retreat,
> Whom you may whisper, solitude is sweet?'

Expected, well enough: – gone, still better. Such attractions
are strengthened by distance. Nor a mistress? 'Beautiful
mask! I know thee!' When I can judge of the heart from
the face, of the thoughts from the lips, I may again trust myself. Instead of these, give me the robin red-breast, pecking
the crumbs at the door, or warbling on the leafless spray, the
same glancing form that has followed me wherever I have
been, and 'done its spiriting gently'; or the rich notes of the
thrush that startle the ear of winter, and seem to have drunk
up the full draught of joy from the very sense of contrast.
To these I adhere and am faithful, for they are true to me;
and, dear in themselves, are dearer for the sake of what is
departed, leading me back (by the hand) to that dreaming
world, in the innocence of which they sat and made sweet
music, waking the promise of future years, and answered by
the eager throbbings of my own breast. But now 'the credulous hope of mutual minds is o'er,' and I turn back from the
world that has deceived me, to nature that lent it a false
beauty, and that keeps up the illusion of the past. As I
quaff my libations of tea in a morning, I love to watch the
clouds sailing from the west, and fancy that 'the spring
comes slowly up this way.' In this hope, while 'fields are
dank and ways are mire,' I follow the same direction to a
neighbouring wood, where, having gained the dry, level

greensward, I can see my way for a mile before me, closed in on each side by copse-wood, and ending in a point of light more or less brilliant, as the day is bright or cloudy. What a walk is this to me! I have no need of book or companion – the days, the hours, the thoughts of my youth are at my side, and blend with the air that fans my cheek. Here I can saunter for hours, bending my eye forward, stopping and turning to look back, thinking to strike off into some less trodden path, yet hesitating to quit the one I am in, afraid to snap the brittle threads of memory. I remark the shining trunks and slender branches of the birch trees, waving in the idle breeze; or a pheasant springs up on whirring wing; or I recall the spot where I once found a wood-pigeon at the foot of a tree, weltering in its gore, and think how many seasons have flown since 'it left its little life in air.' Dates, names, faces come back – to what purpose? Or why think of them now? Or rather, why not think of them oftener? We walk through life, as through a narrow path, with a thin curtain drawn around it; behind are ranged rich portraits, airy harps are strung – yet we will not stretch forth our hands and lift aside the veil, to catch glimpses of the one, or sweep the chords of the other. As in a theatre, when the old-fashioned green curtain drew up, groups of figures, fantastic dresses, laughing faces, rich banquets, stately columns, gleaming vistas appeared beyond; so we have only at any time to 'peep through the blanket of the past,' to possess ourselves at once of all that has regaled our senses, that is stored up in our memory, that has struck our fancy, that has pierced our hearts: – yet to all this we are indifferent, insensible, and seem intent only on the present vexation, the future disappointment. If there is a Titian hanging up in the room with me, I scarcely regard it: how then should I be expected to strain the mental eye so far, or to throw down, by the magic spells of the will, the stone-walls that enclose it in the Louvre? There is one head there of which I have often thought, when looking at it, that nothing should ever disturb me again, and I would become the character it represents – such perfect calmness and self-possession reigns in it! Why do I not hang an image of this in some dusky corner of my brain, and turn an eye upon it ever and anon, as I have need of some such talisman to calm my troubled thoughts? The attempt is fruitless, if not natural; or, like that of the French, to hang garlands on the grave, and to conjure back the dead by miniature pictures of them while living! It is only some actual coincidence, or local association that tends, without violence, to 'open all the cells where memory slept.' I can easily, by stooping over the long-spent grass and clay-cold clod, recall the tufts of primroses, or purple hyacinths, that formerly grew on the same spot, and cover the bushes with leaves and singing-birds, as they were eighteen summers ago;[1] or prolonging my walk and hearing the sighing gale rustle through a tall, strait wood at the end of it, can fancy that I distinguish the cry of hounds, and the fatal group issuing from it, as in the tale of Theodore and Honoria. A moaning gust of wind aids the belief; I look once more to see whether the trees before me answer to the idea of the horror-stricken grove, and an air-built city towers over their grey tops.

> 'Of all the cities in Romanian lands,
> The chief and most renown'd Ravenna stands.'

I return home resolved to read the entire poem through, and, after dinner, drawing my chair to the fire, and holding a small print close to my eyes, launch into the full tide of Dryden's couplets (a stream of sound), comparing his didactic and descriptive pomp with the simple pathos and picturesque truth of Boccaccio's story, and tasting with a pleasure, which none but an habitual reader can feel, some quaint examples of pronunciation in this accomplished versifier.

'Which when Honoria view'd,
The fresh *impulse* her former fright renew'd.' –
                              Theodore and Honoria.

'And made th' *insult*, which in his grief appears,
The means to mourn thee with my pious tears.'
                              Sigismonda and Guiscardo.

These trifling instances of the wavering and unsettled state of the language give double effect to the firm and stately march of the verse, and make me dwell with a sort of tender interest on the difficulties and doubts of an earlier period of literature. They pronounced words then in a manner which we should laugh at now; and they wrote verse in a manner which we can do anything but laugh at. The pride of a new acquisition seems to give fresh confidence to it; to impel the rolling syllables through the moulds provided for them, and to overflow the envious bounds of rhyme into time-honoured triplets. I am much pleased with Leigh Hunt's mention of Moore's involuntary admiration of Dryden's free, unshackled verse, and of his repeating *con amore*, and with an Irish spirit and accent, the fine lines –

'Let honour and preferment go for gold,
But glorious beauty isn't to be sold.'

What sometimes surprises me in looking back to the past, is, with the exception already stated, to find myself so little changed in the time. The same images and trains of thought stick by me: I have the same tastes, likings, sentiments, and wishes that I had then. One great ground of confidence and support has, indeed, been struck from under my feet; but I have made it up to myself by proportionable pertinacity of opinion. The success of the great cause, to which I had vowed myself, was to me more than all the world: I had a strength in its strength, a resource which I knew not of, till it failed me for the second time.

'Fall'n was Glenartny's stately tree!
     Oh! ne're to see Lord Ronald more!'

It was not till I saw the axe laid to the root, that I found the full extent of what I had to lose and suffer. But my conviction of the right was only established by the triumph of the wrong; and my earliest hopes will be my last regrets. One source of this unbendingness, (which some may call obstinacy,) is that, though living much alone, I have never worshipped the Echo. I see plainly enough that black is not white, that the grass is green, that kings are not their subjects; and, in such self-evident cases, do not think it necessary to collate my opinions with the received prejudices. In subtler questions, and matters that admit of doubt, as I do not impose my opinion on others without a reason, so I will not give up mine to them without a better reason; and a person calling me names, or giving himself airs of authority, does not convince me of his having taken more pains to find out the truth than I have, but the contrary. Mr Gifford once said, that 'while I was sitting over my gin and tobacco-pipes, I fancied myself a Leibnitz.' He did not so much as know that I had ever read a metaphysical book: — was I therefore, out of complaisance or deference to him, to forget whether I had or not? I am rather disappointed, both on my own account and his, that Mr Hunt has missed the opportunity or explaining the character of a friend,[2] as clearly as he might have done. He is puzzled to reconcile the shyness of my pretensions with the inveteracy and sturdiness of my principles. I should have thought they were nearly the same thing. Both from disposition and habit, I can *assume* nothing in word, look, or manner. I cannot steal a march upon public opinion in any way. My standing upright, speaking loud, entering a room gracefully, proves nothing; therefore I neglect these ordinary means of recommending myself to the good graces and admiration of strangers, (and, as it appears, even of philosophers and friends). Why? Because I have other resources or, at least, am absorbed in other studies and pursuits. Suppose this absorption to be extreme, and even morbid, that I have brooded over an idea till it has become a kind of substance in my brain, that I have reasons for a thing which I have found out with much labour and pains, and to which I can scarcely do justice without the utmost violence of exertion (and that only to a few persons,) – is this a reason for my playing off my out-of-the-way notions in all companies, wearing a prim and self-complacent air, as if I were 'the admired of all observers'? or is it not rather an argument, (together with a want of animal spirits,) why I should retire into myself, and perhaps acquire a nervous and uneasy look, from a consciousness of the disproportion between the interest and conviction I feel on certain subjects, and my ability to communicate what weighs upon my own mind to others? If my ideas, which I do not avouch, but suppose, lie below the surface, why am I to be always attempting to dazzle superficial people with them, or smiling, delighted, at my own want of success?

What I have here stated is only the excess of the common and well-known English and scholastic character. I am neither a buffoon, a fop, nor a Frenchman, which Mr Hunt would have me to be. He finds it odd that I am a close reasoner and a loose dresser. I have been (among other follies) a hard liver as well as a hard thinker; and the consequences of that will not allow me to dress as I please. People in real life are not like players on a stage, who put on a certain look or *costume*, merely for effect. I am aware, indeed, that the gay and airy pen of the author does not seriously probe the errors or misfortunes of his friends – he only glances at their seeming peculiarities, so as to make them odd and ridiculous; for which forbearance few of them will thank him. Why does he assert that I was vain of my hair when it was black, and am equally vain of it now it is grey, when this is true in neither case? This transposition of motives makes me almost doubt whether Lord Byron was thinking so much of the rings on his fingers as his biographer was. These sort of criticisms should be left to women. I am made to wear a little hat, stuck on the top of my head the wrong way. Nay, I commonly wear a large slouching hat over my eyebrows; and if ever I had another, I must have twisted it about in any shape to get rid of the annoyance. This probably tickled Mr Hunt's fancy, and retains possession of it, to the exclusion of the obvious truism, that I naturally wear 'a melancholy hat.'[3]

I am charged with using strange gestures and contortions of features in argument, in order to 'look energetic.' One would rather suppose that the heat of the argument produced the extravagance of the gestures, as I am said to be calm at other times. It is like saying that a man in a passion clenches his teeth, not because he is, but in order to seem, angry. Why should everything be construed into air and affectation? With Hamlet, I may say, 'I know not *seems*.'

Again, my old friend and pleasant 'Companion' remarks it, as an anomaly in my character, that I crawl about the Fives-Court like a cripple till I get the racket in my hand, when I start up as if I was possessed with a devil. I have then a motive for exertion; I lie by for difficulties and extreme cases. *Aut Cæsar aut nullus.* I have no notion of doing nothing with an air of importance, nor should I ever take a liking to the game of battledoor and shuttlecock. I have only seen by accident a page of the unpublished Manuscript relating to the present subject, which I dare say is, on the whole, friendly and just, and which has been suppressed as being too favourable, considering certain prejudices against me.

In matters of taste and feeling, one proof that my conclusions have not been quite shallow or hasty, is the circumstance of their having been lasting. I have the same favourite books, pictures, passages that I ever had: I may therefore presume that they will last me my life – nay, I may indulge a hope that my thoughts will survive me. This continuity of impression is the only thing on which I pride myself. Even L—, whose relish of certain things is as keen and earnest as possible, takes a surfeit of admiration, and I should be afraid to ask about his select authors or particular friends, after a lapse of ten years. As to myself, any one knows where to have me. What I have once made up my mind to, I abide by to the end of the chapter. One cause of my independence of opinion is, I believe, the liberty I give to others, or the very diffidence and distrust of making converts. I should be an excellent man on a jury: I might say little, but should starve 'the other eleven obstinate fellows' out. I remember Mr Godwin writing to Mr Wordsworth, that 'his tragedy of Antonio could not fail of success.' It was damned past all redemption. I said to Mr Wordsworth that I thought this a natural consequence; for how could any one have a dramatic turn of mind who judged entirely of others from himself? Mr Godwin might be convinced of the excellence of his work; but how could he know that others would be convinced of it, unless by supposing that they were as wise as himself, and as infallible critics of dramatic poetry – so many Aristotles sitting in judgment on Euripides! This shows why pride is connected with shyness and reserve; for the really proud have not so high an opinion of the generality as to suppose that they can understand them, or that there is any common measure between them. So Dryden exclaims of his opponents with bitter disdain –

'Nor can I think what thoughts they can conceive.'

I have not sought to make partisans, still less did I dream of making enemies; and have therefore kept my opinions myself, whether they were currently adopted or not. To get others to come into our ways of thinking, we must go over to theirs; and it is necessary to follow, in order to lead. At the time I lived here formerly, I had no suspicion that I should ever become a voluminous writer; yet I had just the same confidence in my feelings before I had ventured to air them in public as I have now. Neither the outcry *for* or *against* moves me a jot: I do not say that the one is not more agreeable than the other.

Not far from the spot where I write, I first read Chaucer's *Flower and Leaf*, and was charmed with that young beauty, shrouded in her bower, and listening with ever-fresh delight to the repeated song of the nightingale close by her – the impression of the scene, the vernal landscape, the cool of the morning, the gushing notes of the songstress,

'And ayen, methought she sung close by mine ear,'

is as vivid as if it had been of yesterday; and nothing can persuade me that that is not a fine poem. I do not find this impression conveyed in Dryden's version, and therefore nothing can persuade me that that is as fine. I used to walk out at this time with Mr and Miss L—[4] of an evening, to look at the Claude Lorraine skies over our heads, melting from azure into purple and gold, and to gather mushrooms, that sprung up at our feet, to throw into our hashed mutton at supper. I was at that time an enthusiastic admirer of Claude, and could dwell for ever on one or two of the finest prints from him hung round my little room; the fleecy flocks, the bending trees, the winding streams, the groves, the nodding temples, the air-wove hills, and distant sunny vales; and tried to translate them into their lovely living hues. People then told me that Wilson was much superior to Claude. I did not believe them. Their pictures have since been seen together at the British Institution, and all the world have come into my opinion. I have not, on that account, given it up. I will not compare our hashed mutton with Amelia's; but it put us in mind of it, and led to a discussion, sharply seasoned and well sustained, till midnight, the result of which appeared some years after in the Edinburgh Review. Have I a better opinion of those criticisms on that account, or should I therefore maintain them with greater vehemence and tenaciousness? Oh no! Both rather with less, now that they are before the public, and it is for them to make their election.

It is in looking back to such scenes that I draw my best consolation for the future. Later impressions come and go, and serve to fill up the intervals; but these are my standing resource, my true classics. If I have had few real pleasures or advantages, my ideas, from their sinewy texture, have been to me in the nature of realities; and if I should not be able to add to the stock, I can live by husbanding the interest. As to my speculations, there is little to admire in them but my admiration of others; and whether they have an echo in time to come or not, I have learned to set a grateful value on the past, and am content to wind up the account of what is personal only to myself and the immediate circle of objects in which I have moved, with an act of easy oblivion,

'And curtain close such scene from every future view.'[5]

Written at Winterslow Hut, 20 February 1828.
Printed in *The London Weekly Review* (March 1828) and reprinted by Hazlitt's son in *Winterslow* (1850).

NOTES

My First Acquaintance With Poets

1. p.43. '*W—m*' – Wem, Shropshire.
2. p.50. '*Tom Wedgwood*' – son of the potter. Both he and the Mackintosh mentioned here belonged to the Coleridge circle.
3. p.54. '*that other Vision of Judgment*' – a reference to Byron's poem of that name which had just been published in the first number of *The Liberal*.
4. p.55. '*I went to Llangollen Vale*' – Hazlitt spent his twentieth birthday here (10 April 1798). He describes it in his essay *On Going A Journey*. (p.142)
5. p.55. '*Tom Jones and the adventure of the muff*' – Book X, Chapter 5 of Fielding's *Tom Jones*.
6. p.56. '*. . . who gave him the free use of it*' – Wordsworth actually rented Alfoxden for £23 per annum.
7. p.57. '*the ballad of Betty Foy*' – Wordsworth's *The Idiot Boy*.
8. p.59. '*Haydon's head of him*' – 'I now put Hazlitt's head into my picture looking at Christ as an investigator. It had a good effect. I then put Keats in the background, and resolved to introduce Wordsworth bowing in reverence and awe. Wordsworth was highly pleased, and before the close of the season (1817) the picture was three parts done.' – B. R. Haydon, *Autobiography*.
9. p.63. '*the merits of Caleb Williams*' – *Adventures of Caleb Williams* by William Godwin had been published in 1794.

On The Pleasure Of Painting

1. p.70. '*Wilson said*' – Richard Wilson (1714–82), landscape painter.

2. p.70. '*One of the most delightful parts of my life*' – at Winter-slow in 1809.

3. p.70. '*The first head I ever tried to paint*' – this portrait and that of his father (p. 76) are now in Maidstone Museum.

4. p.73. '*Richardson*' – Jonathan Richardson (1665–1745) tells this story in his *Essays*.

5. p.77. '*Mr Skeffington*' – Sir Lumley St George Skeffington, a friend of the Prince Regent and author of the drama *The Sleeping Beauty*.

6. p.77. '*the window . . . the chapel where my father preached*' – Hazlitt's home and the Unitarian chapel where his father was minister can still be seen in Noble St, Wem.

7. p.77. *but he himself is gone to rest* – the Rev. William Hazlitt died on 16 July 1820. Asked to supply a formal obituary notice, his son wrote this essay instead.

The Fight

This splendid piece of sporting writing was nearly turned down by the *New Monthly Magazine* because it was thought vulgar. It describes the battle between Bill Neat and Tom Hickman (the 'Gas-man') which took place at Hungerford on 11 December 1821. It is also a roll-call of Georgian boxers – James Belcher, Cribb, John Gully, Gentleman Jackson, Scroggins, Turner, etc.

1. p.83. '*Mr Richmond*' – Bill Richmond, a coloured boxer who may have taught Hazlitt himself to fight as in a further reference he is called 'my old master'.

On The Knowledge of Character

1. p.99. '*a rude, half effaced outline*' – a portrait by W. Marshall of John Donne, aged eighteen, and painted in 1591.

2. p.99. '*The Duke of W—*' – Wellington.

3. p.101. '*C—'s face*' – Coleridge.

4. p.101. '*the greatest hypocrite I ever knew*' – Sarah Walker (see p. 32).

5. p.109. '*Oh! thou . . . thy heavenly looks*' – Sarah Walker.

The Indian Jugglers

The act described here was billed at the Olympic New Theatre, Newcastle Street, Strand during the winter of 1815. The joy inherent in the essay shows Hazlitt emerging from the black despair he experienced after hearing of Napoleon's destruction at Waterloo that summer. The essay ends with a tribute to another of his heroes, the great rackets-player John Cavanagh.

1. p.124. '*You may make indeed as many H—s and H—s*' – three portrait painters who were contemporary with Sir Joshua Reynolds. They were Hayman, Highmore and Hudson.

2. p.128. '*Jedediah Buxton will be forgotten; but Napier's bones will live*' – John Napier (1550–1617) had invented a calculating device known as 'Napier's bones'. He also invented logarithms.

3. p.129. '*John Hunter*' – the great surgeon (1728–93), whom Hazlitt appears to have seen operating.

4. p.132/3. '*Rosemary Branch*' and '*Copenhagen-house*' – these were taverns at Peckham and the Caledonian Market respectively. Hazlitt liked to sit, thinking and silently observing, in a bustling bar.

5. p.133. '*Mr Powell*' – known as 'One-eyed Powell' on account of his losing an eye when playing rackets.

6. p.134. '*John Davies*' – Hazlitt thought Davies the finest rackets player in the world.

On Going A Journey

1. p.139. '*My old friend C—*' – Coleridge.

2. p.140. '*L— is for this reason*' – Lamb.

3. p.142. '*Gribelin's engravings of the Cartoons*' – Simon Gribelin published his engravings of Raphael's Cartoons in 1707.

4. p.142. '*Paul and Virginia*' – the celebrated novel by Bernardin de Saint Pierre, published in 1788.

5. p.142. '*Madame D'Arblay's Camilla*' – *Camilla*, by Fanny Burney, 1796.

Why Distant Objects Please

1. p.152. '*Mr Leigh Hunt has treated it so well*' – in an essay called 'A Nearer View of Some of the Shops' (1820).

2. p.153. '*the taste of barberries, which have hung out in the snow*' – Hazlitt's only memory of America.

3. p.154. '*See Wilkie's Blind Fiddler*' – *The Blind Fiddler* by Sir David Wilkie, in the National Gallery.

4. p.158. '*An acute observer complained*' – Charles Lamb.

5. p.159. '*You are told that a person*' – Hazlitt is referring to Blackwood's description of him as 'pimpled'.

On Different Sorts of Fame

1. p.165. '*the author of Junius's Letters*' – perhaps Sir Philip Francis (1740–1818).

On A Sun-Dial

1. p.172. '*the account given by Rousseau*' – in the *Confessions*.

On Good-Nature

1. p.180. '*Lord Shaftsbury somewhere remarks*' – in *Characteristics, an Inquiry concerning Virtue or Merit*.

2. p.182. '*It gives them a cutting sensation*' – this sentence originally read, in the *Examiner* version, 'It gives them a cutting sensation to see Mr Southey, poet laureate; Mr Wordsworth, an exciseman; and Mr Coleridge, nothing.'

3. p.184. 'a good hater' – a phrase which Hazlitt borrowed from Dr Johnson, and which he came to like very much. According to Mrs Piozzi's *Anecdotes*, Dr Johnson once said, 'Dear Bathurst was a man to my very heart's content: he hated a fool, and he hated a rogue, and he hated a *whig*: he was a very *good hater*.'

4. p.185. '*Mr Vansittart is a well-meaning man*' – Nicholas Vansittart, Chancellor of the Exchequer from 1812–22.

On the Disadvantages of Intellectual Superiority

1. p.188. '*C*—' – Coleridge.
2. p.193. '*after a diatribe in the* —' – the *Quarterly Review*.
3. p.193. '*a thing called Prince Maurice's Parrot, and an Essay on the Regal Character*' – the first of these essays was published in the *Examiner* (1814) and the second in *The Yellow Dwarf* (1818).
4. p.195. '*L*—' – Lamb.
5. p.195. '*L. H.*' – Leigh Hunt.
6. p.195. '*the celebrated Count Stendhal*' – Hazlitt met Stendhal in Paris in 1825 and frequently referred to him afterwards as 'my friend Mr Beyle'. Stendhal, who was not a count, greatly admired Hazlitt's *Characters of Shakespeare's Plays*.
7. p.195. '*Mr Powell's court*' – the fives court in St Martin's Street, where Hazlitt spent some of the happiest hours of his life.
8. p.198. '*Scholars should be sworn at Highgate*' – the Highgate oath was administered by innkeepers to travellers on stage-coaches. It was 'Never to kiss the maid when you can kiss the mistress'.

On Gusto

1. p.201. '*Albano's is like ivory*' – Francesco Albani, (1578–1660).
2. p.203. '*the Orleans Gallery*' – Hazlitt saw the great collection of old masters belonging to the Duke of Orleans when it was

put up for sale in Pall Mall in December 1798. It was here that he was 'staggered . . . a mist passing away from my sight'.
3. p.203. '*Acteon hunting*' – it was at the above sale that he saw Titian's *Diana and Acteon* (in the collection of the Earl of Harewood).
4. p.203. '*Mr West*' – Benjamin West, P.R.A. (1738–1820).
5. p.203. '*the St Peter Martyr*' – by Titian. Hazlitt saw this painting first in the Louvre in 1802 and at Venice in 1825.

On Familiar Style

1. p.208. '*I have been . . . loudly accused of revelling in vulgarisms and broken English*' – the *Quarterly Review*, in its first notice of *Table-Talk*, found it necessary to 'borrow from the vocabulary of our transatlantic brethren' in order to call Hazlitt a 'Slang-whanger . . . one who makes use of political or other gabble, vulgarly called slang, that serves to amuse the rabble.'
2. p.209. '*Mr Cobbett is hardly right*' – Cobbett advised, in his *Grammar of the English Language*, 1818; 'Use the first words that occur to you, and never attempt to *alter a thought*; for that which has come of itself into your mind is likely to pass into that of another more readily and with more effect than which you can, by reflection, invent.'
3. p.211. '*Erasmus's Colloquies*' – the *Colloquia* (1519).

[The Lake School]

1. p.216. '*the Deucalions*' – Deucalion, son of Prometheus, saved his life by taking refuge on the top of Mount Parnassus when Jupiter flooded the earth.

Mr Wordsworth

1. p.224. '*stately recollections of Cole-Orton*' – Coleorton, Sir George Beaumont's country house in Leicestershire. Coleridge

and Wordsworth assisted in laying out the garden here, and Sir George's memorial to Sir Joshua Reynolds in the park was the theme of one of Constable's greatest paintings, *The Cenotaph*.

2. p.225. '*He* [Wordsworth] *has probably realised Milton's wish*' – in *Paradise Lost*, VII, 31, Milton requests 'Fit audience let me find though few !' Wordsworth quotes this line in his poem, *The Recluse.*

3. p.227. '*To modernize some of the Canterbury Tales*' – Wordsworth's *Selections of Chaucer Modernised* was written in 1801.

4. p.227. '*Mr Wordsworth himself wrote a tragedy*' – *The Borderers* (1795-6).

5. p.228. '*a perfect Drawcansir*' – Henry Fielding's pseudonym was 'Sir Alexander Drawcansir', which he took from a character in Buckingham's play *The Rehearsal*.

6. p.228. '*Waterloo's sylvan etchings*' – Antoine Waterloo, a seventeenth century Flemish painter.

Mr Coleridge

1. p.235. '*At sixteen he wrote his Ode on Chatterton*' – Coleridge was in fact eighteen when he wrote this poem.

2. p.238. '*the John Bull*' – a right-wing paper founded by Theodore Hook.

3. p.238. '*the picture of the Triumph of Death*' – by Giotto.

4. p.239. '*sang for joy when the towers of the Bastile*' – Coleridge's poem, *Destruction of the Bastile*, was written about 1789.

5. p.239. '*swallowing doses of oblivion*' – a frank reference to Coleridge's drug-taking.

6. p.239. '*a poet-laureate or stamp-distributor*' – reference to Southey and Wordsworth.

Mr Southey

1. p.245. '*the author of Parliamentary Reform is an Ultra-royalist*' – Southey published an essay *On Parliamentary Reform* in 1816.

2. p.246. '*recommends the Suspension of Habeas Corpus and the putting down of the* Examiner' – Southey had written, in his essay 'On Political Reform', 'Why is it that this convicted incendiary [William Cobbett], and others of the same stamp, are permitted week after week to sow the seeds of rebellion, insulting the Government and defying the laws of the country? . . . Men of this description, like other criminals, derive no lessons from experience. But it behoves the Government to do so, and curb sedition in time.'

   Habeas Corpus was suspended in 1817 and Cobbett was forced to flee to the United States. Although in greater peril than ever for his liberalism, Hazlitt never ceased to hit out at the injustice and reaction of this period. This was the time when Southey, now a hard-line Tory, was embarrassed by the unauthorized publication of a revolutionary drama, *Wat Tyler*, which he had written when he was nineteen and, like Wordsworth, a radical.

[*Mr Crabbe*]

1. p.249. '*Mr Crabbe's earliest poem of the Village . . . Dr Johnson*' – *The Village* (1783) was Crabbe's third published work. It was preceded by *Inebriety* (1775) and *The Candidate* (1781). His patron was Edmund Burke, who introduced him to Sir Joshua Reynolds and Dr Johnson.

2. p.252. '*Tityrus*' – a mythological Greek giant whose body covered nine acres of land.

3. p.252. '*the only leaf of his books . . . the Rutland Family*' – Crabbe was at one time chaplain to the fourth Duke of Rut-

land at Belvoir Castle. *The Borough* is dedicated to the fifth Duke, and *Tales of the Hall* to the Duchess.

4. p.253. *'with misery, grief and fear'* – from *Peter Grimes* (Letter XXII, *The Borough*).

[*Mr Lamb*]

1. p.256. *'We believe ... the subject of Guy Faux out of his hands'* – Lamb wrote his essay on this subject for *The London Magazine* in 1823 but it was Hazlitt who began the interest in Guy Faux by writing three papers about him in the *Examiner* two years before this.

2. p.256. *'He does not go deep into the Scotch novels'* – Sir Walter Scott's fiction based on Scottish history. The first was *Waverley* (1814). A new novel appeared almost annually until 1830 and they became the rage of Europe as well as of Britain.

3. p.257. *'a fine Titian head'* – Hazlitt painted Lamb in a Titian costume (National Portrait Gallery).

4. p.258. *'to dine at a select party with the Lord Mayor'* – Lamb dined at the Mansion House in November 1823. The Lord Mayor was Robert Waithman (1764–1833), the political reformer.

[*The Times Newspaper*]

In 1785 John Walter (1739–1812) started a newspaper called *The Daily Universal Register*. Four years later its name was changed to *The Times or Daily Universal Register*. Three months later, on 18 March 1788, it became simply *The Times*. Hazlitt worked on it for the best part of 1817, startling the world by the brilliance of his dramatic criticism.

1. p.260. *'Mr Walter'* – John Walter the second (1776–1847).

2. p.261. *'he happened to have a writer in his employ'* – this was Dr John Stoddart, Hazlitt's brother-in-law. He also left *The Times* in 1817 and founded his own newspaper, *The New Times*. Dr Stoddart's loud support of the Establishment –

'Legitimacy', in Hazlitt's vocabulary – was to bring him a knighthood and his brother-in-law's disgust.

3. p.261. '*Dr Sacheverel*' – Henry Sacheverel (1674–1724), a High Church Tory clergyman who was impeached for his scandalous attacks on the Whigs during the reign of Queen Anne but turned into a hero, mainly by right-wing mobs.

[*Dr Johnson*]

1. p.264. '*He ... abused Milton and patronised Lauder*' – William Lauder (d. 1771), a literary forger who introduced Latin translations of *Paradise Lost* into the works of two seventeenth-century Latin poets, Masenius and Staphorstius.

2. p.264. ' "*the Ebro's temper*" ' – 'It is a sword of Spain, the Ebro's temper' – *Othello*.

[*Montaigne*]

1. p.270. Michel Eyquem de Montaigne (1533–92), born in Périgord. Books I and II of the celebrated *Essais* appeared in 1580 and Book III in 1588. They were first translated into English by John Florio in 1603. Montaigne's persistent question was 'Que sais-je?' Hazlitt is the English writer nearest to him.

[*William Shakespeare*]

1. p.273. '*He had "a mind reflecting ages past"* ' – Hazlitt is quoting the dedicatory poem which was added to the Second Folio of Shakespeare's plays (1632).

Romeo and Juliet

1. p.280. '*may find all this done in the* Stranger *and in other German plays*' – *Menschendbass und Reue* by A. F. F. von Kotzebue (1761–1819).

2. p.281. '*Ode on the Progress of Life*' – Wordsworth's *Intimations of Immortality*.

Coriolanus

1. p.284. The entire tone of Hazlitt's criticism of *Coriolanus* is heavy and bitter with his view of the world now that the rhetoric needed to prosecute the Napoleonic wars has ended. In Britain, there is famine and confusion, and the repeal or suspension of laws which had for centuries guarded the common rights of the people. A form of press censorship had been set up and Hazlitt's views on freedom were attracting accusations of sedition. Shakespeare's apparent personal detac ment when describing a similar calamity troubles him.

2. p.285. ' "*Carnage is its daughter*" ' –

> But Thy most dreaded instrument
> In Working out a pure intent,
> is Man – arrayed for mutual slaughter –
> – Yes, Carnage is Thy Daughter !
> – Wordsworth, *Ode*, 1815.

3. p.288. '*what is sport to the few is death to the many*' – in *On Living to One's-Self* Hazlitt wrote, 'Poor Keats ! What was sport to the town was death to him.'

On the Beggar's Opera

1. p.289. Nothing gave Hazlitt so much pleasure as the frequent revivals of the *Beggar's Opera*, first produced at Lincoln's Inn Fields on 29 January 1728. John Gay (1685–1732) also wrote librettos for Handel. His tomb in Westminster Abbey is inscribed :

> Life is a jest, and all things show it;
> I thought so once, and now I know it.

2. p.291. '*Miss Hannah More's laboured invectives*' – Hannah More (1745–1833), among whose moralizing plays were *The Fatal Falsehood* (1779) and *The Search after Happiness* (1773).

It was her tracts such as *An Estimate of the Religion of the Fashionable World* (1790) which irritated Hazlitt.

Liber Amoris

1. p.292. Hazlitt's marriage broke up in 1819 and in 1820 he took rooms in a boarding-house at 9 Southampton Buildings, Chancery Lane. On 16 August 1820 he first set eyes on his landlord's daughter, Sarah Walker, and immediately fell deeply in love with her. The difference in their social position, since made so much of by enemy and friend alike, was subtle, since Sarah's sister Martha had made a very happy marriage with a previous lodger, the North Country banker and man of letters William Roscoe.

Sarah's defence against the unwanted courtship by the early middle-aged writer was a mixture of scrupulous politeness and a careful lack of response. Hazlitt, crazed with a sexual desire which his experience told him could probably be satisfied but knowing that if he used the girl in this way she would not be able to believe in his love, interpreted her coolness as innocence and purity. This view of Sarah was destroyed by a series of obsessions and revelations culminating in his overhearing Sarah knowingly join in the laughter following a bawdy observation made by her teenage brother. A more exquisite climax to his distress occurred when Hazlitt met Sarah out walking on the arm of a handsome young man. His description of this incident is masterly.

In 1822, he converted the entire experience into fiction while on his way to Edinburgh, where he intended to allow his wife to divorce him under Scottish law. Incredibly, while on this same worrying journey, he wrote nearly all the essays in the second volume of *Table-Talk*. The divorce was settled in July and he returned to London, now quite determined to marry Sarah. She refused. A few months later – May 1823 – *Liber Amoris* appeared. It was published anonymously, with a picture of the first 'conversation' on the title-page. Some of the critics respected the anonymity but *The Times* published

Hazlitt's name and called him, among other things, 'this impotent sensualist'.

2. p.314. The 'C. P.' to whom Hazlitt poured out his misery was Peter George Patmore, a journalist friend and the father of the poet Coventry Patmore.

3. p.327. *'my favourite beverage'* – tea.

4. p.328. *'the prince of critics'* – Francis Jeffrey (1773–1850). Founder, with Sydney Smith, of the *Edinburgh Review*. It was Jeffrey who began a review of Wordsworth's *Excursion* with 'This will never do . . .'

5. p.346. The 'J. S. K.' of the final letters was James Sheridan Knowles, a friend of Hazlitt's then living at Glasgow. These letters were not actually sent to Knowles but were conceived as a device to end the story.

6. p.350. *'I walked out with my little boy'* – Hazlitt's son was then twelve. Earlier that fatal year he had written to him *On the Conduct of Life, or, Advice to a Schoolboy*.

7. p.365. *'R— met me'* – Ritchie of the *Scotsman*.

[Man is a Toad-Eating Animal]

1. p.383. *'And we saw three poets in a dream'* – Wordsworth, Southey and Coleridge.

Character of the Late Mr Pitt

1. p.387. *'Hobbes'* – Thomas Hobbes (1588–1679), philosopher.

2. p.387. *'the schoolmen'* – writers such as Albertus Magnus, Peter Abelard, Thomas Aquinas, Duns Scotus, etc., who taught theology and metaphysics based on the techniques of Aristotle and the early fathers of the Christian Church.

3. p.388. *'Fox'* – Charles James Fox (1749–1806), brilliant whig statesman.

4. p.388. *'Sheridan'* – Richard Brinsley Sheridan (1751–1816), dramatist and politician. A supporter of Fox.

[*To William Gifford*]

1. p.390. William Gifford, to whom Hazlitt addresses himself with unparalleled abuse, was editor of the *Quarterly Review*. Originally a poor boy – a shoemaker's apprentice – Gifford was assisted through Oxford by a rich patron. He was a florid reactionary even in his youth and became an early hater of the Revolution and all the intellectual liberalism which sprang from it. He grew to be a brutal scourge of all that was new, young, hopeful, experimental and radical in every shape and form. Hazlitt was not only thinking of Gifford's vicious attacks on his own reputation when he made this slashing reply, but of a whole generation of mainly youthful writers, including John Keats, who had been grossly savaged by Gifford in his magazine.
2. p.392. '*the Rev. Gerard Valerian Wellesley*' – Rector of Chelsea and brother of the Duke of Wellington.
3. p.392. '*the Rev. Weeden Butler*' – a Chelsea schoolmaster.
4. p.392. '*a Jacobin stationer*' – William Rogers, a Chelsea stationer, who was deprived by the authorities of his letter-box because he held radical views.

On the Pleasure of Hating

1. p.397. '*the admirable* Lines to a Spider' – 'To a Spider Running Across A Room' by Leigh Hunt (1823).
2. p.399. '*Panopticons*' – Jeremy Bentham's name for his designs for mixed prisons.
3. p.400. '*Mr Irving, the celebrated preacher*' – a Scotch evangelist, whose mixture of good looks and hell-fire rhetoric drew huge congregations to the Caledonian Chapel.
4. p.403. '*John Scott*' – editor of *The London Magazine*.
5. p.404. '*Mr Washington Irving*' – American writer and diplomat (1783–1859).

6. p.406. '*Mr Moore's Loves of the Angels*' – a poem by Tom Moore, published in 1823.

7. p.406. '*Sitting in my window*' – from Beaumont and Fletcher's *Philaster*, Act V, scene v.

8. p.407. '– *play* [sport] *with Amaryllis in the shade . . . Neaera's hair*' – from *Lycidas* by John Milton.

9. p.407. '*Fonthill*' – the gothic retreat built by William Beckford in Wiltshire. Hazlitt visited it in 1822 when he was touring picture galleries. He later saw the contents of this strange house auctioned. John Constable was also at Fonthill about this time and, from the top of its tower, saw the spire of Salisbury Cathedral darting up into the sky 'like a needle' fifteen miles away.

10. p.408. '*a young female head looks from it*' – Hazlitt is describing one of a number of paintings called 'Titian's Mistress'.

Letters of Horace Walpole

1. p.418. '*Princess Amelia*' – daughter of George II.

2. p.418. '*George Selwyn*' – George Augustus Selwyn (1719–91), a great wit and Walpole's greatest friend.

3. p.418. '*Mr Chute*' – a member of the Walpole circle (1703–76).

4. p.420. '*Horace Walpole . . . is always Pam*' – the knave of clubs and the best trump at Loo, a popular Georgian card game.

5. p.421. '*brave Balmerino*' – the sixth Lord Balmerino who was beheaded in 1746 for his part in the '45.

Brummelliana

1. p.430. '*Beau Brummell*' – George Brummell, dandy (1778–1840).

2. p.433. ' "*They put me to bed to a damp —*" ' – i.e. whore.

3. p.433. '*the year 1815 was fatal to . . . three great men – Byron, Buonaparte, and Brummell*' – Byron married in 1815, Napo-

leon was defeated at Waterloo and Brummell lost favour with the Prince Regent.

Fashion

1. p.436. '*Mr Malthus*' – Thomas Robert Malthus (1766–1834), a clergyman whose *An Essay on the Principle of Population* aroused immense controversy when it was published in 1798 and 1803. Malthusian ideas dominated much nineteenth-century social thinking. They were anathema to Hazlitt.

Country People

1. p.461. '*a better mode of education than either Bell's or Lancaster's*' – Andrew Bell (1753–1832) and Joseph Lancaster (1770–1838) were rival educational reformers.

On the Fear of Death

1. p.470. '*When Bickerstaff wrote his Essays*' – Sir Richard Steele (1672–1729) signed his essays in the *Tatler* with the name 'Bickerstaff', a fictitious character invented by Swift.
2. p.470. '*the firing at Bunker's Hill*' – the battle on a height near Boston where, in 1775, the British beat back the American revolutionaries.
3. p.476. '*I could then write on my tomb – GRATEFUL AND CONTENTED*' – Hazlitt's friends remembered this sentence when they erected his memorial and had it carved on the stone over his grave in St Anne's Soho. The stone was removed in 1870 and the present one substituted.
4. p.476. '*Chantry's monument*' – Sir Francis Chantry's *Sleeping Children* in Lichfield Cathedral. Hazlitt lost two baby sons, at Winterslow in 1811, and in London in 1817.
5. p.481. Hazlitt's only surviving son added a final paragraph to this essay:

I will add a remark, which in some degree breaks the abruptness of the transition from life to death, and renders it less shocking to the imagination than it usually appears. Death is commonly represented as a monster that devours the whole man; the grave as swallowing us entire; not only our future projects, but our past enjoyments as its prey, and all the pleasures of our lives collected together to make a rich banquet for the grim tyrant. But, in truth, Time has already anticipated the work of Death, and left him but half his spoils; for we die every moment of our lives. Death can only rob us of the future, the past he has no power over: our being gradually and silently slides from under us: our momentary pleasures follow each other as bubbles rise and disappear on the water, or the snow that melts as it falls: our attachments and friendships and desires wear out and are forgotten: the objects of them are dead to us, and we outlive not only them but ourselves. We ourselves have drunk up the cup of life, and have left only the lees. The stroke of death does not level the stately tree with all its blooming honours full upon it, but strikes the bare trunk and crumbling branches, and a few withered leaves. A shadow is all that remains of what we were, and we drag about a mockery of existence long after all the life is flown. It is the sense of self alone that makes death formidable and that hinders us from perceiving that our fleeting existence is long ago lost in itself.

A Farewell to Essay-Writing

1. p.484. '*as they were eighteen summers ago*' – when Charles and Mary Lamb visited him at Winterslow.
2. p.486. '*Mr Hunt has missed the opportunity … a friend*' – Leigh Hunt had written a somewhat forthright article on Hazlitt and had shown it to him, perhaps when the two men met in Florence in 1825, but eventually he decided not to publish it.
3. p.488. '*a melancholy hat*' –

   > In the dumps John Ford alone by himself sat
   > With folded arms and melancholy hat.

   > Sir John Suckling, *A Session of the Poets.*
4. p.490. '*Mr and Miss L—*' – Charles and Mary Lamb.
5. p.491. ' "*And curtain close such scene from every future view*" ' – from William Collins' *Ode on the Poetical Character.*

READ MORE IN PENGUIN

In every corner of the world, on every subject under the sun, Penguin represents quality and variety – the very best in publishing today.

For complete information about books available from Penguin – including Puffins, Penguin Classics and Arkana – and how to order them, write to us at the appropriate address below. Please note that for copyright reasons the selection of books varies from country to country.

In the United Kingdom: Please write to *Dept. EP, Penguin Books Ltd, Bath Road, Harmondsworth, West Drayton, Middlesex UB7 ODA*

In the United States: Please write to *Consumer Sales, Penguin Putnam Inc., P.O. Box 999, Dept. 17109, Bergenfield, New Jersey 07621-0120.* VISA and MasterCard holders call 1-800-253-6476 to order Penguin titles

In Canada: Please write to *Penguin Books Canada Ltd, 10 Alcorn Avenue, Suite 300, Toronto, Ontario M4V 3B2*

In Australia: Please write to *Penguin Books Australia Ltd, P.O. Box 257, Ringwood, Victoria 3134*

In New Zealand: Please write to *Penguin Books (NZ) Ltd, Private Bag 102902, North Shore Mail Centre, Auckland 10*

In India: Please write to *Penguin Books India Pvt Ltd, 210 Chiranjiv Tower, 43 Nehru Place, New Delhi 110 019*

In the Netherlands: Please write to *Penguin Books Netherlands bv, Postbus 3507, NL-1001 AH Amsterdam*

In Germany: Please write to *Penguin Books Deutschland GmbH, Metzlerstrasse 26, 60594 Frankfurt am Main*

In Spain: Please write to *Penguin Books S. A., Bravo Murillo 19, 1° B, 28015 Madrid*

In Italy: Please write to *Penguin Italia s.r.l., Via Benedetto Croce 2, 20094 Corsico, Milano*

In France: Please write to *Penguin France, Le Carré Wilson, 62 rue Benjamin Baillaud, 31500 Toulouse*

In Japan: Please write to *Penguin Books Japan Ltd, Kaneko Building, 2-3-25 Koraku, Bunkyo-Ku, Tokyo 112*

In South Africa: Please write to *Penguin Books South Africa (Pty) Ltd, Private Bag X14, Parkview, 2122 Johannesburg*

READ MORE IN PENGUIN

A CHOICE OF CLASSICS

Armadale   Wilkie Collins

Victorian critics were horrified by Lydia Gwilt, the bigamist, husband-poisoner and laudanum addict whose intrigues spur the plot of this most sensational of melodramas.

Aurora Leigh and Other Poems   Elizabeth Barrett Browning

Aurora Leigh (1856), Elizabeth Barrett Browning's epic novel in blank verse, tells the story of the making of a woman poet, exploring 'the woman question', art and its relation to politics and social oppression.

Personal Narrative of a Journey to the Equinoctial Regions of the New Continent   Alexander von Humboldt

Alexander von Humboldt became a wholly new kind of nineteenth-century hero – the scientist–explorer – and in *Personal Narrative* he invented a new literary genre: the travelogue.

The Pañćatantra   Visnu Sarma

The Pañćatantra is one of the earliest books of fables and its influence can be seen in the *Arabian Nights*, the *Decameron*, the *Canterbury Tales* and most notably in the *Fables* of La Fontaine.

A Laodicean   Thomas Hardy

The Laodicean of Hardy's title is Paula Power, a thoroughly modern young woman who, despite her wealth and independence, cannot make up her mind.

Brand   Henrik Ibsen

The unsparing vision of a priest driven by faith to risk and witness the deaths of his wife and child gives *Brand* its icy ferocity. It was Ibsen's first masterpiece, a poetic drama composed in 1865 and published to tremendous critical and popular acclaim.